THE ARRIVAL

THE PRIDDEN SAGA: BOOK ONE

J. M. TIBBOTT

Copyright ©2017 by J. M. Tibbott
All Rights Reserved

No part of this publication may be reproduced or transmitted in any form or by any means, electronic or mechanical, including photocopy, recording or any information storage and retrieval system without the written permission of the author and publisher, except by a reviewer who may quote brief passages in review.

Disclaimer:
All characters in this book are fictitious, and any resemblance to actual persons, living or dead, is purely coincidental.

Cover Art by Deranged Doctor Designs

Substantive Editor: Laura LaRocca

Library and Archives Canada Cataloguing in Publication

Tibbott, J. M., 1943-, author
    The arrival / J.M. Tibbott.

(The Pridden Saga ; book one)
Issued in print and electronic formats.
ISBN 978-1-927890-16-5 (softcover).--ISBN 978-1-927890-17-2 (PDF)

    I. Title.

PS8639.I355A89 2018   C813'.6   C2018-900175-5
                                                                                C2018-900176-3

Printed in Canada

Published by Sun Dragon Press Inc., Canada
www.sundragonpress.com
First Edition, 2017

THE ARRIVAL

THE PRIDDEN SAGA: BOOK ONE

J. M. TIBBOTT

DEDICATION

R. R. Kleiber for his constant belief and encouragement.

J. M. Tibbott

ACKNOWLEDGEMENTS

Special thanks to:

The River Writers for their continuing help in keeping me on track, and focussed on the story;

Tyler Omichinski for his help with understanding the gaming world;

John Truby for his extraordinary writing workshops, without which I would never have attempted to write a novel.

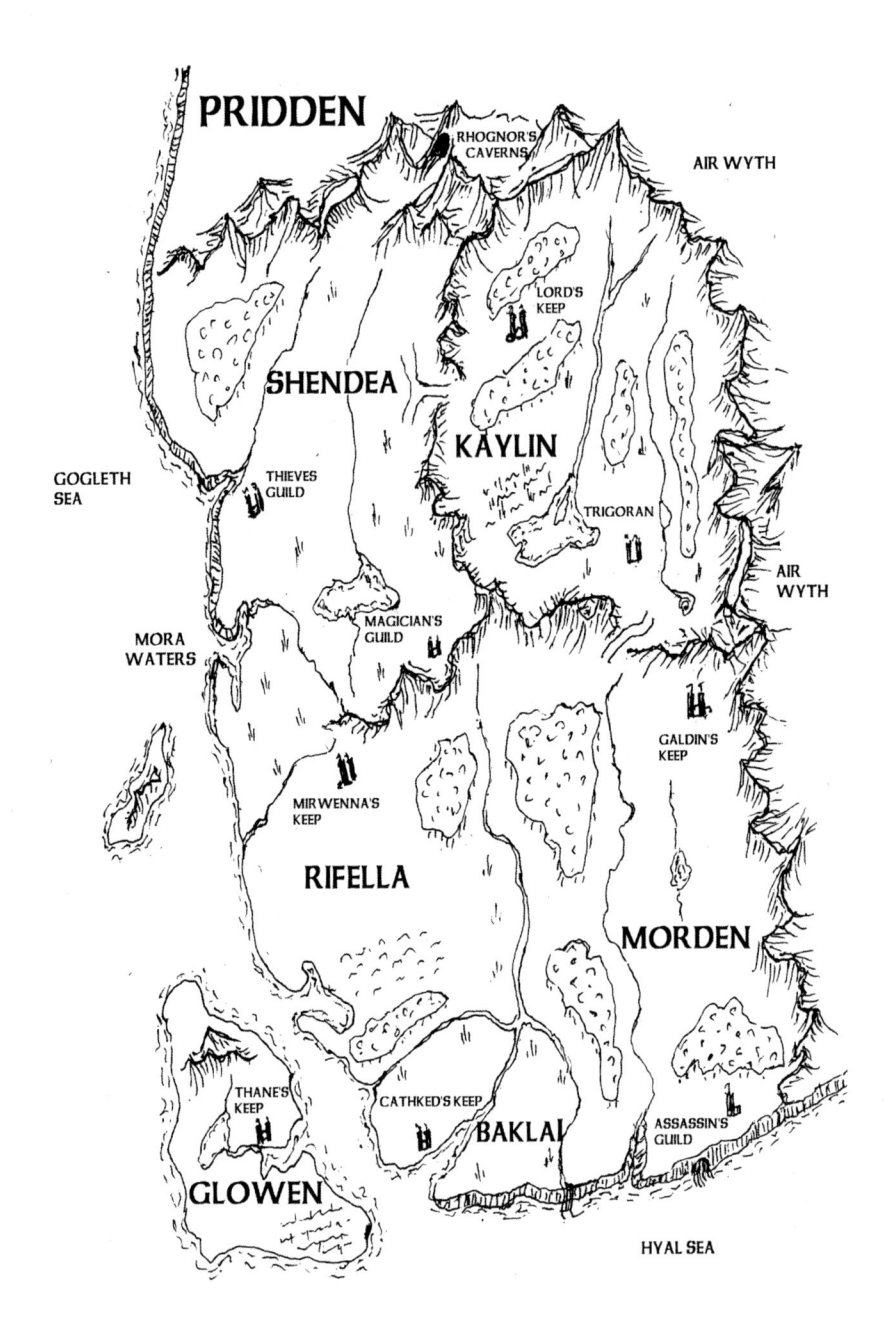

J. M. Tibbott

The Arrival

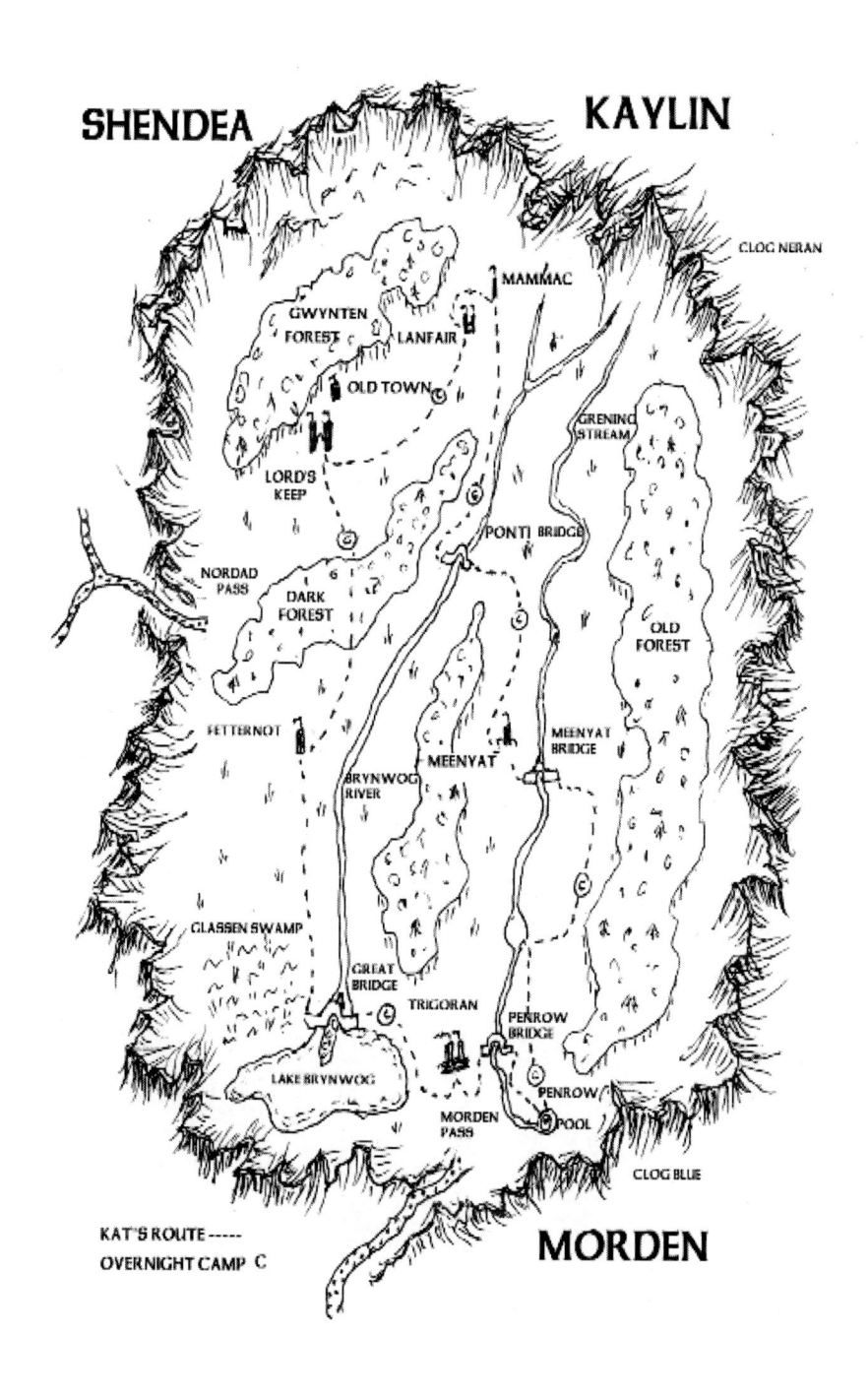

J. M. Tibbott

PROLOGUE

A bitter cold draft sidled into the room, and the short man shivered, despite the mouse-grey cloak which covered him from head to toe and concealed his face.

Where was Galdin? He hastily corrected himself. *Where was the Master?* This old stone tower terrified him, and the Master always insisted they meet here. He shivered again, but this time from fear: raw, trembling, bowel-loosening fear. His first attempt had failed. Would he be allowed a second? The woman, unlike any in this world, smart and quick, displayed the temper of an enraged *hissar.*

He shuddered, remembering his only encounter with a hissar. A small animal, about the size of a farm cat, but those teeth and the howls loosed from the throat of that evil creature had liquified his spine, and sent him fleeing for his life. *I do not remember what I did to annoy the fearsome animal, but then I do not think they need a reason to attack anyone or anything. Even horses run from them.*

My task for the Master is just as fearsome. It is unlikely I can lure the woman here with ease. I will need to employ some of my best tricks to fool her.

"About time you appeared, Mouse." The voice, the soft hiss of a serpent, wrapped him in ice. "I thought perhaps you might flee my temper."

Mouse whirled and sank into a clumsy bow. "Master!"

"You slimy little rodent, where is the woman? I cannot decide which serves me better, to eliminate you or give you another chance."

"She presented an unexpected challenge. This time I will be able to bring her to you. I swear I will complete the task." He shrank back against the freezing walls.

The flash of ebony pin-point eyes beneath Galdin's velvet hood penetrated Mouse's fluttering heart and transfixed him in place.

From the folds of the full, dark robe a stark white hand slithered out, long black nails glinting in the faint glow of the moon peering through the firing slits in the walls of the tower. As the Master's forefinger touched his forehead, his brain burned like fire, and Mouse cried out and dropped to his knees.

"Get up you fool. This woman is the only one who can bring me the heart, alive and still beating. I need her to take control of what is mine by right."

Mouse rose shakily to his feet, twitching violently. "I will succeed Master, I promise."

"I can read you, you foolish little creature. I sense everything about you. I shall perceive immediately if you attempt your slippery, pathetic tricks on me. One false move and death will be painful, and exquisitely slow. Remember that, if you are tempted. My knowledge of your perfidy will be immediate. Go now!"

"Yes Master." He lowered his head, waiting for a blow that never came. When he raised his eyes and scanned the room, he stood alone. The only sound, the low moan of the wind in the narrow arrow slits, sent shivers up his spine.

How does he disappear like that?

CHAPTER 1

Kat stuck her head through the doorway of Nick's office and tapped on the wooden frame. Although the floor to ceiling windows behind him, and Monet reproductions on both side walls, created a bright cheery office, a sense of apprehension enveloped her. When he called her to come to his office first thing in the morning, things rarely boded well. *Working with Nick has always been fabulous, but in the last few months he's been testy.*

Nick caught sight of her. "Kat." He raised his arm, summoned with two fingers, and waited for her to enter. "Are you trying to be fired?"

"Fired? What? No." Without asking, she plunked herself in the chair opposite him. "What's going on?"

His blue eyes hidden behind the reflections off his glasses, gave no clue to what had elicited this question. "You were assigned to the *War* series team, and you chose not to attend the last three meetings. Are you intentionally ignoring me?"

She glanced, brow wrinkled, at the file in front of him with the words 'Your Eyes Only' yelling at her in blood red from the cover. "No, I'm not. What meetings are you talking about?" She plowed on without waiting for a reply. "Wait a minute. You promised me I could finish *Berenga* first. But I ran into a small problem and I'm not completed."

"You're obviously not reading your email about anything else that's going on. The meetings were listed. And as far as *Berenga* goes, you told me the same story four months ago." He shook his head in apparent frustration. "You made everything clear in the past how much you dislike teams, and now I'm suspicious. Are you deliberately dragging behind on your own project, so you won't be forced to operate with the team?"

"Of course not. I promised I would join them, and I will. Look, Nick, I wouldn't ignore you. I'm not going slowly on purpose. Honestly." *I can't believe he's acting like this. What's with him?* She scowled at him. "What is this sudden need to establish teams everywhere anyway? You never used to be like this."

He blew out a long breath. "It isn't all of a sudden. When you came to work here, the company was small and we could operate in an informal way, because I owned it, Kat. I first explained about the concept over a year ago. I thought I expressed myself plainly."

"But I loved working the way we did. We did so many great projects."

"Things are different now. You must understand this. When OSA purchased the company, they never intended to keep the firm small and casual. They want a return on their investment. The Japanese have used the team concept for years with unceasing success. We're now working for them, which means we must change the way we've always done everything."

"Personally I think teams slow things down and cause problems."

"Most of the problems, Kat, are caused by you. As part of a team, you need to think before you act. Think before you speak. You can't continue to run roughshod over other people, including me. You report to me, dammit."

She gaped at him, her mouth open. "I... I... I don't mean to do that. But recently I'm put in teams where some me-too who won't follow directions is always present. You know they're not as capable as I am." *What's going on here? He's always been on my side in the past.*

The tip of his nose turned white, always a sign he was furious. The huge desk between them appeared to expand, and became a major barrier. "I'm aware it's more demanding being a female in the gaming business, but you can't always dismiss other people's ideas. You're a brilliant designer, but even the best people need input. I thought you could handle the pressure. I hoped to count on you to be professional."

"I am a professional, but those dweebs won't do what I want. I'm not a newby, and you know my games appeal to more of the women gamers – and they get high ratings among moronic teenage boys who are aroused by strong females. The guys need to listen. So many of them depend on hacks, and they wouldn't recognise original coding if it was written on their foreheads. Their cheats are lame, as well. It's one thing when someone else's project is at risk, but on my own games? I should at least be able to expect their attention on my stuff." *I'm confused. What's going on? He's usually so fair.*

"You don't get this, do you? You're your own worst enemy. You can't dismiss people. If they do tramp on a favorite idea of yours, you must learn to deal with them with diplomacy."

"I can be diplomatic."

Nick's face softened and he laughed. "Diplomatic? Red, all too often you're about as diplomatic as a kick in the head."

She frowned at him. "Very funny… not."

He put his elbows on the desk and leaned his chin on his clasped hands. "When you first came to me for a job, Red, I nearly didn't hire you."

She sat back, unsure of where the conversation was headed. "Why?"

"Well, when you walked into my office, you came across as prickly as a little cactus. I couldn't figure out at the time whether you would fit with the rest of us."

Kat frowned. *Prickly? Multiple foster homes, my rat of a husband, who I only married to escape that last foster place. Who wouldn't be.* "Well I'd had some challenges."

"Well, you certainly arrived with pile of baggage."

"But I was good at what I did." She grimaced. "Anyway, if I looked so prickly, why'd you hire me?"

"Because the expression in your eyes resembled those of a smacked pup."

Kat glared at him and humphed.

"I figured you needed a break. Plus, your portfolio bordered on exceptional."

"Thank you for noticing, 'cause it was." She stared at him. "You're angry at me?"

He sighed "I'm not angry. I'm disappointed in you." He leaned back in his chair. "Kat, my contract with OSA demands I work for them for one more year. But if I can't make this company produce what they expect, my final payout will suffer. They tend to judge me by my staff. And let's face it, kiddo, you're an important part of my staff."

I would never purposely hurt Nick I thought he knew that. "I didn't realize what you needed me to do."

"Kat, this isn't something I would share normally, but I can't afford to lose my investment, particularly with three mouths to feed. I need you to cooperate."

"I'm trying Nick."

"Your actions don't appear to indicate you are. Think about the bigger picture? Eventually, I'll leave, and you pos-

The Arrival

sess the potential to play an important role in this company." Nick sighed again and rolled his eyes. "But if you continue to be such a thorn in OSA's side, you're not promotable. I would love to present you as a possible team leader, but until you learn to control your temper, be less judgmental, follow orders, and play nicely with others, you'll never be successful." He held up two fingers about an inch apart. "You're this far from being fired. By them. I too have to follow orders. As capable as you are, I can't protect you any longer."

Her heart felt squeezed in her chest. "But... ."

"No buts." He slapped the desk. "You need to change your attitude. It sucks. Take a week off and decide what you truly want out of your job. Or... if you still want your job."

***

The next afternoon, Kat leaned on her architect's desk, staring at the drawings the young illustrator handed her. He'd caught her intention with *Berenga* perfectly. *Remember what Nick said ... attitude.* "Um... um, thank you, Carlo. The designs are terrific. You can begin the coding for these now."

Carlo stared at her open-mouthed, stammered something unintelligible, and scuttled out of the room.

Is Nick right? Don't I give people positive feedback when they do a fine job? She'd spent a sleepless night thinking about their conversation. *Is he also feeling caught in a box with the OSA people?*

"A dollar for your thoughts."

She jumped and turned, at Nick's unexpected words. "I didn't hear you come in."

"Sorry I startled you. I was rough on you yesterday, but before I left for work today I glanced in the mirror and noticed a lot more grey hairs. I'm convinced they're your fault. I hate to watch your talent go to waste."

"I'm not wasting anything."

"You are, though. After that first year when things got better for you, you fitted in so well, but now you're in a bigger pond, and you seriously need to adapt to these new circumstances. You are one of the most talented designers here. But you're hurting yourself with some of your attitudes. You must learn to work with anyone and everyone, if you want to make your mark as a major cog in the gaming wheel."

"Okay, Okay. You can stop drilling. You've struck oil." Kat screwed up her face and frowned at him. "I've been noodling about everything you said, and I will take a week off. I'll also think long and hard about what I should do."

"I'm glad." He handed her an envelope. "Karen and I talked about you. That wife of mine is an exceptional woman and has decided you need protecting and comforting, and she suggested I use some of the special cash reserve I set up years ago. So, we want you to go to someplace sunny with a beautiful beach and a decent hotel. We figured you earned this over the years. Consider it an early bonus."

Kat peeked in the envelope and gasped at the wad of money. "Oh wow, this isn't necessary." She attempted to clear the lump from her throat. Unsuccessfully. *They're both so... so...*

"I think it is. And so does Karen. You and I have played at this company for many years, and I find it difficult to come down hard on you. I'm hoping you'll opt to stay in the job. Please, Red, I don't want this to be a parting gift."

"Nick because we've been friends for so long, I have trouble adjusting to this new demanding boss. You and Karen have always been like family." She swallowed. "I promise I'll spend the time thinking about my future here. I want us to stay friends." *I don't want to lose this family too.*

Nick smiled, reached over and rumpled her short red curls. "Me too. You'll do well, Red. You're a good kid."

She pushed his hand away and raised an eyebrow at him. "I keep telling you, I'm not a kid. I'm twenty-six years old." She tugged at her ear. "I won't let you down, but in the end I must choose what's right for me."

J. M. Tibbott

CHAPTER 2

"Shit." Fat beads of sweat prickled through Kat's hair, then rolled down her forehead into her eyes. Blinded, she shifted her computer to the shaded table beside her beach chair, whipped a hair band out of her bag, and pushed her curls back. The last thing she needed was moisture on her keyboard. Unable to focus, she grabbed a bottle of water and generously doused her eyes and dried the salty mixture with her towel. She picked up the bottle again to drink, but only a few drops emerged. She frowned, licked dry lips and tossed the bottle on the ground beside her.

Retrieving the computer, she immersed herself back in a world of dragons, monsters, magicians, and fierce battle princesses -- a world she created. She loved to bring life to new beings and to help or hinder her heroines. On rare occasions, she challenged herself by forcing them into horrific, mind-numbing situations. She smiled, remembering how *Anfarra*, the red-headed Amazon, had faced not one, but three, of the biggest dragon-lords, and persevered to win the crown and save her people. *Anfarra*, her seventh game for Nick, and her second for OSA Corp, would generate enough for her to live on for almost two years. She appreciated the big perk of this job -- a pay check to design and play games, with bonuses for best-sellers -- the peak dream come true in her world. *Except for those damn teams.*

She patted her laptop. Next to Nick and his wife and kids, this machine, the ultimate in computers, was like family. When not on her desk, her favorite piece of equipment routinely lodged in a place of honor beside her on the bed, in case she woke in the night with an idea. Other than the very best in technical goodies, she required few luxuries. "Just think of all the bling I could buy with what you cost." She glanced around self-consciously, hoping no one heard her. The computer, of course remained silent. "Not to worry, you're worth every penny. I really should stop talking to myself."

Nick had been right to suggest she use her time off as a vacation. He appeared pleased when she said she was heading for Tortola instead of the frenetic social whirl of Paradise Island. *I'll bet he thinks I chose Cane Garden Bay because it's a relaxing place.* She sighed. *OK I did, 'cause I hate when he's not happy with me. I'm sure I'll relax any time now.*

She'd brought her computer, because *Berenga* was flowing so well, she couldn't drop everything now, even though her future remained in a serious state of flux. So reviewing what she'd already coded was important.

This is a super beach, but so what. The threat of being fired squatted on her mind like a noxious gargoyle and she couldn't see a way out, so instead of enjoying the beauty of the island, she distracted herself by working.

Wish we could go back to the way we used to do things. Not possible. She sighed with an audible whoosh of air. *So what do I want?* Still reviewing almost automatically, she squinted at the screen. *Of course, — control my own life, and make my own rules. I'm a terrific game designer, and people should do what I want them to. Don't like boxes.* Her thoughts took off in a new direction. *Jack, the creep, trying to stick me in his nasty idea of a box. I really thought he'd be different.*

She paused. Whenever Jack rose unbidden in her

The Arrival

thoughts, the sharp taste of bile on the back of her tongue reminded her of his lies and his cheating. The bastard had managed to empty their joint accounts before he slithered off to his blonde bimbo's arms. The struggle to keep afloat after the divorce convinced her that men had only one acceptable point. Sex. From that day, she only indulged in sexual play on her terms. *Stop thinking about that idiot. Work now.*

She re-focused on her laptop as it beeped at her. *Oh, hell, I wrote the wrong code sequence and Berenga's in a trap. I shouldn't be thinking about scumbag Jack.* She shook her head impatiently. *I need to get her out of this. Perhaps... a unique gift? Damn! An ability means I'll need to go back and recode the introduction. Better write some notes.*

A shadow fell across her keyboard. She glanced up.

"Why would a gorgeous woman be engrossed in a computer on such a beautiful day?"

Hmm. Tall and tanned, but his line? Pathetic. One of those men. They figure they're just the gift any female pants for. An artful curl dropped from his perfectly coiffed black hair. The grey felt sailor's hat gave a weird vibe though, so perhaps he didn't have that much success with women. *What an idiot.* She glared at him. "I'm busy." She resumed her work.

"How can you sit in front of a computer screen when you're on one of the most idyllic beaches in the Virgins?"

Persistent, I'll give him that. She pretended not to see him and continued pecking at the keyboard, but evaluated him in her peripheral vision. *A potential one-night stand? Perhaps.* He still stood beside her. She moved her laptop sideways so he wouldn't be able to view the screen. He didn't move. If she ignored him long enough, he'd get bored and leave. She gave a quick glance at him again. *I don't believe it, he's wearing fuzzy grey shorts. Everyone wears white or khaki. Where the hell did he ever find grey ones, or fuzzy ones for that matter?* Another glimpse at her computer and Kat groaned. *Oh crap, Berenga's buried in it now. I must pay attention. Won't he ever leave?*

"Can I at least buy you a drink? A Pina Colada or a Mai Tai?"

She refused to answer, convinced he would give up and go away.

"So, no drink. How about dinner later?"

She gave him her snake-eyeing-a-rat stare. "No," she said. The no was also an answer to her own inner question. "I'm not interested."

Apparently astonished at her refusal, he stammered. "But..."

"Which part of 'I'm not interested' didn't you understand?"

He stepped back, blinked, waited a beat, shrugged his shoulders, turned and walked away. He appeared smaller, and it almost appeared her comments had robbed him of stature.

Kat followed his retreat and allowed herself the tiniest of satisfied smiles. *He deserved that, thinking anyone would fall for his stupid line. Kinda cute, but what an ass!* She chuckled to herself. *But his ass was not bad.*

Her labors interrupted, she stretched her back, and winced. *Ouch, my legs.* She had overindulged the sun-tanning session. *Damn. Just as well, I've got Berenga stuck in a dungeon, werewolves at the door, and I haven't figured a way out yet. I think the heat is interfering with my brain. I can code in comfort in the room.*

She packed her bag to return to her air-conditioned room. She could labor in cool air and slather something healing to

The Arrival

her tender, cherry-red skin, and persuade her grey matter to work again. She rose from the chair, glanced at her watch, and stared. *My god, I've been sitting here for three hours!*

***

A cooling shower plus gobs of aloe-enhanced sunscreen and Kat sighed. She admired herself in the mirror. "You look good, woman. A few more days and you'll have a suitable tan." A call to the kitchen, a new pair of soft stretchy jeans and a fresh T-shirt restored her ability to face the world. Kat reached for the odd little necklace with the strange symbol carved on the surface of the green stone. The young girl in Roadtown had given it to her and refused money for the simple leather cord and gem.

Before Kat hooked the piece of jewelry around her neck, a knock heralded the arrival of room service. Food demanded her immediate attention, and she dropped the little stone on the desk.

She opened the door and a thin young waiter pushed his cart into the room. "You ordered the chef special, Miss? We have curried goat in the sandwich today. Most wonderful. The kitchen has also supplied a most delicious Mango smoothie drink for you." He handed her the bill and a pen without meeting her gaze.

"Thanks... ," Kat peered at his name badge, "... Souris. That's an interesting name."

"Thank you, Miss." He kept his eyes lowered, tucked the signed bill into the pocket of his grey apron, and scurried from the suite.

Kat sat down to feast on the fat, juicy sandwich, and by the time she finished, refreshed in mind as well as body, she prepared to rescue *Berenga*. When she rose from the table, she groaned. Three hours in the cramped quarters of the plane two days ago, plus today's lengthy session on the beach, stiffened her muscles. She needed movement and exercise. At the moment her body behaved like one belonging to some old goat. She burped indelicately and decided that having just partaken of one, the word 'goat' was ill advised. *A brisk walk will be the perfect thing to loosen muscles and clear my lungs of stale plane effluvia.* She smiled in satisfaction. She had used her word for the day in a reasonable sentence. *Effluvia! A superior one.*

At the door, she glanced back at the computer. *Should I take it? She shrugged no to herself.* She ignored the necklace beside her computer.

Normally, she forced herself to run, despite the fact she hated the boring repetition. *A walk through the uneven grounds behind the resort will loosen my poor bod and that's exactly what I need. While I walk, I can... cogitate on the problem of the dungeon without distractions. Ha, cogitate was yesterday's word, and I finally used it.*

Narrow paths through the jagged scrub on the island were the only way to hike if Kat wanted to avoid the nasty thorns on many of the low-growing plants. "Goats might do well over these rocky bumps, but sandals are hopeless here. I should've worn something sturdier. Ouch." She stumbled again.

Picking her way around small cacti, she remembered the young waiter, and wondered why any sane parent would saddle their child with a name like Souris. She snorted. *He did kinda look like a little French mouse, come to think of it. Damn another rock.* After tripping for the umpteenth time, she considered turning back. The rumble of thunder cemented her decision, and she changed direction.

The Arrival

Oops. The ominous, dark clouds foretold a nasty storm headed her way. The flashes of lightening and rolls of thunder were definitely unfriendly. *Uh oh, do I have time to get back to the hotel?* A short distance to the side, she spied the ruins of an old building. *Maybe I can get to shelter before I drown in the deluge. Ha and double ha, I did it again. Deluge, my Tuesday word.*

She ran the last few yards, stubbing her toes a number of times, and dashed into the building just as the rain hammered on the remains of the corrugated tin roof over the ruined walls. Despite the metal overhead, the structure of the stone enclosure struck her as bizarre. "This place is weird. I remember seeing forts like this in Spain, or was it Portugal? I wonder what it's doing here? Something is strange about the design." Kat reached out and touched the cold damp stone. "I'm talking to myself again, but at least I'm having a conversation with someone intelligent." She grinned at her own words.

The clay and earth floor flooded with the water, which poured through myriads of holes in the roof. Heavy drops of rain splashed on her head, and she hurried further into the building. Alcoves led from the main area in which she stood, so she began to explore. The room ahead loomed dark, with no window openings, but squinting in the gloom, she barely discerned the faint outline of a door at the far end. She chuckled to herself. *I should have worn the necklace, 'cause the gal on the beach said it would keep me safe. Maybe from the storm? Yeah sure. Don't really believe it, but you never know about weird superstitions.* She moved closer to the door. The ornate, old and weather-beaten barrier, boasted a large iron knob of a handle which had the worn patina of many grasping hands.

She grabbed the metal grip, turned the old knob, and pushed it open. When she stepped through the archway, thousands of sparks lit up her limbs. Brutal air pressure pushed her into the darkness beyond, and ripped consciousness from her.

CHAPTER 3

Pain.

Kat's head throbbed in agony. She slit her eyes a fraction and breathed deeply. *Relief, dim warm light, no lightening.* She sighed and inhaled the scent of freshly washed linens and stroked the silky smoothness of expensive sheets and something soft and furry beneath her hands. *Hmm weird. Where am I? A hospital? Not Cane Garden. They don't use sheets like this.*

She allowed her eyelids to close again, and listened intently for any sounds to orient her. No thunder or rain pummeled on the roof. All she remembered was a sense of being violently drawn into a dark vortex, and then blackness. Her temples ached. *I don't dare move my head.*

"I can tell you are conscious. I watched your eyelids flutter." The voice, pleasant and comforting, reminded her of her grandmother's Christmas puddings.

Kat snapped her eyes open, and stared.

Beside her bed, stood a tall, plump woman, dressed in a long blue robe.

"Who are you? Where am I?"

The woman's smile radiated warmth. "I am your healer, and you are in Lord Eduardo's keep. In the guest quarters."

"What's a keep? Is it like a castle? And why am I here?"

"You do not remember what happened?" The woman furrowed her brow.

"No. I remember a storm and I ran to find some place safe. Then something pulled at me and everything went dark."

The woman sighed. "They found you lying outside the forge hold. No one knows how or why you arrived, and",— she gestured to jeans and T-shirt on a chair,—"your clothing is most peculiar."

Kat startled, thrust her hands beneath the furs on the bed and found the soft folds of a fine linen garment. She could tell the clothing, which she assumed to be a nightgown, extended the full length of her body. *Good. I'm not naked. I hate when I am naked in a dream. And this must be a dream.* She drew her hands from beneath the coverings, impressed by the delicate lace on the long white sleeves.

She pushed back the covers as she sat up to get out of the bed. Her head spun and she swayed, nauseated as her stomach heaved. *Wait, what's going on?* She sank back as the woman gently pushed her into the enveloping folds of the bed linens.

"You cannot arise so soon. You need to rest and recover. Tomorrow or the next day will be enough."

"You don't understand, I must leave. Now. I'm flying home in two days."

The woman's eyes widened. "Flying? Are you then a Wielder?"

"What are you talking about? What's a Wielder? And who are you? Where am I?" *This is the weirdest dream I've ever had.*

The woman put her hand on Kat's shoulder again, and sat in the chair beside the bed. "Perhaps we had better start again. I,"—she put her hand on her heart, —"am Wynneth. I am appointed by the Healer Guild, but I look to Lord Eduardo's keep. You are now in his keep as I told you before."

"Where is this keep? Is it in the Virgin Islands, on Tortola?"

The Arrival

"I possess no knowledge of an island of virgins. I never heard of an island named Tor... whatever word you used. This is the land of Kaylin."

"Kaylin? What country is it in?"

"Country? What a strange word. We are not on an island."

This is definitely a dream — thank god, I'm in one of my games.

Kat lifted her head from the pillow to gaze at her surroundings, but without warning, an entire Japanese drumming corps began a concert inside her skull, and everything threatened to explode. She winced and clasped her head in her hands in an attempt to halt the eruption. *Oh god, my brains are going to scatter all over the room.* But nausea overcame her again, and this time she leaned over the bed and retched fiercely into a basin Wynneth produced. Kat continued to gag, but on an empty stomach, the dry heaves aggravated the pain in her head. *This isn't a dream, it's a nightmare. I knew I shouldn't have created all those werewolves to trap Berenga.*

The woman used a warm cloth to wipe Kat's face and placed a cool dry hand on her forehead. "You poor thing. You must rest or you will be extremely ill."

Kat sank back on the pillow. Wynneth's gentle hand stilled the pain and brought relief.

"Sleep now."

Unable to resist, Kat closed her eyes, and everything faded as she drifted into blessed unconsciousness.

***

The murmur of voices and the sound of birds penetrated the grey cloud in her mind. Kat kept her eyes closed, afraid to allow the headaches to take hold again.

A man's voice, a chocolate river, both rich and deep, vibrated in the room. "Who is she?" Delicious. Major delicious.

"I have no idea my lord."

Kat recognized the voice of Wynneth.

"Two stewards found her unconscious at the forge hold, so they brought her to me. When she first awoke, so ill, she gave me little information."

"Well, I'm sure such a small woman will be no trouble for you."

"Well... ."

"Well what? What are you trying to tell me?"

"She mentioned flying. Do you think my lord she could be a Wielder?"

What the heck's a wielder?

Chocolate man snorted. "Impossible. There has never been a female Wielder in all our records. Plus, Wielders are rarely those of common birth. How could she be one?"

"I cannot guess, my Lord. But she is from neither Kaylin nor Shendea, and despite the red glow of her hair, she does not look to Rifella. I am sure she does not hale from our world. Her clothing is most strange, and even her accent is odd. She did mention an island of... of... virgins."

"Healer, that is not an appropriate topic for discussion. I am sure she only confided such a thing with you as another woman."

"Forgive me, my lord, but I felt you should be familiar with what she revealed to me." Wynneth sounded tentative. "One other thing. One of her eyes is the color of newly risen grass, and the other, the brown of your steed. Do you think, my lord, she could have been placed here by Morden's Thane?"

"Power forbid that should be the case."

At the obvious horror in chocolate man's voice, Kat opened her eyes. "Who the hell is Morden Thane, and why would he place me anywhere?"

The Arrival

At her words both Wynneth and a tall man turned toward her. Silhouetted by the light behind him, she couldn't see his face clearly.

Wynneth moved to her side. "How are you feeling now?"

She sat up in the bed and discovered her head was pain free. "My headache is gone. I feel okay."

"Okay? What an odd word. What is the meaning?"

Uh, oh. Something is exceedingly weird here. How can someone not understand what 'okay' means? Dream? Nightmare? Been spending too much time with Berenga. "You really don't know?"

"If I did, I would not ask."

"It means excellent, great, fine. But you didn't answer my question. Who is Morden's Thane?"

"He rules Morden."

"Oh." Puzzled, Kat pushed back the covers and put a foot on the floor, then caught sight of the tall man as he turned quickly away.

"I will leave you to manage the situation, Healer. Some important items require my attention." With those words he slipped out the door.

Kat, puzzled by his hasty exit, queried Wynneth. "Why did that man leave so suddenly?"

The healer smiled a little. "You are a stranger to him, and are not attired in day clothing. For him to remain in the room, would not be seemly."

Not seemly? Whoa. This is getting weirder and weirder. I better I wake up… and soon. "Who is he?"

"He is Lord Eduardo. Now, what is your name, young woman."

"I'm Kat. Kat Karim."

"You have two names? How interesting."

J. M. Tibbott

CHAPTER 4

Kat pushed the covers off her, and stood on the rug. She sank up to her ankles in soft, cozy fur. "Oh, this is lovely." She wiggled her toes in the furry warmth.

"Be careful." Wynneth reached out to stop Kat from falling.

"I'm fine. Truly. I'm happy to stand on my feet again without everything spinning." She scanned the room. "I need to get dressed, but… " Her clothes were gone.

"Your own garments are being cleaned, but they are not appropriate for a woman to wear in Kaylin. I put a fresh outfit for you in the personal room." Wynneth pointed toward an ornate door to the left of the bed. "You may also want to refresh yourself."

Personal room? Puzzled, Kat pulled at the door and went in. *Oh, this is a bathroom.* She walked to a clear, tall cylinder made from some translucent stone or crystal. *A shower!* She sighed and smiled. Dropping her nightgown on a seat next to a pile of clean clothing, she stepped inside. Disconcerted by the number of valves and handles, she spent a few minutes twisting and turning shiny knobs, jumped back and forth from scalding and freezing water, received a face-full of suds, and at last found a setting of a warm rain of water issuing from spigots ranging from head to toe. She gingerly operated the suds handle again and luxuriated in the joy of being squeaky clean. *This feels so glorious.* She groaned with delight. After she reluctantly turned off the water, toasty air issued from a different set of valves, drying both her hair and body fully. *This is a super good dream.*

She left the shower, found a mirror set in the wall, and tentatively peered at her reflection. Surprised and pleased to find her hair in relaxed curls instead of expected frizz, she turned and picked up the garments from the seat behind her.

Burying her nose in the clothes, she smelled the fresh scent of outdoors: sunshine, rain, and clean air.

Somewhat perturbed when she put on the long dress, she turned to the mirror and figured Wynneth was an excellent judge of size. *The fit is perfect. Except, I haven't worn a dress since I was five.*

The healer rose from her chair as Kat re-entered the bedroom. "The garment looks well on you."

Kat grimaced. "It's a dress, Wynneth. I never wear dresses."

"Wearing dresses would serve you better when you are in Kaylin. The people here express strong opinions on the appearance of both women and men."

"Is that why the guy with the dark hair left so quickly?"

"He is Lord Eduardo, and you would be equally well served to remember his name and title. He is the ruler of Kaylin."

"So, he's a big deal here, right?"

"A strange phrase, but if you mean is he important, then you are right. Not only is he the Lord of Kaylin, he is also of the blood."

Kat frowned, puzzled. "And what exactly does that mean?"

"This will take some time to explain. Sit, and I will call for food and refreshment so we can spend some time. I will attempt to give you enough information about this land to allow you to understand the people who live here." She walked to the wall and pulled on a long tassel descending from the ceiling.

Kat sat at the small table, and waited until Wynneth joined her.

"Lady Kat, I will attempt to make this brief but as informative as possible."

"Wait a minute, my name is not Lady Kat. I can't claim royal blood."

"Perhaps not, but it will not hurt for the people of Kaylin, and perhaps even other lands, to think of you as being... what were the words you used... 'a large deal' too. You do possess hair the color of the royal descendants in Rifella. I suspect you are destined to play an important part in our lands." Wynneth stopped at the sound of a slight tap at the door. "Come."

A small woman with straight brown hair entered with a tray of food and drinks and deposited them on the table in front of Kat.

Wynneth smiled. "Thank you Mayda, we will call you when we are finished."

The woman bowed her head and left the room.

"The girl is quite different from you. Is she also from Kaylin?"

"No, Mayda comes from Baklai. They are darker in color, as you can see, and are much smaller than either the Kaylins or those from Shendea, where I come from. Her male parent is Horse-Master here."

"I see." *Horse-Master? I wonder, does he train horses or raise them, or race them? Wow, when I wake up from this dream, I've got the makings of a fantastic new game. I hope I can remember all this. This just might save my job.* "Interesting." *Sort of.* "But tell me more about the men and women being so straight-laced, and this blood thingy."

The belly laugh which erupted from Wynneth was startling. "You do speak in the oddest way, which I find amusing, and I quite enjoy." She grinned. "Blood thingy — yes, it is a humorous way to refer to the Wielder blood line."

Wynneth poured a cup of tea and settled back in the chair. "In the history of our world, the six lands did not always exist. The entire world was ruled by a family of Wielders of Power. Their line began with Lord Argelwyd. Over many turns, sons and daughters were born, but only one in each generation could rule the world of Pridden and it caused internal strife in the family. Therefore, hundreds of star turns ago, the then ruling Lord, Argelwyd divided our world into six lands, which he gave to his six progeny to rule." She held up six fingers. "Over time, changes occurred within each land, caused by, in some cases deaths of the known blood rulers, who left no progeny of their own. In others, the strength of the line decreased by bonding of the blood with non-blood peoples. Now only three Lords of the original line exist. The two most powerful are Lord Eduardo and Lord Rhognor of Shendea. This is why a deep connection exists between our two lands. True, Rifella is also ruled by a Lord, but the blood-line is weaker."

"So, is Eduardo a Wielder of Power?" *Good game stuff, I must remember this when I wake up.*

"Indeed. Remember he is *Lord* Eduardo."

"So that's the skinny on the blood thingy."

Wynneth appeared puzzled. "Skinny? What do you mean by thin?"

"Um… skinny is an expression we use to mean information."

"How curious."

Kat shrugged. "Whatever. Now what is all this about men and women being appropriate?"

"Well, as each of the lands became more isolated from the others, they grew in different directions. Over much time, skin color changed, ideas changed. Of course, the height of the mountains and width of the rivers of our world created barriers behind which, each of the lands continued in their own paths. I suspect the extreme isolation of Kaylin sent them in a direction of unparalleled rigidity of behavior between males and females. The social rules are no man or woman may see each other in any state of undress until they are bonded."

"I guess they don't get regular sex?"

Wynneth blushed and swallowed. "Forgive me, living in Kaylin for so long, I am startled by speech so open about the subject. You may talk with me about this, but refrain from this discussion with others in this land. It is important you do as I say."

Wow, everything is adding up to one huge sucker of a game. I should wake pretty soon, as I will need to get started on the outline. But these Kaylins need to change. They're just plain weird. Kat glared at Wynneth. "Why should I behave differently from my normal self? This is ridiculous. Simply because they're embarrassed by sex and bodies and such, why do I need to pretend to go along with all this nonsense?"

"This is not nonsense, Lady Kat. You are a guest in this land." Wynneth held up her hand to forestall Kat's objection. "This is their land and their customs and their rules. You cannot afford to make enemies here. Not adhering to these customs is disrespectful, but can also be dangerous. It is important you fit in with the way the Kaylins do things."

"Sounds like rubbish. And I hate operating by other people's rules. I don't like anyone expecting me to follow what other people do all the time." She rose from the table and paced. "I wish for once I could do what I want… and only what I want." *This is my dream, after all.*

Wynneth shook her head. When she spoke, there was pity in her tone. "We all want freedom from rules. Sometimes though, following someone else's customs may achieve a greater end. I urge you to keep your counsel on this to yourself. The time may come when you will need the Kaylins on your side."

"Alright." Kat grimaced. "I will. But I don't like it." *This game better be worth all this annoying stuff.*

CHAPTER 5

Wynneth hurried down the stone passage to meet with Eduardo. The thick rugs underfoot silenced her footfalls.

The young guard at Eduardo's quarters, aware of all who passed his way, grinned as she approached him. "Healer Wynneth, Lord Eduardo is expecting you.." He ducked his head inside the door. "Lord Eduardo, Healer Wynneth is here as you requested." He motioned her into the room.

"Thank you, Dafid." *He's becoming a fine young man. His parents must be proud of him.* Wynneth entered and the guard closed the door behind her.

Eduardo, already standing, moved from behind the desk to greet her, clasping her hands affectionately. "You are smiling. Why?"

"Requested, not ordered. I perceive your intention to reduce the unnecessary formalities are beginning to take hold." She freed one hand and patted him on the cheek. "At least with the younger ones."

"You noticed, but most do not, which is exactly the way I want the changes to take place." He led her by the hand. "Come sit with me, I need questions answered, and I ordered... ." He laughed. "I mean, I requested refreshments for us."

Sitting comfortably in a well-padded seat, a sizable cup of tea and a sweet treat at hand, Wynneth turned her attention to Eduardo. *No matter how grown up and lordly he becomes, he will always be my baby.* "I assume you need to talk."

"About the woman, of course."

"Indeed. What do you wish to find out about her?"

"Everything. This could be vital to Kaylin, and the rest of Pridden as well."

"In what way?"

"Wynneth, I am afraid we are approaching a major challenge among all our people. I constantly receive reports of unrest, not only within our land, but also incidents between the other lands as well."

"I hear many rumors, Eduardo, and I am concerned too."

"The difficulties with Morden were minor until Galdin's male parent instituted the Assassins' Guild. We see a growing and dramatic increase in fear of Morden, particularly among the Baklai. However, the truth is, those from Baklai tend to be fearful people."

"But Baklai receive the support of the Rifellans?"

"They do, but they fear Rifella may not respond quickly enough. In the meantime, Lord Rhognor of Shendea, your own land, contacted me with many tales of troubles among his people. Morden is most often at the base of these."

Wynneth sighed. "I cannot envisage only Morden is at fault."

"True, each land possesses their own peculiarities. People who moved to other lands because they found lucrative positions due to their skills, are now confronted with prejudices. Therefore, even within each land, acrimony exists among the residents who hale from elsewhere."

"Then how do you see Kat as a potential solution?"

"Ah, Kat is her name?"

Wynneth nodded.

"I believe she may be more important than either of us realize. Do you remember when you brought me here to Lord Lanerch, you brought him a message from Healer Deleth?"

The Arrival

"Yes. Deleth directed me to bring you here, and to stay on as the healer for Kaylin. She was most insistent I observe you as you matured."

"And you have done a fine job, Wynneth." He reached over and patted her hand again. "What she neglected to tell you, is she gave another message to my Lord Lanerch. One he was to make sure I received upon his death."

"By Caleesh, Deleth always had a habit of holding back from me. What was the message?"

"First, she explained the circumstances of my birth. She then went on to advise the unrest in Pridden would increase each star turn. A time would come when the survival of our world and the lands would be in peril."

Wynneth nodded. "Deleth is blessed with the farsight."

"She told me there was hope. She told me of a prediction that if Galdin and his ilk found a way to pursue their goals, it was possible they would directly, or indirectly, attract a visitor from outside our known world. This visitor could possess the ability to defeat Galdin and his followers and bring harmony back to our lands."

"And you think Kat is the person Deleth spoke of?"

"She may well be. She is certainly not from this world, is she?"

Wynneth rubbed her hands over her face. "I am convinced she is not, but this is a large hope to place on the head of one woman. A young woman, I might add, who needs to learn much about our lands and our customs. She is extremely headstrong, and she dislikes rules. And as for bringing harmony, I am not sure she is able to be sensitive and non-confrontational."

"Not ideal."

33

"You are right, it is not. But I find one thing most peculiar about her."

"What?"

"She must come from a land quite different from Kaylin. Plus, many things are obviously new to her. She is in a strange and new place, and yet she shows no surprise or fear of anything. I believe this is most unusual."

Eduardo reached over and took Wynneth by the hand again. "I cannot stress how important it is that you find out all you can about her. Perhaps she does indeed hold some power. Let us hope so. This is crucial to the survival of our lands and our world."

CHAPTER 6

Unaware Wynneth had left the room, and grumbling to herself, Kat paced the room. *Wait a minute.* Abruptly, she stopped dead. *I'm not angry. I'm experiencing a dream. How wonderful to write everything down -- lots of emotions. This game will be bigger with women than any of the others. Nick will be super impressed.*

Kat glanced around. "Wynneth… " No answer. *Oh. I didn't hear her leave. Of course you never notice those things in dreams.* Kat spied the remnants of the lunch at the table and poured herself another cup of tea. A few small cookie/cakes still rested on a plate, and she popped one in her mouth. It reminded her of the buttery flavor of Cinnebons. *Gloriously addicting. Wow, this is the first time I can remember tasting stuff in a dream.* She picked up a second, examined it, put it down again, and walked over to the mirror and examined her reflection. *I can live with this. The dress is not bad. But my heroine'll need to don her warrior role later.*

Kat strolled to the window, and hands on the ledge, leaned out and gazed at the scenery. Soft rolling green hills, turned to sharp and massive mountains in the distance. *I could live in a place like this. Kaylin, though, is too full of rules and boxes, but perhaps one of those other ones Wynneth mentioned. I could be a… potentate. Yes! I've been waiting for weeks to use that word.*

As a child, Kat always experienced rich dreams in full color, replete with sensations and emotions. The dreams she had after her father died, were at first soothing, then turned to terror and lasted nightly for more than a year. In dreams, she heard and felt what transpired. She remembered when the dragon bit her. After she woke from the dream, the sensation of the bite lasted most of the day. *I'm experiencing more things in this dream than ever before. Major chill.*

Kat could gather more information for her game if she remained in the dream state longer. *I believe I'll explore, so first the castle or keep (whatever) and then outside.*

She grabbed one more cake, strode to the door, flung it open and walked into the passageway. She halted. *Oh, oh. Something's wrong. Out-of-this-world wrong.* She had never ever been able to walk through doors into another room in any dream before. She always had to stop the scene and then re-imagine herself in the next room. *This is wrong.* A hollow sense of terror chewed at her stomach. She needed air. The cake dropped from her hand.

At that moment, Wynneth appeared in the hallway. "Good, you are well recovered."

"Are you kidding?" Kat pressed herself against the wall. "Wynneth, this isn't a dream, is it? I think I'm dreaming, but I'm not? All this is real. I'm not dreaming, am I?" She slid to the floor, horrified. "I want to go home."

Wynneth hurried over to Kat, who shuddered as she sat on the floor. "You are not dreaming. Yes, this is real, but you are safe." She put her hands out to raise Kat to her feet. "Come, you need to sit down to absorb this."

Slowly Kat rose, shaking, and allowed Wynneth to lead her back in the room. "This is all real. I'm not in a dream. I'm in a nightmare. How did I arrive here? How do I return? I need to find my way home. But how?" She babbled on but couldn't stop herself.

The Arrival

Wynneth drew back her hand and delivered a stinging slap to her cheek.

Kat responded, from her years of martial arts training, with a vicious punch aimed at the healer's face.

Wynneth equally fast, raised an arm to protect herself, fending off the blow.

Kat stared at her in horror, no longer panting in fear. "Oh hell, I'm so sorry, I reacted from instinct." She wrapped her arms across her chest and held herself protectively. "This is real but I can't figure out how I got here. I don't even know where here is."

Wynneth wrapped warm arms around Kat "You are safe, and you need to sit and think and we can decide what to do."

Gratefully, Kat allowed Wynneth to seat her in one of the comfy chairs. *I can't believe this. How can I exist in a nightmare?*

Wynneth took the chair beside her and the two of them sat in silence for a few minutes.

"So I am not in my own world, but where am I and how did I arrive here?" Kat deliberately kept her breathing normal. After all, she owned a black belt, third dan, and had trained to take life in stride. She snorted to herself. *Yeah, right.*

"Let us begin by finding out a bit about your land. Tell me what you were doing shortly before you awoke in that bed." Wynneth gestured toward it.

"Well, I was vacationing in the Virgin Islands…"

A faint blush colored Wynneth's cheek.

"Sorry. Yeah, the sex thing. But that's what they're called. Back to my story. I ate my lunch in the room, and went for a walk. It's the rainy season and I got caught in a storm and ran for shelter in an old stone building." Kat stopped and gazed around her. "This is kinda weird, but the stonework looked a lot like this place."

Wynneth motioned for her to continue.

"Well the roof leaked buckets, so I needed to move out of the water. I hardly did anything. I reached to open this odd-looking door, and something pushed me and pulled me and everything went black. The next thing I knew, I awoke here." She couldn't repress a shudder.

"You mentioned you were going to fly." Wynneth peered at Kat with obvious curiosity.

"Yes. I flew to the islands a couple of days ago and I'm due to fly back home in about three days."

Wynneth's eyes widened at this statement. "Do any others of your people fly?"

"Oh sure, lots of people do. If you can afford it."

"Many of your people fly? Are you all magicians?"

"No. We fly in planes."

"Playns? What are playns." Wynneth's eyes grew bigger.

Oh god, how can I explain a plane? "Well, a plane is like one of those big carts I see down on the roads." She pointed out the window. "The difference is they carry lots more people, with engines installed, and wings which allow them to be lifted into the air. They are made of metal and they travel fast. People can go to far away places quickly."

"I do not quite understand these playns," said Wynneth, "and I do not think it would help for you to attempt to explain this further."

"I don't understand exactly how they work either, but I once met some of the people who designed them. They understand how birds can fly and they used the same principles."

"Enough." Wynneth held up a hand. Her eyes were as large as dinner plates now.

"I must figure out how I can return to my home, because I don't understand how I got here."

"I think you should speak to Lord Eduardo. He is versed in many subjects and also wields much power. He is the logical place to begin."

"I'd like to talk to him. Can you arrange it?"

"I will request an audience for you with him. I do believe he wants to meet you, but you must give him time to gather his cleverest and most trusted advisors to help him, and that may take a few turns."

"I don't want to wait, I need to know now."

"You have no choice, Lady Kat. Plus this will give you time to view the beauty of our land and meet the interesting people in Kaylin."

She's right. I can still make notes on the new game, and I'll keep all the notes for when I arrive back. She shuddered again. *If I arrive back.*

She gazed at Wynneth's eyes. "You want me to be patient, don't you." Kat humphed. "I'm terrible at being patient."

J. M. Tibbott

CHAPTER 7

Wynneth's report on Kat intrigued Eduardo. "So you are positive this woman is not from any other land on Pridden?"

"I told you, Eduardo, her name is Kat. And yes, there is no question she is from elsewhere."

He smiled at Wynneth. He adored this gentle soul. However, the news she brought troubled him. *How am I to deal with this woman... with Kat?* "Thank you for the reminder. Forgetting people's names, does not serve. What else did you learn?"

"The inhabitants of her world are quite amazing. They all can fly."

"What?"

"Yes, but not like our Wielders can sometimes. They use some form of mechanical devices called... called... playns. Truly, I think if you let her explain this directly to you, you would understand better than me. She attempted to convey what they are, but I could not understand her explanation."

"Fine. You can bring her and I will interrogate her."

"I think it would be best if you talk to her, rather than interrogate. I must add, she is a strong woman. I misled you when I said she showed no surprise at being here. I now know she thought she was in a dream state. When she understood the reality of her situation, she became visibly upset, but her recovery was swift. It does appear she is blessed with much inner strength. I think her main desire now is to return to her own land."

He jumped to his feet. "By Morden's black eye, how am I expected to achieve this?"

Wynneth stood, put her hands on her plump hips and glared. "Eduardo, you do not need to curse at me. If you were not far too old now, I would turn you over my knee and deliver a spanking."

At the thought of himself bent over Wynneth's knee, Eduardo concealed his grin with enormous effort. "My sincere apologies, I was startled. This is a sizable challenge. At the current time, I do not hold the knowledge of how to return her." He gestured at the chair. "Please sit."

Wynneth sat back down. "Of course, you will need help. And if you decide she is the one to visit the lands, she will need an exceptional guide. As I said, she is a strong woman — strong willed, strong minded and physically strong as well, I suspect."

"No doubt, you are correct. I am sure she is the one spoken of in the prophecy, and if so, she could help us. However, we cannot allow her to blunder her way through the lands without supervision and guidance." He stroked his chin. "I believe I have an idea." He had a mischievous notion. "Unless, Wynneth, you would agree to act as her guide?"

"If you attempt anything of the kind, Eduardo, I would be willing to curse you myself."

"Forgive me again, I was merely indulging in humor." He reached over and pulled on a tassel hanging from the ceiling.

The young guard poked his head around the door. "Yes Sire?"

"Dafid, would you please send a request for Counselor Drainin to join me in my quarters?"

"Yes, Lord Eduardo." He disappeared and the door closed.

The Arrival

Wynneth rose. "I will leave you to meet with your counselor."

"No, please stay. I want you to bring Drainin up to date with your knowledge of the... of Kat. Pour some more tea while we wait."

***

Two cups later, Dafid tapped at the door.

"Come."

Dafid's curly brown head appeared. "Counselor Drainin is here as you requested, Sire."

Eduardo motioned with his fingers to admit his visitor.

Drainin appeared in the doorway. "Lord Eduardo." He inclined his head.

Eduardo had always envied Drainin his commanding tones. He owned a voice which issued from somewhere below knee level. The gravel sounds summoned up visions of lords commanding vast hosts of armed men to attack at dawn. He imagined Drainin could boast many conquests, despite the Kaylin's severe condemnation of relationships between men and women before bonding.

"Counselor Drainin, welcome. I need advice and counsel. Please sit."

"I am at your service, my Lord." He moved to a chair which sat at a higher level than Wynneth's.

Eduardo gestured toward Wynneth. "My healer advised me of what she learned of our new visitor."

Wynneth inclined her head at Drainin, but only the barest flicker.

Eduardo caught the minuscule flash of anger in Drainin's eyes. *These two don't appear to like each other. Interesting. I've not noticed this before.*

"Healer Wynneth, I heard a woman of unknown origin arrived in Kaylin. I am sure you were able to find much of interest." Drainin's voice hinted of something dark.

Interesting. He demonstrates hints of the powers of voice command. "I asked the healer to remain here while we discuss what the ramifications of the woman's appearance at this time may mean for Kaylin, and possibly for all Pridden. You and I already discussed the challenges among our people, plus those of neighboring lands and how we might address them. This woman's arrival may be a coincidence, but I am hoping we can use her."

"In what way, my Lord?"

"I am considering sending the woman... Kat is her name... to investigate the reports of unrest, and to determine if a common factor exists."

"An unusual task to hand to a stranger. Is she the right person to do this? And, will she even consider performing this for you?"

"I believe the fact she is a stranger is to our advantage. I also believe between the two of us, Counselor, we can persuade her to help." Eduardo smiled at him. "I am aware of your success with the female residents of Kaylin."

Drainin waved a dismissive hand. "They are simply young women seeking a bond mate. I doubt their interest is resolute. Mine, with certainty, is not."

"Nevertheless, Counselor, the unrest is reaching serious proportions, and the time has arrived when we must attempt to unravel the problem. The important part is, to persuade Kat to aid us. We need to assure her this will be in her best interest to undertake the challenge."

"In that case, my Lord, I suggest we send her to Morden first. I myself will volunteer to be her guide."

The Arrival

"Some difficulties arise with your suggestion. First you will find Kat is not a 'young woman seeking a bond mate.' Second, although you may be the best person for the job, I do not wish to spare your counsel for any length of time, your continuing help is too important to me. I am considering a number of other appropriate guides, and I will wait until she meets them all to determine who I choose. Finally, Lord Rhognor contacted me and indicated his strong desire for her to first visit Shendea. Given the close ties between our two lands, I must honor his request."

"But surely my Lord, the unrest in Morden would dictate her presence there is more important than placating Lord Rhognor."

Eduardo laughed. "Lord Rhognor is not easily placated, and our continuing relationship requires I accede to him. You have obviously never been in his company when he is irritated. We must send her to Shendea first." *I wonder why he is so eager to go to Morden with Kat?*

"As you wish, Lord Eduardo."

"Perhaps, Counselor you can begin the logic of planning a route and supplies for the trip through Kaylin. If you are familiar with other guides you suspect would be well suited for a woman who is a stranger to our land, I would appreciate a list of names to consider. Of course, I would be grateful if you can devise a plan to discuss the trip with Kat, so when we meet with her, she will be compelled to say yes to our appeal."

"Of course, my Lord." His body was stiff, apparently with disapproval.

He bent his head once more and strode toward the door.

Wynneth rose to take her leave.

Eduardo stopped her. "Healer, I would ask you to remain, I am irritated by a minor physical complication requiring your ministration."

Drainin barely broke stride at this comment. But the pause hung suspended in the room.

Wynneth regarded Eduardo with the barest hint of a smile. "Of course."

Eduardo waited until the door closed behind Drainin, and his footsteps retreated down the passageway. He turned to Wynneth. "You disapprove of him. Why?"

"A vibration surrounds him which gives me discomfort. I do not know why, but be careful Eduardo. I fear Counselor Drainin cleaves to his own agenda."

"Your words are true. He possesses a decidedly specific agenda. As a highly ambitious man, everything he does is for his own advancement and benefit. He is, however, clever, intuitive, and I have often observed him helping some of the apprentices with their studies. His counsel is almost always excellent, and I trust his abilities and his logic, if not his undying loyalty."

"I should have sensed you would be aware of his intentions."

"One never knows another's true intentions, but I do understand much about him, and I value his contribution." Eduardo patted Wynneth's arm. "Go and advise Kat I will meet with her tomorrow."

CHAPTER 8

At the sound of a tap on the door, Kat glanced up from her thoughts on how she would design the new game. *Why not—Wynneth uses it?* "Come?"

Wynneth entered and strode over to her. "Are you now well recovered?"

Kat smiled and nodded hesitantly. "Yes... I am, mostly." She gestured toward the small table against the wall. "Thank you for the writing equipment. How useful, although it did take some getting used to. Particularly this." She held up a finely carved piece of what appeared to be ivory, and which ended in a sharpened point.

"The writing instrument is carved from a tooth of a cathnog." Wynneth held up a finger. "I will explain a cathnog. They are the most dangerous creatures in Shendea, and they live among the lesser mountains. They may have originally been related to our vermin-catching cats, but they are many times larger. Their teeth are quite long, as you can observe, and they are most vicious."

Visions of enormous mountain felines prowled through Kat's thoughts.

Wynneth continued. "People rarely encounter them as they feed upon the hydodds when they can win a fight against them."

"High-dods?"

"Ah, yes. Hydodds resemble large deer, but they are much bigger and muscular and sport magnificent antlers. When a cathnog and hydodd fight, no one can be sure who will win."

"Are the cathnogs dangerous to people?" *So no dragons here, but huge ferocious animals will add to the game. My ideas will keep me occupied while I'm figuring how to get home.*

"Very dangerous, but these cats will only venture lower down their mountains and prey on the people when they are injured or extremely old. Our young males attempt to find and kill the creature when this happens. To fight a cathnog is the highest rite of passage a young man can achieve." Wynneth picked up the pen. "This particular instrument came from my male parent, who killed his cathnog when he was younger than most."

"Wow. So this is valuable."

"True. But do remember, objects like this are meant to be used, not hidden away or displayed in a case somewhere." Wynneth fondled the fine white carving, seemingly lost in thought. She glanced at Kat. "Do you have sufficient writing materials?"

"Plenty. Thank you."

Pieces of parchment lay about the desk, covered in spidery writing, and spattered generously with blobs of the black substance the Kaylins used as ink.

Wynneth picked up a sheet. "What secret runes are these you use? I cannot recall their like before."

"Er… they're not runes, only English." *I know my writing's bad, but runes?*

Wynneth nodded. "In-glish." The expression on her face reminded Kat of the phrase 'a deer in headlights.' *I wonder why she looks fearful. Are their runes dangerous?*

"Yes. Of course." Wynneth shifted in place. "I cannot read it, but no matter."

Now this world is weirder than I expected. Kat shook herself mentally. *How is it possible we understand each other, but she can't read my writing?*

Wynneth cleared her throat. "Kat, Lord Eduardo has agreed to meet with you on the morrow. He will send a messenger after your morning meal."

Kat's mood lifted further. "Wonderful."

Wynneth continued. "After your meeting with him, I also requested Mayda give you a tour of the keep and the grounds. I believe you will find them both interesting." She paused. "If you would like to continue with recording your runes, I will come later to escort you to our evening meal."

***

Near the end of the day, Wynneth guided Kat through a maze of corridors, and finally entered the doors to the hall where the meal was to take place. Kat was assaulted by color and noise. Hundreds of people, dressed in bright clothes, and seated at benches and tables, chatted avidly with each other. The sound reminded Kat of the flocks of geese at her grandfather's farm. Usually uncomfortable in crowds, and despite the sensory overload of brilliant greens, bright yellows, reds and the stunning blues of their apparel, Kat found herself caught up in the warmth and camaraderie of the people in the hall.

Mayda, seated beside a short, dark, but well-muscled, man, waved at her, and Kat asked Wynneth who he was.

"He is Mayda's male parent, and he is the Horse-Master of the keep."

"He's not very tall, but he looks strong."

"He needs to be. The animals he handles are much bigger than he is."

Wynneth led Kat through the crowd to a table with four other women and introduced her. "Lady Kat, this is Brith. She is responsible for your clothing while in Kaylin."

The tall woman with the severe hairstyle, about the same age as Kat, inclined her head. "Well met, Lady Kat."

Kat remembered Wynneth's instructions on courtesy in Kaylin. "This dress is beautiful and fits perfectly, Brith. Thank you."

Wynneth gestured to the next woman. "This is Bronwyth, who arranges all Lord Eduardo's functions for important visitors. She is from my home land of Shendea."

"Well met, Lady Kat." Bronwyth's curls bounced as she inclined her head.

Wynneth introduced Kat to Clune, the Kaylin woman who functioned as clerk in Lord Eduardo's offices, and Sherwyn the head of house for the keep. Both women lowered their heads in greeting. Although their dresses were similar, each had a badge sewn on the right shoulder. When Kat inquired, they advised her their badges indicated their place and function in the keep. With their rich brown hair and dark brown eyes, they looked so much alike, Kat's only way of telling them apart was the way they wore their hair. Clune wore her hair tied back in a meticulous bun, but Sherwyn's hair, gathered away from her face, contained in a snood hairnet, was decorated with a matching bow for her dress.

Once everyone was seated, young men and women appeared and began serving beverages.

Their efficiency impressed Kat. "The green coats they're wearing — is this a uniform for the keep?"

Sherwyn answered her. "Yes. But this uniform is for these young ones who are apprentices. They spend eight seasons living here, and assist in all crafts, learning about possible careers they might pursue. Some find their calling within the keep, some in the metal-works, or quarries. But most return to their homes and farms with a wealth of knowledge to help them live successful lives with their families, and later with their own bondings and pairings."

"When do they eat?"

"They have already dined, Lady Kat. Lord Eduardo is most adamant on this. Hungry servers cannot be expected to do their chores well."

Kat turned to Wynneth. "Does everyone in this keep eat together every night?"

Wynneth laughed. "No — that would be far too difficult to arrange. Lord Eduardo designated a gathering like this, once each time the seasons change, as a celebration. Only the apprentices and those of us who live within the keep eat meals together. All others dine with their families."

Kat sipped the clear liquid in the glass beside her. The drink tickled her tongue with an unknown sweet and mildly alcoholic flavor. She had never been one to imbibe much, so even the slight amount of alcohol made an impression. "What is this? It's delicious."

Brith answered her. "It is Orenberry wine from Glowen. We need to mix the wine with water to make it palatable here in Kaylin. We only partake of the Orenberry at these seasonal gatherings."

The young apprentices appeared again bearing huge platters of food, which they proceeded to distribute to the tables and benches. Kat sniffed the air and drooled at the tantalizing smell, reminiscent of backyard barbecues dripping on hot coals. Her stomach rumbled in anticipation. The women at her table passed the two huge platters to her first. Wynneth gave her a subtle nod, so she served herself a small amount of everything.

Brith offered to identify the various foods on her plate, and Kat accepted with gratitude.

Unfamiliar but delicate flavors flooded her mouth. Her favorite, a meat with a minty sweet taste, Brith identified as wullawerth.

"Wullawerths are valuable creatures. Their fine hair is spun into the beautiful soft fabrics from which most of our clothes are made. Your dress," Brith continued, "is wullawerth hair."

"It's cuddly, and soft, and comfortable." Kat stroked her skirt. *It reminds me of rabbit fur.*

"I would be glad to show the wullawerths to you, Lady Kat."

"I would like that, Brith." Kat repeated the names of the others in her conversation as much as possible. She was hopeless at remembering names, and this was her own trick as a memory aid. *Nick would never believe I'm having a lengthy conversation with a bunch of women. I don't have many women in my life, so I don't believe this myself.*

By the time the apprentices began clearing the tables, Kat yawned, unable to stop herself.

Wynneth rose. "Your day has been long and full, Lady Kat. I will return you to your rooms."

Kat said goodnight to her table companions and followed Wynneth. The comfortable bed beckoned her.

***

The night, dark as the color of Kaylin ink, concealed all. Kat, leaned over the balcony of her room and waited for her eyes to adjust, but only faint light of stars provided any definition of the shadow shapes of the landscape below her.

The Arrival

Something appeared at the edge of the tree line moving toward the keep, black and formless. The shadows stopped, and roiled and boiled into a tall hooded figure. The malevolent apparition drifted forward, silent and barely perceptible. It radiated fear and loathing. Kat consumed by an urge to run, to scream, was transfixed, unable to flee. Straining to yell for help, she opened her mouth wide, and... .

Kat sat up in bed, gasping and drenched with sweat. *A nightmare. But why and who?* Kat glanced toward the arched window. The faint glow of dawn beckoned her. She crept out of bed and tiptoed over to the light. Outside the first golden rays of the sun lit up the landscape below her. She breathed a sigh of relief. All was green and clear below, but she couldn't go back to sleep with the hooded creature so fresh in her memory.

J. M. Tibbott

CHAPTER 9

Still haunted by the remnants of her nightmare, Kat remained at the window, breathing in the green scent of cut grass. *I'll write down game stuff. The task should keep me awake.* She shivered. *And sane... the game will keep me sane.*

Her heartbeat back to normal, a faint gurgle in her stomach urged her to pull the tassel to summon breakfast. *Tea will be perfect now.*

***

The food and tea had not calmed her and unable to write, Kat paced the room. The nightmare made no sense. *Who was the spooky figure, and why did I feel so afraid?* She shivered again.

A faint knock at the door.

"Come."

Wynneth entered, beaming with friendliness.

Kat glanced at her. "I'm glad you're here. I had this crazy dream last night... well... more of a nightmare, and I want to find out why." She continued her pacing.

The healer's tone was sharp. "Good morrow to you too, Lady Kat."

"Oh yeah. Morning. Whatever. I'm telling you the dream was a truly weird one and... ."

"Stop now."

Kat stared. "What?" She ceased pacing.

Wynneth glared at her. "People of Kaylin greet each other politely before they start a conversation about their day.

They acknowledge each other before they begin talking. You were rude when you ignored me and jumped directly into your own concerns."

"Oh." *Crap, there I go again. How do they ever get anything done here. They waste so much time on silly conventions.*

"Lady Kat, for some reason, you do not appear to understand what I am telling you. Surely your own people are not all this rude?"

Uh oh, she's angry. I better re-think this. She's my only contact in this weird world. I guess I should apologize. "Wynneth, we're very busy people, and perhaps we don't spend as much time on these things as you do. So, I'm sorry if you thought I ignored you. I didn't realize this mattered so much."

"Matter? Absolutely. It is not courteous to ignore people. I tried to tell you. Being polite is important, not only in Kaylin, and it seems a difficult concept for you."

Kat hung her head. She wanted to appear contrite.

Wynneth sighed heavily. "Kat, Kat, Kat. Your attempt to appear apologetic is impossible to be construed as genuine. Obviously, you do not follow the rules of conduct which are significant in our world. However, it is imperative you practice—even if you do not agree with these requirements. You are going to need many people to help you return to your own world. If you continue to be discourteous, no one will be willing to do so."

She's right. I think this is what Nick always meant about following some rules to achieve the end you want. "What you say makes sense. I will do my best to fit into the rules of Kaylin. I suspect I'm going to need a great deal of your help. Will you do this?"

Wynneth's expression softened. "Of course I will. Your heart is staunch, Kat. In many ways, you are similar to a gemstone in need of polishing. I am willing to help to polish you."

Polish me? I wonder if she can hear my internal snort of disbelief? "Thanks, then it's a deal?"

Wynneth blinked rapidly, apparently confused, and then a sly grin turned up the corners of her mouth. "Okay."

Kat relaxed at once and laughed. "Your sense of humor is wicked." *I'll get her using all my expressions before she's aware of it.*

Wynneth snorted. "Lady Kat, I am not wicked, but I do find much to amuse me in my life. Now enough of this discussion, Lord Eduardo is waiting to speak to you. Come and I will take you to his quarters."

"Before we do, Wynneth, can you get me a light so I can see when it gets dark outside?"

"You do possess light in here. See." She pointed at globes attached to the walls. "All you need do is clap your hands once, and they will illuminate your room."

Kat stared at the globes and clapped her hands. The room brightened as the globes illuminated. "How do they work? You don't seem to enjoy electricity."

"I do not know what this eelek… sisity is, but the globes come from Shendea. Our Magician's Guild discovered them deep within the caverns of the highest peaks of Clog Neran. They learned how to use the globes to create light. and they used their own type of wielder power to allow the light to activate at a clap of one's hands."

"What happens when the globes run out of the ability to supply light?"

"No globe has ever failed, at least, not to my knowledge." Wynneth shrugged. "We really must attend Lord Eduardo. He is waiting."

***

Kat perched on the edge of her chair across from Lord Eduardo, unsure of how to proceed, and experienced the sensation of a bug on a slide under a microscope. *Does the first to speak lose?* "I assume you understand why I'm here"

"Indeed. You wish help to return to your own world. Wynneth gave me information about you, and I am convinced you do come from elsewhere."

Mmm—a definite chocolate voice — but dark chocolate. Nice looking too. "I'm definitely not from here. Can you send me back?"

"Before we discuss the possible positive or negative outcomes from such an event, let us attempt to discover all the practical needs for an endeavor like this."

"What do you mean?"

Eduardo leaned forward, his elbows on his desk, and steepled his fingers. "What, Kat, are you willing to do, to achieve your return to your own world?"

"Well, anything. But I didn't bring myself here, so I don't see what I can accomplish."

"You can accomplish much, but not necessarily in the way you anticipate. Let me list the challenges and the possible solutions for you."

"Fine, I'm listening." *Oh boy, more talk, less action. Again.*

"I believe Wynneth informed you a number of people on our world are able to wield power."

"Yes, and she said you and the guy in Shendea are the only people who still retain much of the original ability."

The Arrival

Eduardo visibly winced. "You mean Lord Rhognor."

Oops, they like their titles. "Yeah, Lord Rhognor."

"A reasonably true statement. However, many on Pridden hold power to various degrees. Because of this fact, I believe at least six people with a reasonable amount of wielder power will be needed to return you to your world."

"Surely enough power exists, because somebody brought me here initially."

"Also true, but I surmise a number of people worked together to bring you here. The challenge is I do not know where the responsibility lies, or why they did this."

"Well you understand who on your world has power enough to send me back, why can't you ask them to come here and perform this power thing?"

He sighed. "Not as simple as you might imagine." He drummed his fingers on his desk. "Let me explain what is occurring on our world."

Kat sat down in the chair and waited.

"For many star turns our lands are beset with minor skirmishes, and in some cases the fights lead to death."

"How does this affect me?"

"I believe only an outsider can discover what the real problems are."

"Wait a minute, I'm not a diplomat." *Is he nuts?*

"From what Wynneth told me, Kat, I am well aware of your short-comings in the area of diplomacy." He held up his hand to forestall her. "However, we need a stranger to travel through the lands, and meet with a variety of the inhabitants to discover who, or what, is at the root of the trouble. You could be the very stranger we require. And," —he held up his hand again— "while you do this, you can discover who possesses sufficient power, and," he held up a hand, pointing at the ceiling, "is willing to work to return you to your home."

"So basically it's extortion."

Eduardo shook his head and sighed again. "No, not extortion. Mutual help, Kat. Mutual help."

Kat considered his answer and let the silence between them stretch. "I guess you're right. I'm willing to help." She deliberately emphasized the word help. "But make no mistake, I'm only doing this to return home."

"I understand."

"You're dropping this huge chore on me, but how will I know what to look for and what to say to the people I meet? How big an area do I need to cover? Where do I start?"

"Relax. I am not sending you anywhere without help. I will find an appropriate guide for you, and in each place you go, the people in the various keeps will give you more information. As to what to say or do with the people you meet, I believe we should allow your instincts to determine who you talk to. Primarily, this is a task of observation, and I will leave it up to you, with help from your guide, as to how you conduct yourself."

"Doesn't sound very efficient or practical."

"I'm aware of that. However, I believe you were meant to be here, and therefore, things will arrange themselves accordingly."

This sounds so nuts to me. He hasn't given me anything specific at all. "If that's what's required, but where do I go first?"

"After a tour through Kaylin, we will start with Shendea because Lord Rhognor and I enjoy a close relationship. He will be anxious to meet you."

I'm not crazy about this deal, but... "Fine."

Eduardo continued. "Once people are aware you are going to Shendea first, you may find many will attempt to

The Arrival

persuade you to go elsewhere. Do not listen. Believe me, this is your most important first visit to another land. Do not let anyone dissuade you from Shendea. I will send Lord Rhognor a message advising him you will accept this challenge. We need to give him time to prepare."

This isn't a plan, it's a joke... but I guess I can research for my game too.

Eduardo left his chair and walked to a small covered cage in the corner of his office. Lifting the protection, he raised a latch, reach in and scooped out something tiny and round. He returned to his desk and deposited a furry ball on the polished wood.

Kat stared at the strangest animal she had ever seen. The grey ball of fur shook itself, stretched its body, extended a pair of leathery wings, and yawned broadly, exposing a long pink tongue and two rows of tiny white teeth. Kat laughed. "What is that?"

Eduardo raised his head from his missive. "This is a messenger pyrock."

"It's adorable." Kat was sure she had a weirdly sappy smile people get when confronted by something cute, but she couldn't help herself.

"Adorable?" Eduardo displayed puzzlement on his face. "Merely a simple way to send messages over a distance."

Kat reached out to stroke the little creature.

Eduardo barked at her. "Do not touch!"

Startled, she snapped her hand back from the pyrock. "Will it bite me?"

"No." He cleared his throat. "Forgive me for raising my voice. Pyrocks easily lose their concentration and become distracted, so they are only handled by one person during their lifetime."

"Why?"

"Their abilities are limited and they tend to only be comfortable around a single owner. I alone feed and touch this one, who will always return to me when the message is delivered. Their mind-to-mind communication is minimal, so pyrocks need focus."

"What's its name?"

"This one is called Blink."

"How does Blink understand where to go?"

Eduardo smiled at her. "I picture in my mind the person to whom the message is to be delivered, and Blink can instantly locate the specific individual. Before you ask, the recipients only touch her enough to retrieve the message. Plus, no one else would feed another's pyrock. Since Blink is always hungry, she heads straight back to me once her task is done."

"Oh, I want one. I really want one." *Oh boy. I'll bet I'm still smiling idiotically.*

"I agree, you should be assigned a pyrock of your own. You will need one in your travels. Blink has an egg in her cage which I will give to you in about fifteen star turns or so."

Terrific, about two weeks, I can wait two weeks.

"You should have enough time to establish communication with your future pyrock." With those words, Eduardo rolled up his note, which he inserted in a small tube.

Blink held out her foreleg, and Eduardo clamped the tube firmly in place on the tiny harness she wore. Blink eyed him, head tilted almost upside down, gave a small chirp, halfway between a purr and a bleat, and airborne, she flapped her wings briefly and disappeared with a distinct pop.

Mouth open, Kat stared at the place where Blink had been. "Wow."

The Arrival

Eduardo reached for the summoning tassel. "Now Lord Rhognor is informed, I will introduce you to your first guide."

***

Dafid ushered a tall man with straight black hair and a pale but handsome face into Eduardo's rooms. The man greeted Eduardo and turned to stare at Kat. He had the eyes of a wolf — light blue with a dark ring around the edge of the iris. Kat experienced an involuntary shiver at his feral expression.

Eduardo stood. "Lady Kat, this is Drainin, my Chief Counselor. He will be able to give you additional information about your intended trip."

Drainin moved toward her. "So you are our visitor from another world." His voice came out of some deep gravel pit. His words resonated with power.

Kat rose from her chair to greet him. *Aha. A typically arrogant male and he likes to control women.* She wanted to keep distance between them and so laced her reply with as much ice as possible. "I believe so."

"Lord Eduardo requested I help you in your visits to other lands, and I would suggest we begin with Morden."

In her peripheral vision, Kat caught Eduardo observing her closely. She straightened to her full height. "No Counselor Drainin, I plan on Shendea as my first stop. My mind is quite made up."

She caught an infinitesimal flash of annoyance on his face.

I don't like this man and my gut says don't trust him. He doesn't like to be crossed or refused. Is it why he is upset at my words?

J. M. Tibbott

CHAPTER 10

At the time promised previously, Mayda arrived at Kat's room ready to take her on her first tour of the keep and the adjacent area.

"I would like you to show me the stable where the horses are kept, Mayda. At my home, I often ride."

"I am a little afraid of the horses, Lady Kat. They are all so very big."

Kat suspected Mayda was a little afraid of many things. Her small face and straight brown hair reminded Kat of a chipmunk -- quick and nervous. "Not me, I find some of my best ideas when I am out in the fresh air, hearing the horses hooves. I love the rhythm of the ride. It's super cool."

"The weather is actually warmer today, but I will be glad to take you the stable, Lady Kat."

Rats, I keep forgetting they don't understand my slang.

Mayda continued talking. "We only need to take a short walk past the wullawerth meadow. Haydar is the Horse-Master and he is most knowledgeable."

"I believe he is your parent?"

"Yes. They called him the best Master of horses in Baklai, and when offered this position, our family moved to Kaylin. Life on Baklai is much harsher, and here we live a better life. My family much admire Lord Eduardo and because of him we are most comfortable here. The ways of Kaylin were a little strange at first, but we found our place and are settled."

"Terrific, let's go." *Oh boy, I think she's gonna be a talker.*

***

Kat strolled along the paths with Mayda, listening with only one ear to her eager guide's chattering. The shy young woman, once she relaxed in Kat's company, was unable to use words sparingly. *Great, she's never going to stop talking. Perhaps I should ask her questions I want answered.* "What are those?" She pointed at some bulky wooly sheep-like creatures two fields away.

"Oh those are wullawerths. They are wonderful for eating, and their hair is extremely soft. The clothing we make from them is the best on all Pridden." Mayda chattered on, supplying Kat with facts and figures about wullawerth farming. Many facts and figures.

Finally Kat had enough. "Stop Mayda. I don't need so much information. Let's just be quiet, because I need to think."

Mayda bent her head, concealed her eyes, and blushed as she did so. "I talk too much. Everybody says so. I talk because I am nervous, and I do not know what to say to people. And I…"

Her voice trailed off as Kat put a finger to her lips.

They continued to walk in silence, Kat watching Mayda in her peripheral vision. Every time she opened her mouth to speak, Kat held up a hand to stop her. At last Mayda managed to relax enough so she could walk and keep her chattering to a manageable level.

The sun toasted Kat's face, and the air, sweet with the scents of newly cut grasses, green and clean, and enhanced with a gentle aroma of manure lingered as she inhaled. It was the scent of grass feeders, not of those who ate meat. The sounds of birds and other creatures tickled her ears, and tiny, multi-colored insects darted to and fro in the warm breeze. Kat turned to Mayda. "Let's sit for a while on the grass."

"But the stable is only a little further. You can see the buildings from here." She gestured toward a number of low-slung wooden structures, surrounded by paddocks populated with horses, all munching grass or gazing into the distance — stationary, except for moving jaws, flicking tails and twitching ears.

"Mayda, the day is warm and smells lovely. I find this so peaceful and want to enjoy the view. I want to totally relax. Please sit down as well. This is a time for sitting." *Plus this is perfect for planning the background for my new game. Although truthfully, I'd just like a rest from having to limit Mayda's constant nattering.*

Mayda nodded mutely.

Kat chose a soft clump of grass, and leaned back against the rock behind her. The sun, pleasantly balmy, was delicious, and her imagination brought to mind a symphony with the birds' songs and the buzzing of insects as the instruments.

Kat experienced a wave of lassitude and her limbs became rubber. They flowed and melted into the soft comfortable grass. Even Mayda remained silent, and when Kat glanced her way, her eyes were closed. Kat's own eyes grew heavy and as her lids shut she drifted into a languorous sleep.

***

Kat followed the skirmish of two armies of brightly clothed horsemen as they rode to battle. She found the action exciting and heart-stopping as they moved in swirls of color and the clash of armor and weapons. The sounds increased as they rode towards each other. Drums pounded in rhythm, horses neighed and pranced, and as the armies closed the gap between them, the drumbeats slowed and stopped. The leader called to Mayda.

"Mayda, wake up you lazy girl."

Kat woke with a start and jumped to her feet. A short distance away stood the largest, most powerful horse she had ever seen. The animal had to be twenty or twenty-one hands high. Seated on his back was the man she had seen at the communal supper, whom she now knew as Haydar. Although dwarfed by the horse, he appeared completely in control of his massive mount.

Beside her, Mayda stood brushing bits of grass from her clothes. "Forgive me sir, but Lady Kat needed to sit and think and we fell asleep in the sun."

She calls her father sir? Weird. I wonder how I should address this guy? Well, here goes. "You must be Horse-Master Haydar. I am pleased to meet you."

Haydar stared at her with eyes so dark brown, they were almost black. They held no warmth.

Hmmm. Suspicious guy.

"So you are Lady Kat." He bowed his head a touch. "Well met, my Lady."

He's one person who doesn't seem subservient or impressed by my presence. Perhaps, he could be a model in my game for the hero's battle companion. "Thank you. Mayda and I were on our way to see you, and I hope to be able to ride one of your wonderful horses."

"Of course. However, I must complete the exercising of Brack, and I will return to the stable after. Then we can determine which animal would suit you."

"Thank you Horse-Master."

He wheeled the horse around and set off at a canter, the hooves of the mighty Brack pounding a drum beat once more in the hard-packed earth.

The Arrival

Kat turned to Mayda. "Well, let's go."

Mayda stood pale and trembling. "I should not have fallen asleep. He is displeased with me. He will punish me."

Damn, is he one of those abusive fathers? So much for him being a hero's sidekick. "Nonsense. I won't let him. You only fell asleep because I insisted we stop. I'll make sure he knows."

"Thank you, Lady Kat." Mayda, however, frowned and her lower lip quivered.

***

The stable was a short walk. As they approached, Kat smelled the earthy aroma of horses. She suggested Mayda, who'd already expressed her fear of the large animals, wait outside and she entered the structure alone. Spotless orders of leather bridles and polished saddles lined up along one side of the building. Opposite were a number of individual stalls, with huge horses pointing interested noses at their visitor. Most of the horses were tan, but one flaunted a rich, earth-brown coat, and a white star on his forehead. He was also the biggest. Kat adored horses. She loved their power. She walked to the brown, but even though he bent his head to her, she could barely reach his nose. She spied a small stool, dragged it over to the stall, and stood to reach the horse. "You are a beauty, aren't you?" She put her hand on his soft velvet nose and stroked. He blew a warm, hay-scented breath at her.

"That one is Blayth, and he looks to Lord Eduardo."

Kat whirled around, nearly falling off the stool, and caught the gleam of pride in Haydar's eyes as he gazed at the beautiful animal.

She stepped down. "He's gorgeous, but I assume you would want me to ride some other animal." *I'm good with horses, but this one is a bit bigger than I'm used to.*

"Indeed. The animals in this barn all belong to special owners, and they only reside in this structure when they need further training, or exercising. There are more out here."

He grabbed a nearby rope, strode to the opening at the other end, while Kat scurried to keep up with him. For a short man, he moved incredibly fast.

At the exit, Kat stopped abruptly, enthralled. The stables were a rider's dream, with paddock after paddock, filled with horses, dozens more than she'd seen from the distance. *They're glorious, and the whole set-up is enchanting.* She laughed in delight.

"Those in the paddock next to the barn," Haydar indicated the nearest, "look to Lord Eduardo's personal guard, while many of those" — he indicated the enclosure a little further away— "are for the army. At the base of the hill, there are horses for general use. We will find one for you to ride."

Kat hurried after him and stared open-mouthed as he moved into the enclosure and shouldered horses aside, until he slipped the rope over the head of a smaller mare.

"Come." Immediately, the animal responded to his order, almost as if the line around her neck did not exist.

No one in Kat's experience had demonstrated such power over so many horses. *He's incredible. Perhaps this is why Mayda fears him.*

He glanced at Kat. "Follow me." He walked toward the buildings next to the first set of paddocks.

She followed. *Well, perhaps he can be the sidekick after all. He likes giving orders.* "Why do none of the horses I see have shoes?"

He turned back to her, puzzlement etched on his face. "Shoes? Why would we put shoes on horses?" He pointed at Kat's feet. "Do you think leather such as you are wearing

The Arrival

would last long on a horse? Plus, I am sure wearing it would annoy them."

"I didn't mean leather. Where I come from we have metal pieces shaped like this… " she drew a horseshoe in the dirt at her feet. "which the farriers attach to the hoof with nails."

"Nail a piece of metal to a horse's hoof? I find the idea barbaric. Your people sound very odd. And I have never heard of a faree-er."

"I guess your horses don't need them." *Oh hell, did I just put my foot in it? I haven't seen any tarmac or concrete, so maybe they really don't need shoes.*

"Odd." He shook his head, continued walking and stopped at the edge of the stable.

He handed the rope to her. "This is Ferth. Hold her while I locate a saddle." He turned to the horse. "Stay."

The animal nodded her head two or three times and snorted at Haydar.

He tapped her nose lightly, and shook his own head.

Ferth dropped her head a little and nickered softly.

Haydar smiled, turned and entered a structure next to the main stable. After a few minutes he returned carrying a simple, but well-polished saddle, and a bridle slung over his shoulder. He swung the saddle up and over the Ferth's back, and grabbed the various straps from underneath and proceeded to tighten the girth. He stood back and eyed the horse. "No, you do not." Without warning, he gave her a beefy punch in the stomach. Ferth exhaled with a grunt, and he tightened the girth even more. He turned to Kat. "This one has a sense of humor. She enjoys watching her riders slide down and hang beneath her stomach."

Kat laughed. "I've had a similar thing happen to me. It's embarrassing when a horse bests you."

He pulled a stool from the side of the building and set it beside Ferth's head. Stepping up, bridle now in hand, he slipped the leather straps over her head and adjusted everything. Back on the ground, he moved the stool beside the animal and turned to Kat. "Up you go."

Needing no additional suggestion, she stepped on the stool, gathered her skirt up around her thighs and swung up into the saddle. She glanced down at Haydar.

His brown face appeared almost white, and his mouth hung open.

A nervous glance behind her to locate who or what had caused such horror in his expression, revealed no one. Kat stared down at him.

He spat at her with rage. "How dare you expose yourself like this? Get down this instant."

Kat, astonished by the change, made no move to dismount.

"I said, get down from that animal. Now." Flecks of spittle flew from his mouth.

Ferth moved restlessly from side to side, her ears flat back, snorting and whistling.

Haydar's face turned red, his black eyes mere slits, and narrow lips drawn back with teeth bared. He resembled a wild animal. "I said. Get. Down!"

Kat slid off Ferth's back to the ground. "What are you on about?" *He's gone crazy.*

The red in Haydar's face had changed to a virulent shade of purple. "You are no Lady. You exposed your limbs. It is forbidden. I will not allow you to ride here. Go." His anger was so violent, he hissed at her. "Now. Never return." He pulled on Ferth's rope and hustled her back to the paddock.

Was he afraid the horse might become infected with some vile disease if she remained next to Kat?

What the...? This is insane. What is going on? I must find Wynneth.

J. M. Tibbott

CHAPTER 11

Eduardo marched up and down his office, waiting. Night had swallowed the light some time ago, and the inhabitants of the keep slept soundly. He paused at the sound of a cough outside the door. He assumed the noise came from his guard, and resumed his pacing, sure he would wear out the floor. *Where is he?*

A slight creak, the door opened a crack, and closed almost immediately as Mouse shimmered into existence.

Eduardo smiled and strode forward, arms outstretched. "Mar— .

Mouse telepathically stopped him. *Do not speak aloud. Many in Morden say, 'the stones hear and see more than we know'.*

Eduardo lowered his arms and took Mouse's hand in both of his. "…Mouse. Thank you for coming." *I almost forgot to use thought. I remember now, you fear Galdin's apparent ability to perceive your words from a distance.* Eduardo smiled. *But, it is so wonderful to be together in person again.*

I cannot afford to forget, so we should not speak aloud when we need to conceal information from him.

"You are well met, Mouse. Many years have passed since we last were in each other's company."

"Indeed, Lord Eduardo. By the way, your guard is superb. I had to wait for him face the other way so I could slip through the door."

"He didn't notice you?"

"His mind was simple to cloud."

Eduardo frowned.

Mouse's mouth twitched in a half-smile. *Galdin thought he taught me this technique, so I could perform tasks for him, unseen by others.* "Thane Galdin taught me to be able to blur myself when necessary. A small thing, but my ability is equally small."

"You must appreciate Thane Galdin took the time to teach you."

"Indeed, I am most grateful for receiving his tutoring. But, Lord Eduardo, you called me here. I assume you have a reason, as you and I do not normally socialize."

"A excellent reason, indeed, but before we discuss business, I am sure you would appreciate food and drink. Please sit down and enjoy some light refreshment."

"Thank you, Sire."

As they sat, Eduardo poured tea into a cup and handed it to Mouse. *We will use the time to conduct our business in silence while we both eat.*

You are faced with a challenge?

Eduardo sighed. *All Pridden is challenged. Fights between residents of different lands are occurring almost on a daily basis. The fighting happens over small reasons—reasons which never existed before.*

Mouse clenched his jaw. *I noted the same struggles in my travels and I harbor a strong suspicion none of this is accidental. Groups exist who move from land to land, inciting people's fears of those who are different.*

Do you believe a conspiracy is behind this?

I do. My prime suspect is Morden's Assassins' Guild.

Eduardo raised his left eyebrow. *What about proof?*

Not yet, but each day they are bolder in their sowing of distrust among the people. A man with a clever tongue can

The Arrival

persuade another, his neighbor, whose appearance is different, is an enemy. The members of the Assassins' Guild are well versed in verbal manipulation.

"Mouse, you are well refreshed now?"

"Yes, Sire, my thanks."

Eduardo stood and strode around the room again. "So, down to business. You may be aware of rumors of unrest and fighting in a number of the lands. These reports are of concern to the other Lords and Thanes. We spoke and decided we must act to prevent a total war between the people of our lands."

"I am somewhat aware of unrest. Do you believe this is significant?"

"I do. The number of border skirmishes rose threefold in the last season. Injuries and deaths occurred during the encounters, and the citizens of all the lands are demonstrating grim prejudices. We cannot allow the downward spiral of anger to continue. Now, reported rumors of food item shortages in every land appear daily."

"What are your plans?"

"I considered sending an emissary to attempt to root out the problems. I think fate intervened. An unexpected visitor appeared in Kaylin, and she is obviously from some other world. I believe if we send her out as a completely neutral person, the possibility exists she will discover what is causing the disagreements among our people. Hopefully she can stem the growing need for violence."

Mouse, lips pursed, gazed up at Eduardo. *You are not aware I, along with limited help from Galdin, am primarily responsible for her appearance?*

What? I did not know this. How and when?

Someone informed Galdin of the rumor of a prophecy about a woman from another land who would help him take over Pridden. But I was privy to the information you received from Lord Lanerch after his death. I searched the nearby worlds and I located this woman. Something about her caught my attention — a type of power perhaps, a strength of character, I'm not sure. Whatever she brings, I believe she may be the one mentioned in the letter. Mouse walked over to the table. "With your permission, Lord Eduardo, I am still thirsty."

"Please, help yourself."

Mouse drank. *I persuaded Galdin I needed help in bringing her here. Finally with aid from him and others, we managed to bring her to Pridden. He thinks he was the primary force, and required little from me. I am happy to let him take the major credit for her appearance.*

By the spirit, you are always a revelation. "We are placing a large amount of faith she may well be the one who can help solve these problems."

Mouse grinned at Eduardo. "Even in Morden we get reports about this woman from another land. This is why when your request for my presence arrived, my Master, Thane Galdin, urged me to come to your aid."

"For which I am most grateful. Be sure to convey to Thane Galdin my appreciation." *Do not inform him I dislike him intensely. I wonder if he may the one who indulges the Assassins' Guild in their machinations.*

"I will indeed, Sire." *What you don't know is Galdin is convinced your visitor will give him what he needs to defeat you and all the other land rulers. He will then hold ultimate power in Pridden. I suspect he means to be an Argelwyd reborn, even though there is absolutely no indication of any connection with that particular bloodline in his family.*

The Arrival

I have long surmised he considers me a barrier to his ambitions. Do you expect he is privy to the truth about my bloodline… or yours for that matter?

No. I am sure he is not.

Eduardo coughed. "My idea, Mouse, is to request you act as this woman's guide. Your knowledge of many of the lands is well known to be excellent. I am positive Thane Galdin relies on your council regarding the common people, and this expertise will be valuable in this quest."

"I am honored you consider me to be worthy of this, Lord Eduardo. Since my Master sent me to you, I am sure he will be the first to welcome this visitor to Morden."

"I am sure he would. However, her first visit must be to Shendea to meet with Lord Rhognor."

"But Lord Eduardo, since I came here directly from Morden, it would make sense to go there first." *I must do my best to sway you towards Morden as Galdin expects me to do so, and I need a satisfactory excuse for taking her elsewhere. Sorry to appear to be a boulder in the path, but it is necessary to keep him from suspecting any collusion between us.*

Eduardo gave Mouse a small smile. *Understood.* "You must go to Shendea first. You may not know Lord Rhognor the way I do — but when he is insistent, he will move the stars and the earth to achieve what he wants. We enjoy many mutual trade agreements, and fighting him on this is not worth the potential economic loss. However, the biggest reason is our visitor — she is called Lady Kat — insisted Shendea be her first stop. You will find she is strong-willed in the extreme. Fighting her on this is also not worth the energy required."

"I understand, Lord Eduardo. You are sure we cannot visit Morden first?"

"I am sure, Mouse. Lord Rhognor can be most stubborn."

"If this is the case I will return to Morden and advise my Master of your plans. We will wait to for you to apprise us as to when I should return to accompany the Lady Kat on her journey."

"Excellent. Please convey to Thane Galdin this journey by Lady Kat is most urgent. The reports I receive are upsetting. Our own people in Kaylin are involved in fights with people from other lands, specifically those from Glowen. They always considered the Glowens as shameless, gluttonous, and wanton. Four riots, which I know of, erupted in the past month. Each one appeared to be encouraged by unknown factions who preached racial hatred to the crowd. And, maybe more I have not yet been informed of, plus I receive regular and similar reports from the other Lords and Thanes."

"I will convey your concerns, my Lord, to the best of my ability."

"Perfect. Now, sit and complete your meal, while I write a note to your Thane."

"Thank you, Lord Eduardo."

Mouse how have you been, working so closely with Galdin in the beast's lair?

I encounter days when things are more difficult, but he thinks I am but a little man with a few minor powers, who can cause him no harm. He is suspicious of all the Lords and Thanes of Pridden, but from me he anticipates only fear and some lying. He does not suspect who I am.

Mouse rose from the table. "Many thanks for the refreshment Lord Eduardo."

"You are most welcome. Keep well, and I will contact you when I need you to accompany Lady Kat to Shendea."

Mouse laid his hand on Eduardo's arm. *Spirit protect you, brother.*

Eduardo gripped Mouse's hand. *And you. Your position is far more fragile.*

CHAPTER 12

Kat hurried into her room, and without pausing to refresh herself, knocked on what served as the adjoining door to Wynneth's quarters. She barely waited for permission to enter, and burst through. "Wynneth I need help. Big time."

Wynneth's welcoming smile changed to a brow furrowed with concern. "What is wrong Kat? You seem most upset." She closed the book on her lap, dropped it on her desk, and hurried over to Kat.

"I don't know what to do. He became so angry, he frightened me. Can he be dangerous?"

Wynneth clasped Kat's hand. "Who are you talking about? Who is angry?"

"Haydar, the Horse-Master. He freaked. I've never seen anyone so furious. His face got all red and he screamed at me. I thought he would get violent."

Wynneth blinked and led Kat back to her room and a nearby chair. "Sit, and explain this to me. First, what does freecked mean?"

Kat refused the chair, shook off Wynneth's hand, and paced. "Oh…well… the meaning is a description of a person who becomes really irate, starts a screaming fit, and can't control themselves."

"Haydar is an excitable man. But please sit down, your agitation is making me nervous." Wynneth walked to the ceiling tassel and pulled down twice. "I will request some calming tea." She returned to her usual chair. "You will sit and breathe, and then you will tell me what occurred."

Kat inhaled and then exhaled slowly. The breath did relax her, so she sat opposite Wynneth, with the table between them. "Okay."

Before she could continue, a knock at the door to the corridor elicited "come" from Wynneth. A young woman, a stranger to Kat, entered with a tray which contained a steaming pot of fragrant tea, and the cookies Kat thought of as Cinnebons.

Wynneth glanced at the girl. "Thank you, and please make sure we are not disturbed." She urged Kat. "Pour yourself some of the tea and sip, and when you are ready, start at the beginning."

Breathing a sigh of relief, Kat followed her suggestion. The tea soothed with a warm lemony taste, comforting her as she swallowed. Her fingers twitched, and she reached out and popped a cookie in her mouth. The combination of the flavors of both were heavenly, and she lost herself in the sensation of the moment.

She glanced at Wynneth who regarded her with a bemused expression.

"The cookies are delicious, no? They contain a spice we also use to lessen anxiety. If you are ready to speak, I am ready to listen."

Kat began to recount her walk with Mayda, and she chuckled as she spoke of the girl's constant chatter.

Wynneth, despite a slight twitch at the corners of her mouth, appeared stern. "Young Mayda is most unsure of herself, and it is important you treat her gently. Baklai women are not looked upon as bright by their male counterparts. The young suffer more from this. Although I must tell you, her female parent is a strong woman. She rules the household with a broom of iron, and keeps Master Haydar very much in check. He may be the ruler of the stables, but in his home, he leaps when his bond mate requires him to."

"Maybe the reason why he gets so upset at such silly things?"

Wynneth straightened up in her seat. "What do you mean by silly things?"

Kat recounted Haydar's reaction when she mounted the horse.

"Oh my." Wynneth covered her face with both hands. "Oh my." She glanced up. "You, Kat, threw the equivalent of a cathnog among the wullawerths. Screaming chaos is what you unwittingly created."

"I don't understand."

"This is a delicate situation. Let me explain about Haydar. Baklai is not a wealthy land to begin with, and Master Haydar, despite his talent, lived in greater poverty than the average. But his abilities far surpass those of other men. He is one of the most talented manager of horses in the entire land of Baklai, even though he is shorter than most of the others who live in the land. Lord Eduardo heard of his talent and sent one of his Rifellan guards to offer the position of Horse-Master to him. For Haydar, his dream came to fruition. Compared to his life in his own land, he is now a man of stature and wealth, and he is much appreciated by all who know him. His life changed dramatically."

Wow, I guess he had a tough life. But everybody's got problems. He needs to buckle on a couple.

"The fact is, his temper is short." Wynneth's apparent attempt to suppress a grin at her own humor, failed. "He is a genius when it comes to horses. I am sure Lord Eduardo suspects he bears a distant power bloodline which enables him to bond with his charges so completely."

"What does this have to do with me and how he acted when I got on the horse? His reaction was hair-raising and rude."

"You must understand the difference in his living conditions generated an almost fanatical reverence towards Lord Eduardo and all things Kaylin. He is more rigid in Kaylin doctrine than the majority of Kaylins, most of whom are gradually moving toward a more liberal view of men and women." Wynneth scowled. "Not so, Haydar. When you exposed your limbs, which might in many cause blushes, and perhaps a sharp word or two, to Haydar it seemed the mighty Spirit would descend and smite him if he did not berate you. And, of course, berate you most severely."

"Oh rats, how am I supposed to be familiar with this?"

"I am not sure what rats have to do with Haydar, but this time, for a change, you were innocent in your actions. However, we should consider how we might ask for his forgiveness. I will think on this, because you will need to have a horse to travel to Shendea, which I am aware is what Lord Eduardo requested you do."

"Let me think about this too. I'm familiar with dealing with aggressive, arrogant men."

"Wait a minute. Before you do anything, we should consult on this together."

"Wynneth. I'm not going to barge over and get into another argument with him. Give me some credit."

"I do trust you to do your best, but you are still not aware of all our customs. Admit it, Kat, you possess a tendency to act like a hydodd in a glass blower's shop."

Kat glared at her. "I'm not that bad."

"At times, unfortunately, you are. For now, I suggest you ask Mayda to take you to meet Praetor Bardu who is the

The Arrival

head of Lord Eduardo's personal guard. He is from Rifella, is most familiar with those from Baklai, and respects Master Haydar. He will give you more insight into the Horse-Master's character."

"Do you think Mayda will want anything to do with me after seeing Haydar's reactions to me?"

"I am sure she is used to him and his ways. I also believe she is relieved he directed his anger at you, not her."

"Fine, I'll ask her tomorrow." Kat rose and headed towards the door. "This has been a long and trying day, and I think I will go back to my rooms. I want to write down some things." She paused and turned back to Wynneth. "Thank you for your council. I must be a frustration to you." *I always managed to frustrate Nick. I wonder if he was forced to deal with the Japanese for the consequences of my actions?*

"No, not a frustration. You resemble a child who needs to learn about life. This is strange for you, and I would only ease your path to knowledge of our land."

Hmmph. Child. I don't think so. Kat scowled. "Before I go, is it acceptable if I eat my supper in my rooms?" *How's that for diplomacy?*

"Of course. Simply tug on the tassel three times. This means you desire a meal, which will be delivered to you, with enough variety so you find everything both filling and nourishing. The young woman who looks to your quarters will soon learn what you like best."

"Thanks." Kat smiled at the healer as Wynneth rose and returned to her own rooms.

***

Caught up in the journaling of her ideas for her new game, Kat, startled by an ominous rumbling, remembered she skipped the noon-day meal. *OMG, my stomach's yelling.*

87

Must be time for supper. She walked over to the tassel and tugged three times. *What am I going to call the game? Female heroes always work well, and I usually find names among ancient women warriors. Which ones haven't I used? Boudica? Blenda? Hyppolyta? Nope.* "I'll keep on thinking."

At the faint knock on her door, Kat called out, "Come."

A striking blonde with azure eyes, entered, carrying a tray loaded with food and drink. "Shall I lay this out for you, Lady Kat?"

"No, please put the tray down." She gestured toward the table near the window.

The young woman did as asked, and turned to leave the rooms.

"What is your name, and where are you from?"

She stopped and gazed back at Kat. "I am called Laylin, and my family come from Shendea. My parent is the head of the metalworker forge here at the keep."

"Perhaps you will take me to see him and the forge where he does business. I would like to see his work."

"I would be glad to, my Lady."

"Before you go, Laylin, can you tell me what each of the dishes on the tray are?"

The young woman gave Kat the names and history of every dish. Kat recognized most from the communal feast she attended with Wynneth. Familiar scents and remembered flavors promised a memorable meal.

When Kat's stomach rumbled again, she thanked the girl, said goodnight, and settled down to fill the complaining hollow inside.

Later, Kat leaned back in her chair and burped loudly. *Oops, as usual, I ate too fast.* She burped again. *Wait a minute, the drink tastes a little like ginger. Probably excellent for digestion.* She drank. *Ah, yes. Relief.*

Kat got up, stretched, groaned a little, walked over to the window, and leaned out over the ledge. *Hmm. Dark already. But the air smells like the night-blooming jasmine I remember from Turkey. What a day. Loads of stress.* She yawned broadly. *I could sleep now.*

She turned toward her bed, beckoning with puffy comforters. *Leave the stress, wake refreshed, because as Scarlett would say, "Tomorrow is another day.*

CHAPTER 13

The bird-song chorus penetrated the edges of Kat's consciousness, but she lingered longer in the warm embrace of soft blankets. Lazily entertaining thoughts of games, horses, and the tasks awaiting her, she blinked and sat up. A blinding shaft of sunlight forced her from the bed.

With a stretch and a lusty vocal yawn, she headed for the shower.

***

Refreshed and sated from a satisfying breakfast, she and Mayda discussed their plans for the day. *At least Haydar didn't take out his anger on his daughter. She still talks as much as ever. Wynneth said I must be patient.* Kat snorted. *I'm not adept at patience. Don't really wanna be.*

"Lady Kat, Praetor Bardu will be in his own quarters with his bond mate after the noon-time meal. Now he is with the other guards and we cannot go to them. Those rooms are off limits and no one but Lord Eduardo's personal guards may enter their part of the keep. The Praetor is a well-regarded man, and all respect him. He and Horse-Master Haydar are friends, and … "

"TMI, Mayda, TMI."

Mayda frowned and raised a puzzled eyebrow. "Forgive me. What is this tee-em thing?"

"TMI?" *I must remember to avoid using expressions I have to explain all the time.* " TMI means too much information."

"Too much information? But Healer Wynneth told me you need much information. I only followed her council."

Kat sighed. "I am sure she did, but if you give me too much all at once, I become muddled." *And bored, and you make my ears bleed.* "I would prefer if you gave me answers to my questions instead." Kat stopped at Mayda's expression of regret.

"Oh."

Kat imagined she could see the wheels moving inside Mayda's head. *Oh crap, I've hurt her feelings.* "You understand I need time to process your information, which is why I ask this of you?"

"I could do that, Lady Kat, to help you." Mayda's happy puppy face returned.

"Thank you." *I think I just became diplomatic. Hah.* "So did Bardu know your male parent before your family came to Kaylin?" Kat rummaged in her desk for paper and her special pen. *I'll need to take some notes. I wish to god they sold smart phones here.*

"Yes Praetor Bardu was most kind to us. He told Lord Eduardo my male parent excelled at the training of horses. Because of him, we received the invitation to move here."

Kat continued to ply the young woman with questions until she received the information about both men she needed. *Keeping Mayda on track is tough work, but I think I'm fine with what I want for the moment.*

After a light lunch in Kat's room, they strolled around the edges of the keep where many of the other craft journeymen had erected their well-constructed homes of stone and thatch. Each house, surrounded by a plot of growing foodstuffs, with front yards filled with vibrant flowers and trees heavy with fruit sat in the center of small plots of land. The

The Arrival

air vibrated with children's laughter. Rich scents of fragrant clean earth, perfumed blooms and aromas of meals cooked on open hearths, reminded Kat of cottages she recalled experiencing in many European villages. Every place announced a pride of ownership — of happy satisfaction with life.

The homes changed slightly as they rounded the keep toward the rear entrance. Now the roadways were cobbled with larger stones carved with strange but exotic icons.

"Why are the stones in these roads carved with symbols?"

"Lady Kat, this is where Lord Eduardo's guards reside. They often ride their horses along this road. When rain falls, the horses hooves cannot grip the path. The carvings prevent them from slipping and falling. Horses are most valuable and they are protected from injury by everyone."

"Interesting." *No wonder everyone tiptoes around Haydar.*

They headed toward a larger home, with a wooden roof, rather than the more common thatched ones. Next to the house, stood a smaller building and Kat assumed this to be a stable, because the construction emitted the strong aroma of horses. "Does this one belong to Bardu?"

Mayda's face reddened. "Yes, that is where Praetor Bardu and his family reside."

Something clicked in Kat's brain. *They all look so uncomfortable when I simply call people by their names. They're always using titles. Bugger. Navigating rules and regs here is tougher than facing dragons and werewolves.* She sighed mentally. *I wonder how I can use weird social customs as scary problems in my game?*

They approached the door of the home. "Mayda, please knock and introduce me to Bardu and his mate." *Oops I didn't use his title. Well, they should become used to my ways, as well.*

Mayda lifted the heavy knocker and banged three times. The door opened and Mayda introduced Kat. "Praetor Bardu, this is the Lady Kat who requests a visit with you." She hung back, and headed for the garden.

Bardu stepped out of his doorway. A pair of blue eyes the color of a Mediterranean sky caught her attention.

Kat stood transfixed. *Holy crap. He's a god."*

More than a mortal man, his deep-bronze body, bare to the waist, with sculpted muscle, glistened with his own skin oils. She smelled the musk of sexual male. Her mouth dried up abruptly. His arms and hands, strong and masculine and his shoulder-length hair caused her body to vibrate with need. His platinum mane, thick and lustrous and bound with strips of leather which tamed all but escaping wisps, enticed her. She imagined removing the ties and running her hands through the mass of hair, feeling his body against hers, blood pounding in her ears. *Oh my god, he could take me right here — I am... my body is... everything is more than ready.* She wanted him to grab her and possess her, grinding his hips into hers, up against the wall, or anywhere else. All she wanted was him.

His mouth turned up in amusement. "Come in, Lady Kat." The sound of him rolled around her — hot, enticing, beguiling. He stood aside, inviting her in.

She couldn't move. She licked her lips, desperate for moisture, which had fled to other parts of her body. Vital parts.

"Bardu, behave yourself." A woman's voice — throaty and seductive.

The sound startled Kat sufficiently so she moved into the room. She turned toward the woman, and stared again.

She was glorious, a goddess in her own right. Her skin, sun-kissed to a deep gold bronze, covered intensely feminine curves, hinting at supple strength. Her hair, as blonde as her mate's, likewise bound in leather strips, created a halo around her from the freed tendrils.

Kat had never experienced an attraction for a woman before — an intoxicating, demanding attraction. *She's gorgeous and I want her.* Kat stared back at Bardu. *A threesome. Yes, a threesome. Am I drooling?*

The woman hastily walked... *hell, she's gliding...* to a table and lit a stick of incense.

As the odor of sweet spices scented the air, Kat's head cleared and her intense sexual attraction faded to a more manageable level. *What just happened?*

The woman turned back to Kat. "Our apologies, Lady Kat, we should have prepared better for your visit. The Kaylins are not often affected by our physical presence, as you are. In the past, only the Glowens reacted this way. But they appear to be excited and affected by almost everything. Perhaps because they are under the influence of prodigious intakes of Orenberry wine. Yours was an unusually strong response." She turned to Bardu. "You should have known better, bond mate."

Bardu grinned wickedly. *He's enjoying my discomfort. What a rat.*

"Lady Kat, I am Irina, bond mate to Bardu. Welcome to our home."

"Thank you Irina, and Bardu." *I'm certainly not going to give him his title.* The heat faded from her body, and she gained control over her physical responses. She avoided looking directly at Bardu. Even without the effect of the Rifellan's highly active pheromones, he was one hot looking guy.

Irina beckoned Kat over to a chair beside a stone fireplace. "Please be seated. I will bring you tea containing Karri-san, which is what you detect in the incense. Originally the herb grew only in Rifella and Baklai, but the Kaylins need Karri-san, considering their ideas on love."

Kat grimaced. "I discovered it myself."

Bardu chuckled at her words. "I imagine you encountered trouble with this attitude of theirs. You obviously do not think the same way." *Can he read thoughts as well?*

Irina slapped his hand as she passed him and placed a plate of small cakes on the table. "Behave yourself. Lady Kat's discomfort is not a matter for laughter. She has much to do, and much to learn, and her lack of knowledge should not bear the brunt of your wicked sense of humor."

Bardu lowered his head in mock shame, but as Irina passed by him again, he grinned and slapped her on the buttock.

She whirled and grabbed his little finger and twisted.

"Ow, woman. That hurts. I'm sure Lady Kat enjoys a joke."

"Enough, mate of mine." She shook her finger at him. "You need to drop the humor. Wynneth sent me a message to say Lady Kat needs your help and information with her problem. You will give this to her, or tonight you will find yourself sleeping outside… with the horses."

Bardu threw up his hands. "As you wish my dear one." He leaned toward Kat. "She is a most vicious mate and would think nothing of gelding me."

Kat couldn't help herself. She laughed and the tension drained from her. *They adore each other. Mind blowing.* The tea, and the laughter erased the last dregs of sexual heat from

The Arrival

her. *I could never be involved with Bardu. I respect Irina too much, plus— she could be a scary enemy.*

She grabbed another small cake and sipped the Karri-san tea. "You found Haydar in Baklai. Tell me about him."

The two of them sat opposite Kat and shared the tea from the table between them.

Bardu began. "We visited my friend, Makinti, who moved to Baklai to become Praetor of Thane Cathked's personal guard.

Kat must have appeared puzzled, because he explained.

"Makinti and I grew up together on Rifella, and we remained long-time friends."

"Why would he go to Baklai, if you came here?"

"Both of us are of the Warrior clan on Rifella. The rulers in each of the lands are most anxious to hire us to be personal guards. Makinti and I were well matched, and we always knew we were both Praetor material and would therefore be in different lands."

"Makes sense, but who is Cathked?"

"He is the Thane of Baklai."

"Why isn't he a Lord like Eduardo?"

Bardu winced. "Lord Eduardo, we believe, is of original blood of the great power wielder, Argelwyd. Plus, he is a fine man, and a excellent steward of Kaylin. We respect him enough to use his title. He deserves our respect."

Hmm. A pointed statement.

"But to answer your question. The rulers of the lands are either Lords, which indicates their power abilities, or Thanes. The latter do have some power, but not the strength of a full power wielder. Only three lands are ruled by Lords — Kaylin, Shendea and Rifella. Shendea is ruled by Lord Rhognor, and our own land, Rifella, is ruled by Lord Murwenna."

"Murwenna? A woman? In Pridden?"

Irina interjected. "All lands in Pridden do not share the same ideas about men and women, Kat. Rifellans believe males and females are equal in their abilities, and in Rifella, the succession of Lordship is always the eldest, regardless of sex."

"I like the sound of Rifella." *My kind of place.*

"I believe you would. In appearance you are much like the Rifellans of the north. The shade of your skin is not unlike ours, but the the flame of your hair is similar to the those who work the mines, or manage our land. Lord Murwenna's hair is also like fire."

"My skin is similar to my father's, but the hair came from my mother."

"Most interesting. You use the same words for your male and female parents we use in Rifella. Are you sure you do not hail from our land?"

"No, my world is totally different."

Bardu butted in. "Lady Kat, you asked about Haydar. I became aware of him because I saw him at work with some horses which were being prepared to be sent to Rifella. I had never seen anyone relate to animals so easily and quickly. He appeared a runt, even for the Baklai, but he moved among those large creatures pushing them aside like puppies in a kennel. They were not afraid of him, but apparently thought of him as merely another horse, albeit a small one."

"I saw him do the same thing, when I went to the stable."

"I sent a message at once to Lord Eduardo, and he replied almost immediately and requested I bring Haydar and his family back with me when I returned to Kaylin. They were living in grim poverty, unable to find much employment. The

The Arrival

Baklai did not believe such a short man could control a herd of huge animals."

"I now understand why he is so loyal to you and to Eduardo…" She caught another wince from Bardu. "Sorry. Lord Eduardo. Perhaps I should tell you my problem and hopefully you can make a suggestion."

Irina rose. "Let me get some more tea. You should consume as much of the Karri-san as possible to get you acclimated."

Kat's face flushed with warmth when she remembered her initial exposure with the two of them. *I wonder if they'll ever forget my most embarrassing moment? Probably share it with their Rifellan friends as an example of an inept alien.*

Irina sat down again, and Kat related her encounter with Haydar and his reaction to her raising her skirt to her thighs.

Bardu roared like an hysterical lion. "Poor Haydar, he absorbed the worst traits of the Kaylins. I wish I had been able to see his face." He laughed again.

Kat glared at him. "It's not funny, I need him to give me a horse. Eduardo asked me to travel to Shendea and I need transportation."

"I am sorry Kat, but this is funny." He must have seen the glare. "Of course, be assured I will help you."

Humph. He dropped my title. Apparently I'm not due the same respect as Eduardo.

Irina added. "Haydar is most defensive in his views. We will consider the best way to get him to supply you with a horse, and will let you know when we have a plan. Perhaps he will listen to Bardu."

"Kat, whatever you do, do not approach him on your own again." Bardu sobered. "To do so would be like applying stinging nettles to a bleeding wound. And if you enrage him further you might need to send to Baklai for a horse, which, of course, would be madness."

As they all rose and walked to the door, Kat said. "Wynneth warned me in almost the same way."

"You are lucky to have Wynneth as your friend. She is wise and loyal." With these words, Irina hugged Kat goodbye. *She smells fabulous. I wonder what she would be like? But I'm not hugging Bardu. Too hot. Too tempting.*

She strode outside. Mayda lay fast asleep on a long chair in the garden.

"Mayda. You didn't need to wait, I could've found my own way back."

The young woman jumped to her feet, instantly alert. "Wynneth told me I should wait, Lady Kat. I rested a bit."

They neared the roadway, when Irina came running after Kat.

"Wait Kat." She handed her a bag of seeds and dried leaves. "This is a good supply of Karri-san," She smiled. "In case you meet more Rifellan warriors."

"Thank you. I will use it." Kat snorted inwardly. *Unless… unless the Rifellan is unattached.*

CHAPTER 14

Wynneth stood in front of her herbal cupboard, with two clear containers in her hands. *I must get these refilled. With three new offspring at the forge hold, they will need my relaxing tonic. New parents often sleep too little.* She put down the containers, picked up her herbal remedy book, and made a note in it.

A loud knock at her door startled her, and she chuckled to herself. *Only Kat knocks with such volume.* "Come."

Kat entered. "Wynneth, I think I should join the members of the keep at the evening meal. Would you show me the way?" *Oops, I forgot again.* "Please?"

"I will." *I wonder what happened. She's different somehow.* "Are you sure you are ready?"

Kat's tone was defensive. "Of course."

Oh dear something happened and she is not happy. "Naturally I will escort you." Wynneth hesitated. "I believe you and Mayda visited Praetor Bardu and his mate today. Did the visit go well?"

Kat studied her hands. "Yes, very well."

Well, I never thought... . She is uncomfortable. Wynneth raised her eyebrows. *Oh, I forgot, they are Rifellans, and I doubt Kat consumed sufficient Karri-san in her diet. Perhaps she experienced a strong reaction... and an unexpected one.* Wynneth kept her expression as neutral as possible. "I only realized now, Kat, I forgot to advise you to consume certain spices. I apologize if this caused you any discomfort."

"The visit was fine. I got the information about Haydar I needed."

"Good. Let me wash my hands as they are covered with the ink from my book." Wynneth put down her book, moved the empty jars to another table, and went to her own personal room. *I believe young Kat does not enjoy being out of control.*

When she returned, she reached for Kat's hand. "Come, let us dine together."

***

Kat, completely absorbed in her own thoughts about her embarrassing encounter with Bardu, entered the small room, and did not spare a glance at the other diners. Wynneth led her to a table for two along one wall.

When the young server approached their table, Wynneth ordered for both of them. She suggested Kat try a new dish. "I know you enjoy the wullawerth stew, and this will be the perfect accompaniment." She addressed the server. "Also bring a sizable pot of Karri-san tea. We are both especially thirsty this evening."

Kat groaned. *Hell, she knows.* "Did that jerk Bardu tell you what happened?"

"I have not spoken to Bardu since your visit. What is a jurk?"

Kat groaned a second time. *Explaining expressions is exhausting.* "Yes, a jerk is… well, person — usually a man — who is annoying and frustrating. They're also arrogant and infuriating. They always think they're right, even though they're not."

"I understand. I think, Lady Kat, although you may be judging him unfairly."

Crap - she only calls me Lady Kat when she lectures me.

Wynneth continued. "Bardu is a strong, confident man.

The Arrival

He is used to being in command of a group of guards. Of course, he is not so in control with his mate Irina. She is commanding in her own right." Wynneth smiled. "Perhaps you misjudged his intentions."

I don't think I did, but I'm not going to argue with her, since I need her help again. "Perhaps." Kat took a drink from her cup. "Wynneth I would like to ask a favor of you."

"Of course, anything."

"Could you ask the seamstress to meet with me to make some new clothes? I think her name is Brith."

"Excellent, Kat. You remembered her name correctly. I am becoming convinced you will be of much help to us in the task Eduardo set for you."

Ha. I knew the idea to record everything I could, would be an excellent one. I believe I accomplished the impossible. I impressed Wynneth. Good one. "Wynneth, I notice when you're with me you rarely use anyone's titles. Not even Eduardo's. Why?"

"You are more astute than anyone else realizes, are you not?" She didn't wait for Kat's answer. "First, titles are not something you find comfortable using, so I do not perceive a need to complicate our conversations. Second, in any land, the Healer is for all practicality, the equal of the ruler. Finally, in Eduardo's case, he and I enjoy a unique relationship which existed from the time he first came to Kaylin. We transcend titles."

Kat leaned back in her chair. "Makes sense." *I must pursue her exact relationship with Eduardo. But later. Stomach takes precedence now.* "I love the food. What is the new vegetable in the stew?"

"It is a type of legume called brocca. I thought you would enjoy it." Wynneth rose. "Now, if you will excuse me, I will pass your request to Brith to meet with you on the morrow after the morning meal. No doubt she will wish you to connect with the weavers. Plus, I would appreciate an early night. I am weary."

"I am tired myself, so I won't be far behind you." *I'll get some Karri-san tea sent to my room. I do not want to run into Bardu-the-fink without being prepared. Bardu-the-fink. He probably doesn't deserve the title, but he did take much enjoyment from my embarrassing meeting with him.*

***

After a pleasant morning meal spent listening to birds, and planning what she would ask of the seamstress, Kat rose from her chair at the faint knock. "Brith, do come in. Would you care for some tea before we start out?"

"No tea, thank you. Healer Wynneth mentioned you would wish to visit the weaver to determine the cloth for some additional clothing for you. We should set out at once, before he becomes too embroiled in the weaving for the day." Brith wore a severe dress of her own, with a collar which crawled high on her neck to her jawline, and cuffs to the edge of her wrists. Plus her hair, drawn back and arranged in two rolls on either side of her head, broadcast to the world, 'do not touch'. Not a single strand escaped.

They left the room and Brith headed away from the living areas of the keep. After winding through many corridors, they emerged in a small courtyard. A young man waited for them, seated in a two-wheeled cart drawn by the oddest and ugliest horse Kat had ever seen. The creature was the size of an oversized pony, but with massive hooves and a head belonging to a much bigger animal. The poor ungainly brute appeared to have been constructed by a psychotic Doctor Jekyll.

The Arrival

"What is that?"

Brith didn't seem astonished by the appearance of the oddity before them. "A ponti. They originally come from Shendea and are bred for travel in their mountainous regions. They're incredibly sure-footed, and only a few Kaylin families have them. Master Weaver Thontook can afford to have the best for his bond-mate and their offspring."

"Ponti? It does strike me as sure-footed." Kat climbed into the cart after Brith. *I know I mustn't laugh, but this is the weirdest looking horse ever. I absolutely must come up with something similar for the game.*

***

The weaver's cottage, vaster than most, sprawled over four normal lots. A substantial horse-drawn wagon, sat waiting at the furthest building, as two men offloaded piles of golden wullawerth hair to a hand cart. The cart, when full, entered the building, and as Kat and Brith approached closer, returned empty for more.

"The building second from the last, is where the hair is cleaned and prepared. The closer one is for spinning into thread, and the coloring of the hair."

Kat gaped in fascination. "Can we get a tour?"

"Of course. The building closest to us is where Master Weaver Thontook and his apprentices weave the fabric. His own home is the one set back at the furthest end."

"He has apprentices?"

"Indeed. They are well regarded as craftsmen in their own right when they leave Master Weaver Thontook's employ. Many then go on to work with Tapestry Master Godrith in Shendea."

"How long do they work here as apprentices?"

"Twelve to sixteen seasons, depending upon their own

desire to learn additional skills."

The cart stopped and Brith hopped out and offered her hand to help Kat, but she had already jumped down. Kat's dress caught on the edge of the cart and tore a small hole in her skirt. "Oh hell." *Damn skirts catch in everything. I need pants.*

Brith examined the rip. "I can repair the tear for you. Women need a trick to descend from a cart, which I planned to show you." She paused and cocked her head. "And what does hell mean?"

"Hell's not a what, but a where. Hell is a… " *Here we go again. Damned explanations.* "a… a pretend place where everything bad happens."

"Why would anyone want a pretend place where only bad happens?"

"We also have a pretend place where only happy things happen, called Heaven."

Brith shook her head. "Where you come from must be quite strange."

"Perhaps." *If they only knew how strange this world is to me.*

Brith's face brightened. "Your hev-in, though, sounds much like Lan-Kloon, where the Great Spirit, Caleesh, who lives within each of us, brings us when we depart this life. In Lan-Kloon, those who wish to, may choose to return to Pridden as new beings. Many do not choose to do so, because Lan-Kloon is a place of peace and pure joy. It is not, however, a pretend place, though we cannot experience the benefits until we depart."

"Interesting." *Change the subject. Now. I don't do religion.* "Can we meet the weaver? You did say he might get busy later."

The Arrival

"Yes indeed."

They entered the closest building. The clack of looms and swish of the Kaylin version of shuttles created an hypnotic rhythm. The fingers of the young men and women flew across the looms as they wove bright reds and golds, rich blues and greens of glorious fabrics.

Brith approached an elderly man dressed in a long brown robe. His hair, shoulder length, and his beard were streaked with grey. "Master Weaver Thontook, I would present Lady Kat, who arrived on Kaylin from a different world. She desires to choose cloth for clothes, as Lord Eduardo requested she travel to other lands on his behalf."

Thontook bowed a touch and his eyes twinkled at Kat. "Well met Lady Kat. News of your visit preceded you and permeated my studios. My apprentices and I will be delighted to show you a variety of cloth, in anticipation you find many which will meet with your approval."

Kat liked Thontook instantly. He had a wonderful face with every line indicating pleasure in life. "Well met to you too, Master Thontook." *Oops I left off the weaver bit. Hope he doesn't take offense.*

Thontook took her hand in both of his and his smile glowed like a child at a party. "I believe my dear, conversation would be less cumbersome if we were Thontook and Kat to each other. I prefer not to stand on ceremony as I find it tiring."

"I'd like it immensely." *Oh frabjous day - a normal, older man whose with it. He would make the perfect grandfather.*

Keeping hold of Kat's left hand, Thontook led her past bolts of material hanging from wooden posts.

"As you will observe most of the fabrics we produce here are for clothing."

Kat, unable to resist, fingered soft, delicate fabrics,

smooth, silky ones which gleamed in the lamps of the studio, coarse ones with nubs, others when touched, reminded her of rabbit fur, and strong tough material which brought memories of work clothes. "They're beautiful."

Thontook beamed with pleasure at her words. "What type of clothing are you considering?"

"Well, I'll be traveling a lot on horseback, so I think I'll need something strong."

"Of course, my dear. However, you will also, no doubt, be required to attend functions at the various keeps, so I would also recommend some of the thinner fabrics for hot weather, and at least one bolt of the richer ones for more formal events. For the cold lands, you will definitely need something similar to the thick one. It may give the impression of being heavy, but is light to wear."

***

With the bolts of cloth scheduled to be delivered to Brith's quarters, the two women retired to Kat's room to settle upon the clothing her trip would require.

Brith brought her measuring tapes, and a variety of sketches.

"Brith I'm not sure how I pay Master Thontook for the cloth?"

"You will not need to worry about it, Lady Kat. Lord Eduardo has, I believe, assigned you a task. As such, the costs of your clothing will be absorbed by the keep." She indicated the sketches. "Do you approve of these ideas?"

"These are fine, Brith. Am I going to need to use this thick outer coat?"

"There is no question about this. Although I have not been to Shendea, Wynneth is well acquainted with her home, and Lord Rhognor's keep is high in the mountains. After the harvest season, the winds and the cold can bite through ordinary Kaylin clothing."

"Fine. I don't like being cold. I have one more thing I wish you to make for me." Kat rose and went to a waist high table with four drawers. From the lower one, she withdrew her old jeans which she'd stored, positive she would need them to return home. "I need another pair like these made from a similar strong fabric, so I can ride a horse in comfort."

Brith's face registered astonishment. "Lady Kat, I cannot make you those. Only men don trousers. Men and women do not wear each other's clothing. I cannot sew this type of garment."

"Brith this is madness. I have to travel a long way on horseback." She held out the skirt of her dress. "This is lovely, but totally impractical for such a journey. I will be uncomfortable the whole way."

"I said I cannot do it, and I will not."

Another one? They're determined to be a huge fat pain in my butt. "You must. You are the seamstress. This is your job." *These damn people and their twisted version of men and women.*

Brith quivered with rage. "You are not allowed to tell me what my job is. I answer only to Healer Wynneth and Lord Eduardo. And neither of them would ever order me to make such an abomination."

"We'll see about that." Kat shook with her own sense of outrage.

Brith rose and moved swiftly to the door. "Instead of running to either of them, I suggest you will be better served to find another seamstress. I will not work with you." She opened the door and as she exited, slammed it shut behind her.

J. M. Tibbott

Bloody hell, not again.

CHAPTER 15

Wynneth heard Kat's door slam, and tapped on the connecting door. *I am most surprised she did not come to tell me of her trip to Thontook.*

She entered at Kat's "come," but stopped short when she caught sight of a deeply furrowed brow. *Oh dear, I do believe she experienced another challenge. If possible, I would swear she might shoot flames from her eyes.*

"How... how.." Kat balled up her hands into fists. "How do any of you get anything done with these ridiculous rules?"

On second thought, perhaps she can shoot flames from those flared nostrils. "Kat, my dear." Wynneth reached for her hand.

"Don't. Don't try and soothe me. I'm so mad I could spit."

Then again, perhaps flames from her mouth. "What happened?"

"Brith. She's just as bad as the damned horse guy."

"Before we talk about this, I believe you need to settle yourself, and then tell me the details clearly, and calmly. You are most red, so I would suggest a cooling shower. I will order tea for us and we can sit down and you can tell me all."

Kat glared without answering, but she stalked to her personal.

Wynneth sighed and tugged once on the tassel.

When Laylin appeared, Wynneth asked for tranquilizing tea and Kat's favorite cookies.

By the time Kat emerged from her shower, her face less red, and her body less tense, the tea and cookies rested on the table near the window. Wynneth drew up chairs on either side, and she motioned to Kat to be seated.

"Before we begin, I need to question a word. You referred to Haydar as 'dammed', which puzzled me. I am familiar with dams. We often use them on our smaller streams to create ponds. I am not familiar with a person referred to as a dam."

The sigh from Kat, weighed heavy with frustration. "Damn is just a curse word."

An odd word for a curse. I will explore curses with her later. Eduardo gave this young woman an enormous task. She possesses the strength, but can she handle the difficulty. Spirit help me to assist her. "So tell me what happened."

Kat sipped at the tea, and consumed three cookies while she recounted her morning with Brith.

"Kat you must forgive me for not giving you more information about Brith. I did not realize you would request she make you men's pants."

"What's the big deal? They would cover my legs so I wouldn't inflame the weird desires the men in this land seem to possess."

Wynneth tried to hide her smile.

"This is not funny, Wynneth. It's pathetic."

I must be delicate in how I explain this. "You are correct. It is not funny. I smiled at your wonderful phrasing — your legs inflaming desires. An amusing picture came to my mind."

Kat cocked her head, then laughed. "I guess it was pretty funny. But I don't understand why she became angry so fast."

Excellent. The tea and cookies are working. "I would not normally reveal such personal information, but in this case, I am convinced understanding the circumstances of some of

The Arrival

the beliefs Brith holds, are important for you to know. Her childhood contained much to challenge her. Both her parents were fanatics about the separation of men and women before bonding. As a young child, Brith and a neighbor's son got caught together, naked. Children are naturally curious, which in Shendea we know is quite normal. But for Brith's parents a grave abomination took place. They whipped both of the young ones quite severely. Brith still bears faint marks on her back."

Kat grimaced. "How horrible. How can anyone do such a thing to children? And what did the other parents say about their son being whipped?"

"They were horrified. Brith's parents did not see anything wrong with their treatment of the children. The neighbors reacted violently, as both of them were more liberal in their thinking — and accepted the young are curious. They believed the best way to handle this incident would be to talk to their son and explain society's viewpoint. The fact that Brith's parents took it upon themselves to whip their son enraged them beyond reason. The two male parents fought each other. Both possessed weapons, and they both died from their injuries as a result." *If only I had known about their views. Perhaps I might have prevented what happened.* "The tragedy affected everyone in the keep. We do our best to forget such a terrible time."

"What? Unbelievable. No wonder Brith is so rigid. What happened then?"

"The female neighbor gathered her friends about her and they shunned Brith's female parent. She eventually decided to depart this life, leaving Brith to be raised by others. Even though the replacement parents were more liberal in their thinking, Brith, so traumatized by the incident, still accepted the viewpoint of her original family."

Kat rubbed at her forehead. "I understand why Brith and Haydar are so unyielding. How do you stand all this, Wynneth? How do you live with these narrow-minded people."

Underneath all, she is endowed with a noble heart. Poor woman, she is struggling. Wynneth reached across the table and took Kat's hand. "I am a healer. Shendeans enjoy wonderful relationships between men and women, without the necessity of being in bond. Healer's, specifically, are trained to allow others to be who they are, without judgment. It matters not to me what others believe. They are free to do so, even though I might not believe the same. But I will not, and cannot make light of their beliefs, not through my speech nor my actions."

"Do you mean none of them ever got mad at you?"

Wynneth laughed. "My dear, I often made mistakes when I first arrived in Kaylin. But I apologized and asked forgiveness. I used as my excuse my initial ignorance — based on my Shendean background."

"You hide yourself in their little boxes? How is it possible for you to do that?"

"I do not hide myself Kat. I believe in everything I do." *How to explain this concept?* "Perhaps I can illustrate this. You have seen the pollinator insects flitting between the flowers?"

"Yes."

"The flowers reproduce when the pollinators move the pollen between the plants. Every flower smells sweet, and this is what attracts these insects. If you place two dishes on a table outdoors, with one dish containing sweet-smelling liquid, and the other containing something very sour, the

The Arrival

pollinators will flock to the sweet dish and ignore the sour smelling one. People are the same. They will be attracted to the sweet and repelled by the sour."

"Point made. We have a similar saying in my world."

"And yet, and forgive me for saying this, you do not follow a precept like this?"

"Other people have tragedies in their lives too."

"What do you mean?"

Kat squirmed and lowered her eyes. "I lost my parents as a child."

Wynneth's mouth dropped open. "Oh." She blinked. "You lost them? How can you lose two people?"

"Wynneth?" Kat frowned. "I didn't physically lose them. They died."

Wynneth's eyes opened wide. "Oh by the Spirit. By this word died, do you mean they departed this life?" *I am beginning to understand more of this young woman. Tragedy affected her life as well. She is blessed with a deep strength because of what she experienced.*

"Yes, they departed living." Kat sighed. "Being raised in a strange house is always difficult. I fought for everything. My own parents loved me, the replacements did not. Being sweet didn't win over anybody in the family."

"I am sorry you had a difficult childhood. But now you are full-grown."

"So are Haydar and Brith. Why don't you expect them to overcome their upbringing?"

"Because you, Kat, are more intelligent, and a much stronger person. The potential to grow beyond old prejudices is yours if you should decide to accept it."

Kat glared at her. "Everybody here wants me to jump through hoops. I think you're all only worried about your world... not about me."

J. M. Tibbott

CHAPTER 16

Deep in thought the following morning, Kat wandered outside the keep, unconscious of the bustle of the daily lives of the people about her. Everyone walked with purpose, destinations firmly fixed and intention in every stride. She accidentally bumped into a young man in apprentice clothing.

"Sorry." She moved out of his way.

"My fault, Lady. Please forgive me." He bowed deeply in apology.

"No problem. I failed to watch properly."

He backed away and walked around her.

She followed him with her eyes. Soon he disappeared in the crowds of people around the small shops dotting the roadway. Kat envied their determined yet unhurried movements. They knew where they were going. *Their lives are simple, they know what their place is in this world, and they feel at home. I'm out of place and out of my time, and everyone wants me to fit in and do what they want me to.* "The whole thing's unfair."

Kat realized she'd spoken aloud when a farmer passing her, stopped in place, then leaped backwards and stared at her wide-eyed. "Pardon my Lady?"

"Nothing. It's nothing." Hot in the face, she hurried away from him. *I'm losing my marbles. All I get are lectures from Wynneth, and assignments from Eduardo. Somehow I need to regain control.*

Kat headed away from the built up areas of the keep and finally ended up at the edge of a copse of what resembled oaks. She found a massive tree and lowered herself to the ground, settling back against the rough brown bark, perfectly designed to support her. She faced away from the keep. *I'm overwhelmed by Kaylins for now.* The clean, green scents of nature, the sounds of rustling leaves and chirping of birds hidden in the leafy head of her tree, lulled her. A sense of peace enveloped her. *This is better than the tranquilizing tea Wynneth makes me drink.*

A crackle of underbrush interrupted her thoughts. Kat tensed, ready to jump and run.

A small pink nose and bright eyes peered from under an overhanging dock leaf. Slowly the creature crept out and approached. A cat covered in brown, orange and white fur, padded over to her, sniffed at her feet and glided up to sit at her side. With tilted head the tiny animal regarded her with the type of solemn curiosity only a cat can achieve. Kat reached out to pet it, and the beastie inched up and rubbed her hand with its head.

Without pause, the animal sidled on her lap, circled twice, digging heavy paws into her legs, and curled up. Kat idly stroked the little body which vibrated with purrs, loud enough to emulate heavy machinery.

Peaceful. Animals never expect anything from you. People expect everything. Touching the soft fur soothed and comforted her.

Kat's thoughts drifted back to conversations with Nick. Many of Wynneth's words echoed his admonitions.

She remembered him being particularly frustrated one day. *Poor Nick. I always created challenges for him.*

***

The Arrival

"Red, you must stop prejudging people. Dealing with folks this way doesn't serve you, and doesn't serve me or the company either. We've got people working here from all walks of life, and each enjoy their own abilities. You need to see they all fill different places in the company. Those who don't possess what it takes, won't last long. So although you may meet some of these guys, be patient. Everything will work out."

"There're some scary creeps working here, Nick, and I don't want to be anywhere near them and especially don't want to work with them. I'm always reading about crackpots out there who are violently anti-female regarding game designers."

"This is nothing new."

"One of the reasons I keep a low profile when I attend conventions is the harassment of female designers — and even the death threats. I don't know if some of the weirdos who work here are potentially violent nut jobs."

"I already said this is nothing new. OSA is well aware of the problems, which is why they put their future employees through rigorous scrutiny." Nick threw up his hands. "But come on, Kat, all who work in gaming are somewhat peculiar, including you. This is the exact thing which makes us so good at our jobs."

Kat extended her lower lip. "Hey I'm not peculiar."

Nick laughed. "Oh yes you are. And your pout is the worst I've ever seen."

She laughed. Nick's sense of humor always kept her in balance.

He sighed. "Red, this is important. Have you received any threats?"

"Well, no. But I prefer to keep my distance with everyone

of them."

"You don't need to become bosom buddies with anyone. I never suggested you do. But if a guy you think is stupid or odd, is a talented coding engineer, why wouldn't you make use of his abilities?"

Kat shrugged.

"Look, it comes down to the old saying. 'You can catch a lot more flies with honey than with vinegar.' So try using honey for a change."

***

A wet tongue on her hand brought Kat back to the present. Cat engrossed in cleaning her paws, occasionally licked Kat's fingers, and tickled them. *She's a delicate little thing.* Kat automatically thought of her as female. *I guess that's a prejudice, isn't it?*

She sighed. *Honey. He always mentioned honey. I used to love my discussions with Nick, even when he lectured me. I liked being able to talk about my work. No one here can understand anything about what I do.*

She and Nick continually disagreed with each other. On some occasions they yelled, but every problem eventually solved itself. Now, away from him, she missed him. She missed his wisdom, she missed his laughter, and she missed his criticism.

Cat butted her hand for more petting. Kat laughed. "You're a greedy little guts, aren't you?" *I guess cats do expect things from you.*

I suppose if Nick were here, he'd tell me the same thing about the Kaylins — I'm being too prejudiced, and I'm not giving them the benefit of the doubt. This may be true, but they don't give me the same benefit either. They aren't willing to understand I also think differently. They're just as preju-

diced as they believe I am. What it comes down to is, I'm expected to be more open-minded, but they're wearing bigger blinkers than anybody. At least Nick understood me. Damn I miss him.

Kat pushed the cat off her lap and rose. She brushed the leaves and grass from her skirt and decided to return to the keep. She shook her fist at the sky and yelled. "I wanna go home."

The sound of her voice startled the cat, who arched her back, hissed and darted back into the bushes.

Hmph. The cat's a critic as well.

J. M. Tibbott

CHAPTER 17

Wynneth awoke, startled by the groans coming from Kat's quarters. *What is that?* She jumped from her bed, hurried to the adjoining door and tapped lightly. The moans continued.

A voice cried out. "No. No. No. Don't come any closer."

Wynneth burst through the door and rushed over to Kat. *She's having a night-dream.*

She was thrashing around in her bed, while sweating profusely. Wynneth reached out nervously, afraid Kat might hit her accidentally, and shook her shoulder, encouraging her to wake. "Everything is alright. You are safe. Kat, you are safe."

Kat's eyes flew open and she sat up, gasping. "What?"

"You were having a night-dream. An unpleasant one, I would think. But you are safe. You can relax."

She blinked rapidly and rubbed her eyes. "I dreamed about a horrible trap. I couldn't escape."

"What did you envision in your dream?" *Fear is unusual for her.*

"A black figure in shadow, coming toward me. I felt danger and hatred. Then I saw the eyes." She shuddered.

"Is there anything else you can remember?"

"No. Only those eyes. I wanted to run from them, but I couldn't move."

"Do you normally experience such unpleasant night-dreams?"

"No, not since childhood. My dreams are usually about things I am planning to do, and are always pleasant. I never have nightmares any more."

"My dear Kat, I think you should go back to sleep and you will wake refreshed in the morning."

"I can't sleep. Those eyes are burned into my mind. Besides the sun will be up soon. I hear birds. I'll do some writing instead."

"Do what you wish. I should be up for the day myself, and I have much to do."

Wynneth hurried from the room. *I must talk with Eduardo. Something is wrong. Something or someone is after Kat.*

***

"Eduardo, forgive me for coming to you so early, and without making an appointment…"

"Wynneth. I never insisted you make an appointment to meet with me. Particularly since you appear to be quite agitated. I assume this is important?" He gestured toward a chair. "Shall I pour tea?"

He is always aware of what I need. Sometimes I think Eduardo plays the healer role with me. The son becomes the parent. "Please."

He poured her tea from a pot on a table in the corner of his office. "Drink, and tell me what upsets you."

Aware her forehead wrinkled with tension, Wynneth massaged it to smooth out her brow and then breathed deeply to relax herself. "I am concerned — concerned about Kat. Eduardo, you ask a lot from this young woman. She is a stranger to our world and our customs, and yet you have pinned your hopes on her ability to save our lands. This is not an easy task for anyone, and I catch her constantly challenged and continually battling our customs. She is stressed by this." *And so am I.*

"I am fully acquainted with the degree of difficulty involved in what I requested of her. I would willingly ask this

The Arrival

of another. Any other. But I cannot ignore what Deleth predicted."

"Of course. But I am afraid for Kat. Sometimes I am not sure she will be able to cope with what awaits her."

Eduardo leaned toward Wynneth and held her shoulder. "I believe she is a far stronger person than you may understand. She is stubborn, strong-minded, and appears to possess much physical strength. I detect the warrior in her. Both Irina and Bardu speak highly of her, although Bardu cannot help laughing when he describes their first meeting."

Wynneth managed a smile. "I hope he does not laugh in her presence. He would be most unwise."

"Of course not. Irina would reprimand him, and she is the only person in all Pridden around whom Bardu walks carefully." Eduardo held out his hands as though in supplication. "Understand, Wynneth, I believe Kat is more capable than any of us realize. Deleth's letter to me described her well. Everything I see and hear is Kat will live up to our expectations and more. I am convinced of this."

She relaxed a bit with his words. "You do make sense. She does learn quickly and picks up nuances about people very clearly and accurately. Given enough time, I also believe she will be of help. I worry, however, you are asking her to move too fast."

"Why do you fear for her safety?"

"She experienced some bad night-dreams. She calls them 'nightmares', although I do not understand how female horses relate to dreams."

Eduardo raised an eyebrow.

Does he think I am becoming senile? "I am quite serious Eduardo. Kat uses some strange expressions I find puzzling." *Has Eduardo forgotten many night dreams are in truth, visions of what is to come?*

"I also found the same thing about her use of words, but sometimes to make progress I find if we ignore the expressions and concentrate on what she means, we better understand her."

Wynneth raised her hands to her face. "I am sure there is something sinister about these dreams she experiences."

"What information did she give you about these 'nightmares' of hers?"

"She gave a vivid description of her dream. She described a robed figure, all in black, gliding toward the keep. She claimed she experienced a strong sense of malice emanating from this creature. The most extraordinary things were the eyes. She claimed they froze her in place, leaving her unable to move or call out, despite her desire to flee."

"Do you know if these types of dreams common for her?"

"She claims not."

Eduardo rose and paced the room, hands clasped behind his back. "Do you think, Wynneth, this is a foreshadowing?"

Oh my. Is he worried too? "I am fearful it might be. This is why I came to you immediately."

Eduardo ceased moving and turned to her, his brow creased. "Do you think Kat is in real danger?"

Wynneth sighed. "I do not know." She reached out with her hands, palms up. "I do not know. But I fear she might be. Eduardo, we must give her more help."

"I think it is time for Kat to be traveling. I will send her on a number of trips within Kaylin, accompanied by Drainin. This way she can experience the feel of the challenges facing her, but we will be able to observe her during this time."

"I am not sure Drainin would be the best guide for her. I suspect he holds a different agenda than you do."

"I am well aware Drainin considers himself first in all he does. However, his advice is always excellent, he is clever and resourceful, and he is much admired by women. He often acts as a mentor to some of the apprentices. As a fighter he is formidable, and as such will make a fine body-guard."

"I really do not think his usual attractiveness to females impressed Kat. I believe she is uncomfortable in his company. She once indicated her dislike of men who think they are attractive to females."

"I do not plan to send her off with any single person without additional protection." Eduardo sat at his desk and began writing a note. He glanced up at Wynneth. "I remember Liandock, our metalsmith, collects some interesting gems from Baklai."

Thank the Spirit, he is aware. He will protect Kat. "Indeed. They are said to contain emanations to help and enhance the abilities of those who wear them."

"I am writing to him and will ask him to prepare one for Kat which she can carry with her constantly." He held up his hand. "Do not worry, I will ask him to give her whatever he designs when Drainin is not about, because I would not wish him to understand we fear for Kat's honor in his presence."

"Thank you, Eduardo. I need to remember you always anticipate challenges. Although I suspect Kat is more than capable of protecting her own honor."

"No doubt. I will also advise Liandock of the fearful dreams she experiences. I am hopeful one of his gems may help Kat with this as well."

Eduardo rose from his desk, went to the cage in the corner and drew out the furry ball called Blink. The little creature yawned, stretched, and extended each wing in succession. It then settled on the desk and presented its foreleg. Eduardo rolled the note into the tube and fastened it to the harness.

He gently stroked the furry head. "Thank you Blink. Go to Master Liandock at Lanfair."

Blink rose, lifted her wings, flapped them twice to lift off the desk and popped out of existence.

Eduardo regarded Wynneth. "Satisfied?"

He is such a fine man. He knows what soothes. "Yes."

CHAPTER 18

Fear.

Kat stood at the open window. The night, overcast, moonless and with the stars hidden, blanketed the land with shadow. Beyond the meadow, she hardly discerned the line of trees moving restlessly. A black hooded figure materialized, moving silently toward the keep. Face concealed, robes fluttering slightly, the form glided, rather than walked, across the dark landscape. Icy fingers clutched at her throat, preventing any outcry. Her heart drummed and thumped and her blood roared through her veins. She dreaded the specter would hear the noise and come after her.

He stopped. The figure struck her as male. He slowly raised his head until she could see his eyes. Pools of dread, rivers of terror, and she could not turn away. He resumed moving toward the keep. The scream she wanted to unleash died within her. Everything turned to stone. Incapable of screaming, or moving. She was helpless.

Someone grabbed her from behind calling out her name.

"Kat. Kat." Wynneth shook her, eyes filled with concern, her forehead lined with worry. "You are alright. You are safe. Kat, you are safe."

Kat gasped for breath. "I couldn't escape. A nightmare." Sweat trickled through her hair and down her spine.

The healer asked her to describe her dream — she called them night-dreams, and Kat told her all she remembered. The memory, stark and real, haunted her. She kept blinking trying to clear the visions from her mind.

"My dear Kat, I think you should go back to sleep and you will wake refreshed in the morning."

Kat refused. "I dare not close my eyes. He's still standing, waiting to come back. I must stay awake."

Wynneth excused herself. "I need to handle some things."

So do I. I think I'll work on the game. It'll take my mind off those eyes.

But even after Wynneth left, Kat's concentration on writing failed.

Birds chirping, and the sky is getting light. I think the best thing is to go for a walk. After my walk, I'll eat breakfast. Things will be normal again.

***

By the time Kat emerged from the keep, the sun peered over the horizon, and the birds sang with morning gusto. Kat always loved this time of day. Back home, animals began their days, but the streets were never cluttered with people. Like home, Kaylin was similar. In addition to the songbirds, Kaylin boasted a small, self-important bird similar to the starlings. Kat loved watching them. They tended to walk about like pint-sized pompous people, intent on some vital mission of their own. When they gathered in a group, they called and shrieked and indulged in obvious arguments. She remembered once attending a local council meeting, and these birds were doubles for the agitated, puffed-up members of the local political scene. She had fled, head aching from all the nonsense and chattering. *All this pontificating is exhausting.* Kat grinned to herself. *Ha, I finally used pontificating in a sentence. This word sat waiting for me to use for ages.*

Her mood improved and the dregs of the nightmare dissipated, Kat strolled along the avenue of the shops. The locals opened up for the day, and she took time to examine each tiny shop. Shoes and jewelry and artwork on racks, were all displayed at their most advantageous. *I wonder what they use for currency? I'm not much into shopping, but there're some interesting things.*

The smells of fresh-baked breads and hot drinks drifted toward her. She salivated. *Time to go back for breakfast.*

As she turned around abruptly, she bumped into Drainin.

"Forgive me, Lady Kat."

The extraordinary voice again. "My pardon, Counselor Drainin, I didn't watch where I was going." *Darn, I used his title — the lack of it might have taken him down a notch. I goofed.*

"You are about early, Lady Kat. Would you like me to give you a tour of the market?"

He genuinely thinks he's Gods gift. He regards me like a snake viewing a bunny meal. I nearly said no, but perhaps I can use him. "Why yes, I would like a tour."

Drainin pointed out the set-up of the marketplace as they strolled through the alleyways of shops and stalls. "The shopkeepers tend to keep in groups with their own people. You will observe as we travel through the merchants' stalls, each land specializes in their own crafts. This area of the market is the Kaylins' section."

"I saw much of the cloth at Master Thontook's." *I'm going to make sure I use titles for everyone else, so he will notice when I drop his. Something about him I don't trust.* Kat allowed herself a hint of a smile. "The clothing they offer is new to me."

"In the next stall you will see the excellent leather products they produce." Drainin walked over to the display and extracted a blue leather belt and held it up against the sleeve of Kat's dress. "This would go well with your gown."

Kat's stomach growled, loud enough, she was sure, for Drainin to detect. "Sorry, I think I must cut our tour short. Breakfast is calling."

"Brek-fast? What is that?"

Rats, another explanation needed. "I use this word for the morning meal."

"Of course. But you do not need to return to the keep. Come." He dropped the belt back on the display, took her arm and practically dragged her to a stall in the next alley.

Annoyed by his presumption, she prepared to wrench free, when he stopped at a shop offering a variety of foods. The odor, beyond wonderful, curled in Kat's nostrils, and her stomach groaned in protest again.

"Do you like wullawerth meat?"

"Yes, but... ."

He ignored her and turned to the shopkeeper. "Two plates of your wullawerth special, and your regular tea."

He must be in control. Arrogant. He's being very nice to me, but I can't help it, I don't like him.

The round faced, pudgy merchant hastened to fill the order. "Certainly, Counselor Drainin. On the keep record?"

"Yes."

The stall-keeper handed Drainin a large tray with two plates of something appetizing, a pot of tea with two cups, and the necessary eating implements.

I think the owner of this stall consumes a lot of his own wares. But he seems a happy person.

Drainin nodded toward the open space beside the stall. "Over here are tables where we can to sit to eat."

The only thought in Kat's mind was delivering the contents of the plate to her demanding body, so she moved to a table and sat, while Drainin placed food and tea in front of her.

"Thank you, Counselor." *I can't be too rude yet, since he did just buy me breakfast.* "I've got no money, so I thought I would need to return to the keep."

"You use some strange words. What is munny?"

"It's what we use to give people in exchange for their goods."

"We do not use this munny. All goods are traded. If someone does not possess a trade item at the time, the seller writes out a record, which the purchaser signs. Eventually all records get cleared. We all need something others produce."

"Sounds complicated."

"Not really. Trading works for our world." He finished his meal and pushed the plate away. "Is your hunger satisfied?"

"Yes, I loved the food."

"Shall we continue our tour?"

"I'm curious to look at more."

"We must return to the leather shop. The blue belt bears your name."

"Counselor, I own nothing to trade."

"The merchant will add the belt to the keep record."

"I don't think that's right. I haven't any trade items of my own."

He turned to her, shaking his head. "Lady Kat, you are a guest here. Everything you need will be absorbed by Lord Eduardo. He would expect you to purchase items as you need them. Did you not wonder about the new clothes you are wearing?"

"Briefly. But it's been a whirlwind of new experiences. I guess I assumed I'd need to pay for them later." *Then again, they did bring me here and now want me to help them. I guess these are my wages.* She followed Drainin back to the stall with the blue belt.

133

The shopkeeper wrote the sale on the keep record. "It suits you my lady."

The belt, soft and supple, glowed with the beautiful blue of a jay's wing. The only challenge was her discomfort when Drainin insisted on tying it around her waist. *He's much too close. But he does smell marvelous. Male and sort of hot.* Kat raised her eyes to his. His smirk drove all thoughts of admiration from her mind.

"Fine, Counselor, thank you." His smug smile annoyed her.

"You are welcome, Lady Kat." He dipped his head. "We should visit the rest of the market."

Kat agreed and they set off again, wending their way through the alleyways of fascinating shops selling leather, glorious crystals, beaded shoes and more kiosks selling foods. Although Drainin suggested various items she should consider purchasing, Kat refused. *I don't have place to store stuff in my rooms, and what will I do with everything when I go home?*

They lapsed into silence.

I wonder if I should ask for his help? He's arrogant, thinks of himself as a chick-magnet and likes to control, but he's been kind to me this morning.

"You are not from Kaylin, are you?"

"No, I birthed in Morden, and I only reside temporarily in Kaylin."

"Do you miss Morden?"

"In some ways, I do. When one wishes to advance, they need to travel wherever the opportunities are. Lord Eduardo offered me the position of Counselor, and I enjoy my life here. I would be deemed foolish to refuse the option."

The Arrival

"I know how you feel. I miss my home a lot. But I didn't receive a choice like you did. I want to go home, but I don't know how. I asked Lord Eduardo, but nothing happened. Please, Drainin, can you get him to help me?" *Oh bugger, I left off his title — this was not the time to insult him.*

"What makes you think I can persuade Lord Eduardo to help you?"

"You're his Counselor. He listens to you, doesn't he?"

"He listens to me when we discuss matters of importance to Kaylin. Not when some woman is pining for something she will never obtain."

"What do you mean 'never obtain'?"

"You are not the only person to arrive in Pridden from elsewhere. You are not unique."

She recoiled from him. "Others? Did they go back to their homes?"

"No one ever returned to their original lands. I suggest you stop thinking about what you want, and concentrate on becoming a useful citizen of Kaylin or some other land." He glared at her. "You might as well accept your fate. You are here to stay, Lady Kat. Accept it." He turned on his heel and marched away from her.

Kat stared at his back. *No. He's got to be wrong. I don't want to be stuck here. I hate him. What a freaking arrogant man.*

J. M. Tibbott

CHAPTER 19

When Kat returned to her quarters, she sat at her desk to write, and scribbled angry thoughts on her parchment. Her game notes turned into a journal, and everything she experienced, no matter how trivial, became grist for something extraordinary. Plus she was frustrated. She had headed immediately to Wynneth's quarters. Unfortunately, Mayda advised her the healer and a patient were in consultation.

Kat put down her Cathnog pen, pushed back her chair and paced the room. *I must talk to Wynneth. I don't do patience. People are mad at me and won't co-operate, Eduardo made promises but nothing happened, and Drainin's mind is limited to only one thing. If I get home... no, when I get home, I'll never complain about OSA again.*

A light tap at the door and Kat swiveled her head toward the sound. "Come."

Mayda peered around the door. "Healer Wynneth can see you now, Lady Kat."

"Terrific." Kat ran to the connecting door, tapped, and entered without waiting for Wynneth's reply. "Wynneth, I need your help. That Drainin guy is... is... ."

Wynneth's eyes were closed and her hand pressed against her forehead, furrowed in evident frustration.

Rats, I forgot. "Sorry. How are you Wynneth?"

She gazed up at Kat. "I am well." She smiled. "Social niceties are so difficult for you. I do understand, but others will not. Please practice."

Kat did her best to appear embarrassed. "I will try and remember."

"You mentioned needing help. What troubles you now?"

She thought she caught a sigh from Wynneth. "I met Drainin at the market, and we spent some time together. He almost appeared to be a nice person. When I asked if he could persuade Eduardo to help me return home, he told me no one who came here from elsewhere ever returned to their own world." Kat spread her hands in anger. "Why didn't anyone tell me others came here before me?"

"Kat, there were only two others, and they came from far beyond our lands from the area we call Air Wyth. We have no idea how they came to cross the mountains of Clog Neran. They did not wish to return. They liked being in Pridden. One woman is now living in Shendea in training to become a healer, and the other is in Glowen."

"Why didn't they want to return?"

"I am unaware of their reasons. I assume they chose to stay because this world is better than where they came from. Glowen certainly offers many pleasant distractions."

"Drainin didn't inform me they chose to remain."

"Counselor Drainin adheres to his own agenda, particularly with attractive women. He is a man who thrives on the admiration of females. The challenges in Kaylin, because of the repression of relationships outside of bonding, do not give him the opportunities he would prefer."

"I already figured out he's a horn dog."

Wynneth's mouth dropped open. "A what? What does this mean?"

How do I put this without offending her sensibilities? "A horn dog is a man who is continually on the lookout for women with whom he wants to mate. He's not discerning, either."

The Arrival

Wynneth cocked her head, seemingly deep in thought, and then smiled. "I like this expression. Horn dog. Yes, I do find it amusing."

"Drainin also told me I might as well resign myself to being here, because I will never be able to find my way home. I hated him right then. Believe me, he will never... ever... ever be able to compromise me."

Wynneth still grinned. "I never considered for a moment you would fall under his spell." She laughed, a deep belly sound. "Horn dog. I like this. The phrase suits."

Kat, although pleased Wynneth found the expression amusing, was impatient to get her questions answered. "Is he right? Will I never return home?"

"Drainin is unaware of all Eduardo can access. If Eduardo gave you hope, do not abandon what he conveyed." Wynneth's face was serious. "I think we should arrange for you to meet again with him, if only to ease your mind. I will arrange things so Drainin is not with him at the time, and although I understand you are not blessed with patience, please attempt to be so."

"I'll wait, because I really want to speak to Eduardo again."

***

Dafid's face lit up when Kat walked up to Eduardo's door the next morning. "Lady Kat, I am please to meet you again. I will inform Lord Eduardo you are here." He turned, pulled at the door and peered in.

He's such a cute young guy. All those curls and bright shiny smile. But not for bedding, for admiring. He's adorable and sorta cuddly.

Dafid stood aside to allow Kat in, and she smiled and thanked him. *Yup, cute as a button.* She entered the office. *Oh yes, niceties.* "Good morning, Lord Eduardo."

139

He chuckled. "You are most formal today, Kat."

"I always seem to be annoying people, who then refuse to do what I ask, so being formal appears to be the sole way to achieve what I need."

"This must be a challenge for you."

"You're attempt at sympathy, Eduardo, is not successful. Your eyes are laughing at me."

"Forgive me. I am remembering I went through much of this myself when younger. Fortunately I had the protection of being the Lord's heir, plus Wynneth acting the part of cub safety."

"Well don't tell me to be patient. The word raises my hackles."

Eduardo laughed. "What a delightful expression. I envision a picture of one of our hunting dogs when they are aggressive. The hair on their backs does indeed raise, although we do not call them hackles." He motioned Kat to a seat. "Enough of the pleasantries of the day. Wynneth informed me you had a disagreement with Drainin about your return to your world."

"This was no disagreement. He told me others had come here from elsewhere and none ever returned home. He insisted I could never go back."

Eduardo leaned back in his own chair. "To my knowledge, only two others ever came to Pridden, from a land outside the Clog Neran and neither wished to return to their own worlds. They remained here out of their own desire."

"Yes, Wynneth told me."

"Their coming here is quite different from your appearance in Pridden." He leaned forward. "I know you find Drainin annoying, but I would urge you to be… ." He stopped when Kat glared at him. "I was about to speak the word you despise, but truly, you will need to practice patience with Drainin as well." He spread his hands toward her. "Kat, many people enjoy some small power on Pridden, but few hold the knowledge and ability Lord Rhognor, myself and a number of others do. What this means is Drainin is unaware of all the possibilities."

"What you're saying is, he doesn't have all the facts."

"Well, yes. I would urge you to accept him as he is. While he is convinced of his abilities with females, he is also a shrewd and capable man. He has been my advisor for some time, and his advice is always valuable. He can be quite charming when necessary, and he is extremely familiar with Kaylin."

"Why are you trying to sell him to me?"

"What I am trying to do is tell you I wish you to give him another chance. He can prove useful to you."

What's Eduardo up to. Something tells me I'm not going to like this. "In what way?"

"What I ask of you, Kat, is you travel around Pridden helping to uncover the reasons behind the problems we are all facing, and simultaneously, locate people you believe have the power... and the desire to help you in your attempt to return to your own world."

"You've covered this before. You told me I must go to Shendea."

"True. Before you do go to Shendea, it is important you travel through Kaylin."

"Why? Don't you own sufficient power to help me?"

"Possibly I will be the one from Kaylin to act as Power Wielder. However, someone else maybe better suited. And, you need to complete the first part of your task for me in this land."

"This is getting too complicated. And too demanding."

"Are you prepared to do this to obtain what you want?"

Kat glared at Eduardo for a moment. "Fine. I'll do it. But I'm not happy about this."

"You will be less happy when I tell you your guide through Kaylin is to be Drainin."

"What?" Kat shook her head. "No, I don't want him with me." *No freakin' way.*

Eduardo sighed. "Kat, you are making much more of this than is necessary. Drainin is an excellent guide and is acquainted with Kaylin like one born here. He can be diplomatic when called for. He is in contact with many people and can open doors for you. He is organized, skilled, and can also function as a bodyguard for you, should you need those services."

"No. Absolutely not. I do not want to travel with him." *Damn him.*

Eduardo closed his eyes and rubbed at his forehead. "You need to do this with Drainin."

"You can't make me." *I can't believe he is doing this.*

Eduardo spread his arms, with palms up. "You said you were willing to do what ever necessary to achieve what you wanted."

"Well… yes."

Eduardo leaned forward again and pointed directly at her. "This is necessary."

"Drainin thinks he can get any woman he wants. He's going to try the same thing on me."

"What? By the Spirit, surely you do not expect me to believe you are incapable of fending off unwanted attentions?"

"Of course I can."

"Then what is the real problem?"

The Arrival

"He's arrogant. He thinks he knows everything, and I don't like him."

"Those may be the exact things you will need on this trip. As far as your dislike of him, you will need to put this aside, if you wish to accomplish your task."

Even in another world, people still do everything they can to control me. Eduardo's being a twit now. What choice do I have though? "You're quite clear on what I am required to do. But I don't like it."

"You do not need to like this, Kat. If you fight less, and perhaps attempt to find some pleasant things, you may find the experience less frustrating. Your own attitude will ease this journey for you."

"I've said I will do what you want, and I will go with Drainin. What I don't require are any more lectures from you."

Eduardo sighed. "I will excuse your unpleasant reaction as coming from frustration, but you will be better served to keep your temper under control when you look for help in the lands." He rubbed his right eyebrow. "I will hand Drainin the information, and he will begin planning for the journey. It would be best if you return to your quarters."

Kat rose, turned on her heel, and left without further comment. *I thought I had Eduardo on my side. Will Wynneth do the same thing to me? I can't stand this. Doesn't anyone understand how much I need to go home? Damn them all!*

J. M. Tibbott

CHAPTER 20

Mayda bounced into Kat's room after knocking. "Healer Wynneth instructed me to help you pack for the journey, since I am to accompany you."

Oh terrific. I receive the pleasure of traveling with the chatterbox as well as arrogant Drainin. Gag me with a spoon. Although having Mayda along isn't such a bad idea. She'll be the buffer between us. I'm still mad with Eduardo about this, but he's given me no choice. "Thank you, Mayda. What do I need to take?"

"Counselor Drainin said we will first travel to the mining community near the Clog Neran mountains, and you will be able to meet Master Liandock who is the Master Metal-Smith in Kaylin. Healer Wynneth said to tell you he is from Rifella because this would be important for you to know."

Right. Must take lots of the Karri-san stuff.

Mayda continued talking. "The air near Clog Neran is often quite chilly, particularly after dark, so you will need warmer clothing. After Clog Neran we will travel to Trigoran, which is the biggest village in Kaylin. Even I have not been so far away from home. It will be so exciting. Trigoran is located toward Clog Blue, which are what their mountains are called, and is hotter than the keep."

Tuning out Mayda's on-going prattling, Kat laid out her clothes, including one dressy outfit. *I better also take my writing stuff. I should find more material for the backgrounds for my game. At this rate, I'll bet I've got enough material for at least three new games. Nick will be major happy.*

Mayda handed Kat a type of duffel bag made from leather. "This should hold all you need to take. Mine is packed."

Together they loaded Kat's bag, Mayda speaking faster than ever. Watching her reminded Kat of a puppy, wriggling with excitement at the prospect of an adventure.

A knock at the door elicited "Come" from Kat.

A tall young Kaylin man with curly hair like Dafid, entered. "Good morrow, Lady Kat. Counselor Drainin sent me to take you and your luggage to the courtyard to meet him." He picked up both the bags. "If you would follow me, please." He paused, a little flustered. "My apologies, I did not introduce myself. I am called Bannon, and I will be the wagon handler."

"Thank you, Bannon. This is my friend, Mayda."

At the word friend, Mayda squirmed with pleasure.

I guess no one ever called her friend before. I suspect Haydar discourages friendships for his daughter.

"Well met, Mayda." Bannon turned and walked out the door and down the corridor. Kat followed, with Mayda almost scampering to keep up with Bannon's long-legged stride.

***

All three arrived at the courtyard, where waiting for them they found a wagon with a covered section over a driver's bench and immediately behind, a pair of benches facing each other. Two pontis were harnessed at the front. The rear of the passenger section extended to an area for luggage. Already stowed were two sets of baggage, plus three long and two short parcels wrapped in a heavy type of canvas. Attached to the back of the rear seat were a couple of quivers containing arrows plus two items which resembled crossbows.

The Arrival

Drainin leaned against the wagon. "Did both of you bring head gear?

I guess he means hats.

"You will need protection in the daylight."

"Yes, Bannon added them to the luggage for both of us." Kat glanced again at the weapons. "Are we expecting trouble?"

Drainin laughed. "You mean the arrows and the springbows? Not trouble, but we will be staying some nights in tents, and while we do carry food with us, when we arrive at Clog Blue, the mountains which run from east to west, we can hunt the gornogs, which make fine eating. They are not easy to find, and they fight well when cornered. If we do manage to kill one, we can sell the tusks in Trigoran to the jewelers. What we cannot eat, we will dry and sell in the village as well."

"How long will this trip take?"

"About thirteen or fourteen star turns, Lady Kat." He motioned to Bannon to load their bags. "One other thing. We may encounter some Kithras when we are near Trigoran. They are not large, but they can be vicious. Bannon packed additional weapons to help if they attack us."

"So what are gornogs and kithras?"

"Well, gornogs resemble our pigs, but are much bigger, with long tusks and if cornered are unpleasant foe. They are also exceedingly ugly." He smacked his lips. "But their meat is sweet and worth the effort of the hunt. Kithras, however, are formidable animals. They are no larger than a dog, but since they prefer to hunt in packs, and their teeth are razor sharp, we avoid them if possible. They do not make pleasant eating."

"I hope I never meet a kithra." She leaned up to touch one of the bows. "I'm familiar with the long bow, but, I would like to learn how to use the spring-bow. Will you teach me?"

"I will, but there is no time to do so for the next four or five star turns. It is interesting you mention long bows. The only people who use them exclusively are the Rifellans, because the long bow is easier to handle from horseback."

Bannon handed Mayda and Kat their hats, extracted a folded up version from his back pocket and donned headgear so it flopped over the back of his neck and completely shielded his face.

"I will help the females, Bannon. Take your place." Drainin held out his hand for Kat and then Mayda to be helped aboard. "I will sit in the seat facing forward, because I wish quick access to the weapons if needed."

"I thought you said you weren't expecting trouble?"

"I am not. But this means both of you are protected, front and back… in case."

Drainin is back to being his ever-so charming, women-fall-under-my-spell, self again. Fourteen days. I wonder how this is going to work out. He doesn't strike me as being a patient person. How is he going to react to Mayda's constant talking?

Once all were seated, Bannon clicked once, shook the reins and the two sure-footed little pontis obediently trotted forward.

As soon as they were moving, Drainin pointed out the containers attached to the seats. "Make sure you drink plenty of water, the wind and heat will dehydrate you quicker than you anticipate."

Boy, he is being charming. I don't trust charming men. They always have a hidden agenda.

The Arrival

***

The wagon rocked gently for most of the day, and a number of times, Kat drifted in a half sleep. A change in pace woke her fully and she found herself in shoulder-high grasslands, dotted with occasional bushes and trees.

Bannon stopped the wagon in a small clearing, surrounded by rocks on one side, and trees on the other two. Close by, a pool of clear water shimmered in the sun. Bannon filled the wagon's water containers, then released the pontis from their harnesses and took them to the pool to drink their fill. Once they were sated, he hobbled and tied them to a line strung between two trees so they couldn't wander off.

While Bannon worked, Drainin dismounted and stretched. "We will stop here for the night. This way we will arrive refreshed at Master Liandock's settlement."

"Master Liandock? He's the Metal-Smith, correct?"

Before Drainin could reply, Mayda jumped in. "He is, and his creations are much prized in our land."

Kat glanced over at Drainin, whose mouth set in wry amusement, merely rolled his eyes at the young woman.

I thought he'd be furious with her for interrupting. "Thank you, Mayda. Counselor, is our destination much further? Why stop now, there's still plenty of daylight."

"The amount of light is deceptive. We would be unable to reach the settlement before dark." He addressed Bannon. "I think you can set up the tents over by the trees." He pointed to a flat clear space. "Build the fire in the center of all three." He looked over at Mayda and Kat. "Fire building is necessary and requires help. Would each of you search for small pieces of wood, and for kindling. Bannon and I will find the larger pieces."

They all set off to gather fire making materials, and by the time Kat and Mayda returned, Bannon had set up three tents. His own, the smallest one, was set close to where the pontis were hobbled, comfortably munching on the sweet grass around them.

Drainin pointed at the middle tent. "That one, Lady Kat is for you and Mayda, and one on the outside is mine."

Kat grinned. "I notice Mayda and I are protected on both sides again."

Drainin raised an eyebrow at her. "Of course." He smiled back at her.

Oh no you don't. I'm not falling for your machinations. Kat entered her tent and set up her bedroll and comforter, watching Mayda for hints. *I never did like camping, but perhaps this will be OK. My idea of roughing it was always finding warm champagne in a luxury hotel.*

Outside again, she watched carefully as Bannon set up a circle of rocks, and stacked the wood and kindling inside. Once satisfied with his set-up, he withdrew a small rod from his pocket, which he tapped twice on a stone, pointed the rod at the kindling, which caught fire at once.

Kat's mouth gaped at him. "How did you do that? What is the rod made of?"

Bannon glanced up. "This is a tinder rod, Lady Kat. You tap it twice on a rock to excite the metal so the small sticks can ignite. Most people own one. We use them for lighting our fires and stoves within our homes."

She held out her hand. "Can I see, please?"

"Of course." He gave it to her.

The rod was a dark metal, and the end was roughened, and it fascinated Kat. "This is amazing. How can I find one?"

"Mayda should be able to obtain one for you from the Head of Housekeeping."

The Arrival

After handing the tinder back to Bannon, Kat entered her tent, found her writing materials, and took a small stool outside, which she set up near the warm flames. She began recording what she had learned about lighting fires.

Shortly Mayda and Drainin emerged from their tents, both placing stools of their own.

Drainin rose to peer over her shoulder at her page. "You can write in runes. Impressive. Where did you learn?"

They really can't read my writing. Weird. This I'm not going to attempt to explain. "I learned as a child. My parent taught me." *Well, dad did teach me how to write my name. It's sorta true.*

Kat continued writing while Bannon prepared their meal. Soon the delicious aromas rising from his pots persuaded her to put aside her paper and to dig into the a bowl of what appeared to be wullawerth stew. Bannon had added some unusual spices, plus at least two savory root vegetables, one of which tasted sweet on the tongue. Together they created a delightful flavor combination. "This is wonderful, Bannon. I'm hungrier than I realized. Could I have some tea now, please? I brought some with me in this bag." She handed her personal stash to him to prepare.

Drainin smirked at her. "Karri-san. I observe you are aware Liandock is Rifellan."

She glared at him without answering. *He can't help it. He's been pleasant all day, but the annoying rat part can't be concealed for long. Hmmph.*

Kat took her tea with her to her tent. By the time she blew out the light, night had fallen and she couldn't help yawning as she cuddled into the comforter. Moments later she heard Mayda creep into her own bed. The orchestral sounds of the night reminded her of the tree frogs in the Virgins. One of the pontis nickered softly and some far away thing grunted. Her eyelids fluttered closed. She slept.

***

Kat woke before the rest, and treated herself to a brief bath in the pond. Cleaning herself did not come easily in the full-length bathing robe Mayda had packed, but she welcomed the cover-up, when Drainin suddenly appeared.

"My pardon, Lady Kat. I will withdraw until you return to your tent."

Yeah, right. He's probably dying to cop a peek. Kat hurried back to her tent, dried off and dressed. Mayda was up and busily packing their things. The wet bathing clothes and towels went into a special waterproof container.

"We will be able to spread these out on the back of the wagon when we set out, Lady Kat. They will dry swiftly."

After a substantial breakfast, and another cup of Karri-san for Kat, Bannon cleaned the area, packed up all their belongings, and they boarded the wagon once more. The day was bright with sun, and the air a little crisper than the one before.

The shawl Kat brought with her to cover her shoulders kept her cozy.

Drainin called to Bannon to stop the wagon. "I wish to pick up some items. Slow down a little and I will catch up to you." As the wagon stopped, he hopped off, taking a quiver and one of the spring-bows with him.

The wagon lurched forward again, but travelled slower than before.

"What would he be looking for, Mayda?"

"I do not know, Lady Kat."

Kat estimated they travelled for about twenty minutes, when suddenly, Drainin appeared running along side the

The Arrival

wagon. Bannon must have seen him, because he stopped the pontis long enough for Drainin to board.

He replaced the quiver and bow in their positions, and opened a small bag at his waist. He emptied the contents into his hand. The rough stones in various colors, sparkled in the light. "They are much sought by Master Liandock for the jewelry he makes. He always appreciates receiving new ones."

"They're beautiful. I suspect when they're polished they are even more attractive." Kat wanted to touch them, but was reluctant to make contact with Drainin's hand.

"You may wish to purchase some of Liandock's jewelry, so take two of these stones for him."

"But you found them. Don't you want to use them?'

He laughed. "I find them constantly. Plus, I possess plenty of items to trade for what I want."

I hope he doesn't think two stones are enough for me to... Kat reached out reluctantly and picked two stones. "Thank you."

Drainin then offered his hand to Mayda. "Pick two for yourself. You may want some jewelry as well."

Mayda shrank back. "Master Haydar would never allow me to wear adornments."

Drainin rolled his eyes. "Then pick two and purchase something for your female parent as a gift."

Mayda shyly plucked the stones from his hand. "I would be allowed to do so. Thank you Counselor Drainin."

I wonder why he's being so kind to Mayda. She will never allow him liberties. She's much too afraid of Haydar. Am I being overly suspicious of him?

The pontis slowed their gait, and Bannon leaned back. "We are approaching the village, Counselor."

A village? There are only a few houses. "I didn't realize this was a village. What's the name?"

Out of the corner of her eye, Kat caught Mayda's mouth opening to reply.

Drainin answered her question first. "The name is Lanfair. Because we are close to both the rock and metal mines, the metal-smiths and the builders live in small villages adjacent to each other. I'm sure you noticed most of the homes are built from rock. These mountains boast stone which is extremely hard, streaked with crystals and yet easy to work with, so this is where the materials for building are quarried."

"I did admire the stonework at the keep — and the elegant construction. I suspect Kaylin's builders are in demand."

***

At the entrance to the Metal-Smith's home in his village, Drainin took his leave from Kat. "I have other business to attend to, so I will leave you in Mayda's capable care. She will cover your introduction to Master Liandock, and he will make arrangements for your accommodation. I will be staying with someone else. We can meet for the evening meal in the Master's eating room. On the morrow, we head for the stone-cutter's village where I will introduce you to Master Builder Penrow."

"Fine." Kat waited at the entrance to Liandock's quarters.

Mayda's knock was met with a roar. "Come."

Wow, he sounds like a lion. A lion with an incredibly deep voice.

Kat and Mayda entered the rooms which acted as workshop and display areas. A forge burned brightly in the corner, and the Metal-Smith worked with a type of soldering iron glowing red from the furnace. He bent and curved silver metal into shapes and in several places, joined them with the iron.

The Arrival

He put his tools aside and glanced at the two women.

He even resembles a lion. A mass of blonde hair tied back, with a face red from the heat, and bare to the waist, exposing thick blond chest hairs, he is sex personified. He's gorgeous, but Karri-san is keeping my temptation manageable. Do all Rifellans resemble gods?

He rose and strode over to Kat, the brown leather kilt-like garment he wore, swaying with each step.

Good Lord, he displays the swagger of some Highland piper, with the awesome strong legs of one too.

His leather boots, laced up the front to his knee, make no sound on the wooden floor. With her attention on those sexy legs, Kat was startled when he grasped her hand in his.

"Lady Kat, you are expected." His voice, melodic and deep, vibrated in in the pit of her stomach, more a purr than a roar.

One of his eyes is yellow... no, more gold. "Er... yes." *OMG did I just moan a little?* "I... er... have some crystals for you." She held out her other hand.

Liandock took them from her. "Excellent specimens. Come. We will find a suitable pendant for you." Still holding her hand, he led her to chairs in front of a display of fine stones and silver chains. His gold eye laid bare every thought and dream she possessed. "You are not from here, and you are facing many challenges. No? You are also under much stress."

How does he know this? Did Wynneth tell him? OMG, can he read my mind?

Liandock released her hand and picked up a number of chains, which he held up against her, brushing her skin each time. He gave them names, none of which penetrated her flustered state.

She chose a delicate one he called Fere, perhaps because he held this to her throat longer than the others.

"Now a stone to meld with the chain." He reached for a deep emerald-green crystal, carved on the top with a rune which Kat found familiar. He held the stone to her face, at her temple. "The color of the stone and your eye compliment each other. This is the one." He held the stone and chain together and regarded them closely. "I will make them one."

Oh his glorious voice. I wish he would talk forever.

As he worked, she stared at his hands — strong, yet gentle enough to handle the fragile silver wire, without breaking it. *I wonder what those fingers would feel like on me? Stop Kat. Stop now. Get ahold of yourself. Remember you are supposed to be in control.*

She swallowed and cleared her throat. *Where have I seen that rune? Wait a minute it's the same as the one on the necklace I bought in Tortola.* "The shade is beautiful, Liandock."

"So you do know my name."

"Oh forgive me, I forgot to use your title."

"Titles mean little, Kat." He held the stone, now cradled by silver wires. "This pendant is made specifically for you, and will serve you in the journeys to come." He held up the chain. "Please, let me?" Without waiting for permission, he put the chain around her neck and clasped it at the back, his fingers brushing her neck, sending frissons of electricity down her spine.

He is so enticing and I haven't had sex in a long time. I wonder if his 'talents' match his voice?

"This will help you with some worrying decisions, and will protect you from many challenges. Wear it well. And listen when it speaks."

The Arrival

Speaks? Kat turned around to stare at him, their faces inches apart. The sparks between them were palpable. She barely breathed. "Thank you."

"No thanks are needed." He traced a finger down her cheek. "We are not yet done. You have other needs which require fulfillment."

"Yes?" Kat, unsure if her reply was a question or an assent, remained spellbound. She was sure she had squeaked the question.

Liandock broke the mood and stood. "Ah. Your companion traded for some jewelry of her own, so one of my assistants will show you to your room, while I help her decide."

Kat rose to her own feet, slightly unsteady at first. The necklace warmed and comforted as it lay against her skin. Except for the the attraction to Liandock, she felt peaceful. His assistant led her to her room.

I just remembered something else. The symbol on my stone resembles the norse rune for warrior. How curious, that's exactly the talisman I chose for Berenga in my latest game.

CHAPTER 21

Liandock had not joined them for dinner, pleading work which required his attention. The four travelers dined in silence, each immersed in their own thoughts. After a quiet evening meal, each headed for their rooms: Bannon to the stable master's home; Drainin to whatever quarters he had arranged; and Mayda and Kat to their rooms in Liandock's home.

Undressing in the room she'd been assigned, Kat snuggled into the soft bed, the comfort of the emerald stone resting between her breasts. She had forgotten to unpack night clothes, and reveled in the soft folds of the bedding enfolding her naked body. The sounds of tree frogs and the scent of night-blooming jasmine lulled her, and she drifted into slumber.

Liandock came to her in the night. He stroked her face gently, his warm breath in her ear. When he slid beneath the covers, the heat of his bare flesh against her was so intense, she groaned with desire. He stifled the sound with his mouth, giving and taking, his tongue seeking and finding. She tasted the honey of his lips, and inhaled the spicy scent of clean, strong male. His magic hands coaxed pleasure from every fibre of her body. Time bent and twisted. Juices flowed, and finally he slid into her.

As wave after wave of the most extraordinary climax she had ever experienced took control of her, his guttural cry of triumph woke her fully. With his face inches away, his golden eye mesmerizing her, she gazed back in awe, mentally stunned and unable to perceive anything but the aftermath of exquisite release.

"Liandock?" *Is this a dream? Is this real?*

The faint light of Pridden's moon revealed his smile. "High stress and mutual need existed between us. Sleep well, Kat." His lips brushed hers, then he slipped from the bed and disappeared from her room.

Not a dream. Wow. Certainly not a dream. I've just met him and... this's a first for me. Kat smiled to herself. *Sleep well? I bet I will.*

Every limb heavy, languor overtook her body, and she slept. Again.

***

A shaft of sunlight poking through the gap in the curtains, stabbed at Kat's eyes. She yawned, stretched like a cat, threw back the covers and slithered out of bed. She would have purred, if possible. *I'm not sure what or how Eduardo thinks I should accomplish his task. But last night ensured I do find the trip worthwhile.*

Mayda knocked at the door, announcing herself. "Counselor Drainin sent me to help you pack, Lady Kat."

Kat hastened for the personal to wash away the evidence and scent of the night. "Come in." After a brief shower, she gazed in the mirror and found, to her delight, the small frown lines had vanished. Her face, smooth again... and glowing, smiled back at her. Dressed, she joined Mayda to help with the packing.

"You appear well rested, Lady Kat. The air here must agree with you."

"The bed was comfortable and my sleep peaceful." *I hope I'm keeping a straight face while lying this badly.*

The Arrival

When packed, they headed for the eating room in Liandock's buildings. On their way, Drainin joined them.

"I trust you both slept well?"

Kat caught him examining her closely. *Does he know or suspect? I'd better put on my bland face.* "Very well, thank you, Counselor."

Liandock loped into the room, the great lion satisfied. *Thank god, he's wearing a shirt.*

He joined them at their table and summoned his staff to begin serving. "I receive enormous pleasure from guests. We do not enjoy visitors often, so this is a change from our routine."

At least he's keeping discreet about our nighttime sexercise. She allowed herself a small inner smirk. *I wonder if my made up word counts in my word game? Anyway, Drainin can't really suspect anything. Can he?*

Liandock gestured toward the dishes. "My assistants prepared a special meal for you. Let us dine."

"We appreciate your hospitality, Master Liandock." Drainin growled his reply.

"I thank you, Counselor Drainin." Liandock tipped his head, his smile akin to a baring of fangs.

Oops. I don't think my 'lion' likes Drainin. They're like two beasts sizing each other up before beginning battle. I suspect though, if they did fight, the Metal-Smith would win.

The meal continued, with little conversation from the two men, but Mayda, her normal self, chattered away about everything she had seen the day before.

Kat compared the males on either side of her. *These are two fabulous characters for my game. I would create the Drainin character with a sense of menace. I'm not sure how I could instill in the Liandock character the degree of*

161

hotness he possesses. Pictures and sensations from the night before flooded her mind. She lowered her gaze to the food in front of her and attempted to concentrate on eating. With the lion sitting on her right, tearing her thoughts away from the memories of his hands on her body became impossible. And the scent of him, spicy, hot male… *I better drink some more Karri-san. Now. Although I think this goes beyond the normal Rifellan pheromones.*

Liandock rose from the table. "Forgive me for leaving you momentarily, but I must set the work schedule for my staff in the metal shop. I will see you all before you leave, and Mayda, your brooch will be ready, so perhaps you can collect your jewelry."

They all acknowledged his apology, and Kat almost breathed a sigh of relief. Drainin still had her under the microscope of his suspicious scrutiny.

***

With their meal finished, and their belongings packed, the two women left for the metal-smith's shop again, leaving Drainin and Bannon to load the wagon for the trip to the stonecutter's small village.

This time, the door had been left open, so Kat and Mayda walked in.

Liandock greeted them and brought a lovely brooch to Mayda, which he wrapped in a soft cloth. "Your maternal parent should be delighted with this. Your discernment is excellent."

Mayda blushed furiously at his compliment. "Thank you, Master Liandock." She retreated from him and with self-conscious movements, examined some of the other jewelry on display.

The Arrival

"Lady Kat." His voice, the deep throaty rumble of a big, satisfied cat, enveloped her. He took her hand in both of his. "We are well met. I thank you." His faint smile made the Mona Lisa look insipid. "I hope we may meet again."

Kat, emboldened, smiled back at him. "That would also be well met, Liandock."

He spoke quieter. "Then, farewell for now, Kat." He dipped his head, the golden eye staring at her from under the blonde brow. He drew back from her, one finger stroking the palm of her hand as he released it.

She didn't expect the sudden surge of heat in her body. Even her pendant grew hot. *If I don't walk out this door now, I'll never leave.* Her farewell emerged as a croak, and she backed out of the door, calling to Mayda to come.

The wagon waited, with Drainin already seated. Bannon helped both women into their seats, and scrambled up to the driver's bench. The wagon lurched forward as they travelled without talking, each locked in their own thoughts.

This isn't a comfortable silence. Drainin's got his blank face on. Well, if he suspects what my lion and I did, it's none of his business. "Mayda, I didn't get a chance to examine your lovely brooch. May I see it again?"

"Of course, my Lady." She drew the carefully wrapped parcel from a pocket and handed the piece of jewelry to Kat.

The intricate work on the brooch was breathtaking. Three brilliant red stones tucked in among the silver and gold wires gleamed in the sunlight.

"Your parent will love this. Master Liandock is right, you do have excellent taste."

At the mention of the Metal-Smith's name, Drainin scowled.

Ha, I think our Counselor is jealous. He wants to be the centre of attention with women. And this time he wasn't. Mischievously, Kat held up the brooch to show him. "Don't you agree Counselor?"

His only reply, a grunt.

Mayda swiveled around. "See there, Lady Kat. We are almost at Mammac village, which is where Master Builder Penrow lives."

As Kat turned to catch a glance, Mayda pointed at the massive range of mountains. "Clog Neran is the range of mountains behind the village. The best stone in Kaylin is cut at this site."

The buildings of the settlement tucked themselves into the foot of the magnificent mountain range. The trees further up grew in darker shades of green and climbed partway up the slopes, giving way to grasses and strange stunted plants, until all faded into gray rock, streaked with crystals in a myriad of colors. Beyond the immediate peaks, bare rock soared in saw-toothed spires high above the land, the furthest ones covered in snow. Mountains, rocks and trees stretched across the horizon, never ending.

Kat glanced back at Drainin. "I feel I'm surrounded by mountains."

"You are."

"Whatever do you mean?"

Drainin settled into his seat, once again the epitome of a man in control. "A legend says, more star turns ago than we can count, most of Pridden was covered in tall jagged mountains, hostile to animals, and possessed of little vegetation. One night, a star streaked across the sky and as it approached Pridden, broke into many pieces, and the largest part came down in what is now Kaylin. When the star hit, fires and

The Arrival

explosions reduced many of the mountains to rubble leaving behind small rocks and dirt. When the land healed, grasses and trees took hold in the rich soil, and Kaylin became a lush bowl of land, ringed by huge mountains."

The story fascinated Kat. *Sounds like a comet or a meteor struck the planet and Kaylin received most of the impact.* "What a wonderful story. Is it true?"

Drainin shrugged. "There is no recorded history about this. However I travel extensively throughout Kaylin, and I discovered, if you follow the base of the mountains, you travel in a circle and eventually end up where you began."

Mayda piped up. "The information comes from the writings of the Spirit Caleesh."

Drainin responded, his voice dry and humorless. "Not all believe in everything attributed to the Spirit."

Mayda blushed and relapsed into silence.

Kat reached over and patted her hand. "Whatever the truth, the story is interesting."

The wagon neared Mammac village, which consisted of less than a dozen sturdy stone buildings. Bannon steered the pontis toward the biggest set of three structures. As utilitarian as they seemed, the sun glittered off crystals imbedded in the rocks, which suggested a lighter, more spritely quality.

As they pulled up to the entrance of the most extensive one, a burly, barrel-chested man hastened from his door, calling to them. "Counselor Drainin and Bannon, welcome. We have been waiting for you, and we prepared a luncheon feast."

Drainin hopped down, grasped the enormous outstretched hand and clapped his host on the shoulder. "Master Penrow, well met. Let me present Lady Kat and her friend Mayda."

Penrow reached up to help them from the wagon, but instead of simply extending a hand, put two massive paws around Kat's waist and swept her to the ground. He then did the same for Mayda and stood beaming at them. "Lady Kat, Mayda, well met. Hasten now, the feast waits for no one."

Oh my, he's like an enormous teddy bear. With the thick beard, wild brown head, hair all over his arms, and tufts poking from his shirt, he almost resembles a giant grizzly.

The man, a powerful whirlwind, gathered them in his wake as he lumbered into his home.

Bannon excused himself. "Master, I must always settle the pontis before I eat. I will return as quickly as I can."

"Of course you must." Penrow grabbed Kat's arm and tucked it into his. "Such odd little creatures. Nothing but a sizable horse would support me." He burst out laughing.

He's not only a bear, he's a jolly bear. He swept Kat, too startled to object, into the dining area. She glanced at Drainin to see how he responded to this force of nature. He was grinning. *I think everybody likes this gentle giant.*

Penrow made sure all were seated comfortably and as Bannon appeared again, roared at him to join them at the table.

Servers scurried in with dishes of food, moving fast, but all beamed in pleasure. They attempted to serve Penrow, but he growled at them to attend to the guests first — beginning with Kat, whom he had managed to plant in the seat beside him.

The meal, a madhouse with dish after dish of food, and of humorous stories from Penrow, punctuated by roars of laughter, overwhelmed them all.

His appetite was prodigious, and he kept putting tasty tidbits on Kat's plate. When she begged him to stop because she

The Arrival

was full to bursting, he laughed at her. "Nonsense, you are far too thin. You need to fatten up." He poked her upper arm.

Kat eyed him as severely as she could manage, desperate to stem the laughter bubbling up inside her. "Master Penrow. You cannot possibly fatten me up with one meal. This is illogical and impossible."

He stared at her. "Well, how astonishing. I believe I have met a woman with spirit." And roars of laughter overtook him again.

At last, with the meal over, Kat was unsure if her ribs ached from laughing or from eating far too much.

Penrow rose from his seat, towering over them all. "Lady Kat, one of my assistants will show you all to your rooms so you may rest from your journey. I must retire for my afternoon nap. Please feel free to walk the grounds and explore. I will see you for our late evening meal." With no further ado, he lurched off to his quarters.

Wow.

Her three companions, eyes glazed, appeared they'd outlasted a hurricane.

Drainin, first to speak, summarized their experience. "You have just enjoyed the pleasure of having the massive wagon of Master Penrow roll over you. If you survive this, you can survive anything."

Well I'm astonished. Drainin's got a sense of humor.

Bannon rose unsteadily to his feet. "It is best I unpack the wagon and make sure the pontis are settled, as I also have eaten and drunk too much. With your permission Counselor, after I deliver your things to your rooms, I would like to nap as well."

"You have my permission, Bannon. You are not alone in that desire."

***

Kat woke, refreshed from a wonderful deep sleep. *I hope I haven't missed too much.* She left her room, and wandered down the hall toward the sounds of hammering and loud voices. She tentatively entered a work room, where Penrow argued with a tall, muscular young woman. She resembled Penrow, except she was more slender and her body much less hairy.

The builder glanced up as he spied Kat. "Ah, Lady Kat, you are well rested?"

"Indeed, thank you."

"Come here and tell me what you think of this magnificent building I designed. Unfortunately, my argumentative offspring disagrees with me."

The woman growled back at him. "I am telling you, the placement of the kitchen is too far from the eating area. The food will be cold by the time the assistants bring the meal to the diners. And if the female who lives in this building is the one to cook, it separates her too much from her guests."

Kat edged forward and peered at the small wooden structure perched on the table. Both Penrow and his daughter pointed out the kitchen and eating areas.

"We are waiting for your input." He pointed at the young woman with the wild hair like her father. "This is Illian, my eldest offspring. She is apprenticing to be a builder. Though why she does not marry and give me grandchildren, I do not know."

Illian snorted and smiled indulgently at her parent.

They both studied Kat expectantly.

"I believe, Master Penrow, I must agree with Illian. As a woman, I would not want my kitchen so far from the eating area."

The Arrival

Penrow glared at her. "Hmph. Women. They always side with each other."

Illian grinned. "Ignore him. He does not like to lose." She beckoned to Kat. "Let me give you a tour before the evening meal."

Kat and Illian spent the balance of the afternoon touring the facilities and Illian explained why she had become interested in joining her father in his business. "I have always loved designing structures. As a child I would build little houses from pieces of wood and stone I found in the workroom." She smiled, perhaps remembering. "Both of my male siblings were quick to leave home. I am sure my parent could not believe his luck at least one of his offspring desired to join him in his profession."

Later, in the eating room, Illian and two other apprentices, joined them. The feast, generous as before, and filled with joyous mirth, extended well into the night. Although the staff had watered down Orenberry wine, Kat found herself mildly unsteady when she headed for bed. As she walked from the room, she caught Drainin and Illian in deep conversation, heads together. *I think Drainin will be occupied tonight. But Illian is no naive young Kaylin. She is clear about what she wants and will get it — without strings.*

Kat slipped into her comfortable bed. *I've got my stone, and memories of my lion to keep me warm. That's enough for now.*

The Arrival

CHAPTER 22

The morning meal at Penrow's home proved as chaotic as the evening before, with assistants and servants running from table to kitchen, and the builder bellowing at everyone and everything. "Come sit here, Kat. You belong beside me."

Kat caught Mayda blanching at his lack of formality, but the others appeared to take his words with humor. *He's a well-loved man. They are convinced his loud voice, demands and commands are an act. He enjoys playing the role of a tough guy. I must fit him into my game, somehow.*

Both Illian and Drainin sat like pillars of calm, while drama eddied around them.

They did the dirty. Sex with no strings. Super. Maybe Drainin will be a little less annoying today.

"I notice you wear Liandock's jewelry."

Penrow startled Kat and her hand went to her neck. *I thought it was covered.*

"I caught a glimpse of a silver pendant, Kat. I recognized his work. Did you enjoy your visit to Lanfair?" Penrow's words contained a hint of humor.

Kat glanced at him to catch one eyebrow raised and a definite twinkle in his eyes. *Bland face, remember, bland face.* "I did indeed. Master Liandock is extremely talented. I only traded for this one piece, though his shop contained so many lovely objects."

"Liandock is talented in many ways." Penrow nudged her in the ribs, eliciting an 'oomph' from her. He wiggled his eyebrows. "Unfortunately, I cannot impress you with fine crystals, and I doubt stone or buildings will win your heart either."

Kat laughed aloud. "You, Master Penrow, are being a rascal." *He's so adorable. Very cuddly, but a little stronger than he realizes.*

The meal continued with much laughter, until Drainin stood and addressed Kat and Mayda. "Despite the hospitality, we must follow our schedule, and so we need to depart soon." He turned to the builder. "Master Penrow, our thanks to you and your assistants." He glanced at Bannon. "If you would load the wagon, and be prepared to leave, the females and I will make sure we are packed and will meet you within the hour."

Bannon set off to do his chores, and Kat and Mayda rose and gave thanks to the builder for allowing them to stay at Mammac.

Penrow again expressed how much their visit pleased him, and in an aside to Kat, asked her to meet with him before she left.

***

Kat completed her packing, and told Mayda to go to the wagon and she would join them in a few minutes.

She located Penrow in his workshop. "You asked me to come to you before we left. Why?"

The builder came over to her and took her hand in his huge paws, his touch, gentle. "I believe, my dear, you are embarking on a journey with many challenges. I wish you to understand I am your friend, and will aid you at any time, should you need me."

"Thank you, Penrow. This is unexpected but most welcome."

The Arrival

"Liandock and I are united when your safety is at stake." He pressed a small wrapped package into her hand. "Here. He sent a gift for you. Our messages for you are the same. There may be some dark times ahead, but you possess excellent instincts. Trust them."

"I will. I find this often difficult in Kaylin, but I'll follow your advice. And please, thank Liandock for his gift." *I wonder if they have the power to help me get home? Not now, but something to think about.* In Penrow's presence the stone in her pendant warmed against her skin.

Kat left his workshop and as she strolled toward the wagon, smiled when she heard him singing as he worked. *His voice is brilliant. Deep, but lovely melody. He sounds so joyful.* She put her hand over the stone hidden beneath her clothing. The gentle heat soothed her. *I have the protection of a lion and a bear. How perfect.*

***

They travelled the first part of the journey in silence, the swaying motion of the wagon lulled Kat and she drifted into the half sleep she always thought of as 'alpha' rhythms.

A rustling brought her awake, and she opened her eyes to find Drainin consulting some sort of map.

When he noticed she was awake, he pointed out the route they would be taking. "This is the Ponti Bridge, and over here is Meenyat, which is a village of only a hundred souls. We will attempt to stop for midday meals whenever possible, but on occasion may eat while traveling."

"Can our food be eaten while traveling?"

"Yes, we packed plenty of dried rations, but we will live more from the land whenever possible. We will fill up all our water containers at the Brynwog River, and again as we cross the Grening Stream. Water is important because the heat will increase after Meenyat. You and Mayda should drink plenty of liquid."

***

When the sun was high overhead, the wagon stopped beside a swift-running river, cascading around rocks and eddying in pools close to the shores. The rumble of the waters, like a heart pounding and the susurrus of wavelets on the sand in the pools, sang in Kat's ears.

Bannon released his charges from their yokes. "Counselor, I will deal with the pontis before I prepare our meal."

"Fine." He addressed Kat and Mayda. "I will show you some of the interesting plants in this area."

Bannon took the pontis to one of the eddies, and they drank their fill. He then drove a stick into the ground and attached lines from their harnesses, allowing them sufficient room to graze in the sweet green grass.

While Bannon filled the water containers, Drainin dug around a bright yellow flower, and drew out a deep ochre tuber. "This is excellent eating, starchy and filling, and especially delicious when roasted."

Kat dusted off what looked to her like a yam, and examined it closely. "What do you call it?"

"I am not sure of an official name. Everyone refers to this as yellow flower root. If you would like, we can dig up a few and dine on them for our evening meal."

While Mayda helped Drainin dig tubers, Kat strolled to the river and bent down to reach the stream flowing over a small rock. She cupped her hand and sipped. Cold, clear and refreshing, so she drank her fill.

At last Bannon call them to eat. "Master Penrow's assistants prepared this for us."

Kat gazed at the sizable plates of food set on the rocks. "What a feast. I think, Counselor, Master Penrow forgot he would not be with us. He gave us enough for two meals at least."

"Not quite, Kat, but with the tubers we dug today, our evening meal will be plentiful."

The meal done, and on their way again, Mayda's chattering ushering them along the pathway, they approached a bridge spanning the broad river.

Kat stared across the river. "What an amazing and beautifully crafted bridge. An engineering masterpiece. Was Penrow involved in the building?"

Mayda jumped in. "Master Penrow designed and helped cut the stone. Everyone admires the craftsmanship."

Drainin rolled his eyes and sighed. "You are knowledgeable, Mayda. Most knowledgeable."

I suspect Mayda's constant talking is getting to the mighty Drainin. Serves him right.

As the wagon rolled across the extensive bridge, they all remained silent gazing down at the rapids below. The river rushed through a canyon at this point, and the waters roiled and boiled over rocks far below them.

I'm glad these weird little horses are sure-footed. I'd hate to fall from this height. I'll bet the water's damn cold too.

***

They travelled only a short way from the bridge and the wagon slowed. They prepared to camp for the night in a clearing in the trees. Bannon brought buckets and served the pontis their water and fastened them to a line strung between two trees so they could move about and munch on grass.

Kat eyed the spring-bows attached to the back of the seats. "Will we have enough time before dark for me to learn to use the spring-bows, Counselor Drainin?"

"Not this night, Lady Kat, but we will spend morrow night in Meenyat, and we might a find a place for you to practice. Now, it would be best if we gathered firewood." He turned to Mayda. "If you will help gather the kindling, we will have enough for a good fire."

By the time they amassed a sufficient supply for the night, Bannon had erected the tents and set blankets out to sit upon, around the circle of stones where the fire would be.

"Bannon, when the logs are in place, will you allow me to light the fire with your tinder rod?"

"Of course, Lady Kat."

He was as good as his word, and with two taps on a stone, Kat lit the kindling with ease. She handed the rod back to Bannon, grinning to herself. *What fun, and it works better than matches.*

With the meal over, Kat washed her face and hands in a small basin, wishing she'd been able to swim in the river earlier in the day. *Boy, I miss the personal at the keep. I like feeling clean all over.*

In her tent, she reached into her pocket for the package Penrow had given her. A silver bracelet with an emerald stone, marked with the same rune, nestled in the soft cloth. When she tried the bracelet on, it proved far too big. *Oh, not a bracelet, an anklet.* She reached down, wrapped the chain around her left ankle, and fastened the clasp. The stone in the silver chain nestled cozily over her ankle, and she admired it, briefly turning her foot to each side, delighting in the sparkle. She then slid into her bed, happy and sleepy.

I wonder what the dark times are Penrow talked about. Never mind. A lion and a bear are on my side. I'm safe with them.

***

The Arrival

The following day, after eating lunch while traveling they arrived at Meenyat in the early evening. The small town, although sturdily built, lacked imagination. The colors drab and without personality, weighed Kat down giving her the impression she carried an enormous burden on her shoulders. The inhabitants, men and women alike, all wore pale grey robes. They appeared solemn, and smiled rarely. Even the young children, dressed in similar robes, did not run and play and squeal with delight like others Kat met elsewhere. However, despite the somber appearance, men and women touched and hugged each other affectionately, different from the way Kaylins normally behaved.

When Drainin introduced Kat to the leaders of the village, however, they became quite animated, and invited them all to an evening feast. They also provided them with the finest quarters in the town. Bannon chose to bed down at the stables because he was uncomfortable leaving his precious pontis to the care of the Meenyat stable-master.

After a subdued dinner, Kat discussed their hosts with Mayda. "The people seem less restrained in their personal relationships, but they're calm and quiet. Are they truly Kaylins?"

"Healer Wynneth advised me they are deeply spiritual, and consider Caleesh the most important aspect of their lives. Master Haydar disapproves of them because they do not adhere to all the rules of Kaylin, but the healer says they are untroubled people. They leave us alone, and we do the same for them."

Regrettably, Kat had opened Pandora's box, which released Mayda's chatter. After suffering longer than she desired, she interrupted and suggested they turn in for the night.

A comfortable bed, a light breeze blowing gently through the open window, and the hooting and shuffling sounds of various creatures, eased Kat into a deep sleep.

***

At their brief morning meal, with the eating room filled with curious observers, Kat asked Drainin why so many of the villagers attended the meal.

He snorted. "They are aware you are from another world. I expect they want to find out if you own two heads or four eyes, or some such other nonsense."

The leader of the village rose and spoke to all, raising his cup to Kat. "Lady Kat, we waited long for Caleesh to send you to us. We are most grateful she has done so. Now you are here, we will enjoy plentiful harvests and much celebration. The people are happy the prediction is finally fulfilled."

Prediction? Whoa, this sounds weird. "How can my brief visit be of value to you?"

"You are here to live among us. This Caleesh has promised us. She foretold a woman would come to us, a woman who possessed one green eye the color of summer grass, and the other the color of the wood of the Old Forest trees."

"Forgive me but that is impossible. I need to make a journey, and I must return to my own world."

He smiled at her like a parent to a naive child, but his eyes remained cold and hard. "There is no question of leaving. You will stay. Caleesh has deemed it so."

Vigorous alarm bells pealed within Kat's head. "But… ." About to declare she would not stay, some sense of foreboding struck her and she decided not to contradict him. "Ah, Caleesh. Of course." She leaned over and whispered to Drainin. "We should leave as fast as possible. Something is not right." *The stone on my pendant feels suddenly cool,*

The Arrival

perhaps this could erupt into an unpleasant situation. Is this one of those dark times?

"I think you are correct. Something is not right. The way they regard you is strange. We should leave now."

"How soon can the wagon be available to leave?"

"It is ready now. I asked Bannon to be prepared to depart early, because my intuition said we should leave directly after the morning meal." Drainin rose and gave a deep bow to the residents of Meenyat and made a short speech of thanks. Quietly, he leaned over to Kat and gave her instructions. "Thank them and bow as low as I did. I hope you can keep them calm… for now. Praise them as much as possible in your speech, but do not indicate we are leaving the village"

Kat rose from the table and did as he suggested, requesting the villagers excuse her for a short period because it was time for her meditation.

After her words to them, the people applauded using the backs of their hands. The three travelers, pretending to return to their rooms, sneaked at once out the rear entrance. When they found Bannon with the wagon hitched to the pontis, they climbed aboard and immediately departed.

As they pulled away from the village, a young boy caught sight of them leaving, and dashed into the inn. Their escape discovered, the villagers pursued them on foot, shouting for them to return, and calling on Caleesh to bring them back. Bannon drove the pontis as fast as their odd little legs could manage, and eventually Meenyat and its inhabitants faded into the distance.

Mayda stared at Kat, with huge worried eyes. "Lady Kat, I found their actions most strange. The Meenyats acted angrily. What were they planning?"

"I'm unable to guess." *What was that all about?* "Counselor, any suggestions?"

"What plans they have, I do not know. I believe your obvious refusal to remain in Meenyat angered them. From what they were calling after us, it appears they believed you are part of a prediction by Caleesh." He coughed. "With many beliefs, people often tend to be erratic. I am not sure if they would resort to violence to keep you. It was best not to find out."

The three lapsed into silence, each caught up in their own thoughts.

Kat's stone warmed her skin beneath her dress again. *We're OK now. Why does everyone want me to remain on Pridden when I want to leave? But Eduardo was right, Drainin is very capable in odd situations.*

They approached a narrow bridge, just wide enough to allow the wagon to proceed. Bannon asked them to descend and walk across ahead of him and the wagon. "I am not sure how sturdy the bridge is, and I would prefer none of us ended up in the Grening Stream below."

Simply being on foot made the bridge more than rickety enough for Kat. Mayda was pale and quiet as well, as they negotiated the unsteady overpass.

On the other side, after the wagon joined them, they boarded and set off toward Trigoran.

Drainin told them about the next leg of the journey. "We will camp in the late afternoon beside the Old Forest. And, before you ask, Lady Kat, I will show you how to use the spring-bow." He drew a packet from a bag beside him. "There is food in the bag to eat on the way, and the water containers are full, so make sure you drink your fill."

He handed a packet of food forward to Bannon. "On the morrow, we will stop for our mid-day meal at a small pond

The Arrival

formed in the Grening. We will fill with water, and you ladies may wish to bathe. We have sufficient time, and Bannon can set up a temporary tent to allow you to change."

Mayda murmured her thanks.

"We will then proceed to the camp for the evening, on this side of the Penrow Bridge. You will also be able to view the Penrow Pool, although you cannot bathe in it."

"Penrow? Is it named after Master Penrow?"

Again Mayda jumped in to reply. "Indeed, Lady Kat. Master Penrow was born in Trigoran, and the Trigorans are most fond of him. The town already possessed a name, so they gave him the honor of a bridge and a pool."

Kat rode in silence, barely hearing Mayda prattling to Drainin who nodded, rolling his eyes occasionally.

After another moving lunch, they continued toward what appeared to be a line of dark green trees nestled at the foot of mountains wearing snowy caps.

Approaching the trees, the wagon stopped and Kat, stiff from sitting for so long, jumped down, waiting for neither Drainin nor Bannon to help her. She stretched gratefully, and rolled her neck and shoulders to ease the cricks.

Drainin hopped down and helped Mayda to descend. He turned to Kat. "While Bannon feeds and waters his animals, and then sets up our camp, you and I will use the springbows. I only hope you are strong enough to set the spring."

Does he think women are weak and helpless? He is such an ass.

He handed her a quiver and a bow, took a set for himself and strode long-legged toward the line of trees. He stopped beside an old rotted trunk.

"This will be our target." He walked back about 90 feet. "And this will be where we stand. The quarry we hunt are

181

powerful and ferocious, so we should shoot from as far away as possible. This is an excellent distance, although experienced bowmen can shoot from twice as far. But in the forest, if you are that distance away, you might experience difficulty spotting your prey through the trees."

Drainin showed Kat how to step on the stirrup and pull the line back to hook over the trigger mechanism. Without a struggle, she armed the bow, inserted the arrow, and took aim.

"You are stronger than you look, and I perceive by your stance, you have used a bow before. You will find this one shoots a little to the right, so compensate for the error in alignment."

The air was still in this part of the day, so Kat shifted slightly, sighted along the flight groove and pulled the trigger. The arrow flew and hit the tree trunk with a resounding thunk. They both walked over to the tree and Drainin pulled out the arrow. The metal tip entered the wood for about 6 inches. He regarded Kat with raised eyebrows. "I do not think you need much practice. When we arrive in Trigoran, we should trade for a quiver and bow for you. If we are attacked by anything, you will prove most helpful." He smiled at her. "You are full of surprises, Lady Kat."

Despite his smile, my stone cooled. I wonder what he means.

Drainin eyed her speculatively.

What's he up to now?

"I think we could consider hunting for a gornog. If we catch one, we will feast tonight, and still retain enough to use as trade in Trigoran."

"I'm willing, Counselor."

They armed their bows, slung their quivers over their shoulders and set off into the forest.

The Arrival

Drainin showed Kat some droppings which indicated the presence of their intended prey. "This narrow trail is one these creatures created. When we come upon a fresh track, we will know we are near, so be as quiet as you are able, and be vigilant. Gornogs are dangerous creatures."

They advanced silently through the trees. *Man, Drainin can sure move quietly.* Kat who attended many outdoor survival courses while researching for gaming design, was familiar with the ability to slip through a forest with stealth. *My damn dress keeps catching on the brush. I hope it won't make noise.*

Drainin whispered more instructions. "Aim for the jugular, or for the heart. Those are the animal's weakest points. We are close now."

At his words, the creature exploded from the bushes, howling in fury. With a body the size of a jaguar, the grey and black monstrosity was covered in stiff bristles, and the two sets of tufted ears put those of a jack rabbit to shame. Only thirty feet away, the beast charged on six clawed feet and left no time for finesse. The nightmarish animal was almost upon her when Kat raised her bow, sighted, and shot for the blood-red eye. The gornog howled in pain and dropped, writhing and attempting to dislodge the object. But the arrow pierced the brain, and with few further convulsions, the brute lay still -- the red of the eye fading to a milky white.

Kat shuddered at the sight of it. The tusks and razor sharp teeth, yellowed, fierce, and at least twelve inches long protruded from a mouth ringed with warts. A dripping snout, the color of dung, would win this gornog no beauty contests. Kat trembled from the excess adrenaline in her system.

Drainin rounded on her, his voice booming with rage. "I told you to shoot at the jugular or heart. I thought you could aim. You are incredibly lucky to shoot it in the eye. You will need to practice a fair amount before you ever go hunting again. You cannot fathom how lucky you are to be here and be alive." He grabbed the front legs of the gornog. "Grab the hind legs, we must leave at once before any 'friends' appear. I am sure others heard its screams."

When they reached the edge of the forest, he called to Bannon to help with the butchering of the animal. He ordered Kat to dig a deep hole.

"Why?"

Drainin's temper was still vile, and he spat his reply. "We do not want the remains to attract the kithras."

Kat dug.

Bannon, thoroughly carved up their kill, and placed a number of pieces of the meat on a spit over the fire to begin roasting for their meal. The balance of the meat, he hung from a line, over the flames, to be cured by the smoke. Everything else he and Drainin disposed of in the hole prepared by Kat. The area was pristine once more.

The gornog, nasty in appearance, tasted delicious. Kat could not remember ever eating such a sweet, tender meat. The tubers, roasted in the fire, accompanied the meal perfectly. She ate far too much and relished every bit, but now the meal sat heavily in her stomach. She desperately needed to break wind to relieve the sense of having gorged so much food. Her attempt to burp surreptitiously was unsuccessful, and she apologized for her lapse of manners.

"There is no need to excuse yourself, Lady Kat. Gornog flesh causes the same reaction in everyone." With those words, Mayda belched loudly.

Her words encouraged louder eruptions from Drainin and Bannon.

All three of her companions appeared relieved.

I think they waited for me to burp first. Lame. Freakin' lame. Crazy Kaylins. They run from possible sexual encounters, but feel free to emit those incredible deep throated belches in public. Timid little Mayda was louder than the other two. These Kaylins are full of surprises.

While Bannon and Mayda cleared up after the meal, Drainin attacked Kat again for her shooting of the gornog. "How did you manage to miss the jugular after I gave you specific instructions?"

With the adrenaline out of her system, Kat relaxed, and Drainin failed to ruffle her. "I couldn't discern the jugular from where I stood, so I aimed for the eye."

Drainin's jaw dropped. "You aimed for the eye?"

"Yes."

"Unbelievable." He shook his head. "You never used a spring-bow before and you aimed for the eye and pierced it?"

"Yes."

"You aimed for the eye. It was not just luck?"

Kat's hackles raised. "Yes. I aimed for the eye. It wasn't just luck."

He shook his head again. "I may have misjudged your abilities, Kat."

You certainly did, you arrogant fool.

J. M. Tibbott

CHAPTER 23

Kat spent a restless night. The snuffles and growls from the forest reminded her of the vicious, yellowed tusks rushing for her at breakneck speed. *Maybe I ate too much. But, I enjoyed the delicious stuff.* She slept fitfully most of the night, and when dawn came, she woke up grumpy and out-of-sorts.

During the trip to their lunch destination, Kat managed a brief nap, so when Bannon announced their arrival at the Grening pond, she awoke in a much better mood.

I needed extra shut-eye. I feel a lot more human now.

Bannon secured, watered and fed the pontis and then set up a tent so Mayda and Kat could change to swim in the pool. He and Drainin then headed through the trees to a spot further downstream to ensure the women enjoyed privacy.

Kat stepped into the invigorating stream. "Ahh." She moved into the waters up to her neck. "This is marvelous." Despite the challenge of the tent-like swim garment, she managed to use the soap all over. *Heavenly. I feel clean again.*

Abruptly, Kat received a face-full of water. Without thinking, she splashed Mayda back, who promptly squealed and continued scooping handfuls of water at her.

Kat laughed. *I used to play like this with my dad. I wonder when I forgot to have fun.*

Clean, happy and relaxed, they scurried into the changing tent when voices indicated the approach of the two men.

After a brief meal of gornog and the greens which Bannon had gathered, they packed and were on their way to the camp near the Penrow Pool, their damp bathing dresses drying on the back of the wagon.

"Tell me about Trigoran, Drainin." *After his grump at me he doesn't deserve a title.*

He grinned at her. "Well, Kat, there is a lot to tell."

He dropped my title too. I'll bet he suspects I left his off deliberately. I guess he can access a sense of humor. But he's still not my favorite person.

"Trigoran is a cosmopolitan village. People from every land travel there. Also many come from Morden, which as you know is my birth-land."

"Are you the only person from Morden at the keep?"

"Yes, those from Morden tend to keep to themselves, much like the Kaylins. However, you will find more Mordens at Trigoran because it is only a half star-turn to the pass through Clog Blue. On the other side of the pass is my homeland."

"Tell me more."

"I would suggest you keep your wits about you. Trigoran is a strange place. With people coming from every land, often jealousies and old arguments which are simmering beneath the surface, tend to erupt. Do not get yourself embroiled in any disagreements between the various people. The possibility exists for danger to touch us all."

Kat just scowled at him.

"I am serious Kat, walk carefully in Trigoran."

"I don't need a lecture from you. I'll be careful." She turned her back on him and asked Bannon. "How far to where we're camping this night?"

"We are almost at the site, Lady Kat."

In less than an hour, Bannon guided the wagon beside a copse of trees, next to the stream. He helped the women

The Arrival

down, unhitched the pontis and after watering and securing them to a nearby tree, began the task of setting up camp.

Mayda eagerly approached Drainin. "Counselor, can we go to the Ponti pool now? My parents never took me to see these types of things. This is so exciting."

"Of course, Mayda." He regarded Kat with a faint grin. "If you would like to join us, Lady Kat. We should go before dark."

She gritted her teeth at the emphasis he placed on her title. *Sarcasm suits him. Creep.* "I will." She returned a simpering smile of her own.

She found it incredible such a seemingly small stream like the Grening, managed to create this pool. The maelstrom of swirling water poured into a vortex which drained into the earth.

This looks like a giant bathtub drain. "Drainin, this is amazing. I've only ever seen whirlpools caused by different currents coming together. Where does the water go?"

"No one is sure. Some suspect it travels down through the Clog Blue mountains, deeper and deeper and then flows underground to the great waters of the Hyal Sea. Places in Morden exist where an underground river pours through caverns deep in the earth."

"Has anyone ever travelled the length of the waters?"

"If they did, no one has seen them again. The underground torrent is fierce and uncompromising."

"I'm so tempted to jump in and see where I come out."

Drainin paled at her words. "By the spirit of… Lady Kat do not even think about this. Please step back from the pool."

"Relax, I wasn't intending to dive in. I'm curious, but I would need to be much better outfitted to attempt such a thing."

Drainin relaxed, but poor Mayda had faded to three shades lighter and shook visibly.

Kat moved to put her arm around the girl. "Mayda, I'm fine. I'm not going to jump in."

"It is not good, Lady Kat, to make such jokes."

Drainin suggested they return to the camp for their meal, and both women followed him.

Well. Well. He certainly doesn't want to lose me. Is it because Eduardo would punish him? Or is he holding some other agenda?

Their meal in the evening consisted of more gornog, this time in a stew flavored with a variety of herbs.

Kat finished her meal with her usual cup of Karri-san tea. *Rifellans are bound to be in the town, but one 'lion' is quite enough.* She yawned. *I think I'm going to sleep well tonight.*

***

As they crossed the Penrow bridge in the morning, Trigoran filled the horizon. This was not a town of grand design, but a muddle of structures of every size and color. Some buildings were constructed of huge grey rocks with the odd one built of stone from Mammac. The Mammac stones glittered as the morning sun flashed off the crystals imbedded in them. Other buildings were made of wood, no doubt from the forests at the foot of Clog Blue. As they neared the town, their ears were assaulted by voices, musical instruments and hammering on metal and wood.

At the stable master's establishment, Bannon arranged for the pontis to be fed and watered, and the wagon stowed at the rear. He hired a young male to deliver the luggage to the local inn. The smoked meat he unloaded and passed to Drainin. He then handed the tusks and teeth to Kat. Bannon remained at the stable, having settled with the master to stay for the night so he could be near his beloved weird little horses, but agreed he would meet them for the evening meal at the inn.

When they reached the market, Kat, excited by the noise and colors, and anxious to explore everything, had a challenge containing herself. The market area was like a fair, filled with shops of all shapes and sizes, and bustling with people from all the lands. She saw small dark people from Baklai, lovely bronze Rifellans, and at a stall selling potions and herbs, regal healers from Shendea. At one shop, selling bottles of liquid, which Kat assumed held Orenberry Wine, the flushed, fleshy faces of Glowens beamed at them. The stall next to the Glowens was occupied by a pair of disapproving Kaylins who displayed beautiful cloth of all colours and textures. A Glowen approached the cloth-sellers and touched an exquisite gold threaded bolt of material. "How much for this bolt, store-keeper?"

"We do not sell to profligate, self-indulgent people such as you."

The Glowen's face fell.

Kat couldn't help herself. She stepped over to the Kaylin shop keeper. "You are being silly. This man recognizes beautiful work and wants to pay you for it. Why would you deprive yourself of the sale?"

"He is from Glowen."

"So what? He is a customer, and it shouldn't matter where he comes from."

Drainin spoke up from behind her. "Lady Kat, this is none of your business."

At his words, the shop-keeper blanched. "You are The Lady Kat?"

She nodded.

"We are aware of you." He examined her and tilted his head. "What you suggest is reasonable." He looked toward the Glowen, apologized stiffly, and after some negotiation, they completed their trade.

Drainin took Kat by the arm and moved her away. "I told you not to interfere."

She shook off his grip. "He was being foolish. How senseless to deprive himself of a sale because of his weird prejudice."

Drainin shook his head. "Come we must trade the meat." He set off, with Kat matching his long strides, and poor Mayda scurrying in his wake. "We will sell the extra smoked meat to a local merchant in the next lane of shops."

The merchant, pleased with the quality of the smoked gornog, settled quickly for the fresh supply. Drainin appeared pleased with compensation he received.

After completing the trade for the meat, they continued on, and arrived at a stall displaying masses of unusual jewelry. Bright stones of extraordinary clarity glittered in colors of blood red, smoky topaz, cobalt blue, and all shades in between. Necklaces, magnificent brooches and fine chains of silver and gold hung from displays. Odd bones and monstrous teeth adorned other pieces and added to the glorious chaos. Drainin bargained with the jeweler for the tusks and teeth of the gornog.

Each merchant passed them chits of paper, which they now took to a shopkeeper who sold spring-bows of all types and sizes.

Kat faced Drainin. "This is really your trade, Counselor."

"Not at all. You shot the animal, Lady Kat. The trade is yours."

I can't figure him out. Sometimes he's so reasonable, and others so annoying.

The Arrival

The shopkeeper helped match her with the perfect sized spring-bow. The pull to arm it was a little heavier than the one from the wagon. "You possess more strength than I guessed, my lady. This will work well for you." He also supplied two dozen arrows, and suggested she choose a quiver from the many displayed.

She chose a beautifully crafted one of light brown leather, embossed and painted with leaves and vines in green.

"A wise choice, my lady. This quiver will act as camouflage in the forests when you hunt."

Kat, delighted with her purchase, slung the quiver over one shoulder and hung the spring-bow over her back on a strap around the other. *Ooh, I'm powerful. Beware, I'm Kat, warrior queen - watch yourself, weaklings.* She chuckled to herself. *This hunting set-up will be perfect for the heroine of the new game.* As she preened in the mirror the shopkeeper owned, she caught Mayda regarding her with awe.

"Mayda, There are still some trade chits left over. Would you would like something for yourself?"

Mayda shyly suggested a belt she had seen. "It is a lovely dark brown and I adore the shiny buckle."

They returned to the leather shop, and purchased the belt for Mayda. The color almost matched her skin tone, and contrasted wonderfully with her dark green clothing. She wrapped it around her waist, and as they strolled back to the inn where the Elders of the town had placed them, she continually touched the buckle, shaped like a domestic cat, seemingly fearful it might disappear.

Poor Mayda. I don't think she gets many pretty things of her own.

At the lodge they were shown to their rooms, and Drainin agreed to meet them at the eating hall of the inn after they changed and refreshed themselves.

***

The dining hall, filled with people of all heights and shades, with clothing running the gamut of colors from brilliant blues and fiery reds to sunny yellows, vibrated with raucous discussions. The noise of conversation and the heat from the colossal fireplace where a wullawerth roasted on a spit, added to the sense of bedlam. Serving maids ran to and fro, with brimming mugs of frothy liquid, which resembled beer. Bannon who had joined them for the evening meal, was eyeing the crowd with rapt attention.

Enchanted by the pandemonium around her, Kat twisted in her seat to catch the sights and sounds. *How interesting. Everyone is sitting with the people from their own land. They don't mix with each other.* A table of very pale skinned men with coal black hair, eyed Mayda with what appeared to be contempt. Their clothing, opposite to the majority of the people at the inn, was dark and gloomy.

Kat pointed them out to Drainin. "Are those men from Morden, Counselor?"

"Yes, they are."

"I don't like the way they're looking at Mayda."

"Lady Kat, the people from Morden do not care for those from Baklai. They consider them inferior."

"You don't act like them around Mayda. Why?"

"I have been living at the keep for many star turns, where Lord Eduardo welcomes people from all the lands. It makes sense we learn to live with each other. Although I would be uncomfortable in Baklai itself, I respect Horse-Master Haydar and his family. They are valuable assets to the community."

Valuable assets? Sounds like he still doesn't consider them as people. Mind you, Haydar is a pain in the butt.

The Arrival

The muttering among the group from Morden increased. They continued glancing over at Mayda. Finally one of the most vocal rose from his seat and approached Drainin. "You are from Morden?"

"I am Counselor Drainin."

"Why then do you break bread with this filth from Baklai?"

Before Drainin formed a reply, Kat sputtering with rage, jumped from her seat. "How dare you? By your name calling of this young woman, you label yourself as filth."

"I do not know from where you hail, woman, but if you align yourself with Baklai, you are not worthy to speak to me."

"I am the Lady Kat. In my world we would squash you like a beetle."

Drainin jumped up and moved in front of Kat. "Easy, friend. Lady Kat is a well respected member of Lord Eduardo's keep. Her arrival has been prophesied and I cannot allow you to insult her. All who know of her, even Thane Galdin, value her."

The Morden paled at his words, and bowed his head. "My apologies, Counselor. I misunderstood the situation." He pivoted on his heel and hurried back to his seat. A few words from him to his companions and they ceased talking and studiously avoided any eye contact with those at Kat's table.

How weird. He seems almost frightened of the Thane person?

Kat glanced at Mayda whose eyes opened as wide as the plates on their table. She cowered in her seat. Kat sat down again, and patted her hand. "It's fine now, Mayda. You're safe."

Bannon, still at the table, watched the others, but remained silent.

"Lady Kat." Drainin edged his seat close to her so his words would not carry beyond their group. His voice cracked like a whip. "Your interference was ill-advised. You were rude and the situation could have resulted in a physical battle."

"Rude? That vile man from Morden was the rude one. He had no right to be so insulting to Mayda."

"Perhaps. But there was no need to speak as you did." Drainin's wolf-eyes, like icicles, bored into her. "I am from Morden and I can handle others from my land with ease. You had no right to to step in. You owe me an apology."

"An apology? Why?" *Is he out of his mind?*

"You inserted yourself in a disagreement between two men. Women are not entitled to do so. Plus I could have lost face — then you would all be in real danger."

"Oh." *Men are such idiots. He believes I made him lose face. But we've still got a long way to travel, so perhaps I'd better grovel a little. Plus, his nostrils are flaring. I think he's upset.* "My apologies, Drainin." *Crap! I hate apologies.*

"Accepted."

"By the way, who is this Thane Galdin and why does he value me?"

"Thane Galdin is the ruler in Morden. As to him valuing you, I doubt he is even aware of your existence. Some times, however, stretching the truth is required."

"The Morden looked nervous when he heard the name." When she glanced their way, no one sat at the table any longer.

"The Thane is a strong, demanding ruler. Many fear him." He rose from his seat. "I think it best if we all retire.

We will decide on the morrow whether to remain in Trigoran one more night, or continue our travels."

Hmph. He never consults, just decides. I hate to admit this, but Eduardo did put him in charge, and I don't know the area. I'll go along with everything — for now.

J. M. Tibbott

CHAPTER 24

At the morning meal, Drainin informed Kat he decided they should continue their journey without further delay.

"When we leave Trigoran, we will head for the village of Fetternot. We will spend our final night at the far edge of the Old Forest, before we return to the keep,"

"I think it sounds like we still need to do a lot of traveling."

"We do, and you, Kat, may yet put your new spring-bow to use. The areas around Lake Brynwog and the Glassen Swamp, which we must pass, are the habitat of the kithras."

"I'm not sure I want to run into a bunch of kithras, but I'm not into shopping either. We've walked most of the market, so I'm ready to go anytime."

Mayda spoke up. "I like shopping, but I am not sure I like Trigoran. I find this town rather frightening, so I am glad we are going to go home."

Drainin rolled his eyes at Kat, who glared at him and shook her head just enough, so Mayda would not catch his expression. *He doesn't understand Mayda's fears.*

***

The day-long journey along Lake Brynwog passed peacefully, without conversation. Even over lunch, the four companions, lost in their own thoughts, ate sandwiches without speaking. All was silent, but the plop of a jumping fish, in late afternoon, brought Kat from her reverie.

She addressed Drainin. "Are the fish good for eating?"

"Fisshh?" He appeared startled. "I assume you are talking about the lake swimmers." He grimaced. "The few which were caught tasted foul. No one enters the lake itself, because the swimmers' teeth are long and they attack anything entering the waters. We avoid them, and you would do well to do the same, Kat."

Bannon leaned back in his seat. "Counselor, I would suggest we camp for the night in the clearing in front of those trees. Do you approve?"

When they descended, Bannon watered the pontis from the supplies they carried, and tied them down for the night, keeping their lines much shorter than usual, so they were unable to wander far. He set rocks for three fires — one in front and additional ones on either side. With the lake at their backs, their tents and the little beasties were protected on all flanks.

When Kat asked Bannon why he had prepared their camp this way, his brief reply explained everything. "Kithras."

Their evening meal consisted entirely of vegetarian offerings. Drainin explained by refraining from cooking meat when kithras were known to be in an area, ensured a safer journey. "They are drawn to the smell of flesh cooking, or even raw for that matter. While three of us are able to use spring-bows, I feel it still best to avoid any possibility of attracting them."

Kat regarded Mayda shivering beside the fire, despite the heat from the flames. "I suspect you've made a wise choice, Counselor." *Eduardo was right about Drainin's capabilities. I may not like him, but he is a competent guide.*

Bannon fed more wood to the fires when they retired, and Kat heard him in the night, adding further fuel to the flames. The night squeaks and squeals coming from the trees

The Arrival

outside their circle of protection kept her from deep sleep. She relaxed when dawn lit the sky with reds and yellows and the black slowly turned to blue. The arrival of full sunshine gave her a sense of release from the tension of the night.

Bannon prepared everything for departure with controlled speed. Mayda and Kat, hastily packed their own belongings to help hurry their withdrawal from the campsite.

A sense of relief enveloped the group, and once under way, Bannon entertained them with traveling songs. His delightful tenor imbued the light-hearted ballads with a sense of fun. The morning passed quickly, and Mayda's young voice joined Bannon's in a sprightly duet.

Kat moved to the rhythm in her seat, while munching on their luncheon sandwiches.

Drainin's deep voice startled her. "I decided we should eat while traveling. Pausing too long in kithra country is not wise."

Before Kat could answer, Mayda bounced in her seat with excitement. "Is that the Great Bridge, Counselor?"

"Yes, but before we cross, Bannon will fill our water containers slightly upstream with clear water." He smirked. "Free of any long-toothed lake swimmers."

Kat rolled her eyes at him. "Don't. Your flippant words frighten poor Mayda."

"Nonsense. She is aware she is safe with us."

As he spoke, Bannon pulled the wagon on a side trail, brought the pontis to the water to allow them to drink their fill, and jumped down to fill the wagon's water containers. He hastily stowed the water, backed the little beasts from the river, and headed over the bridge.

The span over the water, extensive and well constructed, could allow two wagons to pass each other with ease. Down below, the river, although broad, tumbled and gurgled over rocks and falls, as it split around a long forested island, only to slow as it joined again to flow to Lake Brynwog.

Kat scanned the island for buildings, but found none. "What lives on the island below us?"

Bannon answered from his seat. "Nothing much. Occasionally a creature falls into the river and is swept up on the shore. The only place they can swim to the other shore is just at the entrance to the lake, when the river calms once more. But the lake swimmers are always hungry and they patrol the area with care. It is possible some small tree creatures survive on the island, but no man has ventured to find out. So they live in anonymity."

When they reached the other side of the river, Bannon turned around in his bench. "Counselor, we traveled faster than expected. Perhaps we would be wise to continue on to Fetternot, rather than camp beside the Glassen Swamp. We will arrive in the village at dusk, but in time to find lodgings and food."

"I agree, Bannon. Continue on to Fetternot."

As the wagon rolled on its way, they passed an area dotted with stunted trees, festooned with fungus, strings of rotting vegetation, and what appeared to be spider webs. The miasma of decay and stagnation caught Kat's throat and she coughed. "What a stink. Did something die?"

"Something probably did."

At Drainin's words, a chill ran up her spine, and the hair on the back of her neck prickled and the stone on her pendant lay like ice between her breasts. *What now?*

They travelled about a hundred yards when a high pitched screech erupted from the nearby foliage. An animal about the size of a dog with black eyes, needle sharp teeth, and scruffy

The Arrival

brown hair, sprang from the underbrush, and headed toward the pontis, who squealed and moved even faster. The loathsome beast was followed by three more of these vile creatures, all slavering with foam around their mouths.

Drainin pulled both spring-bows and quivers from behind him, and handed a set to Bannon. Kat reached under her seat for her own. All three set the bows, notched their arrows and Bannon brought the first one down, while two more fell to Kat and Drainin. Kat had scarcely reloaded, when one of the loathsome brutes leaped for her, and she shot without thinking. As the arrow pierced its brain, blood splashed her face and arms, Mayda screamed, and Kat pushed the dead beast off the wagon. As more of the creatures erupted from the bush, the three bowmen loaded and shot until a dozen or more kithras lay dying. Caught up in the maelstrom of a feeding frenzy, the remaining animals turned and attacked their comrades, forgetting about the pontis and the occupants in the wagon. Bannon urged the little animals into a ponti-type gallop, which was the fastest they had managed thus far.

Adrenaline pumping through her, Kat sat breathing deeply, only now noticing, poor Mayda, who in her fright, had slid to the floor of the wagon. Kat helped her up and when she glanced up at Drainin, observed the pulse in his neck pumping fiercely.

He let out a deep breath. "This is one time we do not attempt to retrieve our arrows. We will purchase more in Fetternot." He handed a water container to Kat. "Use this to wash off the kithra blood, we do not wish to attract any more to us."

Mayda helped Kat remove all the unpleasant smelling gore from her face and arms, but her clothing still retained noxious stains.

Once the main danger had passed, Bannon slowed his panting charges, and they all travelled in silence to the village, each allowing the violent thudding of their hearts to slow down.

Kat could not decide if the experience excited or terrified her. *I can't believe I pulled that off. I know I shot at least four of those monsters. It's why my stone lay like ice against my chest. Is that how it warns me of danger? Did my lion decide I would need this kind of signal?*

CHAPTER 25

Late in the afternoon, Fetternot appeared in the distance. All Kat could see was a collection of small buildings, part stone and part wood, set haphazardly about a scraggly square. It possessed a rather run-down appearance, and the fields on the outer edge were filled with low-growing dusty-looking plants.

Drainin warned them Fetternot was a village of limited resources, and the inhabitants constantly struggled to eke out a living from the dry earth. "Not much rain falls here, so the villagers learned to use seed from flax-grass which is familiar with desert-like conditions. The flax-grass is traded at the market at the keep for much of the food stuffs the people require." He paused. "And the weavers prize the Fetternot grass, which they shred and pound into threads for creating tough cloth for field workers. The resultant threads are also perfect for taking dye and are used to create tapestries."

Kat grimaced. "It must be a grueling existence."

"By your standards, no doubt. But the Fetternots are happy and productive people. This type of life is all they know. Every extra they receive, is a great event. The inn, however, has limited rooms, and I hope they can accommodate us since we are arriving earlier than expected."

Dusk descended before the weary travelers arrived in the village, but fortune ensured they found rooms available at the inn. Kat's first step was to head to her room to change her clothing, and remove the kithra stained garments.

When she re-entered the dining area, their host, surprised by their early visit, welcomed them with a late dinner and a warm drink. "We anticipated your arrival two star turns hence, Lady Kat, Counselor Drainin. Luckily we are not visited often, and this is a quiet season for us, so we can accommodate you." He fluttered about, ushering them to a table near the hearth, issuing hurried commands to his helpers and bearing flagons of steaming near-ales to their seats.

The food, and especially the hot drink were most welcome. They were dressed for the weather at Lake Brynwog, and with nights at Fetternot much cooler, the cheery warmth of the inn erased the chill of the evening.

Kat ate little, but requested a cup of Karri-san tea before she staggered off to bed, exhausted from the journey and the disturbed sleep of the night before. She sank into the warmth of a puffy mattress, enveloped in the comforting folds of wooly blankets. Her mind was churning with questions, and sleep would not come easily. *I have been in this place for about two weeks of my time. Are they wondering back home why I haven't shown up? Will they search for me? It's not fair. I wasn't even in the Bermuda Triangle when I disappeared.* She yawned so widely, her jaw creaked. *Stop it Kat, turn your mind off. You need sleep more than trying to... .*

***

The morning sun pierced through Kat's dreams and she sat up in bed and stretched, muscles popping and crackling. The slight breeze through the window was still chilly, and she hastened her entry to the personal for a shower. Not as luxurious as the one in her rooms at the keep, nevertheless it was toasty and cleansing, and when she dried herself, she was one thousand percent more cheerful than the terrifying

The Arrival

time at Lake Brynwog. *I never want to encounter a kithra again.* She shuddered at the memory.

As she dressed, she remembered her confusing thoughts about the night before. *I must try and persuade Drainin to skip camping tonight and travel straight to the keep. I need to make up with Eduardo. I may need to beg him to send me home. He asked me to help with finding out why people are fighting with each other. The trouble is I don't know exactly what he expects me to do about it. Surely it can't be meeting people or talking to them.* Kat folded and packed her clothes in the duffle bag. *I don't believe Eduardo's going to be happy. The only thing I managed to do is make people mad at me.* She straightened up. *Wait a minute, I wonder if that's his plan? Everyone will be mad at me instead of each other, and then they will work to get rid of me. Perfect.*

A timid knock on the door of her room, reminded Kat to hurry with her packing. *Mayda's here. I better move along.*

They walked to the eating room in the Inn, and encountered Drainin in the halls.

He greeted them both, a bounce in his step. "Good morrow Kat. Mayda. I trust you slept well?"

They both agreed they had.

Drainin is acting all conquering, puffed-up peacock. I wonder if he got his jollies? Again? I can use the fact he's in a fine mood.

Bannon joined them at the table and advised Drainin the pontis and the wagon were ready to be reloaded, and he had taken on additional supplies of water and food for the next two days.

Kat saw her opportunity. "Counselor, could we travel a little faster and instead of camping this night, return to the keep immediately?"

"It would make for a most uncomfortable journey. Why would you want this?"

Uh oh. Be careful how you answer. "I'm tired of the travel and I'd like to be back enjoying the amenities of the keep."

"I think we all would, Lady Kat. But as I said, it would be uncomfortable, and we would need to travel during the night. Not a wise choice." He addressed Bannon. "Am I correct?"

"Yes, Counselor. We cannot move fast through the Dark Forest, and the distance from the other side to the keep would be during the night on very rough roads. Plus the pontis cannot pull a load for long without rest."

"Oh." *Rats. I must wait another day before talking to Eduardo again.*

Drainin's humor entertained them throughout their morning meal. He displayed extra courtesy to Mayda, making sure she was comfortable and well fed. He ordered special dishes for Kat. "That is made from the tuber which produces the flax grass. The Fetternots possess a way of pounding it and mixing it with spices to create the thick stew in your bowl. It is filling and the villagers often dry it in strips as food for journeys.

"I like the flavor." *He's being most attentive and funny this morning. I wonder if he did entice some woman to his bed, or... does is it mean another agenda? Can't help it. Don't entirely trust him.*

Bannon rose from the table. "I will finish packing, Counselor."

"Excellent. Take Lady Kat and Mayda with you so you can help them with any more packing they need, and I will settle our dues with the Innkeeper."

By the time Drainin emerged from the inn, they were ready to depart for the Dark Forest. Kat, curious about the name, wondered what they would find. The morning journey was dreary, past endless fields of short, dry flax grass.

Despite a lengthy night's sleep, Kat found herself yawning broadly. *I'm not really tired, it's just boring.* She yawned again, and pinched herself to stop.

When the sun was almost overhead, Bannon handed out food, and they ate lunch moving in rhythm with wagon as they chewed. Drainin made a point of being particularly solicitous with Kat. "That is the dried flax tuber I mentioned at our morning meal."

"You are right, it's very filling." *Am I too suspicious of him? He can be so nice and so funny at times. Then he does his macho crap. I haven't a clue what to make of him. Most of the people are what they seem. But he's an enigma. Weird.*

Bannon called back to them. "This is the entrance to the Dark Forest, and because the trees are so thick, and the trail narrow, the pontis will need to travel more slowly."

Kat grimaced. "Do any dangerous animals exist in this forest? Like kithras for instance?"

Drainin reached over and patted her hand. "No kithras, and nothing dangerous. The forest is benign."

He patted my hand. This is the first time he's touched me. I knew it. An agenda.

The trees sighed and whispered as the wind undulated through the edges of the forest and the wagon slowed as they entered, the pontis delicately picking their way along the narrow trail. The deeper into the trees they traveled, the darker it became. Drainin reached behind him for a strange type of lantern, and passed it to Bannon, who stopped the wagon briefly, touched his tinder rod to the metal on the side of the cart, and lit the lantern. He suspended the light from a frame above his head, and shook the reins for the pontis to continue. The glow gave them enough visibility to remain on the trail, and wend their way through the mass of foliage.

At one point, Bannon stopped the wagon and spoke to them. "Listen."

The silence was absolute. A sense of age, of things too ancient to be counted in normal time, enveloped the four travelers. The trees towered over them watching, waiting for eternity, older than life itself. No needles dropped, no creatures moved. Even the pontis appeared to hold their breath.

Then Bannon broke the spell and shook the reins for them to continue. The only sounds now were the creak of wood, the occasional clink of metal harnesses, and the shuffling of hooves on the thick bed of needles covering the forest floor. Reality existed solely in the pool of light as they moved through the trees.

Kat understood the reason for the name. "I've never been in woods so dense. What or who made this trail?"

Mayda remained silent, allowing Drainin to answer her query. "This forest is, we believe, the oldest in Kaylin. Who made the trail is unknown. It is likely, however, people who wished to move between the keep and Fetternot were responsible, because to travel around the forest would mean going all the way to the Brynwog River, close to Lanfair. That route would add a minimum of four star turns to a journey."

The pontis plodded along the trail, the gentle rocking movement of the wagon lulled Kat into a half sleep. A metallic sound awoke her. Bannon passed the now unlit lantern, which rattled again, back to Drainin to return to storage.

Kat yawned. "Excuse me." And yawned again.

In her peripheral vision she caught Mayda yawning discreetly behind her hand.

The Arrival

Bannon called back to them. "We are exiting the forest, and will be at our camping site shortly."

When they arrived, the young driver, as usual, settled the animals before attending to erecting the tents.

Drainin walked up to Kat. "While Bannon is preparing the camp for the evening, perhaps you would help me gather wood for the fire."

"Do you want Mayda to help as well?"

"No. She can gather the kindling which is in the immediate vicinity. You and I will need to go a short way into the trees to find the best firewood."

Kat suggested to Mayda she begin gathering kindling, and then followed Drainin the short walk into the forest. They picked up some logs and carried them back to the tree line, and then returned to gather more.

Kat spied a clump of pale white leaves in a small clearing. A touch of fiery red sprouted from it. "What a gorgeous flower. What's it called?"

"Kalins name it Flamewort, and this forest is the only place on Pridden where it grows." He strode over to the flower, plucked it carefully from the patch of foliage and holding it at arm's length, brought it to Kat. "Flamewort is known for the extraordinary scent it possesses." He passed it to her. "Inhale the perfume. You will enjoy it."

Kat took the flower from him, buried her nose in the blossom and breathed in. The aroma was heady, and reminded her of the spicy fragrance of Liandock. Her head whirled and she was lost in a memory, all current sights and sounds muffled, as though encased in cotton wool. A tall man stood in front of her, his voice deep and alluring. She wanted to speak his name, but the word 'Liandock' emerged as a faint moan. He moved closer, his lips reaching for hers. Soft. Tempting. But,

211

as the warmth of his lips touched her, a blast of ice stabbed her between her breasts. Shocked and galvanized into action, she pushed away from him. Not Liandock, it was Drainin.

"Stop. What are you doing?"

"Giving you what you want from me. What all women want from me." He pulled her to him again.

Kat drew back her fist and hit him in the face. Her training and her disgust lent power to her blow. He rocked backwards and landed on the ground. "Keep away from me Drainin. I am not one of your little 'doxies'. Keep your distance."

He jumped to his feet. His eyes blazed with fury. "You hold yourself too important. You will regret this." He stepped toward her, hostility in his stance.

Adrenaline coursed through Kat and she trembled with rage, her own voice like gravel and menacing. She raised an outspread hand. "Don't you ever. Ever. Touch. Me. Again."

"Or what?"

"Or I'll report you to Eduardo."

"You are a fool. Who do you think Eduardo will believe? Me, his trusted Counselor, or you, almost a stranger, and totally inept in the ways of Kaylin."

Kat was sputtering with rage, but Drainin must have seen something unexpected on her face. He stopped short, stared at her, and a confused frown creased his brows.

Kat turned and tore away from him back to the camp, forgetting to pick up the wood for the fire. *The swine. Bastard. He used the Kaylin equivalent of 'roofies' on me. How many other women has he done this to? He's a potential frickin' rapist. The pig. He's disgusting.* Kat was so incensed, she couldn't think clearly. She wanted to scream, jump up and down and stamp the ground in her fury. She charged directly to the tent she shared with Mayda, and attempted, unsuccessfully, to calm her breathing.

***

During dinner, Kat sat as far away as possible from Drainin. She couldn't convey what had happened to either Mayda or Bannon. She was on her own. Thank god she shared a tent with the girl. She'd move Mayda's bed closer to the entrance than hers.

Mayda, oblivious to the tension between Kat and Drainin, chattered away about the dark of the forest and how much light Bannon's lantern gave.

Bannon refrained from conversation. He appeared to scrutinize Kat and Drainin, but he did not query either of them.

Desperate to be alone, Kat excused herself and went to the tent. Once in bed, however, she tossed and turned, unable to close her eyes and rest. A part of her was nervous Drainin would creep into the tent. *I'm so glad the icy cold brought me back to reality.* She sat up, *Wait a minute. It was my stone.* She reached under her nightdress and grasped it in her hand. *It's warm now. Was it warning me about Drainin?* She smiled to herself. *Oh, my lion, you were right. I am being protected. Thank you.* With thoughts of Liandock, sleep enveloped her.

***

Kat woke to a glorious morning — mild temperature and bright sun. She emerged from her tent, dressed and ready for the day, and stretched and breathed deeply of fresh, clean air.

The four of them ate a quick meal, before Bannon packed and readied the wagon for travel. Drainin and Kat exchanged not a single word during this time. Kat avoided looking at him.

On board the wagon, Kat manipulated Mayda to sit opposite Drainin, while she made a point of gazing at the landscape on the side away from them.

Bannon turned to the group behind him. "Counselor, we made an early start, and our pontis are fresh and can make excellent time. We could reach the keep for a midday meal if you wish."

"Excellent idea, Bannon. Please do."

They travelled in silence and shortly, Kat's heart lifted at the sight of the keep before them. The beautiful stonework glittered in the full light of the sun. Around the edges, small neat homesteads, with patches of green and splashes of color from the blooms in their gardens, were dotted around the cobble streets which led to the private residences of the Lord's guards. Despite the fact she ached to be back in her own time and place, Kat experienced a small tug of homecoming.

***

Bannon stopped the wagon in the courtyard from which they had left, and began unloading.

Reluctantly, Kat approached Drainin. *I must see Eduardo, and Drainin is his counselor, I'll swallow my pride and ask his help.* "I suppose there is no point in asking you to intervene and request an audience for me with Eduardo?"

His voice was frigid. "Why do you want to see him? And why do you think I would help you?"

"I still wish to return home and I need his help."

"Lady Kat." He spat out the words. "It is time for you to get over yourself. You are here to perform a duty for Lord Eduardo. I suggest you better spend your time learning to befriend the local people in Kaylin, instead of bothering the Lord with the trivial matter of your desires. You are here to help him, not yourself." He glared at her. "Although judging by your actions with me, I doubt you will be able to relate to any of the Mordens." With that diatribe, he turned on his heel and stalked off.

Kat yelled after him. "Bite me." Under her breath she cursed him. "Bastard." *Son-of-a... .* The stone on Kat's pendant was icy again. Watching her nemesis stride angrily into the keep, she turned and headed back to the wagon where Bannon was still unloading. "Thank you, Bannon, for your help and expertise on our journey." She handed him her last remaining chit from Trigoran.

Bannon blushed and ducked his head. "You are most welcome Lady Kat." He gazed at the chit in his hand. "This is not necessary."

"On the contrary Bannon, I want to give it to you."

Bannon blushed an even deeper pink.

Kat smiled and turned away. *Interesting. The stone is cold when Drainin is around, but warms up near Bannon. My stone is a wonderful judge of character.*

J. M. Tibbott

CHAPTER 26

Bannon left to take the pontis and the wagon to the stable master, and alone in the courtyard, Kat paced, fuming at Drainin's words. *He's got his nerve. Telling me I should be friendly with everybody. He probably meant, I should be friendly with him. Creep. Perhaps I should speak to Wynneth.*

Although Kat had explored much of the keep, she got confused about the twists and turns, and found herself outside an unfamiliar room. The open door enticed her to peek in. Brith, with her back to the door, was sewing. Kat paused. *Brith. I wonder. Although I loathe Drainin, perhaps he made a point. Eduardo does want me to help people to work together. I need Brith to help me. I guess I'll have to ask her for her forgiveness. Rats, how I hate having to constantly apologize. But... I want riding clothes.*

"Brith."

The woman, startled, swung around, and glared when she recognized Kat. "What do you want?"

"Please. I need to apologize to you." *Crap this is awkward.* "I never meant to insult you. Please understand I don't know your customs and sometimes, I misinterpret and say the wrong things." *I sound like an idiot. But remember what Wynneth told me about Brith's childhood. Perhaps she can't help being so boxed-in.* "I need you to forgive me, and perhaps we can help each other."

Brith's face softened. "Perhaps you did misconstrue our ways. People from other lands are also not familiar with our customs, and sometimes they make mistakes." She achieved a faint smile. "When those people arrive here, they receive information about Kaylin, so their slips are mild. As I now understand the situation, you were not given such a benefit." Her smile broadened this time. "Perhaps I did not allow myself to consider this. For my error, I also apologize."

Wow. Well I'll be... "Brith, thank you."

"I should have been more understanding. I must have been more forgiving when I encountered others who accidentally broke our customs. Although in my defense, your mistake was bigger than most."

Kat's laugh was rueful. "I guess so." *To get riding clothes, I can pretend to understand her weird reaction.*

"Usually travelers from the other lands research our people before coming here. The exception are those from Glowen. They cannot accept how we live. They refer to us as 'repressed'. Rarely do they visit Kaylin because they find us too different."

"Someone mentioned to me the Glowens are free in their thinking."

Brith grimaced. "Indeed they are. Please come in, Lady Kat. I will order tea and refreshment for us." She stretched for the tassel near her workbench and tugged twice. "Let us sit, and we will talk."

Kat entered the room, which was a feast for the eyes, crammed with bolts of material, some furry and touchable, some with nubby textures, combined with others sculpted with swirls of clipped threads. The colors reminded Kat of rainbows -- from brilliant crimsons to deep royal blues and purples. Neatly stored in bins, matching threads and piping piled along one side. A number of half-finished garments hung on racks in another corner. Across the room, three half-

The Arrival

open doors led from the glorious chaos into: a tidy sleeping room, a formal personal, and a storage area filled with more sewing supplies. As she headed toward a table off to the right, she took the opportunity to caress a fine emerald velvet, and touch a pale cream-colored fur to her face. *I must remember this treasure chest of different shades and styles of fabric so I can advise the illustrator about them for the new game when I return home.*

Brith beamed with apparent pride at Kat's admiration of the wares in her quarters. "They are so beautiful, are they not? Kaylin cloth has a well-deserved reputation for quality and design." She turned at a tap on her door, walked over to the young man standing outside, and took from him the tray laden with treats.

"I brought these right away, Brith. The tea will follow shortly." He bowed his head slightly and excused himself.

After the tea arrived, Brith poured, which Kat sipped. She breathed deeply, feeling the calming effects within minutes. She picked up a cookie. "I love these. They remind me of similar ones I used to get in my own home. The challenge is they are so delicious I can't eat just one."

Brith chuckled. "I understand. I find it difficult to only eat four in a day."

They ate and drank in silence for a while.

"Lady Kat, I am positive you wished to talk about other things with me."

"Yes. I came up with an idea of how you might adjust a dress for me so I can ride comfortably."

Brith regarded her warily. "What sort of adjustments?"

"Let me show you. Can you give me a writing instrument and some parchment?"

"Of course." Brith rose and walked over to a carved wooden desk, opened a drawer and withdrew the items Kat needed.

Kat drew a long skirt. "I'm not a skilled artist, but if you split the skirt down the middle, front and back, thusly, and then sew in a panel to connect the front and back, and leave a space in between the two halves of the skirt, it will make it easier to move. Like so." *Not bad. It does look like a full skirted set of gaucho pants, although I'm better at doing this in computer code.* "This will allow me to ride with less difficulty, one leg on each side of the horse, but without exposing anything. What do you think?"

After examining the drawing closely, Brith turned to Kat, her eyes shining. "I think the idea is amazing. My customers often tell me they wish they could ride horses with less effort. This type of skirt with a split, will make it possible without being disrespectful of Kaylin custom. I must thank you, Lady Kat. You have given me a way to provide my customers with an excellent new option. I will sew this skirt for you at no charge, because your idea will bring me new business. I will have fun designing the skirt to be practical as well as beautiful."

Oh joy. That wasn't as onerous as I imagined.

Brith poured another cup of tea and the two of them chatted, with Kat, having finally persuaded Brith to drop the Lady honorific when they were speaking privately. She shared some of the stories of her travels through Kaylin.

"Kat, I cannot believe you hunted a gornog. Everyone says they are terrifying and fierce creatures."

Kat shuddered, remembering. "They're big and ugly and dangerous. The tusks are razor sharp and can inflict serious damage. When younger, I used a regular bow, so the spring-

The Arrival

bow is easier for me to handle. But my biggest challenge here is my clothing. The long full skirt catches in everything and makes moving fast almost impossible." Kat grimaced. "I would not want to be running away from kithras with all this cloth slowing me down. Kithras are even more terrifying than gornogs."

"I understand with the types of garments the women of Kaylin wear, you would be at a disadvantage. But women in our land do not hunt. Our jobs are to care for our homes and our offspring. Only men hunt and perform manual tasks."

"Brith, I need additional help from you." Kat sighed. "It appears I will be traveling through most of the lands, and I am not sure what challenges I will encounter. I need to be prepared to move freely and fast. So, I must ask another favor."

Brith assessed Kat, her eyes narrowed with suspicion. "What favor?"

Uh oh. Tread gently here. "Can you work in leather? Or do you perhaps keep cloth which is almost as strong as leather?"

"Nothing is as strong as our leather. Why do you ask?"

"I noticed when I visited Bardu and Irina, she wore straight leather pants with a tunic over them which extended just below her knees, and was split down the sides. Since Irina rides with the guards, it makes sense this outfit gives her the freedom she needs in the saddle, and the ability to move easily and noiselessly when on foot."

"But Kat, as a Rifellan guard, Irina is allowed special dispensation regarding her clothing. Plus her limbs are well covered. Her pants are also looser than those you originally showed me."

"Yes, I'm aware of this. Therefore, I would like you to make for me an outfit similar to Irina's, but with the tunic extending no further than the top of my knees." Kat held up her hand as Brith opened her mouth to speak. "Wait, if you will make me an outfit like Irina's, I promise never to wear it in Kaylin."

Brith leaned her elbows on the table, her chin on her clasped hands, obviously in deep thought. She lifted her head and regarded Kat at length. "You do promise you will not wear the outfit in my land?"

"I said so, and I meant it."

"I will do it. You may also have supplied me with an idea to approach the Rifellan females to sew their garments. They are modest enough, and at this time they send to Rifella to purchase their clothing. Some of them may be willing to hire me to make their uniforms here. It appears these ideas of yours create many benefits for me. I thank you for this."

"I'm so relieved you will help me. No thanks are needed."

"Nevertheless when you are preparing to leave Kaylin, I will help you with the wardrobe you will need in Shendea. It would be unwieldy to take sufficient outfits for all the lands." She laughed. "You would need a large wagon following you. Instead, I will give you information where you can obtain what you require when you travel further."

"Thank you, how wonderful." Kat stood and reached out and hugged Brith.

The woman, apparently startled by the gesture, blushed and dropped her head. "Your customs are unusual, Lady Kat."

Oops, I think I overstepped some boundary. Again. She's reverted to being formal. But at least she's prepared to help me. Perhaps Wynneth has a point. People are not always what they appear.

J. M. Tibbott

CHAPTER 27

When Kat's evening meal arrived in her room, she asked Laylin where she might find Wynneth. "I knocked on her door and got no answer."

"Almost everyone is at the concert, Lady Kat. You should look for her at the hall."

"A concert? Where is the hall?"

"The way is simple. You are accustomed to finding Lord Eduardo's office?"

"Yes."

"You head toward his office, but turn to your right at the fifth passageway. Turn to your right again at the third passageway, and this will lead you directly to the concert room." Laylin ducked her head in apology. "I would take you to the hall myself, Lady Kat, but I am required to return to the kitchens."

"Not a problem, I can find my way." She called to Laylin's departing back. "Oh, and... thank you." *Rats, I nearly forgot. Manners are a pain in the ass sometimes. It's a wonder anybody gets anything done in Kaylin. In business we expect things to be done. It's all part of the job, not some special favor.*

A steaming bowl of soup sent tendrils of mouth-watering aromas to curl around Kat's nostrils. *I want to get to the concert, but growling stomachs during a production are embarrassing.* The bowl brimmed with vegetables and chunks of some type of meat, plus the familiar noodles she adored.

She dug in. *Wow. I missed these keep-cooked meals during my travels. Except for the food at Liandock's and Penrow's — and, oh yes — the delicious gornog feast at the camp near the Old Forest. This is heaven.*

After her regular cup of Karri-san, Kat followed Laylin's instructions and found herself outside a pair of tall doors. Beautiful notes from beyond the entrance beckoned her, and she pulled the door enough to slip into the room. The magnificence of the hall and the four young people on the stage caught her immediate attention. Three women and one man, accompanied by two musicians playing odd-looking, stringed instruments were the individuals responsible for the delightful sounds. She stood inside the entrance, awed by the glorious harmonies emanating from the stage, until she remembered her search for Wynneth. At last she spied her three rows in, and fortunately a seat beside her was unoccupied. Kat tiptoed to the chair and eased into it.

Wynneth glanced toward her, a smile lit her face, and she mouthed the word 'Welcome.'

Kat understood she should be silent, so she turned her attention to the singers. Their voices blended in perfect symmetry, and soared and swept over the audience. Not a single member coughed or fidgeted. Kat closed her eyes, soon lost in the joy and rhythm of the music. They reminded her of concerts she attended in many of the parks back home, and an unexpected wave of homesickness swept over her. The heat of tears pricked at the back of her eyelids. To prevent herself from crying, she opened her eyes and blinked as rapidly as possible. *That's a first. I haven't been this close to tears since my childhood when my parents were in the car crash. What's going on with me?*

The Arrival

The music ended and the audience stood and shouted and applauded wildly. Kat stole a glance at Wynneth, who cheered equally enthusiastically. The singers and their accompanists bowed and melted from the stage, and the crowd ambled from the hall, chatting animatedly among themselves.

Wynneth grasped Kat's hand. "Welcome back, Kat. I hope you enjoyed your travels and you succeeded in your mission."

"I'm glad to be back. I missed the amenities of the keep." Kat motioned toward the stage. "I loved the music. Were the singers all from Kaylin?"

Wynneth laughed. "Your change in subject was not achieved with much skill. But to answer your question, the young man and two of the women are from Shendea, and the other woman is from Morden."

"Morden? She is unlike the Mordens I met in Trigoran."

"You must tell me about everything. We will return to your room and enjoy some night time tea."

***

Seated before a table, containing a huge pot of what Kat mentally referred to as 'sleepy tea', and a generous plate of her favorite cookies, she plied Wynneth with more questions about the concert. "Do the group live here at the keep?"

"No, they normally reside in Shendea. Twice a year, they come to Kaylin to perform, both here and in Trigoran. I believe they also give performances in other lands."

"They're extraordinarily talented." *How long can I avoid talking about the trip? What should I say, and how much should I explain to her?*

"Kat, what are you not telling me?"

"I'm not avoiding anything." *Liar, liar.* "I'm not sure where to start."

"Begin with the day you left the keep."

"Well, we drove toward the metal-master's and the builder's villages, but stopped for the night beside a quiet pool. Well, quiet except for Mayda, who tends to talk a lot. Bannon, our driver was so competent, and he's a delightful young man."

"And how did you find the trip with Drainin?"

Boy, she's determined to interrogate me. "He surprised me. Most of the time he could be quite charming, and he found some crystals along our way, which allowed both Mayda and me to trade for jewelry with Master Liandock." To hide the sudden rush of heat at the mention of Liandock's name, Kat withdrew the stone embraced in the silver of her pendant from beneath her clothing and showed it to Wynneth. "The color is gorgeous."

Wynneth regarded the stone carefully. "He created the perfect combination of stone and silver for you." She looked up at Kat. "Do not allow any other to touch this. I believe Master Liandock attuned the stone to you, and you alone. He is a skilled artisan."

Little do you know how skilled he is. Watch yourself, Kat. Hold it together. "He did mention the stone would speak to me, but I'm not sure what he meant." *I hope she doesn't guess what we did.*

"The metalsmith's talent lies in hearing the vibrations of the rocks and metals he works with. I am not sure if he means they speak in words." Wynneth smiled. "I do not possess his talent or his powers of blending stones with fine metals. I suspect you will understand what the stone intends to convey, all in good time."

Kat resumed her tale of their travels. "The next day we left for Mammac and met Master Builder Penrow." She laughed out loud. "What a delight. An immense bear of a man, with an enormous appetite for life. When we finally left him, I was so sore. I had eaten way too much and laughed so hard, my poor ribs ached."

"You have described him perfectly. He is one of the most beloved men in Kaylin. He breaks rules of conduct constantly and not one person finds him at fault. He has a talent for joy."

Kat nodded, remembering. "Next we travelled to Meenyat. Now those people are scary. They decided I had to stay with them because of some prophecy or other by someone called Cally… no, Caleesh. To be able to leave, we had to sneak off and make a quick escape."

"Ah, yes. Meenyat is a poor village, and the people only hang on to their existence because of their deep faith in Caleesh. Somehow they are convinced She predicted a woman would come to live among them and their fortunes would improve. Hopefully, with your hasty exit, they decided you are not the predicted one."

"I hope. The weird thing is they mentioned my hair and eye colors."

"I would not worry. Predictions have a way of being revised to meet changing circumstances." Wynneth patted Kat's hand. "Did you proceed to Trigoran after leaving Meenyat?"

"Yes, but we camped near the Old Forest, and Drainin taught me how to use the spring-bow. So we hunted and caught a gornog. It was the most delicious meat I've ever eaten. Bannon cooked some over the fire, and then smoked the rest of the meat to use as trade in Trigoran. We also kept the tusks and teeth for the jewelers." Kat yawned.

Immediately, Wynneth also yawned. "That is catching. I believe, Kat, it is time to retire. I, too, had a busy day and I wish to sleep now. I will meet you for a meal in the morning and you can continue the tale of your adventures."

Kat yawned again. "Fine. I'll see you tomorrow."

After Wynneth left for her own room, Kat shed her clothes, took a warm shower and slid into bed, totally naked. *This is only the second time since I came here I get to sleep without clothes on. The last time was when I slept at Liandock's.*

Yum. Perhaps I can enjoy a sexy dream about my lion.

CHAPTER 28

Morning came slipping in with bird song and a day bright and shiny with new possibilities. Wynneth knocked at the door connecting to Kat's room.

Kat promptly opened it, a bounce in her step, and smiling her welcome. "Wynneth. How are you today?"

By the Spirit, she is happy. I wonder if Liandock's pendant is helping her with her moods. "I am fine Kat, and I ordered a wonderful morning meal for us. Come join me." She motioned Kat into her own room.

They moved to the table, laden with food and drink, and Wynneth poured the tea. "You are looking well. You obviously slept soundly."

"Oh, yes. I needed to. Camping is not exceptionally restful." Kat, her face lighting up when she glimpsed what dishes waited, served herself from the platters of food. "Wynneth. Wow. You got some gornog meat. How?"

"Traders from Trigoran undertake a hunt every four seasons. They process the gornogs by smoking and drying, and trade at Fetternot and then come directly to the keep, They always find willing buyers here."

"Well I'm glad they do. I love this stuff."

"Perfect. Now my treat will be hearing about the rest of your travels. You last mentioned the result of your hunt." *Perhaps I will hear what she was reluctant to alk about last night.*

In between mouthfuls of food, Kat continued her tale. "Next we visited the Penrow Pool which was awesome.

I would love to figure out where the waters go. Drainin told us they suspect the pool becomes an underground river, which travels through Clog Blue and goes further underground in Morden and eventually empties into… um. I can't remember what name he gave me. I think the water falls into a sea."

"I also am aware of this possible explanation. The sea would be the Hyal." *She is not talking about meeting other people. And she barely mentions Drainin. Why is she glossing over her trip?*

"I think he did use the name Hyal. Then we went to Trigoran where we traded our meat and the tusks, and I bought a spring-bow and a beautifully made quiver to hold the arrows." Kat grimaced. "It's just as well I did, because we were attacked by kithras near the Glassen swamp. I never want to be confronted by one of those monsters again."

"I have never seen one, but I am conscious of the tales." Wynneth glanced at Kat's face. *She's definitely concealing something.* "Trigoran is a substantial village. Did you not meet any of the people?"

"Yes, of course. We met all kinds from everywhere. At the market, we purchased a lovely belt for Mayda." Kat sipped at her tea. "I don't think she receives many things simply because they are lovely. She can be sweet, despite the fact she talks too much."

Did she not interact with others in Trigoran? "Go on."

"I found most of the people polite, but I noticed those from other lands stick together. Four men from Morden were at the inn. They were so rude, especially to Mayda. So I told them off."

Well, well. "How did Drainin react? You do realize he is from Morden himself."

The Arrival

"When they turned on me, he warned them about insulting me. He said someone called Thane Galdin valued me, which I thought kind of weird. But the name seemed to scare the Mordens, and they left soon after."

"He mentioned Thane Galdin?" *How odd.*

"Yes, but he got furious with me. He claimed I was rude and I could have cost him face, and Thane Galdin probably isn't aware of me. I couldn't speak to him. He was in such a foul mood."

Interesting. "Your reaction may not have been the wisest move, but I do understand why you defended Mayda."

"Wynneth, I did apologize to him. I figured we still had a long way to travel back to the keep, and I should humor him."

Some Mordens can be unpredictable, so at least she knows when to use some social skills. Although I notice she only uses those skills when she wants something. "So after Trigoran you fought off kithras and I assume you travelled to Fetternot?"

"Yes and we went through the Dark Forest and camped one more night before coming back to the keep."

"I love the Dark Forest. I believe those trees are the oldest on Pridden. You are never aware of what you might find in the depths of the woods. Only small animals live within the shelter of the trees, and the silence is absolute. Once every four seasons, my fellow healers from Shendea come here and we venture to the forest and meditate for about five star-turns. I return refreshed and renewed." Wynneth sighed, remembering. "During our time away, we exchange what we have learned over the past seasons. No matter what else happens, my renewal in the Dark Forest is the savior of my soul. Did you find the trees relaxing too?"

233

"I did, but I looked forward to returning to the keep."

Oh dear. What is she not telling me. She is frowning the way she does when she is unhappy. Even her eyes appear dark. What happened? "I always feel the same way when I come back. Tell me Kat, did you find your trip successful?"

"I've no idea. How do you classify success on a road trip?" Kat's face brightened. "However, I got something accomplished, but here in the keep."

Wynneth raised her brows in query.

"You'll be proud of me Wynneth. I made up with Brith."

"Excellent." *At least she feels she's made some progress. But what is there about the trip she is not telling me. She changed the subject most abruptly.*

"I went to visit her and apologized, and she agreed to make me some clothing I can wear comfortably when riding. She is convinced the idea I came up with will also help expand her business. I'm pleased she is willing to help me. She appeared to be so rigid before."

Wynneth grinned to herself. Kat has found a way to get what she wants. Again. "I am glad the two of you are talking. Brith is a fine woman. This is a successful accomplishment for you. So now, when does Eduardo want you and Drainin to travel again?"

The abrupt change of expression, and the rage on Kat's face frightened the healer.

"I will never go traveling with Drainin again." Kat's voice dropped to an almost terrifying whisper. "He is rude, arrogant and I loathe him. I would sooner be trapped on Pridden forever than do anything more with him."

"What did he do?" *By the Spirit, she is furious. This cannot be favorable.*

"I don't wish to discuss this. But I do want you to help me to meet with Eduardo. He and I didn't part well the last

The Arrival

time we met. I want to go home, but I'm not willing to be blackmailed into traveling with Drainin. Can you arrange for me to speak with Eduardo?"

Something significant occurred between Kat and Drainin. Eduardo must be apprised of this. "I will arrange something for you. Leave this with me."

Kat rose from the table. "Thank you for the meal, Wynneth. It was delicious and my stomach is very happy. However, now I need to do some things."

Wynneth rose and grasped Kat's hand and patted it with her own. "Please be assured I am here to help you."

Kat's expression softened and a faint smile tugged at the corners of her mouth. "I know, Wynneth. You're my friend. Thank you."

Eduardo is not going to be pleased. But if he wants Kat to continue helping him, he will need to find another guide. But, who?

235

J. M. Tibbott

CHAPTER 29

Early in the afternoon, Kat hurried along the cobblestone path on her way to Bardu's quarters. *I need advice.*

When she knocked, Irina opened the door. "Lady Kat. I am sorry but Bardu is not here."

"It's fine. It's you I want to speak to." *Wow, she's still gorgeous, but I don't feel the incredible attraction this time. Good old Karri-san."*

Irina raised her brows. "Really? Please do come in."

Kat entered the house, and Irina offered her a seat and brought tea and cookies to the table.

"I believe you just returned from a journey around Kaylin?"

"Yes, a lengthy one, and I'm glad to be back at the keep. I don't like camping. Somehow you never get truly clean, and being in a different bed every night means sleeping soundly is difficult."

"I understand the challenge. As guards, we often go on training exercises, and getting back to my own bed is delightful."

Kat smiled and nodded. She gazed down at her hands. *This is not easy to tell. But I must get someone on my side. I'm sure I can trust her.*

Irina broke the silence. "What do you need, Lady Kat?"

"This is a little awkward. I'm not sure how to begin."

Irina smiled at her. "Given the circumstances of our first meeting, I do not think anything should be awkward between us."

Kat chuckled. "You do make a point." She clasped her hands, rested her elbows on the table and placed her chin on her entwined fingers. "I need to tell you something in confidence, and I need advice on how to handle an awkward situation."

"Of course, go ahead. I will not tell anyone if you do not wish me to."

Kat sighed and twisted her fingers together. "I'm here about Drainin."

Irina' eyebrows leaped up her forehead. "Oh."

"I should give you some background on his behavior during our trip. Most of the time he could be charming and helpful. I caught a glimmer of something odd when we went to Master Liandock's village." Kat blew out a frustrated breath. "Liandock and Drainin behaved like a couple of animals about to attack each other. Now I realize Drainin is moody, but I found Liandock... er... helpful. He was not a moody person. The feeling between them was strange to me. I couldn't understand it."

Irina raised her hand to her face, obviously attempting to hide her grin.

Kat was not fooled. "What?"

"Do you think Drainin suspected you and Liandock enjoyed more than friendship?"

Kat's face heated. *I'm sure I'm blushing furiously.* "What makes you say this?"

Irina sighed. "I am not judging you Kat. Personally, I would consider you a fool if you did not take advantage of Liandock's ministrations. I can tell you did. Your face betrays you. I suspect the healer would order a similar encounter for you." She smiled. "The metal-smith is a fine lover."

"Am I that transparent?"

"No, but I am well acquainted with Liandock. He is my sibling, and we delight in a connection which transcends simple verbal communication."

"Oh no."

"Kat I told you no judgment exists on my part. I love him considerably, and I respect you. I am not surprised you two enjoyed each other." Irina's face brightened with a mischievous grin. "But we were discussing Drainin. Most men are usually able to tell when a woman had been with another. I suspect Drainin is interested in you and when he suspected you and Liandock had spent time together, he became jealous. You must admit he enjoys few options here in Kaylin to seduce women."

"I'm positive he and Illian managed to spend a night together when we stayed in Mammac."

"Indeed, they probably did. One thing you should realize about Illian, is her female parent is from Glowen, and the Glowens exhibit few personal restrictions. Illian indulges in sex on her terms. No emotion involved. She would never be subservient to Drainin. Thus when she wants to liaise with him, she does so, but only when she desires to. I would submit Drainin is not entirely happy with the arrangement. He prefers to be in control of women."

"I agree, he does love to be in control, and I believe he thinks of women as playthings. Well he did spend most of the subsequent trip being charming, to Mayda as well, but he got nasty and grumpy when I told off some Mordens in Trigoran."

"Hold. You told off some Mordens?"

"Yes, they were rude to Mayda who had accompanied us, and Drainin claimed I had almost made him lose face. But that was all. Until… ." Kat lowered her eyes and stared at the table between them.

"Until? Do not stop now, I am intrigued."

"Well, we camped for the night on this side of the Dark Forest, and Drainin asked me to help him gather firewood immediately inside the trees. I saw a beautiful red flower, which Drainin referred to as flamewort. He picked the flower, suggesting I should smell the perfume."

Irina's eyes widened and her mouth dropped open. "He did not?"

"He did. My head swam and I was lost in a fog. Unable to move, I existed in something strange and other-worldly place, with no impression of time passing. A man stood in front of me, whom I thought was Liandock, and came toward me and touched his lips to mine. If my stone hadn't turned to ice on my chest, I might have fallen for his trick."

"Wait a minute, Kat. Do you mean to tell me Drainin attempted to use flamewort to seduce you?"

"Yes." *Oh I am lighter now — a weight has lifted from my shoulders. I so needed to confide in someone.*

"That is unforgivable. No honorable man would do such a thing. We must inform Eduardo, or Bardu."

"No, please don't. I came to you because of this. I don't want anyone else to know. I can take care of myself. I let my guard down, and I am almost embarrassed about the incident."

"You have no reason for embarrassment, no person can resist the effects of flamewort. Eduardo should be aware of Drainin's reprehensible behavior."

"If I tell anyone about the incident, I will also need to tell them about my stone."

"I remember, you mentioned your stone got icy cold. Did Liandock create the stone for you?"

"Yes. And it becomes cold around Drainin, but warm around other people. I believe I need to keep silent about what the jewel does."

"May I see it?"

Instead of answering, Kat withdrew the pendant from beneath her clothing and offered her hand toward Irina so she could view the silver-enclosed emerald.

"Gorgeous, Kat. Did he tell you what the rune means?"

"No, it wasn't necessary. In one of the ancient languages on my world, this rune means warrior."

"Perfect. My sibling is endowed with a wonderful relationship with gems and metals. Whether he locates stones which posses powers, or he is able to imbue them with remarkable properties, he, himself, is unclear about the situation. But he is blessed with much talent." Irina reached across and patted Kat's hand. "I understand why you do not wish others to be aware of your pendant and its properties. Liandock created something unique for you. Use this stone well and wisely. But, keep this hidden and never allow another to touch it."

"He said the stone would speak to me. Is this what he meant?"

"I believe he meant there would be a number of ways in which the stone might communicate with you. The cold/warm reaction is a simple way of warning you of those who should not be trusted, and those who should. I do not doubt you will become aware of other functions. Functions you may discover, which do indeed speak to you."

"I hope so. But what should I do about Drainin. I can't tell Eduardo, because I need his help in returning home. Plus Drainin appears to hold much power as counselor in Kaylin."

"If you do not wish to tell anyone else about it, I think it would be wise to avoid him completely. As much as is possible."

"Of course you're right. But it may be difficult."

"And I believe Liandock gave you exactly what you need to cope with Drainin."

Kat rose. "I must go, Irina." She paused. "May I ask you one last question?"

"Indeed."

"You mentioned the connection between you and Liandock... I believe the words you used... 'transcends verbal communications.' Can you describe to me how it works?"

"I shall try. Liandock and I enjoy a mental connection. We do not speak in words, but we receive images and emotions from each other when either of us is experiencing extreme joy, or sometimes, fear. As little ones, Liandock often came to my rescue if I encountered trouble."

Oh, wow, what an amazing experience. "Thank you for sharing, Irina. Thank you also for hearing me out — and for your advice. I will do as you suggest. Avoid any contact with Drainin."

"Excellent idea. You are welcome." Irina walked over and hugged Kat. "You would make a marvelous sibling-in-bond, my dear. Unfortunately it cannot be. I believe it is important you must return to your own world. I think Liandock is aware of this, because the pendant he created for you is powerful and may contain even more properties than he realizes himself."

Kat left Irina's home, turned and waved at her, and headed back to the keep.

I do want to go back. The pull for my home grows stronger every day. But Liandock and Irina make leaving more difficult than I anticipated.

CHAPTER 30

At the knock. Eduardo glanced up, and Dafid poked his head around the door. "Sire, Healer Wynneth is here."

"Show her in. I am always ready to meet with the Healer." *Odd, she usually sends me a message when she wants to see me.*

Eduardo rose as Wynneth entered, walked to meet her and clasped her hand in both of his. "I am delighted you are here. As always." He raised an eyebrow in query. "Your visit is unexpected. What brings you to my office?"

Wynneth sighed. "The person who brings me most often to your quarters these days. Kat."

When Wynneth speaks like this, things are rarely good. "What has occurred now?"

"That is the challenge. I do not know. Kat wants to meet with you. She refuses to go on further journeys with Drainin ever again. She went so far as to say, she would sooner remain in Pridden, never to return home, than be in Drainin's company."

Eduardo dropped Wynneth's hands and rubbed his chin. "Curious. A forceful statement, given all she ever requests from me, is to send her back to her home. I wonder why?"

"I cannot tell you why. I tried to get her to reveal her reasons, but she refused to divulge the cause."

"Is it possible Drainin took liberties?"

"Eduardo, Kat is no blushing or naive inexperienced girl. She is a woman of strong sensibilities." Wynneth giggled.

"And an equally strong sense of humor. She referred to him, before they left on the journey, as a 'horn dog'." She giggled again. "Even though I do not fully understand the expression, you must admit the words do describe him… with accuracy."

He laughed loudly. "A wonderful expression, and you are correct, the description is apt." *Wynneth is delightful when she does her funny giggles at something she finds amusing. The years drop from her, and I remember the younger version who taught me so much.* He frowned to himself. "Apparently we cannot force her to travel further with Drainin. I need another plan." Eduardo moved toward the cage in the corner. As he removed the furry ball from its nest, he spoke to Wynneth again. "Tell Kat I will meet with her in two star turns. I must arrange some things."

"I will. For your information, Drainin constantly attempts to keep Kat from speaking to you." Wynneth squinted. "I wonder if he suspects she may tell you something he wishes to keep from you?"

"A possibility. Use your skills Wynneth. If anyone can discover what Kat is thinking, I believe you are the one."

"I hope you are right. Something is definitely troubling her about Drainin. Since I will be with her later at the evening meal, possibly I may obtain additional news." Wynneth reached out and patted Eduardo's hand. "I will do my best to unravel this mystery." She headed for the door.

As Wynneth took her leave, Blink unfolded her wings, yawned and stretched each leg separately.

Eduardo began composing a note, but paused briefly to stroke the furry head with a finger. He reached into a dish on the desk and offered a treat to the little creature. "You slept a great deal. How is the egg coming?"

Blink gazed up at Eduardo, tilted her head and chirruped a musical note.

The Arrival

He smiled, completed writing on the parchment, blotted and rolled it, and inserted the result into a small tube. "Blink you must find Mouse and deliver this to him." He attached the tube to the foreleg Blink extended.

Once the note was secure, she raised herself, shook out her wings, flapped them twice and in mid-flight disappeared with an audible pop.

***

Later, Mouse slipped through the door into Eduardo's office, who smiled as he caught sight of him. "I gather you confused my poor page again?"

"I did. Keeping my presence concealed from all who reside here is necessary for now. However, you will be pleased to hear Galdin cannot listen to me once I am beyond the borders of Morden. We may speak freely."

"Excellent news. I am aware you are able to use mind-speak with ease, but I always end up with a headache."

"We possess different talents and powers, Eduardo. Incidentally, I believe it would be best if you only refer to me as Mouse. There is always a danger of unseen ears."

"Agreed." Eduardo walked over to Mouse and hugged him. "I am glad you came, as I need your help."

"This is about the woman, correct? Kat, I believe she is named?"

"Yes. She is determined to return to her own world, but I need her because I cannot accomplish anything on my own. Therefore, I made a bargain with her. It is important we discover who is behind many of the challenges occurring among the people of Pridden, so I told her to seek out the problems and perhaps the instigators. I also advised while she did so, she should attempt to locate those who are blessed with sufficient power to help her return home."

Mouse raised his eyebrows at the statement. "I remember you telling me this. A colossal job for one woman. Does she even know what to do?"

"Even I do not know what specifically she should do. Everything I observed about her, and based on what others have told me, I suspect she harbors an instinct which will help us. Big job, yes, but the prophecy exists. However, we have a set-back. A substantial one. I chose Drainin to accompany her, but she developed an antipathy towards him."

"I do not need to read your mind to guess what is coming. You did mention the possibility of me guiding her."

"Mouse, I wanted to protect your position with Galdin, but I now need you to to be her guide. You are the only person on Pridden I trust enough, and who is endowed with enough skills and power to accomplish this."

Mouse sighed. "Not a task I would choose for myself." He crossed his arms. "But this may work out quite well. Galdin wants her to come to Morden to help him defeat you. I already told him how headstrong she is, and she insists she must visit Shendea first. I could keep feeding him information regarding her specific desires about visiting the other lands as well. He will become frustrated." He shrank into himself, bent over and appeared weak and helpless. "He will never suspect small, quaking little Mouse of working against him. He will also believe Kat is in complete command of my movements." He resumed his original stature.

Eduardo laughed at the very thought of anyone truly commanding Mouse. "I would be willing to wager this will work."

"I will embellish the story. I will tell him you requested I accompany her, because you are convinced I am quiet and self-effacing, and will cause Kat no distress."

This time the laughter from Eduardo was loud and long. "You can be most unscrupulous. Perfect."

"I believe this calls for a glass of the Orenberry wine you keep hidden in the bottom drawer of your desk."

Eduardo's eyes widened. "How did you know… ?"

"I did not read your mind, I promise. Wynneth told me many years ago of your little vice."

"Is everyone in your confidence?"

Mouse, suddenly sober. "Just you and Wynneth. We both realize I cannot reveal myself, or our relationship, to any other. We still live in a world which requires we remain secretive."

Eduardo reached into his lower drawer and drew out two glasses and the infamous bottle of Orenberry wine. "We will drink to your cunning and the need for secrets."

Mouse reached over and poured wine into the two glasses and lifted up one. "To brothers."

Eduardo picked up his glass. "To brothers."

They drank.

J. M. Tibbott

CHAPTER 31

On his return journey to Morden, he slipped on the true mantle of Mouse. He changed his character completely, to one of a small man, beset with fears, and nervous of the coming meeting with the Master. He changed all his thoughts to project this agitated creature, knowing full well Galdin had a talent for reading the minds of his minions.

The horse he chose, although smaller than most of those bred by the Baklai, but with the ability to be a swift and tireless animal, ensured his journey would last but two star turns.

Mouse felt the anxious persona settling into his being — the real man, hiding deep within him, far from the scrutiny of any other. Clad in grey, cloaked and hooded, he passed through Kaylin and finally entered the pass through the Clog Blue mountains into Morden, now fully a small grey mouse of a man, apprehensive and jittery.

A half a star turn later he approached the iron gates of Thane Galdin's stronghold. Two guards barred his way at the entrance, so he slipped from his horse and approached them.

The guard on the left sneered. "Oh, its only you, Mouse. About time. The Thane has been asking for you."

The other guard stepped up, smirking when Mouse cringed. "You had better hurry. He wants you in the supplication room immediately." He grinned even wider at Mouse's discomfort. "I suggest you do not keep him waiting."

Oh no, I did hurry. I came as fast as I could, but it

appears the Master is not happy with me. He scurried to leave the horse at the stable, scampered up three flights of stairs, and rushed to the large wooden door at the end of a long passage.

The guard at the entrance to the supplication room held up his pike to stop Mouse. "Wait. I will announce you." He turned, opened the door and spoke to the man inside. "Mouse is here, Sire."

From inside the room, Galdin bellowed. "Send the miscreant in."

Quaking, Mouse sidled into the room, his head lowered.

"Approach." The voice, like hollow tones rising from deep dark caverns of ice, struck terror anew in the quavering heart of the little man.

He moved forward at the Master's command. His heart beat violently in his chest, and though he was always cold in this damp and frigid stronghold, his palms were sweating. He bowed deeply. "Master."

Galdin, seated in a throne-like chair, covered with gold film, hissed at him. "Well? Where is the woman?"

Unable to view those cold hard eyes, Mouse shivered at the words. "She is still in Kaylin, Master. She went on a journey through the land with Counselor Drainin."

"My patience is thin. You should have brought her to me by now." His black eyes bored into Mouse.

The poor wretch shivered. *I am in trouble. The Master holds me responsible for the actions of this stubborn woman.* "Master, I could not approach her as yet. However I can convey some good news."

"About time. What news, you foolish little rat?"

"Lord Eduardo of Kaylin approached me to take the woman to Shendea. I may be able to persuade her to come to Morden instead. It will be difficult, because they say she is headstrong, and claims to possess a friend who haled from Shendea."

"Who would that be?"

"I could not discover the name of her friend. I thought to approach Counselor Drainin, but decided I should consult with you first."

"At least you did one thing right. You are to stay away from Drainin."

A small spark lit up at the farthest region of Mouse's brain.

Galdin growled at him. "Remember, Mouse, I can read your every thought. It is not your place to wonder why I order you to refrain from contacting Drainin. Just know. You are not to speak to him. Under any circumstances."

"Yes, Master." Mouse trembled, icy rivulets ran down his spine, and he lowered his head further, attempting to sink into his own grey robes.

Galdin leaned forward, his left eyebrow raised above a fathomless black eye. "Why did Eduardo request you accompany the woman to Shendea?"

Mouse fidgeted anxiously. "He said because I knew Shendea well enough to guide her, and since I am from Morden, I would be best able to accompany her. He claimed he was convinced I would not cause her distress, nor would I attempt to seduce her."

At these words, the icy voice shattered into splinters of scornful laughter, a sound like fingernails scraping on stone. "You? Seduce her? Eduardo is more discerning than I believed." He pulled a pale hand from beneath his robes and pointed a long black nail at Mouse. "Since the woman is determined to travel to Shendea, you are to concentrate your efforts on keeping the visit brief. Bring her to me and I might let you live, you little weasel."

Mouse cringed further unto his grey robes. He remembered the pain those nails were able to produce if they touched him. He kept his mind blank, avoiding thinking of anything which might be misconstrued.

"Come here."

Mouse shuddered at the command, but moved slowly forward, waiting for a blow.

Galdin thrust a small bag at him. "In here are five messenger moths. You will release one with a report every few star turns. They have been enchanted to return to my quarters, and you will keep me informed of your progress."

Mouse darted out a hand and grabbed the bag, taking care not to touch his Master. "I will, Sire."

Galdin rose from his throne and moved toward his quaking servant. "Do not let me down. You know well what I can do to those who cross me."

Mouse bent almost double to avoid the painful touch. Waiting. Terrorized.

When no blow came, he peeked up, and caught the swirling black of the Master's robes as he swept from the room.

I must must do my best to persuade the woman to come to Morden. Quickly.

CHAPTER 32

As Kat approached Eduardo's quarters, the young man in the corridor pulled open the door, leaned in, and spoke to someone inside.

He withdrew his head and smiled at her. "Lord Eduardo is expecting you."

"Thank you, um… " *What was his name again? Ah yes.* "… Dafid."

He bowed his head and held the door for her.

Eduardo, seated behind his large wooden desk, rose as Kat entered the room. He gestured toward a small table with two chairs. "I requested tea for us, and those chairs are far more comfortable."

He's trying to be less formal. Well, maybe he's not extremely angry with me. She took the offered seat. "Thank you Eduardo."

He poured their tea.

From the faint scent curling up from her cup, Kat recognized the pot contained the relaxing blend. "You people in Kaylin really like your teas. Don't you consume other drinks?"

Eduardo raised an eyebrow. "I never thought about this. We do use other beverages, but we enjoy many types of teas, so we rarely drink anything else. We keep teas to help us sleep, to keep us calm during challenging negotiations, to give us energy, plus others, which possess further beneficial ways to ease us through our days. Many of these originated with the Shendean healers, and since their land is beside ours, their drinks are familiar to Kaylins."

"You're right about the variety. I like a lot of them. And some are... well... they're necessary." *Especially Karri-san when Rifellans are around.*

Eduardo changed the subject abruptly. "Kat, I would like you to tell me everything about how you arrived in Kaylin."

"Why? I thought you knew most of my story."

"I am aware generally of how you came to be here, but I need to understand everything. I asked you to perform tasks for me, and I gave you my word I would do all in my power to return you to your world." He spread his arms. "To accomplish this, I need as much information as possible."

Kat recounted the storm she became caught in, and how she sought refuge in the old stone fort. "The last thing I remember is reaching for the handle of an ornate door. Everything whirled around me and I seemed to be pulled into the next room, and pushed from behind at the same time. At that point, everything went blank." She rubbed her forehead. "The next thing, I woke up in a strange bed, with Wynneth leaning over me. I still don't sense what actually happened."

Eduardo massaged his chin, apparently deep in thought. "I am convinced, whether accidental or with purpose, much power brought you to Kaylin. However, I suspect you may need a greater power to return to your world."

"What does this mean?"

"I already said your task will be to discover why people are developing such unusual enmity with each other. I believe you are able to sense things about people which lie beneath the surface. These problems are occurring all over Pridden, in every land. If not checked, we are in danger of war between the lands. Our entire world could revert to the violent and tragic dark ages legends say once existed. To return to black savagery is unthinkable."

Kat leaned forward. "Is this another one of those prophecies I keep hearing about?"

"What do you mean?"

"Well, I needed to leave Meenyat quickly to avoid being imprisoned because of a foretelling by a god or goddess. Plus, most people I meet are aware I am from another world, and they accept I am here because of some sort of prophecy." She raised her eyebrows. "You all appear to be quite superstitious."

"The prophecy is not about war. Most of our leaders can access the history of their lands. These stories tell of a time of infamy, and of how suspicion and fear among the people, led to violent battles which decimated much of the population. Most of our leaders fear this could be a repetition of those times."

"Oh." *Sounds a lot like periods of Earth's history.*

Eduardo rose and paced around his office. "This is why I asked you to visit each land and determine the cause of the unrest. Plus you will be meeting many people who possess certain powers. It is the combination of these powers I suspect will eventually be able to return you to your home."

She sighed. "I want to so desperately. Kaylin is fine, but I miss my own life more each day." Kat hesitated and held up her hands. "But wait, why should we need so many people with power to return me home? It's obvious to me if there'd been lots of people involved, instead of only one or perhaps two, everyone would grasp what happened, and would mention this to me. You're the only one who appears to think a power from your world brought me here. So why can't you use the same person to return me?"

"I have no idea who the person or persons are."

Kat grimaced and then raised an eyebrow at him. "If you don't know, how am I going to find the people who hold the power to help me?"

"I am convinced you will meet them by the time you leave each land and head to the next."

"Oh come on, Eduardo. How the hell am I going to figure out who has power and who doesn't?"

He smiled. "You are certainly not shy about asking questions, no matter how disrespectful. Plus, the Master Metalsmith gave you a token, did he not?"

Kat drew in a startled breath, and clutched at the pendant through her clothes. "What do you mean?" *Did Irina tell him?*

Eduardo chuckled. "I asked him to give you something to help you. And by your reaction, he acceded to my request."

"He did. Do you think Liandock might be one of people of power to help me when the time comes for my return home?"

"I doubt he can be of help. His talents and powers lie with metals and gems alone."

Oh yeah? He controls more talents than you realize. "Fine." She frowned to cover up the rush of heat to her face.

"Kat, I agreed to help you get to your home." Eduardo paused a moment. "Therefore, you must, in turn, find those whose abilities can help you, while you perform the task I asked of you." He held up his hand to forestall her objection. "Once you leave each land, you will send me, by pyrock, the names of those who agree to aid you. When I feel we have a sufficient number, I will gather them all together, and we will attempt to accomplish your return."

Kat perked up at his words. "By pyrock you said?"

"Yes, which brings me to another item." He walked to the cage in the corner. "The egg is beginning to harden, and I wish you to come to my rooms for the next two star-turns to bond with your pyrock-to-be. Even if I'm not here, come in and touch the egg. I will tell Dafid to expect you." He beckoned her over. "Come." He removed the small furry creature and cupped the round soft little pyrock in his hand. "Reach into the cage and touch it."

Kat did so. The egg was warm, and as she put her hand on it, the pale cream object vibrated, and Kat experienced a flash of intelligence, probing at her mind. She smiled. *She likes me, and she knows me. How amazing.* She sighed with pleasure. *Wait. Weird. How do I know she's a she?*

As Kat removed her hand from the cage, Eduardo replaced his small furry bundle on top of the egg.

"You felt a connection?"

"I did. How wonderful."

"If I am not here, please be very careful not to touch Blink when you reach in the cage. Just request she move aside to let you handle the egg."

"She'll understand?"

"She does, and she has no wish to be handled by any other than me."

"I'll be careful."

"Excellent. When the egg hatches, I will bring you here, and you can imprint on the new pyrock."

Grinning lopsidedly, Kat thanked Eduardo and left his office.

How wonderful. She smiled with pleasure. *This isn't home, but I've got a pendant with a stone which speaks to me, a lion and a bear who want to protect me, and I'll also have a cute little fuzzy pyrock.*

J. M. Tibbott

CHAPTER 33

At the knock on the massive door, Galdin raised his head from his ruminations. "Enter."

A thin, tall man appeared at the edge of the door and slipped into the room. The hood of his long black robe, thrown back, revealed a bizarrely smooth pate. His face, so pale in color, as to be almost white, displayed not a single visible hair. Bereft of eyebrows or lashes, his skin, free of any blemish, stretched taut over his jawline. His eyes, sunk deep in their sockets, and his expressionless face hinted of danger and of hidden evil.

He strode toward the throne and dropped his head in the bow of equals. "Sire, you asked for me."

Galdin stepped down and the two men clasped arms. "Ssarff, I require your expertise."

The man, his face stripped of all emotion, gazed at Galdin from dark ochre eyes, with a vertical slit of gold. An ancient memory of serpents reminded all who viewed him as one who trafficked with the long slithering dangerous creatures of Morden. Other than Galdin, he was the most feared man in the land. "The Assassin's Guild are always more than willing to aid the Thane of Morden."

Galdin nodded, revealing no emotion by making sure his own face remained concealed in the shadow of his hood. *This man is dangerous and powerful, but when well managed, makes a fine ally.* "You no doubt heard of the woman who appeared in Kaylin recently?"

"Yes." Ssarff's speech was rife with sibilance. "Is she the one spoken of by the prophecy?"

"I am convinced she is, and I want her in my presence." He turned away from Ssarff and paced the room. "Once she is here, I can easily manipulate her to bring Eduardo to me. His power, which lies in his heart, must be mine. When I combine his power with my own, Pridden will once again be united and ruled by a Morden male. The prophecy foretells this."

"A considerable ambition."

Galdin whirled toward Ssarff. "And your Guild will own even greater power than ever. I value all you have done, and will continue to do so. No longer will you need to keep to the shadows. Instead your names will be spoken across this world with awe. You will be allowed complete freedom to operate in my name." *But I will never allow you greater power than I possess. I can deal with you, my ambitious viper.*

The thin man's mouth curled in a faint grin. "The thought is pleasing. What do you wish from me?"

"I want you bring her to me directly."

"Have you not already dispatched a servant to do this?"

"What makes you think so?"

Ssarff repeated his grotesque grin. "My followers are everywhere, Sire. We saw the small man summoned here, who then left hastily, obtained a fast horse, and took off in the direction of Kaylin. A natural assumption."

"I forget you enjoy the use of eyes and ears everywhere."

"I gather Sire, you boast no faith in your servant."

Galdin shook his head. "Oh, he will succeed eventually. However, I cannot count on him to achieve what I want in a timely manner. His cowardice and personal fears will always result in a lengthy conclusion to any assignment. I want the woman now, which is why I ask for your help." *Curse Ssarff. I must tread cautiously with him and his guild. I find their minds clouded and I am never sure of their intentions. Their ways in dispatching their enemies are subtle and always unexpected. The Guild must always be watched. Carefully.*

"In what way do you wish me to help?"

"You will not need to work without aid. I own the loyalty of a man deep within the Lord's keep in Kaylin. He knows the woman well, and is trusted by Eduardo."

"Will he be able to separate the woman from others within the keep?"

"Most assuredly. His advice by messenger is the woman is much taken with him. She will gladly do what he asks. He always possessed an ability to please females."

Ssarff appeared puzzled. "Why then would he not request she come to Morden with him now?"

"A question I put to him." Galdin sighed. "Before they met, she had made her decision to visit Shendea, and this is delaying my plans. Apparently she is headstrong to a fault, and even my ally cannot change her mind. He needs help from your guild to bring her to Morden without first heading to Shendea."

"Do you, Sire, have complete faith in his ability?"

"I do. He has long kept me advised of the inner workings of Eduardo's keep, and he immediately notified me when the woman arrived in Kaylin. It will ultimately prove most fortunate she is attracted to him."

"If this is the situation, I accept the assignment. I will meet with my followers and formulate a plan. I will send only seven guild members. Too many Mordens arriving in Kaylin could cause unnecessary speculation and suspicion."

Galdin eyed Ssarff, and nodded. "The usual payment?"

"For what appears to be a fairly simple assignment, the usual will be sufficient." He furrowed his hairless brow. "But if there are challenges, the price will increase. Understood?"

Galdin extended his arm, his palm facing toward the other man. "Yes. Agreed." *Thank Ssayleese, I do not need to make further physical contact with him.*

Ssarff mirrored Galdin's gesture. He too appeared to be reluctant to touch Galdin again. "So agreed."

The two men briefly bowed their heads to each other, and as Galdin returned to his throne, Ssarff strode toward the door of the hall.

At the last moment he turned back. "Oh, yes. How do I contact your ally?

Galdin curled his lip in a faint grin. "That will be easy. He is Eduardo's Counselor. His name is Drainin."

CHAPTER 34

Kat sat at the small table near the window in her rooms. *It's been two days since I met with Eduardo. I wonder what progress he's made.*

Well sated from her breakfast and drinking her daily Karri-san tea, she attempted to plan her morning. *This is so annoying, I can't organize my usual day. I own no computer, no phone, nothing electronic. My brain is going to atrophy from lack of use.* She straightened in her chair. "Atrophy." She spoke aloud. *What a wonderful word. I haven't been using excellent words in sentences for a while. I gotta keep my brain fed. But I don't have my daily computer reminder.* She pursed her lips in frustration. *Damn, what to do.*

She rose from her seat and strolled to the window. The shutters stood open, as the weather was not yet cold enough to close them at night. She leaned out over the ledge and inhaled a deep breath. The slightly crisp air flooded her lungs, bringing new clarity. As she returned to her seat, she passed the collection of sheets detailing the ideas for her next game. Most were tucked into the leather shoulder bag she purchased in Trigoran. The beautifully crafted item had attracted her attention because it reminded her of diplomatic courier bags. Plus the pouch was the perfect size to hold her sheets, her cathnog pen and a sufficient supply of Kaylin ink.

"Perfect. I'll keep a journal of words." *Oh boy, I'm talking to myself. Again. I'm losing my marbles.* The bag held everything. The three sections in the center portion contained her game notes and blank parchment. *My word list can go in the middle section too..*

Kat grabbed a blank sheet, hurried back to her seat and began the list. At the top of the sheet she wrote a title of 'Words', and on the line below, her first word—atrophy. She wrote a second word—egress, and grinned to herself. *Rad. I found a mechanical solution. Once I obtain a plethora of words, I won't miss the computer as much. Hah. I love remembering good words.* She hurriedly wrote plethora on her list.

A knock at the adjoining door leading to Wynneth's quarters disturbed further contemplation.

Kat raised her eyes toward the entrance. "Wynneth, come in."

The door opened enough for the healer's smiling face to appear. "Greetings, Lady Kat. I trust you are well today."

"Thank you, Wynneth. I'm well." *Odd. Despite the smile, she looks concerned, and she's more formal than usual. Is she still wondering about Drainin?* "What can I do for you?"

"I am here because Eduardo would like to meet with you in his office."

"Ooh, the pyrock's hatched?"

"I am not sure, but he does need to discuss a number of items with you, and asked me to send you to him."

"Fine. I'll go now." Kat placed her new list in the pouch and closed the top on the ink. She turned to ask Wynneth what Eduardo wanted to discuss, but the healer had already retreated to her own quarters. Kat shrugged and headed for her meeting.

***

Dafid greeted her as she approached Eduardo's quarters. "Good morrow, Lady Kat. Lord Eduardo is expecting you." He pushed on the sturdy door and ushered her in.

The Arrival

Eduardo looked up as she entered, rose from behind his desk, and strode over and took her hand. "You will be happy to learn Blink's egg is now hatched. The new pyrock is ready to greet you." He led her to the cage in the corner.

"Oh, she's beautiful." Kat beamed at the miniature animal. *I'm sure I'm grinning like a fool again. Why do little-baby-furry-things make such asses of us all?* "She's so tiny. Can I touch her?" *I'm still wondering how I know she's a she?*

"Of course, but let me move Blink out of the way, so you do not touch her accidentally." He reached in and scooped up the bigger furry ball. Blink opened her eyes and yawned.

Kat reached into the cage and with one finger carefully stroked the miniature version of Blink. The little creature woke and stretched. The mother, when fully extended, measured about eight inches in length, but her progeny barely reached four. She butted her small head against Kat's finger and emitted a squeaky purr. Kat felt a connection in her mind, and she figured the pyrock was attempting to communicate. She beamed up at Eduardo. "See? She's winking at me." She addressed the fuzzy beast. "I'm going to call you Wink." At her words, Wink squeaked once more and her parent chirped. *Is she agreeing with me?*

Eduardo, a wry smile on his face, replaced Blink in her cage, taking care not to touch Wink. "I believe they both advised you the name is appropriate."

He closed the cage and moved back to his desk, indicating Kat should be seated. "Your Wink can be transferred to you in a couple of star turns. By then Blink will no longer be feeding her."

Kat could only grin at him in reply. *My own pyrock. How rad is that?*

"Kat, I gather you are pleased with the idea of a pyrock, but we need to discuss your forthcoming travels."

Suddenly sober, Kat waited for more.

Eduardo leaned toward her. "Wynneth informed me you refuse to travel with Counselor Drainin. Why?"

"I do not like or trust the man. I find him arrogant, condescending and annoying."

"Are you talking about something specific?"

Damn, doesn't he listen? "Isn't what I've said enough? I will not travel with him. Can't you accept this?"

Eduardo sighed and rubbed his forehead. "I never intended for you to travel outside of Kaylin with Drainin. I merely would like knowledge if he has been inappropriate in any way. He is, after all, my Counselor. He has been a valuable ally, and never indicated any failings in character to me before."

He would defend him. But I don't think it would help Eduardo by telling him about Drainin's actions toward me. Kat clenched her jaw stubbornly. *Unfortunately, I don't trust Eduardo enough to tell him the complete truth about my stone.* "As far as I'm concerned, nothing is left to say."

Eduardo and Kat sat eyeing each other, the silence stretching to infinity.

The old saying is, the first one to speak loses, but if I don't ask... "So who is going to be my guide to Shendea?"

"I am still investigating who should accompany you. In the meantime, we need to make preparations. I assume you can ride a horse?"

"Yes."

"Your travels in Kaylin took a lengthy time. Pontis, which are surefooted, do not possess speed. You will travel most of the time on horseback, although once you head

The Arrival

to Lord Rhognor's stronghold, you will need to ride on a ponti, as the roads to his residence are treacherous. Ponti's are the only creatures who possess capable stability in the high mountains."

"I assume you will make arrangements for a horse for me, but what do I need to do as part of this planning?"

"Wynneth will help you with proper clothing requirements, and she will also ensure you are able to communicate via a pyrock."

"What do you mean?"

"The healer mentioned when you put words on paper, they resemble runes. Few individuals on Pridden are able to interpret runes, so she will give you some lessons in our letters so you can be assured the messages you send can be read."

"Oh." *This is so weird they can't read my writing. Why? It's not like they speak a different language.*

Eduardo rose from his seat. "I will send for you when Wink is ready to leave her parent. You should request young Bannon to supply you with two cages — one for your quarters, and a small one for traveling. He will also give you sufficient nuts with which to feed your new companion. The primary way to care for Wink is to keep her warm and well fed."

Realizing she had been dismissed, Kat rose. "Thank you Eduardo, I will do as you suggest." *I don't believe it. I'm copying the way they speak. Get real, Kat.*

***

As she approached her room, she caught Mayda exiting Wynneth's quarters. "Mayda, is the Healer in her rooms?"

"Not now, Lady Kat. She is attending a birthing." Mayda displayed excitement at the prospect of a new resident of

Kaylin. "I will tell her when she returns you wish to meet with her."

"Fine, I would appreciate you giving her the message." Kat opened her own door, and stopped. "Oh, one more thing, How I can find Bannon?"

"I am taking some additional supplies to Healer Wynneth, and I will be passing his lodgings." Mayda's face turned a bright pink. "I can give him a message if you wish?"

Hmm she blushed. Does she like him? "Perfect. Would you ask him to come to me?" *Oops, nearly forgot.* "Please?"

"I will, Lady Kat."

Kat sighed as she entered her room. *She can't help herself. She's gone all formal again.*

***

After lunch, Wynneth knocked at the adjoining door and poked her head in the room. "Greetings, Kat. You sought me?"

Terrific, she's her usual ebullient self. "Wynneth, thanks for coming. It appears I need your help." *Oh, I must remember to write down ebullient after she leaves.*

Wynneth raised her brows in a query.

"My pyrock hatched, and her name is Wink. She's adorable and I'm impatient for her to be with me full time. But Eduardo says I must get lessons in writing messages when I send her on a task. He says no one can read my runes."

Wynneth laughed. "You can take a breath. I would guess you are excited about the pyrock."

"I can hardly wait to show her to you. She's adorable."

"Calm yourself, and gather your writing materials. I will get some more from my rooms."

Kat grabbed her cathnog pen, some ink and a number of sheets of parchment, and as she seated herself at her table,

The Arrival

Wynneth returned with additional parchment and a pen of her own. She moved a chair to sit beside Kat.

"If we're side by side, you can better observe how I form the letters, and you will find copying them to be easier."

"Fine."

Wynneth put a blank sheet in front of them and dipping her pen in the ink, wrote three odd squiggles. "This means 'mission is accomplished'. Please copy this on your paper."

Kat dipped her pen, and copied the lines as exactly as possible. "Is this correct?"

"Perfect."

Kat added a dash beside the lines and she wrote, 'mission is accomplished' in english.

"What did you write?" Wynneth's face wrinkled in apparent puzzlement.

"I explained to myself what these lines mean."

"Excellent, Kat. Clever. You are most logical."

Wynneth continued the lesson, giving Kat five more phrases for her to copy, which she managed easily. "You are blessed with a keen eye for things. But we will stop now, and continue on the morrow. I cannot believe overwhelming you with too much at once makes any sense"

I'll file my Kaylin writing with my own list of words. "Thank you, I agree. I'll remember those better if I learn a few at a time."

As Wynneth gathered up her own materials and returned to her quarters, a soft knock sounded at Kat's door.

"Come."

Bannon peered around the edge of the door. "Lady Kat, you asked for me?"

She motioned him to enter. "Yes, Bannon. Eduardo…" Bannon winced at her informality, "… suggested I request you prepare me two cages for my new pyrock. I will need one for my quarters here, and a smaller traveling one. Can you do this for me?"

"Most certainly, Lady Kat. I will make the one for your quarters so that it can be folded. That way you can pack the larger one to use when you stay in one place for a number of star turns. I can bring both to you on the morrow after the midday meal. Will it be time enough?"

"Excellent." She smiled at him. "Thank you, Bannon."

He blushed, dipped his head and slipped out of her quarters without another word.

What an odd young man. He's cute, and shy. I wonder if he is married or whatever they call marriage here? Mayda blushed when I mentioned his name. He would be perfect for her, I think. Kat laughed. *I bet I would make an excellent matchmaker in Kaylin.*

CHAPTER 35

Two mornings later, Dafid knocked and stuck his head in Eduardo's door. "Sire, You have a visitor. Someone called… er… Mouse?"

"Thank you, Dafid. Send him in."

Mouse strode into the room, his demeanor more forceful than the timorous creature who crept out of Morden. "Good morrow, Lord Eduardo."

The door closed and Eduardo stepped forward and clasped arms with Mouse. "You obviously told Galdin I requested your help?"

"Yes, and he is convinced I will be able to persuade your visitor to come directly to Morden, rather than traveling to Shendea first." Mouse smirked. "What he is not aware of, is your Kat is going to prove so difficult, I will be unable to persuade her to change her plans."

"You believe you are joking, but Kat is far more stubborn than you realize. Even if you tried to, I doubt you would be able to change her mind. Plus, for some reason, she developed a strong dislike to my Counselor, who is from Morden. I suspect this will delay her travel to Morden until all the other lands have been visited." He gestured toward the table to the right of the desk. "I ordered Orenberry wine and food is waiting for you.

The two men sat and Mouse poured the wine. "Your Counselor is Drainin?"

Eduardo nodded.

"I have never met the man. I prefer to remain in the shadows when I am in Kaylin. Tell me about him."

"Why do you ask?"

"Only because Galdin made a strong command I avoid him and refrain from contacting him under pain of my death."

"Odd. I wonder why?"

"I do not know. Perhaps because he fears the man is too close to you."

"Perhaps. But to answer your question, Drainin does own the arrogance of a Morden, but his council to me is always solid. But unlike many Mordens, he is on excellent terms with my Horse-Master who is from Baklai. He can be kind and helpful when needed. He is loyal, clever, and knows the ways of the streets, but fancies himself as a man whom women desire. Kaylin must be frustrating for him, because the women here do not dally before mating. I am sure various women from other lands are available for him to enjoy on a regular basis. Apparently, Kat refers to him as a 'horn dog'."

Mouse burst out laughing. "What an interesting expression. Your Kat is blessed with a sense of humor."

"Perhaps, although she rarely demonstrates this in my company. We tend to act more like two hydodds battling for territory. Thank Caleesh she is not a hydodd, her horns would be vicious."

"Do you fear her?"

If only it were fear, that I could handle. But she possesses a strength unknown to me in women. "Of course not. It's more like a sense of deep disquiet. I find her company wearisome for a lengthy period. She is strong-minded, and wishes to control everything in her vicinity. She is also curious to a fault. She needs to have a grasp of why things work the way they do, and will not rest until she gets her way. She blunders

The Arrival

through relationships with the Kaylins, and manages to create additional challenges daily." Eduardo sighed. "I do not envy you. What I am about to ask of you will try you more than any battle you ever fought."

Mouse raised an eyebrow. "I am conscious of the fact you wish me to guide her in Shendea. What more are you asking?"

Eduardo sighed again. "Considerably more. It is imperative she travels to all the lands, and hopefully can unearth the challenges facing Pridden. You are the only one I can think of who can accompany her without losing control." He leaned on the table and rubbed his jaw. "Or your sanity."

"Eduardo, your own sanity may be in danger. If she is this much trouble how can she ever be of help in discovering the causes of the unrest?"

Eduardo sat back in his chair. "Ah, now that is what is so interesting. If you own a container of straw, and you drop a small bead in, you cannot find such a tiny item if you simply scan over the surface. You will need to shake the container for the bead to eventually appear."

Mouse nodded.

"Kat is like the person who shakes the box. She achieves this unwittingly, but most effectively. I received reports from the towns and villages she visited in Kaylin, and her very presence resulted in many shakings. She is able to learn, but she is also a prime manipulator." Eduardo grinned. *A brilliant manipulator.* "Buried somewhere in her psyche is a sympathy for the down-trodden. As a result she managed to change the views of a number of our people. I was surprised, but gratified by this."

"It sounds like you are trying to tame a hissar. A painful and precarious undertaking."

Eduardo smiled at Mouse. "She often does resemble the nasty-tempered illogical and fierce animal. You cannot control hissars, and neither can you control Kat. However, it will be you who will do the majority of the taming." He paused. "Through the next five lands."

Mouse rose from the table and paced the room. "I do not like the sound of this."

"And I do not blame you. But if we are to save Pridden, this must be done. The absolute truth is, no one else possesses the ability to handle her, but you."

"How is she is going to agree to this?"

"Her agreement already exists. Her strongest desire is to return to her own world. She constantly battles me about this. I told her she would need at least one person from each land to work together to send her home. Although I did not tell her I am aware of how she came to be here, I do believe I am correct in assuming at least six persons of power will be needed to return her."

"I suspect you are correct." Mouse reached over to the wine and poured another cup for himself. "You ask an enormous and difficult task of me." He drank and glanced over at Eduardo. "I would not do this for anyone but you."

"I know. This is not something I request lightly. You will encounter difficulty with both Kat, and the circumstances. But you are the only one who can succeed in the undertaking. I dearly wish there were another way."

Mouse stood, moved toward Eduardo and placed a hand on his shoulder. "I understand. You could help if you would supply me with a set of rooms, as I will need to make plans. And shortly you will introduce me to your hissar." He squeezed Eduardo's shoulder. "I agree to this."

Eduardo reached up and grasped Mouse's hand. "Thank you, brother."

J. M. Tibbott

CHAPTER 36

Kat leaned out the window watching the herd of wullawerths munching grass in one of the nearer pastures. Two young ones leaped around the older ones, butting into trees and falling over their feet. *They're quite adorable, gamboling about like idiots. All small animals are sweet.* Kat chuckled. *Hey, I used a great word. Gambol.* She turned back to her desk, grabbed her pen and the list of words, and added the latest idea at the bottom. *This list is working well with more than twenty words now, many of which I haven't used yet.*

A knock distracted her. "Come"

The door opened and Brith peered in. "I come bearing clothes. Can we enter?"

"Absolutely. What are you bringing me?"

Brith and two other young seamstresses entered, each carrying a pile of clothes. As they laid the bundles of clothing on the bed. Kat examined the various blouses, skirts, warm winter coats, and one beautiful formal outfit. "This is like Christmas. I love it."

Brith, who had excused her two helpers, appeared puzzled. "What is krissmus?"

Oops, here we go again. "Christmas is a holiday many people on my world celebrate." Kat picked up the gaucho pants and removed her skirt to try them on. She swung around to face Brith. "This is perfect. I can easily ride a horse without exposing anything the Horse-Master might find offensive." She twirled round, admiring herself in the mirror. "The material is tough but extremely comfortable. I love this blue color." *The blue reminds me of stonewashed jeans.*

"I understand why you suggested this type of skirt, Lady Kat. There is much less material involved, and I surmise why you will find riding easier."

Kat hesitated, moving from one foot to the other. *This is going to be awkward.* "Uh, Brith. I love the clothes and I appreciate the wonderful work you accomplished." Kat felt her face heating. "Umm... Would you mind leaving?"

"What?" Brith's face crumpled in a hurt expression.

Oh crap. "I do want you here, but I'm dying to try on the leather pants and skirt, and I promised you I would not wear them around anyone in Kaylin."

The sun came out from behind the clouds in Brith's eyes. She beamed mischievously. "But I am not just anyone. I am your designer, and I want to observe how well they suit you." She had obviously noticed Kat's frown. "Please?"

No second urging was needed. Kat hurriedly took off the rest of her outer clothes and slid into the garments. They were supple and soft, barely whispered as they glided over her body, and enveloped her in the delicious aroma of well tanned leather.

Brith released the breath she had been holding with a long sigh of appreciation. "You look... well, glorious. You resemble a Rifellan warrior. Many of those who live near the mountains boast brilliant red hair. In the leather outfit, Kat, you could be Rifellan royalty."

"Some Rifellans are red headed? The only ones I have seen here, sport locks of either a deep gold, or the palest yellow — almost white."

"True, because red-headed Rifellans rarely leave their homeland. They all believe those with red hair descend from royalty." A mischievous grin lit Brith's face. "If you visit Rifella, you would be very, very well treated." Brith stood back and eyed Kat up and down. "I do believe I did an excellent job on your clothes."

The Arrival

"You did. Thank you." Kat began disrobing once again. "Now, I must put the split skirt on to visit Horse-Master Haydar. Hopefully, he'll let me ride. But if I show up in the leather outfit, I'll probably destroy all his sensibilities. He might even experience a heart attack." Kat chuckled, imagining the possible expressions he might display.

"Why would your leather outfit attack his heart?"

Sigh. "It's only an expression, meaning he might be completely thrown into disarray."

"I do not think he would. Horse-Master Haydar is a strong minded man."

Double sigh. "You're no doubt correct. You're better acquainted with him than I am."

"I am sure he will appreciate your new skirt." She moved toward the door. "I must leave, as I need to complete three outfits before my evening meal. I am behind in my work." As she started to slip through the door, she turned back. "I shall see you on the morrow, Lady Kat. Please be sure to inform me of Master Haydar's reaction to your new skirt."

Before Kat could agree, Brith left.

***

She walked briskly to the stables, happy her outfit felt lighter and easier to walk in. She was positive Haydar would approve of the new skirt, and would forgive her for the past. She hummed to herself anticipating him allowing her to ride a horse. Finally. The grass along the way, although mostly green displayed brown at the tips of the blades, and a new chill lingered in the air. *I'm glad I wore this light jacket. I think we are heading toward Kaylin winter. I wonder if it snows here? I suspect snow does fall in Shendea, because Brith has supplied me with two coats, one of which is leather and lined in fur. How decadent.* For a moment, she imagined meeting Liandock wearing only the coat with nothing beneath it. Just the thought made her feel warm.

As she approached the paddock closest to the house, Kat spied Haydar working a horse in the ring attached to a building. Other horses watched curiously as Haydar took the animal through a series of turns, starts and stops. *Wow. He's amazing with these huge beasts.*

As she approached, Haydar ceased the training and stared at her. "What are you doing here?" His face contorted in anger. "You are not welcome."

"Horse-Master Haydar." *Remember Kat. He's a stickler for formality.* "I am here to apologize." She pulled at the skirt to show the split, which allowed her to ride modestly. "I can ride with this outfit comfortably, and I will not show off any limbs."

Kat waited.

Haydar's face did not change expression. "Do you honestly think I am fool enough to believe you have changed?"

"But... " *What is his problem?* "Master Haydar, I am truly sorry I accidentally flouted your laws. I was not aware of the expectations of the people of Kaylin. I made a mistake because I didn't know your customs."

"That is no excuse. You should make sure you understand us, before you insult us."

"You are being unfair."

"Unfair? You acted like a harlot. I objected. What is unfair about that?"

"But I didn't know." *He's more than a dumb-ass. How can I persuade him to let me ride?*

"Kat." He spat her name out. "I cannot in all good consciousness call you Lady. You do not deserve the honorific. I said it before. I will not allow you ride any of my horses."

The bastard. The insolent dork. I can't believe it. Who the crap does he think he is? "You are an ill-mannered, insulting excuse

The Arrival

for a man. How dare you be so discourteous?" Kat lost all control, shaking with fury as adrenaline flooded her body. "You possess no manners, and you are a prejudiced runt of a man, who isn't fit to hold the bridle of any horse I ride."

By this time, Haydar's countenance paled. The tip of his nose was white with anger and his black eye's blazed in fury. "You… brazen, vile woman. May Morshag curse you and all your offspring." He jumped down from the horse, and grabbed a crop from the rail. He rushed at her, swinging the switch. "Leave my property. Now."

Unable to fend off blows from a whip, Kat backed away. "You will pay for this, you foul creature. Mark my words well. You will definitely pay."

Haydar raised the crop at her again, but Kat stepped forward and despite the sting, grabbed the switch in his hand, wrenching it from his grasp. She threw it, hitting him in the chest. "Bastard." She spat at his feet.

Before he could react, Kat spun around and stalked back to the keep.

J. M. Tibbott

CHAPTER 37

Kat, hot, tired and furious, stomped her way through the keep to her room. *I can't believe this. I apologized to him. He not only rejected the apology, he cursed me. The bastard.*

She yanked open her door and slammed it so hard, the entire keep gave the impression of shaking.

She paced the room when a knock sounded at the connecting door to Wynneth's quarters. "Come in, Wynneth."

The healer peered around the entrance, her eyes rounded in apprehension. "What is wrong, Kat?"

"I'm so angry I could spit blood."

Wynneth's eyes widened further. "I will order some relaxing tea, and we can sit down and discuss this calmly." She tugged at the tassel for Laylin. "Sit, Kat. Breathe. In… and out."

Laylin appeared and Wynneth ordered.

Kat strode to the table and plopped herself with a thud in a chair.

"I said breathe, Kat. Breathe."

Kat, elbows on the table, held her head in her hands. She closed her eyes and breathed in deeply four times, and out four times. She gazed up at Wynneth. "You're right, I am relaxing a bit."

A tap at the door, and Laylin brought a tray with tea and cookies and placed them on the table. She left silently.

Wynneth poured two cups and handed one to Kat. "Before we begin our discussion, drink this — slowly."

Kat sipped the tea, and without thought, reached for her favorite cookies. She ate three without being aware of putting them in her mouth. *This tea works. I'm exhausted from the fight and the dash back to the keep.* She glanced over at Wynneth. "I went to see Haydar."

"Ah." Wynneth's eyebrows scampered up to her hairline. "I thought you might wait for someone to help you with him. Did you apologize to him?"

"I tried to."

"Please, Kat, tell me what happened. Your monosyllabic replies do not give me much information."

"I know." She held up her hand to ward off further questions. *I need to be calmer before I can explain.* "Wait, please."

Wynneth waited in silence.

"Okay." Kat rubbed her forehead. *The beginnings of a headache. Just great.* "I put on the new skirt Brith made for me and walked to the stables to apologize to Haydar. I wanted to show him I solved the riding problem, and would not expose any limbs for him to stress over."

Wynneth waited. Again. "And?"

"He was training a horse when I arrived, but when I walked up to the paddock, he yelled at me to leave before he gave me the chance to explain." Kat took another deep breath. "I apologized for upsetting him, and showed him the new skirt would not expose any part of me a Kaylin might find offensive." She shook her head. "This was not easy for me, Wynneth, because I always felt he over reacted. And I can't think of anything I did this time, over which he might be displeased. But I need to ride horses, so I told him what I thought he wanted to hear."

"Then what?"

"He refused to believe me and even when I explained I had no knowledge of Kaylin customs, he insisted I should have researched before I approached him."

"Oh dear."

"Oh dear is right. After I told him he was being unfair, he lashed out again and called me a foul name. He then refused to address me as Lady Kat, and things went downhill from there."

"What do you mean by downhill?"

"Well, he insulted me further, and the name-calling escalated from both of us. Finally he jumped down from his horse and came after me with a whip. After cursing me? I had no way of defending myself — other than using my fists, which I decided would not work well for me at the time."

Wynneth sighed heavily. "What else did you do?"

"I snatched the whip from him, threatened him, and came back to the keep."

"This is not pleasant."

Kat glared at Wynneth. "I'm well aware of this fact. However, I need to be able to ride a horse, and the irksome little moron is standing in my way. I won't put up with this, Wynneth. I won't."

"Someone will need to intercede on your behalf. Perhaps we should obtain help from Drainin to…."

Kat interrupted and hissed at Wynneth. "I told you before, I will not deal with Drainin. Your suggestion cannot be considered."

"Please do not do anything foolish."

"Foolish? I must obtain a horse. Not in the future but now." Kat clenched her chin. "I'll have to take this situation into my own hands. I must solve this. If Haydar won't give me a horse, I shall take one."

Wynneth's mouth dropped open. "No, Kat. You cannot. Stealing a horse is a terrible offense, and carries the death penalty in all six lands of Pridden. Do not do this."

I don't want her warning anyone of my plans, I should pretend to back down. "Wynneth I don't intend to steal anything. I require a horse, so I will find someone who can help me. Perhaps procure a horse from Haydar and then turn it over to me." She cocked her head. "Yes. Finding someone else to help would work. And doing this is not stealing is it?

"Correct. If someone else requests a horse, and Haydar gives it to him or her, and if he afterwards discovers you are using the horse, he will become furious, but no stealing involved."

Perfect. She swallowed my suggestion. "By the way, why does stealing a horse carry such a bizarre punishment?"

"All horses are imported from Baklai, and are trained by the Baklai themselves. They are the only asset the Baklai possess, and are considered a valuable commodity in any land. The Baklai insist we can only receive them by adhering to their rules. We possess no load-bearing animals of our own in Kaylin, so it is imperative we maintain sound relations with the Baklai. They are the ones who demand the death penalty for the theft of horses."

"I understand." *No wonder Haydar is such an ass. He believes the Baklai hold all the power when it comes to horses.* Kat did her best to appear completely innocent in any consideration of horse-thievery. "I won't tempt death by stealing a horse from Haydar."

Like hell not. Eduardo would never anything happen to me. He needs my help too. Isn't it always the way? When you want something important done, you have to do it yourself.

***

The Arrival

Kat found Mayda in the reading room, knowing well the young woman loved the stories she found stored there. *The poor girl. She adores the equivalent of Harlequin Romances, Kaylin style. Boy meets girl, nearly loses girl, they persuade parents to bless their union, so they mate and live happily ever after.* Kat snorted. *As if life is like a fairy tale.*

She found the young woman curled up in a chair, her nose buried in a book. "Mayda, I need your help."

Mayda glanced up eagerly. "Of course, Lady Kat. How can I help you?"

"I need to locate a map which will provide me with the route into Shendea."

"Ooh, I can find one. Are you going alone? Do you also need a map of Shendea too? Can I come with you?"

Kat held up her hand. "Just wait a minute. All I need from you is the map, and yes I would like you to get me one of Shendea as well." *No way do I want her to come along. She'd talk me to death.*

"Can I come with you? Please?"

"No, I must go alone. Plus this might be dangerous for you."

"Please? I can help you on your trip, and I can help you pack. I cannot imagine a better adventure."

Frustrated, Kat snapped at her. "Mayda. No. It might be dangerous. Remember the kithras."

The girl shuddered and her face contorted in fear.

"But, I would love you to help me pack for the journey. Can you do this?"

Mayda appeared bereft. "Yes, I can help you pack." Her lower lip trembled. "But I want to come with you so much."

Kat moved toward her and patted her hand. "I know Mayda, but not this time. There will be other opportunities."

Mayda nodded, mutely.

She looks so unhappy. But I can't abide some puppy following me, particularly one who talks so much. I can't even get help from Eduardo. He should have arranged for Haydar to give me a horse. Obviously, he didn't. This, I must do alone.

CHAPTER 38

Kat surveyed her duffle bag. Everything she thought she would need was carefully tucked into the massive carry-all: her leather outfit, a warm coat, gloves and a fur hat, additional changes of clothing, plus assorted toiletries she figured would be needed for the journey. *Mayda managed to be so helpful in the packing She thought of things I might have forgotten. Poor thing. She's not happy since I told her she can't come with me. Plus, of course, Haydar would never agree. And that's a good thing.*

Kat managed to fit items she would need on a more frequent basis into a backpack carrier. The leather worker for the keep did a fine job. He'd worked the leather into a soft and supple bag, with wide, comfortable straps. Finally, the courier bag she used to contain her writing supplies rounded out her travel luggage. The bag, stuffed with the notes for her games, her list of words, pyrock writing notes — plus blank parchment and her cathnog pen and ink, still retained space for additional writings. The two cages she had asked Bannon to obtain for her, completed the pile.

I must persuade Eduardo to give Wink to me soon. I can't leave without her. Tomorrow night, well after dark, I will sneak to the stables and find a decent horse. I'm familiar with the place where Haydar keeps the saddles and bridles so I won't run into a problem. Kat sighed and paced the room. *Now where am I going to keep the horse until I'm ready to leave?*

Kat's stomach growled. *I'll head to supper, that will keep my mind off everything.*

***

Kat, with the help of an apprentice she met on the way, found the communal dining area. The seasonal evening meal was once again underway. The noise of conversation and the clink of dishes and cutlery, assured her she'd reached her goal. When she entered the hall, she searched for an empty seat, and caught sight of Wynneth waving her over to a group of women.

Kat smiled in relief. The women at the table were familiar to her. "Brith, I love the clothing you made for me. The thick coat made from from wullawerth hair is cosy and warm." Kat laughed. "And, I feel like I'm getting a hug when I wear the coat with the fur lining. Your clothing is practical and beautiful at the same time."

The woman sitting next to Wynneth agreed. "Brith made me a paneled skirt which is allowing me to ride a horse more comfortably. She said you gave her the idea, Lady Kat."

I can't remember this woman's name. The two women across from me are Clune and Sherwin. Easy for me to recall because they look so much alike. This one is from Shendea, but the name escapes me. I'll just fake it until someone else uses her name.

"She did indeed, Bronwyth. She possesses a talent for fashion." Brith smiled at Kat.

Kat snorted to herself. *Talent for fashion. Not.* But now, at least, I know her name. "Yes, Bronwyth. I remember now. You're responsible for all Eduardo's functions and dinners when he meets with leaders from the other lands." Kat caught a sharp intake of breath from Clune. *Oh crap, I forgot Eduardo's title. Again.*

Brith jumped into the conversation, and it appeared she was trying to cover up Kat's mistake. "I want to thank you again for your clothing ideas, Lady Kat. I approached Praetor Bardu's bond-mate, Irina, and just delivered new guard-wear, because she and the Praetor leave on the morrow for one of their regular journeys in the north of Kaylin. She promised she will recommend my services to the other Rifellan women." Brith beamed at Kat. "My abilities are now being talked about all over the keep. I need to take on two new apprentices to help fill the orders I received for more of the new attire."

I think I've created a freaking entrepreneur. "Excellent news, Brith." *Hmm, I wonder if I can use her to help me with Haydar? Nope, probably not, she's not a strong personality, and Haydar's a major nutcase. I'll obtain a horse on my own.*

Wynneth turned to Kat. "You did well, Lady Kat." She glanced at the other women at the table, and looked satisfied they were chattering among themselves. She leaned toward Kat and spoke in a low voice. "I am well aware you are anxious to meet Lord Eduardo, and he would like you to visit him. I believe he wishes to turn the pyrock hatchling over to you."

Kat brightened instantly. "Oh fabulous."

Wynneth blinked slightly at the word fabulous, but made no remark. "I know you are anxious to begin working with her, and your lessons in our writings are well advanced." Wynneth patted Kat's hand. "Has Bannon finished the cages?"

"Yes, and he did a marvelous job. He's skilled with wood."

"He is a fine young man, with many talents."

Kat nodded. "He amazed me on the trip. He made us all as comfortable as possible. He's also very sweet and polite. His vast memory for the uses of the local plants impressed me so much. As a result, he kept us well fed." *I should have used the word prodigious. What a super one. I must remember to write it in my word list.*

Wynneth turned to her left as Bronwyth asked her a question, and they began chatting.

A thought struck Kat. "Brith, did you mention Praetor Bardu and Irina are traveling on the morrow?"

Brith glanced toward her. "Yes, Lady Kat. They journey to a different section of Kaylin each season. This time they will be going north, so this route generally takes them about three star turns. Why?"

"I thought they might visit Lanfair, and perhaps Irina could obtain another piece of jewelry for me." *Wow. Quick thinking, kiddo.*

"Unless you contact them this night, you will not be able to connect with them, as they usually leave before sun-up."

"Not a problem. Merely an idea." *So they'll be gone for at least three days. A stable is attached to their quarters. It'll be the perfect place for me to conceal the horse I intend to… er.. borrow from Haydar's stables. Yes. It's amazing how things always work out for me.*

She smiled to herself, barely listening to the chatter around her. *Haydar, you've met your match.*

CHAPTER 39

Mayda's lower lip trembled as she trudged along the dusty path to her home. She seemed to be struggling to keep the tears back. She muttered under her breath. "Lady Kat is being unreasonable. After all, I accompanied her on her trip through Kaylin, and Shendea is a close neighbor and Shendean people are peaceful." One sizable tear escaped and trickled down her cheek. She brushed her hand against her face and wiped the salty drop away, still muttering. "She is not being fair. I am a fine helper, and I am also an excellent traveling companion. She needs me."

She drew in a sizable sniff as she approached the house. The Horse-Master was working with a massive chestnut mare in one of the closer paddocks. She sighed in apparent relief. Master Haydar was absent from the house.

She walked in the rear door of her home, where a Baklai woman stood, preparing a meal at the counter. The woman, who appeared to be an older version of Mayda, turned at the sound of the door opening. "Mayda-kins, what ever are you doing home at mid-day?"

Mayda burst into tears and flung herself into the woman's arms. "Mayrin, Lady Kat is... is... not being nice."

"My dear, sit down and I will bring tea." She led Mayda over to a enormous table, and settled her in one of the chairs carved with vines and leaves and polished to a gleaming brown. "While we drink, you can tell me what upset you so."

She handed a plain linen square to the poor girl. "Dry your eyes, and I will also bring some cakes."

Mayda mopped her eyes and face, while the dark-haired woman returned to the counter and prepared the beverage and snacks. She placed each item on the table in front of her now dry-eyed offspring. She sat, poured the tea, and leaned back. "Why are you upset with Lady Kat?"

"She is going to Shendea and will not let me come along with her. It is not fair. I helped her during the trip through Kaylin, but now she refuses to let me accompany her. She says I am too young and I have no experience."

"Lady Kat possesses wisdom. Haydar and I would not let you travel with her to Shendea."

"Why not? I proved I am capable."

Mayda's parent smiled. "Little one, you were capable on the Kaylin trip because you had excellent guides and protectors. We are familiar with, and trust Counselor Drainin and Bannon. We knew you would be in no danger while traveling with them."

"I did not need them. Lady Kat protected me too."

The woman shook her head. "Mayda, did you lift a spring bow to defeat the kithras?

"Well, no. Who told you about the kithras?"

"As our youngest offspring, we are aware of everything you encounter. This is not Morden where all things are kept secret. You could not survive a kithra attack with only Lady Kat to use a spring-bow."

"But Mayrin, Lady Kat is a perfect protector, and I want to go with her. Please." Mayda teared up once more.

"Mayda-kins, you are our beloved offspring. We do not wish to see you in danger. Lady Kat is unfamiliar with the

The Arrival

lands of Pridden, and knows not what challenges may lurk in Shendea."

At that moment, the door to the house opened and Haydar strode in. "What is this about danger and Lady Kat?"

"Mayda wishes to travel with Lady Kat to Shendea, and I am convinced our youngest would be in danger, particularly since Pridden is unknown to her, and also because Mayda is inexperienced."

Haydar turned to Mayda. *Aha. What is the harlot planning? Before I forbid my foolish offspring to go with her, I should obtain some answers.* "You have already been told no. Perhaps, however, you can tell me more about Lady Kat's plans."

Hope lit the young woman's face. "She is leaving soon to travel to Shendea, and she will need help on the journey. I want to go with her, but she refused me. If you would ask on my behalf Sire, I am sure she would agree to take me."

"Tell me more. How will she be traveling? Who will guide her on this journey?"

"I helped her pack, because she will be leaving on horseback. I did not hear if she will take a guide. She will not go with Counselor Drainin." Mayda added with eagerness in her voice. "I got her the maps she needs for her journey."

"I see." *How does the devious female plan on obtaining a horse? She must be aware I will not give her one. I wonder... no, not possible. She would not.*

Mayda put her hands together in a begging gesture. "Please Sire, I want to go so desperately. Lady Kat will take care of me and I can be of help to her."

"I will do no such thing. You are too young, and the journey is too dangerous. That woman is not one I would choose to allow my offspring to fraternize with. She possesses no morals, and she is dangerous."

Mayda continued to beg Haydar to change his mind, but each of his refusals grew louder.

Mayrin stood wringing her hands, uncomfortable with the situation.

Finally Haydar reached the peak of frustration. He roared at Mayda. "My answer is no. I wish no further discussion on this subject. My word is final."

Her tears flowed again. "You are being so unkind. I want such a simple thing. Please."

"Enough. Go to your room immediately. Never mention the woman's name in this house again." Haydar's blood pounded in his head as he glared at his youngest. "Go now."

Mayda turned white in the face, and fled to the safety of her room.

Haydar grabbed the keys from the hooks near the door and followed her, turning the key in the lock once she entered. He swiveled back to his mate and handed her the keys. "Mayrin, keep her locked up until the disgraceful woman leaves for Shendea."

"I do not necessarily agree she is disgraceful, Haydar. But I agree, Lady Kat is not familiar with Pridden, and Mayda would not be safe to travel with her on this journey. If you would only be more gentle with your young one. She is so sensitive."

He humphed at his mate in frustration, and headed for his office. *Mayrin does not realize the woman is too bold and too stubborn. I am convinced she will think nothing of taking a horse from the stable. I cannot let such a crime happen. I must catch her in the act of her thievery.* He paused at the huge wooden desk, wrote a short note, and then crossed over to the small cage in the corner of the room. He reached in and extracted a small furry creature. The little pyrock yawned, stretched, and held out a plush foreleg for the message. Haydar rolled the note in the tube, which he attached to the delicate leg, and threw the creature upwards, where it raised leathery wings and disappeared with a slight plop.

Praetor Bardu and Irina leave for their guard duties early on the morrow, and I should not disturb them. However, the Praetor's second-in-command, Kadnu, will come at my request. We will prepare a trap for the vile harlot.

Haydar expelled a satisfied breath, sat back in his chair of wood and woven leather and placed his hands firmly on his desk, viewing with pride the sparsely appointed office, and admiring the paintings of horses and scenes from his own land of Baklai.

The brazen creature does not realize this yet, but she has met her match with me.

J. M. Tibbott

CHAPTER 40

Night descended on the keep, and Kat prepared to sneak to the stables at Haydar's home to locate an appropriate horse to use on her journey to Shendea. *I wonder if I'll need a second horse for my luggage? Nope, I think that would be pushing it.*

She gathered any items she might find useful for her night time exploits. *When I pick up the animal, I'll store her in Bardu and Irina's stall, and if anyone notices the horse is not at the Horse-Master's stable, I'll play the innocent.*

Kat glanced at herself in the mirror, admiring her artless expression. *Things are working out for me. Early in the morning when Bardu is expected home, I'll leave for Shendea. This way I'll have time to plan my route from the maps Mayda found for me. I would prefer a guide, but Eduardo's done nothing.*

She smirked to herself. *Haydar you have met your match with me. This should teach him to to treat me badly. Good riddance.*

Silently she crept outside, carrying only a rope with which to guide the horse to Bardu's house. Luckily, with the moon in apogee, and only a sliver of the crescent visible, the night remained dark and silent. She shivered with excitement. *At last I'm on my way. This crazy planning is worth the risks. Plus with another new adventure to write up for my game, I'm one step closer to getting home.*

***

Once she reached her destination, Kat stealthily approached the stable and slipped inside. She reached up to pick a bridle off one of the hooks and moved over to the selection of saddles. She chose a small one, moved outside and placed it on the rack near the paddock. Noiselessly, she moved among some smaller animals, all which were standing, nodding in their sleep. She found the perfect young chestnut horse, rubbed her nose gently and before the mare managed to nicker, offered a cube of solid honey. The horse happily crunched the sweet treat, although to Kat's ears, the mare's chewing sounded like an earthquake. She paused, listening for any sounds of humans.

Easing the saddle on the horse, she gave a knee to the mare's stomach, and with a whoosh of air coming from the animal, the saddle settled firmly in place. She tightened the girth, and then slipped the bridle over the mare's head and adjusted everything to fit. *This is great - I've got a horse, and no one is any the wiser. I think I'll risk riding, instead of leading her on a line. Quicker, because the sooner I get her to Bardu's, the better.*

Kat brought a stool over to the little mare, and used this to give her the lift she needed to mount.

Once aboard, she guided the animal out the gates and set off cautiously down the road, headed for Bardu's home.

Bursting from a secondary building, armed men on horses, carrying lighted torches, surrounded her. Before Kat could react, she was trapped. They were led by Haydar. His face flushed with success and he grinned like an evil goblin.

Oh shit.

"Now we caught you, ... Lady Kat." He sarcastically emphasized her title, and followed with a triumphant smile. "You just earned yourself the death penalty."

The Arrival

Double shit. I can't fight this many men.

Haydar ordered the nearest guard. "Tie her hands. I do not want to risk her fleeing. We will take her to Lord Eduardo to obtain permission for this thief to be put to the sword."

Sword? Holy crap. Nope, not gonna fight... yet. I'm in real trouble now.

***

At the keep, they all dismounted and Haydar ordered one of the guards to now bind Kat's hands behind her back. With a line attached to her, they dragged her into the Eduardo's presence.

Eduardo's eyebrows shot to his hairline, obviously startled to see the woman whose help he needed, in such a predicament. The entire group was ensconced in the interview room, a room normally used for negotiations between Eduardo and leaders of various other lands.

Kat stared around her. Cold sweat trickled down her spine. *This is not okay. I'm caught up in a terrifying kangaroo court. What the hell am I going to do?*

Eduardo coughed loudly in an attempt to bring order to the babble and accusations flying from Haydar.

The confused yammering ceased, and all turned expectant faces toward their leader.

"What is the challenge, Horse-Master?"

Haydar, still sputtering, appeared abnormally enraged at the situation. "Lord Eduardo, this woman stole a horse. I demand the death penalty."

The tip of Eduardo's nose turned white. He glared back and forth from Kat to Haydar. "The death penalty is a most severe request. What makes you think Lady Kat stole a horse?"

"We caught her, Sire. She planned this, and my duty is to demand the full punishment required by the law of this land.

This law is an ancient one. Horse thievery has always been a death penalty mandate throughout Pridden."

"I would like all versions of the story, before I rule on any of this." Eduardo's eyes bored into Kat, his voice icy and controlled. "What do you to say regarding this accusation, Lady Kat?"

Oh boy, here goes nothing. I gotta explain myself, or I'll never get home. Eduardo's not happy, and Haydar's practically foaming at the mouth. "Lord Eduardo." *Time to pull out all the stops and remember all the damn courtesies. OK. OK. A different spin on this situation.* "You asked me to perform a task, and I needed a horse to serve you." She swiveled toward Haydar. "Master Haydar was decidedly unwilling to supply me with one, so I thought I needed to borrow a horse to achieve what you requested." *Ooh thank god, borrow is much better than take.*

Haydar began to bluster again. "No one is allowed to steal a horse, Lord Eduardo." His face was now a fiery red.

He looks like he's gonna experience a stroke. I better think fast. How can I turn any of this to my advantage? "I didn't steal the horse, I only borrowed it."

Haydar, unable to contain himself, was almost incoherent in indignation. "We cannot allow anyone to make a mockery of the law, and take what they want without permission." He swung around and pointed at Kat. "This woman broke a sacred trust of this land, and she deserves to be punished."

Eduardo held up his hands. "Master Haydar what you say is correct, however, I must tell you, there are mitigating circumstances and I pray you will see this incident in a different light when I explain what occurred."

"What possible circumstance can warrant her being a horse thief?"

The Arrival

Eduardo sighed and pinched the bridge of his nose. "Haydar, I requested Lady Kat perform a vitally important task for me, and I fully intended to request the necessary steeds for her upcoming journey. I expected to speak with you in a star turn or two." He held up his hand, again, to forestall Haydar's objections. "Lady Kat, who is unfamiliar with our ways and customs, only knew she needed to fulfill her promise to me as soon as possible. I believe she assumed I spoke with you, so she acted in what she considered an appropriate manner and found a suitable horse to perform her task."

No wonder Eduardo's the lord here. He's pretty damn good. I think I'll let him solve this situation. This is the time to remain silent.

Haydar opened his mouth again.

Eduardo allowed him no time to speak. "I am not finished, Horse-Master. I erred because I did not realize the importance she placed upon my request. I am aware she is a woman who often takes action quickly and unexpectedly, but I did not take this into account. She desired to please me and help the people of Kaylin, and so she assumed I conveyed the necessary information to you. Her heart resided in the correct place, even if her reasoning did not."

"She still is at fault for her actions."

Wow, he's not going to give an inch. How the hell is Eduardo going to handle this?

Haydar stood in front of Eduardo. His entire body fairly vibrated with indignant stubbornness.

Eduardo sighed again. "I do request of you, Master Haydar, you lift this blame from Lady Kat's shoulders and place the burden upon mine where it belongs."

Holy cow, how can he refuse Eduardo after those words?

303

Haydar showed signs of calming. His face now returned to his natural brown color, but his shoulders drooped, and he continued to sputter. "My Lord, I... I... did not understand how many things you were considering." He glared at Kat again. "This woman should know better than to simply remove a horse from my stable."

Eduardo cleared his throat, and stared pointedly at Haydar. "The stable does not belong to you, Horse-Master Haydar, but to the keep."

Haydar had the grace to pale at Eduardo's words. "I merely meant, Sire, it is my responsibility to ensure the safety of all the animals on behalf of the keep."

"I believe in your devoted stewardship of the stables. You must realize, Lady Kat thought her actions were at my bidding, and was swayed by the fact I own the title of Lord."

At these words, Haydar paled further. "Sire, of course, you are correct. Perhaps I acted too hastily in assigning the blame to Lady Kat. I only wish she considered coming to me with her request."

Eduardo raised an eyebrow. "Horse-Master Haydar, look to the truth of your dealings with the Lady. Did she not attempt to do so?"

Haydar hung his head. "I suspect... I suspect she tried, Sire." He faced Kat. "Lady Kat I apologize for refusing to listen to you."

Wow. What a quick about face. Despite his arrogance, he fears Eduardo's power. Interesting. I can afford to be generous now. "Master Haydar, I accept your apology. I presume much miscommunication happened between us." *I still think you're a toad, though, and your apology sounds reluctant.*

"Thank you, Lady Kat. If you will visit me on the morrow, I will find you the perfect horse for your journey."

The Arrival

"I eagerly await the visit." *Eduardo put him in his place, and so well Haydar did not lost face. What a fascinating view of leadership qualities.* Kat glanced at Eduardo's face and caught him regarding her closely. With the barest shake of his head, a minute smile curled the corners of his mouth, but his eyes were dark and furious. *Crap. He knows I lied. I wonder when the heavy boot of Eduardo's wrath will descend on me?*

***

At her morning meal, Wynneth mentioned Mayda had been locked in her room all night and Haydar had imposed a curfew on the poor girl for ten star turns.

Kat sought her out. "Mayda, please forgive me for causing trouble between you and your parent. I never intended to cause you distress."

"I do know this, Lady Kat, but I want to come with you to Shendea."

"You must realize your desire to travel with me is impossible."

"But why? I can be of help to you. Please."

"Mayda, I thought you learned a lesson from the punishment you've received. The trip with me might be long and dangerous. You are too young, and you are well aware, Haydar will never consent to this."

"But…"

"No buts, Mayda. Relax. When I return, I will tell you all about the journey. So even though you cannot come with me, I will relate all the details to you."

"You will?" Mayda's face beamed.

"I will. I promise. When I come back, you can give me a report of what transpired in Kaylin while I was away."

Mayda's puppy wriggle returned in full force. "Oh perfect. I will wait for you and am eager for many discussions about your journey, and about Kaylin happenings."

And that is why, dear Mayda, I'm glad you're not accompanying me. Far too many discussions. Far too much talking.

CHAPTER 41

Kat stood at her window, watching the residents of the keep begin their day, while she drank her regular cup of Karri-san tea. She loved the flavor— a slight ginger taste with a faint tang of cinnamon and honey. *I must remember to pack plenty of this. Rifellans appear to be used as guards, so they will probably be in every land.*

A light knock at her door elicited one word. "Come."

A handsome young apprentice entered and handed her a note.

She attempted to read the contents and grimaced. The writing was pyrock speak. She glanced at the man. "Do you know what is in this note?"

"The missive is from Lord Eduardo, my Lady."

"Can you interpret the writing for me?" She held it out to him.

He wrinkled his brow, but took the note from her and read aloud. "Lord Eduardo requests you attend him in his office once you complete your morning meal, Lady Kat." He handed the note back to her.

"Thank you. Please tell him I am almost finished and will come soon."

The young man bowed slightly and departed, shaking his head in what looked like puzzlement.

***

Mouse and Eduardo, in deep discussion were seated at the small table near the window in Eduardo's office, poring over maps of Shendea, when a slight knock interrupted them.

Eduardo raised his head. "Come."

Dafid stuck his head around the door. "Lady Kat sent advice she is almost finished her morning meal and will be with you soon, Sire."

"Thank you, Dafid." But the young man had disappeared and shut the door behind him.

"We covered most of your movements, and what you will need in Shendea. Some last minute items. I think you should leave my office and come back when I summon you because I need to speak with Kat once more before we introduce the two of you. I also believe you should be 'Mouse' when you are with her."

"I fully agree. You gave me an excellent idea of her personality. I will retire to my room and prepare my packing items, and work out the final route through Shendea."

"Excellent." They stood, clasped arms, and Mouse left the office immediately.

***

Approaching Dafid, Kat smiled. *I think he and Mayda would make an excellent couple. He's so cute. But she did blush when she spoke of Bannon. Who shall I promote her to?*

When Dafid caught sight of her, he straightened his spine, his eyes shining and a slight blush covering his cheeks, he beamed a welcoming smile at her. "Lady Kat, Lord Eduardo is expecting you."

Uh, oh. Don't tell me he's developed a crush on me. You should be after Mayda, goof. Not me. "Thank you." Kat erased the smile from her face and entered the office. *I mustn't encourage him.*

As she walked in, Eduardo stood and indicated she should sit, and as she did so, he returned to his own chair, placing his elbows on the table. He clasped his hands beneath his chin, and the corners of his mouth twitched. "So, Kat. Has Haydar picked out a horse for you?"

"I already thanked you for intervening in that catastrophe. I'm well aware you know I embellished the truth with Haydar."

"Embellished? Is that the word on your world for lying?"

"You know it was the only way to deal with the situation. One, by the way, you grabbed at to solve the problem. I'm aware you saved me from a possible hanging, or beheading. You don't need to rub it in."

He frowned. "Rub it in. Hmm." He grinned. "I see the meaning. I do not receive many occasions for fun in this office, but I admit I enjoy the opportunity to mock you a little. Your reaction is often predictable. Plus you have done the same to me at times."

Kat glared at him. "Excuse me? Mock you? I treat you with the respect you deserve."

Eduardo laughed out loud. "Respect? You are one of the most disrespectful young women I have ever met." He held up his hands as she opened her mouth to retort. "For myself, I am not complaining. You are also one of the few to relate to me as an ordinary man, rather than as the lord of an important land. In a way, I find this restful, and I enjoy the feeling. I am able to drop all pretenses in your company."

Kat gave him her snake-eying-prey stare. "Ordinary man? Hah." *This man hides more than anyone I've met here. I never understand his motives.* "Come on, Eduardo, you blackmailed me into working for you. Yet, if I attempt to do what you want, I get into trouble. You're not as clever as you think. If you were, you would prepare me better for the job you ordered me to do."

Eduardo shook his head. "You are a cynical young woman. And a frustrating one."

"I must be to cope with you Kaylins. You all harbor agendas." Kat paused. "Well, except perhaps for Mayda. I doubt she would know an agenda if one bit her on the nose."

Eduardo grinned at her words. "I understand you are confused by the situation in which we find ourselves. Believe me, I am equally challenged, and your different words and your attitudes are refreshing. I did not intend to blackmail you. I asked you to perform a task, and as my payment, I would attempt to return you to your world."

"Whatever." Kat shook her head. "So what now?"

Eduardo rose and paced the room. "I believe you have what you need to begin the journey through the rest of Pridden, and now all you need is a guide." He stopped at the tassel near his desk and gave two sharp tugs. Dafid peered around the door. "Dafid, can you summon Mouse to my office?"

"Yes, Sire. Right away." He turned and closed the door as he left.

What? he's getting me a mouse? I have a horse, a pyrock and now a mouse? What the hell kind of a journey is this? "What is this guide like?"

Eduardo returned to his seat. "He is familiar with the Shendean customs and is well acquainted with the people themselves."

"Does this mean I'll receive different guides for each land?"

"Not necessarily. He is well-versed in most of the lands."

"If he's so wonderful, why did you saddle me with Drainin?"

The Arrival

"Drainin is a trusted Counselor, and an experienced guard. Plus he is very familiar with Kaylin. Why do you display such antipathy towards him?"

A knock at Eduardo's door interrupted. *Thank goodness. I didn't need to reply.*

The door opened, and Kat stared as a small man, clad in a grey hooded cloak, sidled into the room. *This is the guide? He stands there looking like a puff of wind would blow him over. He's not the kind of guy to handle kithras, for sure. Does Eduardo believe I'm capable of handling all physical challenges, and all I need is a directional guide?*

"Mouse, welcome." Eduardo pointed to a chair in the corner. "Bring the green chair and join us. Lady Kat, this is Mouse. Mouse, Lady Kat.

If Eduardo thinks I'm going to be all formal around this mousey guy, he's mistaken. Kat only nodded at Mouse, not sure what role to play.

Mouse brought the chair and sat. He pulled out a map and spread it on the table. "Sire, my Lady, I prepared a route to cover the most important areas of Shendea. This will take us first through the Nordad Pass and will set us on the best path to pay our respects to Lord Rhognor."

As Mouse continued to cover the routes he planned to take, Kat scrutinized him closely. Something about him struck her as familiar, but she couldn't place his face. He never once met her eyes, which she found peculiar. *He truly is a mouse of a man. No confidence, and he would definitely be unable to handle anything dangerous like kithras or gornogs. Just as well I'll be taking my spring-bow.*

Finally Mouse turned toward Kat. "Lord Eduardo agrees this is the best route, Lady Kat. I will arrange a pack animal with Horse-Master Haydar, and we should be ready to depart in two or three star turns. I will send a list to your room of items you would be wise to include in your pack."

"Thank you Mouse." *Better play nice until I figure this 'mouse' out. He's one character I can't see how to fit into the game.*

They all rose.

Mouse bowed. "Well met, Lady Kat."

He left ahead of her, and Kat followed him with her eyes. *Is there anything on his list I haven't packed? I guess I should allow him to guide me, because Eduardo did recommend him. But then, Eduardo also recommended Drainin. I wonder.*

CHAPTER 42

Drainin studied the note with care. Delivered last night by pyrock, and written in the code preferred by Galdin, he delayed answering a summons by Eduardo. Deciphering the message was top priority.

Drainin smiled with relief. *Galdin calls me to perform my tasks for him. At last. In a few star turns I return to Morden and I will be in my own land with my own people. No more hiding who I really am. A new day for Morden is so close.*

Drainin sobered. *My only regret is I must betray Lord Eduardo. He trusted me and has been an admirable superior. I truly have enjoyed working for him. But the power and position promised me by Galdin is within my grasp, and to disobey him would prove unwise. Most unwise.*

He smiled again. *Kat. Once Galdin is through with her, the woman is mine.* He laughed. *She will regret her arrogance.*

Still smiling, he set about completing the de-coding of the correspondence. So familiar with methods used to conceal the wording of secret messages, Drainin accomplished his task quickly. He pushed back from the table, rose, and strutted around the room, satisfaction coursing through every muscle of his body. He would meet with the first assassin from the Guild at the midday meal, when most of the keep would be otherwise occupied.

Excellent. I must now head to Eduardo and receive his instructions for the day. I intend to keep my secret from him for as long as possible. Eduardo, unfortunately, is a trusting and in many ways a naive fool. He never detected the part I play in Kaylin.

***

Drainin strode into Eduardo's office. "Lord Eduardo, you summoned me."

"Good morrow, Counselor. I require your help. Lady Kat leaves for Shendea in about two star turns, and much final preparation is required."

Drainin raised an eyebrow. "Surely you are not sending her off unaccompanied?"

"No, I assigned a companion." Eduardo hastened to speak further. "I cannot send you, Drainin. Firstly, I need your advice too much to let you leave for such a lengthy journey. And…." He avoided direct eye contact. "Lady Kat finds your company too strong for her."

Too strong indeed. She is not a compliant woman. She cannot understand how exceptional her life would be with me. "Who accompanies her to Shendea?"

"I requested Thane Galdin give me Mouse as her temporary companion."

"Mouse? Lord Eduardo, with respect, Mouse is most inappropriate. He possesses no fighting skills. He is weak and spineless."

"I am well aware of the his short comings. His weakness, though, is what Lady Kat will appreciate most."

By the goddess, is Eduardo nervous of Lady Kat? This will work even better for my plans. "I am surprised, Sire, by your choice, but what you say is valid. Lady Kat does not prefer the company of assertive men."

"You spent many star turns in her company. What is your opinion of her?"

I must be careful in my answer. I still need access to the woman. "She is very tough minded and stubborn. She often ignored my warnings, and exposed herself... and the rest of us... to potential danger." Drainin grinned. "I suspect Mouse will find difficulty controlling her actions."

"I am of the same mind." Eduardo sighed. "When someone is that determined to control everything around her, she must accept the consequences. I need you to pre-arrange the switch from horses to pontis once she and Mouse approach the stronghold of Lord Rhognor. Mouse's familiarity with Shendea will eliminate most challenges, once they cross through the pass."

"Your wish is my command, Lord Eduardo. I will make the arrangements after the midday meal."

"Not a command, Drainin, merely a request. But thank you."

Drainin lowered his head, and took his leave.

***

Drainin headed past the enclave set aside for Eduardo's guards, and into what the locals referred to as Old Town. The buildings here were not well kept, and the air of seedy decay took precedence over the few improvements some of the residents had attempted. This area, established many star turns ago, deteriorated each season, and Kaylins with any sense of self-respect moved to better accommodations, closer to the farms and shops. The alleys between the houses were narrow, grimy tunnels through Old Town, and less reputable citizens chose unlawful ways of living. While the greater portion of the Lord's keep offered clean and pleasant residency, relatively free of crime, the rate of nefarious activities within Old Town was a source of dismay for Eduardo.

Drainin trudged through the dirty, sooty passageways, searching for his Morden counterpart. Without warning, he whirled upon the man following him, thrust him against the filthy brick wall, and brought his knife to the throat of his stalker. *The fool, his boots shuffle and slip on the stones of the road.*

The man smirked, displaying blackened and missing teeth. "Counselor, you are quick indeed. What alerted you?"

"Your smell. It is stronger than the stench of the streets." Drainin lowered his knife. "Who sent you?"

"Ssarff gave me the direct order, but you know the request came from Thane Galdin. Ssarff and five others will arrive by the morrow. My purpose is to plan the abduction of the woman."

So Ssarff himself is coming. This becomes more interesting. "Your timing is excellent. The woman and her guide are to leave in two to three star turns. We have no time to waste. What are you called?"

"Ssarff gave me the name of Salssin when I became a Guild member."

"Fine." Drainin pulled Salssin by the arm, wrinkling his nose in disgust as he did so. "We will retire to the Gould Inn three doors down. The inn contains many quiet dark corners and their custom is light during the day. We can create the perfect plan to seize the woman."

The two conspirators sidled by the buildings and entered the inn. A blast of fetid air curled around Drainin's nostrils, eclipsing the foul aroma of his companion. He dragged Salssin by the arm, across a floor littered with old sawdust and unknown refuse. Halting at a filthy table in the corner he called to the barkeep. "Two of your local ales. Now."

The Arrival

The two sat in silence until the innkeeper slopped two huge glasses of ale on the table. Drainin tossed him a coin, which the publican bit, gave a nod, and pocketed.

Salssin drank half the glass of ale and leaned back in his chair. "So, have you a plan in place on how to abduct the woman?"

"A perfect one." Drainin gulped down most of the ale. "We will put the plan into action well after the evening meal on the morrow. All the staff of the keep will be asleep, and the rest of the Guild members will be here. Send them a message to meet you here to dine, if you all wish to take a chance with this inn's dubious offerings, and you can fill them in with the plans during the repast."

"Where will we bring the woman?"

"You will stay here for the night, and change your appearance in the morning so you are able to easily pass for a Kaylin laborer. Clothing and supplies to cleanse yourself will be delivered to the inn at first light." Drainin leaned forward as he emptied his glass. "Further down this alley is an abandoned building which once housed foodstuffs. The vermin are reasonably small and should give you no problem. You will direct the rest of the Guild to the warehouse before you head for the keep to obtain the woman."

"How am I to bring her? Drug her? Attack her? I would prefer to perform the task noiselessly."

Ah, this one listens and asks the right questions. Our plan will work. "You will take this scarf and tell her a young woman by the name of Mayda is in trouble and is asking for Lady Kat".

"Is Lady Kat the name of the woman the Thane seeks?"

"Yes. Now you must make sure you force her to rush to come with you. Make the task sound urgent so she is not able to call for anyone else to help. Thane Galdin made it clear we must take her before she can reach Shendea." Drainin sat back in his chair, rocking it on the two rear legs. "One more thing." He brought the chair forward so it thumped on the floor. "Your will call yourself Daylin, which sounds more like a man from Kaylin. Everyone would consider Salssin to be a Morden name. If she questions you at all, you are a laborer on a farm at the far end of Old Town."

"An excellent plan."

"Indeed. You must remember to continually rush her along with a significant sense of urgency. She must not have time to question you or to think of calling for additional help."

"Clever, Counselor. Ssarff indicated Galdin's faith in your abilities is serious. I see why."

"We are in accord?"

Salsin nodded and drained the last of his ale.

"Fine. I will head to the warehouse in plenty of time to be included in the welcoming party. Until tomorrow." Drainin rose and headed for the exit.

He smirked to himself. *Kat, you have met your match. You will pay for your arrogance.*

CHAPTER 43

Kat stretched, hearing muscles snap and crackle. She rubbed her eyes. *Time for bed. Everyone else is asleep and my preparations are as complete as possible.* She headed to the personal to change, when someone knocked at her door. *Who on earth is here at this time of night?*

Kat opened the door and found a young Kaylin man — a stranger to her. "Yes?"

"Are you the Lady Kat?"

Kat nodded. "Who are you, and why are you here so late at night?"

The young man gave a deep bow. "I am Daylin, and my sincere apologies, Lady, but she desperately needs you."

"Who needs me?"

"I worked late today, and on my return through Old Town, heard a young female crying for help. When I found her, she had fallen somehow. She is bleeding and in immense distress. When I went to her aid, she told me her name is Mayda, and she asked me to fetch you as fast as possible. I did not want to leave her, but she became most insistent I bring you to her right away."

"Oh poor Mayda, we should find help for her."

"Please my Lady, I did not want to leave her alone, so we must go now." The man held up a scarf, covered in blood. "She asked me to give this to you, to convince you to come immediately. Once you are with her I can find additional help. It is critical you be with her. She has already begun to panic."

Rats, Mayda has done something foolish. Her blood is all over the scarf. I warned her she couldn't accompany me to Shendea, but I think she's attempted to do something to make sure I take her with me. "Well fine, let's hurry. Where is she?"

The man glanced back at her. "Not far. Follow me." He hurried on, leaving Kat to rush to keep up with him.

Kat followed Daylin past the residences of Eduardo's guards. A moonless black night and silence greeted the two as they hurried through the streets.

"Maybe we should stop and ask one of Eduardo's guards to come with us?"

"My Lady, there will be questions, and delays, and saddling of horses and thus time wasted. We need to return to your friend right away. I am most concerned about her. She begged me to find you, and became decidedly upset when I suggested I get help for her first. I worry her wounds need tending to." With this speech he strode even faster. They passed out of the last of the more modern parts of the keep, where no further pole lamps shed any light on the area.

Kat managed to barely discern a series of ancient buildings a short distance away. The edifices, so close together, created narrow, black and muddy alleys. Kat shivered at the thought of heading into the series of tunnels presented. *I don't like this. Those dark doorways might be hiding anything. Does Daylin need to go this way? And why did the silly girl come here in the first place?*

Daylin pushed open an old iron gate, which led into the town, and the rusty hinges shrieked in protest.

"I don't like this Old Town. Are you sure Mayda is here?"

Well into the first narrow street, he glanced back and

The Arrival

motioned her to hurry. "Of course I am sure. She is in danger. We must reach her. Please let us help her, my Lady."

Shaking her head in doubt, Kat entered the tunnel between the dirty black buildings, expecting danger to leap at her from every doorway. *This is creepy. I'm cold and now I don't trust this guy. I should have insisted we bring someone else to help.* "Where is she? How much further?" *I hope I haven't made a mistake following him.*

"Not far. She is in the stone warehouse at the end of this lane. We will be at the building shortly. Your friend is in anguish."

Kat's stone froze and lay like ice against her skin. *My stone is warning me of danger ahead.* She slowed, but Daylin grabbed her hand and pulled her along.

"We must hurry, Lady."

Kat stopped in her tracks. "Wait. Something's wrong."

But he continued to drag her to the building, as he urged her on. "The only thing wrong is Mayda needs our help, and you are resisting."

She pulled her hand free, stopped again, but on hearing a muffled cry, ran the last few steps to the doorway of the old stone structure. A faint glimmer emanated from the interior, and mist swirled and whirled around the entrance, bringing with it the smell of mold and old things, long since lost to the town. *I don't want to go in, but I must find out how badly Mayda is hurt.*

She hesitated at the doorway, when a meat hook of a hand whipped from the entrance and grabbed her by the throat. Kat choked, unable to take a breath. Reflexes eclipsed fear, and she bunched up a fist and struck the unknown assailant on what she assumed was the bridge of the nose. Hot blood gushed over her hand. The pain she inflicted gave her sufficient leverage to free herself from the clutches of the stranger.

Her eyes adjusted to the faint light, and Kat, detecting the scrape of boot on stone behind her, assumed Daylin planned to attack her. She scanned the immediate area for a weapon. *I'm a fool, he's evil. But where's Mayda.* She seized a chunk of old wood and struck Daylin across the head, and turned swiftly to deal another blow to the stranger in front. Both men went down, the fight knocked out of them. Kat wheeled around at the hissing sound from her left, and narrowly escaped another blow.

Footsteps from all sides approached, and Kat whirled and fought and kicked and punched with every ounce of strength she possessed. She roared at her assailants and each yell imbued her body with great force and the determination to remain free. She managed to keep the other assailants at bay, when a cold arm circled her neck and bent her backwards. The strongest attacker by far, this new assault stunned her for a moment, but before she managed to react, something sharp stung her. Her limbs became jelly and bent beneath her. Unable to stand, she attempted to call out for help, but only a croak emerged. *Where is my lion? Where is my bear? I need you.* Slowly her world dissolved to black.

CHAPTER 44

High pitched squeaking from the next room, roused Eduardo from sleep, and he sat up abruptly. Throwing on pants, he rushed to his office. The noise issued from the pyrock's cage. When he removed the night cover, Blink was backed up in a corner avoiding the young Wink who screeched and jumped and flapped her wings.

"What is wrong with her, Blink?"

Eduardo turned his head at the frantic knocking at his door, which he hurried to answer, flinging it open.

Irina, gasping for breath, rushed into the room. "Eduardo. They took Kat."

His eyes wide, he clutched at her arms. "Who took her? Where?"

"I do not know. Liandock contacted me. He conveyed terror and a cry for help emanating from the stone he gave her. He said all went blank and he is fearful for her life."

The words barely left her lips when Mouse burst upon the scene. "Ed... " He caught sight of Irina. "... Sire, I believe Lady Kat is in danger." *That was close. This woman is not aware of me, or my abilities.*

"Irina just brought the same news, and Kat's pyrock is upset as well. Do you have any idea where she is?"

Mouse's eyes clouded over and he searched the vision he received from Kat. "A cry of danger came from... from an old abandoned stone building. All is dark and I cannot pick up her thoughts. But I sense a heartbeat. She is alive. I see many old stone structures, narrow streets, cobblestones… and I sense evil."

Eduardo whirled around to Irina. "Fetch Bardu and ask him to summon the guards, saddled and ready, and advise him I believe Kat is in Old Town. Please ask Liandock for any further visions."

"He is already on his way here, Sire, and he brings Master Penrow with him."

Eduardo raised an eyebrow. "Both Liandock and Penrow? This is most unusual."

"Lady Kat is an unusual woman. Both of them are aware she is important."

"Whatever their reasons, we are grateful for any help they may give."

Eduardo asked Dafid who stood at the door, concern on his face. "Prepare my horse, and leave him at the Northern Gate. Once my horse is ready, hasten to Horse-Master Haydar. Apprise him of the situation and request he meet us at the gate with fresh horses. We may need them, because whoever took Lady Kat, will not wait for us to obtain new mounts for the search.

All the occupants, except Mouse, tore from the room to fulfill Eduardo's orders.

Eduardo turned to Mouse. "You must come with us. You can touch her mind better than any of us, and we must… we will find her."

"I planned on doing so. My mare is stabled beside yours. I will meet you all at the Gate. While I wait I will search for any sign of where she might be."

"Thank Caleesh you are here. I suspect Galdin is behind this. But who would he prevail upon to perform the abduction?

The Arrival

Mouse's answer was grim. "The Assassins' Guild. I cannot conceive of any other."

Eduardo paled. "How did they enter the keep?"

"I will wager they enticed her to come to them instead."

"How? Why? I cannot believe she would go to Old Town in the dead of night. The place is foul and most residents are unpleasant company. It is unlikely she would go willingly."

"We will, no doubt, find out soon enough. Eduardo. Speed is required."

With those words, Mouse left and Eduardo paused long enough to don a jacket over his night shirt, and snatch his long sword from a shelf, before he hastened after him.

***

Eduardo, Mouse, Bardu, and Kadnu with eight more guards rode toward Old Town, and despite the thunder of hooves, all else kept silent. No speech between the riders could overcome their alarm for Kat's safety.

Eduardo became aware, rather than heard, the approach of two sets of riders. From the south Haydar and three of his journeymen appeared with six fresh horses. Following from the keep, four more riders joined them, and Eduardo caught sight of Bannon and Dafid among them.

The party of riders slowed as they reached the rusty iron gate of Old Town, and once entering, they formed a single file to navigate the narrow alleys through the dark, filthy structures.

Eduardo glanced at Mouse and raised a single eyebrow.

Mouse indicated with a nod of his head, the crumbling stone edifice ahead.

Eduardo held up his hand and the band of rescuers stopped, and followed at a slower pace after the two men in the lead. At the entrance, the two of them entered the building, Eduardo with drawn sword. They were met with silence. Empty.

Mouse kneeled down and examined the prints in the dusty floor. "Seven men… no eight came here, and there are signs of Kat."

"Who are they, Mouse?"

Mouse drew in a long breath. *The scent is familiar.* "You are not going to like this."

Eduardo frowned. "What?"

"The Assassins' Guild assembled here, and Ssarff rides with them. And I find the tracks of a man of Kaylin."

Eduardo gasped. "Ssarff! Kat is more important than we imagined. Seven Assassins. A dangerous number." He regarded the group of rescuers. "Do we bring enough men to stop them?"

"The Guild are fierce and vicious fighters, Eduardo. You will need all the men gathered here and with luck, Liandock and Penrow will arrive in time to help win the coming battle." Mouse rose and followed the tracks, and stopped. Puzzled. "This is strange. They are headed to the north gate of Old Town."

"Follow the tracks. We will come behind you."

They continued to track the Guild and their captive, and once outside the northern gate, Mouse paused once more to search for additional signs.

He glanced up at Eduardo and grimaced. "This makes more sense. They turned south for Morden. We must ride fast to catch them before they can cross the Brynwog. If they reach Morden with Kat, we will have lost her."

Eduardo passed on to the rest of the group the vital need to free Kat as quickly as possible. The entire troupe, fired by the importance of the rescue mission, turned as one and spurred their animals forward with renewed zeal.

Mouse led the way, determined his smaller horse would not hold them up. *We must find her. Our futures, both Eduardo's and mine, depend upon her return.*

J. M. Tibbott

CHAPTER 45

The sky painted with the pale grays and mauves of early dawn, revealed the landscape and Bardu called out to the group. "I see them. They are ahead."

From the northwest, Liandock, on a pure white mare, accompanied by Penrow, his bulk supported by a massive black stallion, and two of their assistants, emerged from mist to help swell the ranks of the pursuers.

Encouraged by the appearance of additional support, every man urged his horse to greater speed and the anger of the riders lent wings to the feet of the animals. Hooves drummed and thrummed upon the earth, swords, lances and spring-bows clanked, and horses and men alike, their breath labored, grunted with the effort from the chase. Nearing the fleeing assassins, Penrow, despite his girth, lifted his longbow and shot. The arrow sliced through the air with deadly accuracy, and an assassin fell from his steed.

Eduardo turned on him, horror etched on his face. "Take care, Penrow, we cannot hit Kat."

Penrow puffed at Eduardo. "I only ever hit what I aim at." His frown matched his irritated tone.

The riderless horse in the path ahead, veered and struck another. The second rider fell from his horse, began running, and with a surge of speed caught up with his steed. With one bound he sprang to the saddle again, reminding the pursuers of the uncanny abilities of the Assassins.

Mouse, caught sight of Kat, her hair now flying free, and her wrists lashed, caught in the middle of the fleeing pack. She closed with the first rider-less horse, reached toward the animal with her bound hands, and with difficulty, freed the sword from the sheath attached to the saddle. A foolhardy move, because in doing so, she flew from her perch, landing with a thud, where she lay momentarily stunned. The rider who appeared to be from Kaylin, immediately veered his horse to re-capture her, but as he approached, she leaped to her feet, grabbed the sword lying next to her with both hands, and swung it at the horse's legs. The animal stumbled and the rider pitched forward. He hit the ground, rolled away from the struggling animal, and drew his shorter sword from the scabbard attached to his belt. Kat, staggering under the weight of the sword in her hands, and barely holding it with her arms trussed with rope, began to swing at the man.

Even from this distance the rescuers could hear her screaming at her assailant. Kat and the man fought on the ground, but he appeared to be simply defending himself, without attempting to kill her. She was tiring, and it would not be long before he could overpower her.

Eduardo broke from his group and headed to her assistance. Kat, swinging her sword wildly, was ineffective with her hands bound, and the kidnapper gained ground, inch by inch. Eduardo rode up behind him and plunged his sword into Kat's attacker, who screamed in pain, dropped his sword and sank to the ground, face down, bleeding profusely and writhing in agony.

Pandemonium broke loose among the Guild riders, as the pursuing rescuers caught up with them. Chaos reigned. Men fought and horses went down. Piercing cries of pain from the fallen filled the air and Kat, still swinging her stolen

The Arrival

weapon continued her assault on all the enemies surrounding her. Eduardo defending himself, fought fiercely with a pale assassin, but another horse bumped into his, and the assassin's sword sliced his arm. Both groups of men now crashed into each other and horses and men alike screamed in fear and pain. The Assassins fought savagely, wounding many men, as they slashed and swung with swords. Their numbers, reduced to only four men, put them on the defensive and Lord Eduardo's men garnered favorable advantage and wounded two more.

Two of the assassins rode off and fled to the nearby woods, one wounded and leaning over the head of his steed. He rode only a few more paces, when a spring-bow arrow pierced his neck and he fell, blood spurting from the slash at his throat.

To her left, Kat stared in horror as one of Eduardo' guards executed another assassin by swinging his sword at the throat of his attacker. Blood flew, droplets of red spraying through the air, and the assassin fell, blood pumping from his neck as the head rolled two feet from the body. Kat gasped as the head came to rest near her, blind eyes staring at her. Her stomach heaved, but empty of food, she could only manage dry retches.

The other assassin, who had cut Eduardo, gained the shelter of the woods, and Eduardo shouted to his own group. "Let him go. We must attend the wounded and hold any prisoners." He dismounted and ran to Kat. As he approached her, she raised her sword for a further attack, but dropped the weapon when she recognized Eduardo, not an Assassin.

He cut her bonds.

She grabbed him by the arm, not noticing his wince, and pointed at the writhing man Eduardo had stabbed, and who continued to moan in agony. "Look." She strode over to the kidnapper and lifting with her boot rolled the man on his back.

Eduardo stared, his eyes wide. "Drainin."

"I told you he couldn't be trusted. Wynneth didn't like him either."

"He must have been working for Galdin." Eduardo shook his head. "But I did trust him." He rubbed his hand over his face. "He is paying with his life for his treachery." Eduardo called to one of his guards. "Dispatch him."

Before the guard moved, Kat stepped forward. "Let me."

"No."

"Why not? He deserves to die."

"You should not be the one to end his life, Kat. You will suffer, because killing leaves scars on a person."

Kat sputtered at Eduardo. "I have already killed today. I'm not suffering."

"True. But the man you killed threatened you, and you killed to protect your own life. Were you to plunge the sword in Drainin now, it would only be for revenge, and it will not serve you."

"Isn't it the reason you are ordering the end to his life?"

Eduardo gazed down at Kat, who caught the compassion in his eyes.

He explained. "Even an enemy deserves mercy." He glanced back at the guard. "Dispatch him now. End his cries of pain."

As the guard raised his sword, Drainin raised his eyes to Eduardo. "Thank you," his voice barely heard above the keen of wind and the sounds of the waning battle.

Kat stared at Eduardo, speechless. She swallowed, and lowered her gaze, unable to watch Eduardo while Drainin met his end. She harbored no sympathy for the traitor. *He did get what he deserved, and yet why don't I feel better about it?*

The last Assassins continued to fight, refused to surrender and died because of their fierce intention to fight to the death.

Kat glanced at Eduardo's arm. "You're bleeding."

"It is but a minor cut. I will have it attended to when the more seriously wounded are helped."

He's an extraordinary man. A good leader. I misjudged him.

Kat and Eduardo began to examine the men on the ground... some groaning, and obviously alive. They bypassed the dead assassins, and Eduardo dispatched a mortally wounded one.

"Oh no." Kat ran over to a huge man who lay without moving, with his eyes closed. "Penrow. Don't you dare die on me." Her tears splashed on the face of the builder.

"I will try not to, although it will be difficult with you attempting to drown me." His voice subdued, and his face pale, he attempted a grin.

"This is no time to be silly, Penrow. You're seriously wounded."

Eduardo called over two of the guards. "Prepare a litter for Master Penrow and take him at once to Praetor Bardu's home. Dafid, find Healer Wynneth and request she come to Bardu's house. Ask her to bring all her best healing remedies."

Penrow raised his voice. "Sire, I am wounded, true, but attend to Bannon and Kadnu. They both need the healer's services far more urgently than I do."

Liandock appeared at Penrow's side. "He is correct, my Lord. Bannon is sorely wounded and requires aid sooner. I will attend this rascal until the healer is free. He demands far too much attention."

Kat stared at him, heat rising up her cheeks. "You came."

"You needed me." He smiled at her. "We will talk later. You need attend to another, and I must quiet this corpulent and annoying child."

Penrow sputtered in protest.

Kat surveyed the bodies and spotted Bardu kneeling over Kadnu, who lay on his back, staring up at the sky, now streaked with the pink and yellow ribbons of full dawn. Bardu placed his fingers reverently on Kadnu's eyes and closed them. He motioned to one of his men. "Prepare to transport this brave man to his home. We will mark his leaving of this land on the morrow." With those words, he laid his hand on the heart of his fallen comrade, and bowed his head in silence, as the rest of the men gathered around him. The quiet moment stretched and then Bardu lifted his voice in song. The music rose deep and true. The tale remembered a valiant hero, and the rest of the guards joined in the dirge, adding their voices to surround the words of reverence for their companion.

Kat, who had drifted to stand beside Bardu, experienced the vibrations of the union of magnificent bass voices as they celebrated the life of a fallen warrior with exultant harmony. The men holding lances began to bang on the earth, while others joined in, stamping with their feet. The rhythm increased in speed, and the earth shook with the power and majesty of the sounds, winding among all, nourishing the air with the blending of their voices. She felt the song deep within her solar plexus, and without warning, fat, salty tears rolled down her cheeks.

The hymn for Kadnu soared to a glorious finale and the sudden silence struck like a blow to the heart.

The Arrival

What glorious music. So much love and honor in their voices. I didn't know there could be glory in death.

Shocked by her own emotion, Kat stayed at Bardu's side, awed by these men, as the last echo of the stunning sounds faded. She touched her hand to his arm. He glanced up at her and nodded his thanks.

Bardu stood, and his men bent down and lifted Kadnu on their shoulders and placed him on a cart brought by the healer apprentices. He hardly glanced at the six dead Assassins. They would be placed on a funeral pyre in two star turns.

Kat swiveled her head and caught sight of young Bannon lifted with care on a litter for transport, by two other men. Her heart in her throat, she ran over to them. "How severely is he hurt? Will he recover?"

A man strode up beside her. "He is not well, Lady Kat. I am not sure if the Healer can help him."

She glanced at the man beside her, surprised when she recognized him. "Haydar. Oh rats, I mean, Horse-Master Haydar."

He stopped her words with a hand in the air. "Some times formalities need be forgotten. This is one of those times."

Tempted, Kat wanted to ask him 'who are you, and what did you do with Haydar', but he might not relate to her silly thought, and he had moved on to help one of his assistants who tended another injured man. She was heartsick over Bannon. She remembered his shy smile, his helpfulness and his wonderful knowledge during their trip. An enormous lump formed in her throat, and without warning, she wept for him and for all the other fallen men on that day.

One more time, Kat toured the field of skirmish, wondering if she might be of help to any other. *I can't believe this. The people who came to help me. I could expect Liandock and Penrow but not from so far away. And Haydar? I thought he hated me.* She hastily wiped her eyes. *Kadnu and Bannon put their lives on the line for me. How I misjudged them.*

Mouse joined her. "Lady Kat, I watched you using a sword. I was not aware you were adept with a weapon of such weight."

"I'm not. But because my hands were bound together, they helped me to wield the damn thing."

Mouse gazed around him. "The members of the Assassins' Guild are strong, treacherous fighters, who do not fear death. This makes them more dangerous than most. You handled yourself well."

Kat ducked her head. *I'm not comfortable receiving compliments.* "I've never fought with a sword, but I did study the techniques." She gazed at Mouse. *I never noticed how well or how poorly he did in the fight. Will he be a first-rate guide for me?*

"I will guide you well, Kat. I promise you this."

Crap, did he just read my mind? Please don't tell me he can read minds.

Mouse tapped her on the arm. "Eduardo and his men need to clear this place, and you can do no more. Many fine men have suffered this night. I would suggest you return to your quarters and rest. You experienced an exhausting time, and we leave in two star turns hence."

Hence? Who even uses the word? However, he's right. I'm whacked. Plus Liandock may come. "Thank you, Mouse. You're right. I'm worn out. I'll head for my rooms now, and I intend to sleep 'til I'm slept out."

"I left a supply list for you at your quarters, so when you awake, you may check if you need pack anything more. I will discuss our time of leaving with Lord Eduardo. He may require we meet with him on the morrow to confirm our journey to Shendea."

"Fine. When you two need me, let me know."

Kat caught an Assassins' horse and mounting, rode wearily for the keep, keeping her eyes averted from the bodies and blood on the ground. *Now I have experienced a true battle, the game will benefit. But at such a cost. I wonder how I might ever insert smell into a game, because the stink of battle is ghastly.*

CHAPTER 46

Before climbing into her bed, Kat visited Wynneth's infirmary, and found Penrow healing well from his injuries. He would be ready to travel to his home soon. Bannon, whose wounds were serious, slept deeply, but according to Wynneth, would probably not last the night. Kat asked to sit beside him.

"No, Lady Kat, you must leave."

"But… "

Wynneth caught Kat's hands, her face gentle. "You do not understand how Kaylins view departure from the physical. It is part of life's circle. Their only desire now is to join with Caleesh, and it is tradition they are guided peacefully by a Healer. Your heart is good, but you would be a distraction, Kat."

She stared a long time at both Wynneth and Bannon, but ultimately turned from them and found her way to her room.

She intended to shower before bed, but her body, battered and drained, demanded sleep more than the cleanliness.

***

Kat woke from a health-giving sleep, refreshed in both body and soul. Now rested, she showered and began to dress for the day.

I'm amazed I feel this physically energetic after the last couple of days. Why does this Thane guy want me to come to Morden? Eduardo wants me to go to every land, but I'm going to leave Morden to the end. I have not been impressed by Mordens.

A knock at the door set her heart thumping. *Liandock?* "Come."

Kat did her best to conceal her disappointment when Mayda walked in.

"Oh Lady Kat, I am so pleased you are unharmed. I was so worried, I could not wait to find you and make sure you are well." A tiny half-sob escaped her lips. "I have been told Bannon fought courageously during the battle. I was with him when he left us during the darkness."

A flash of anger. "How did Wynneth allow you? I thought only Healers attending the dying?"

Mayda gazed at Kat, her face gentle, changed somehow. "I assist Healer Wynneth in her duties. I am now her apprentice. Someday I long to be a Healer in Kaylin."

She's changed. There's a new confidence in the way she holds herself. "This is something you wish to do?"

"Yes. Helping guide Bannon to join Caleesh was something I will never forget. His passing was joyous. I hope you are not grieving for him."

Rats I don't want to talk about death. "I'm fine. There's nothing to worry about. I will miss Bannon, and you are correct. He fought most valiantly." She swallowed, keeping her head turned so Mayda could not see her eyes."

Mayda stood staring at Kat.

"Do you have something else, Mayda?"

"Um… Lord Eduardo has requested you join him in his office as soon as you are able."

"Thank you, Mayda. I will finish dressing and go right away."

Mayda stood fidgeting, but Kat stopped her.

"Mayda, please go, I need to finish getting ready."

The young woman sighed and left the room.

The Arrival

Man, she wants to talk about her experience with Bannon, and I can't handle that at this moment.

***

When Kat entered Eduardo's office, he, Wynneth, Mouse, and Liandock were already seated.

Eduardo motioned her to a chair. "Kat, in view of what happened, we consider the matter important enough for you to set off for Shendea on the morrow. Mouse will meet with you in the courtyard after the morning meal, with the horses for your transportation, and he will arrange for Dafid to bring your packed luggage to the courtyard as well."

Mouse nodded at this.

"Thank you." Kat examined each of them. *This is time to bare my soul... and I don't find this easy.* "I want to thank you all so much. I realize I misjudged many people in Kaylin. I am grateful to Master Haydar, to Master Penrow, and you, Master Liandock, for saving my life. I know because of me, Bardu and Irina lost a close companion, and," she swallowed and with a catch in her throat, continued, "we all lost a valued friend in Bannon. Please forgive my misunderstandings." *I'm so close to tears, I guess I really meant what I said.*

Wynneth smiled at her. "Kat, we have nothing to forgive. You were thrust into an abnormal situation, and managed well. I hear you fought as an effective warrior against seven Assassins. That is no small feat. They are deadly fighters, and Eduardo's guards only overcame them because of their greater numbers."

Kat concentrated on her shoes. *These people are... are just plain nice people. I can't believe I didn't see all this before.*

Eduardo stood. "Kat, you will face many challenges in the seasons to follow. I suggest you return to your quarters and ensure your packing is complete, and then rest."

"Thank you, again. I would like to have some time to myself." Kat stood and headed for the door.

Liandock caught up with her as she exited. "I must re-energize your stone, so I will visit you after your evening meal."

She nodded, and left without speaking. *Whenever I'm around him, everything else fades.*

***

After her evening meal, Kat entered her personal and luxuriated in the warm shower, lathering her body and hair with the floral soap she adored. Thinking about Liandock, made her nipples stand at attention. *Damn, the man is hot.* Clean, she threw on a loose dress. *Not going to wear underwear.* She brushed her hair back from her face, which slightly wet, made masses of curls spring everywhere, paying little attention to her desire for an alluring style.

A faint knock set Kat's heart thumping. When she opened the door, he stood still for a minute, displaying his gorgeous, bronze body and loped into the room. He wrapped his arms around her and kissed her gently, and then with urgency. Heat rushed through her and those hidden parts moistened with desire. She wound her fingers through his blonde mane and pulled him closer.

He moved back. "I am here to restore your stone. The gem expended much power to call me to you. I will also teach you ways to refresh the energy on your own, because I may not always be near to help you."

"How do you revive the vitality?"

"I will show you." He found the pendant between her breasts. "Perceive how pale the green and how lackluster the appearance?"

"Yes."

"Now we will re-insert energy." With a mischievous grin, he lifted her in his arms, and carried her to the bed. He lay beside her and caressed her with his lips, his tongue, and his hands, seeking all the delicious trembling places on her body. He nibbled at her ear lobes causing her toes to curl with exquisite pleasure. How he made every part of her a demanding, arousing erogenous zone, she would never understand. All Kat knew was need, and fire, and hunger for him. His touch and kisses on her body, played her like a fine instrument, and at last delivered her to the crescendo of ecstasy.

Her heart pounding, breath clamoring for air, she lay beside him, glowing with moisture. "But you didn't… "

His smile conveyed pure lust. "But I will… " He held up her stone to show her. The green had deepened and the color glowed.

He let the stone drop back to her breasts and bent to use his tongue to tease her nipples, which hardened, sending quivers of heat all over her body. He slid down the bed and picked up one of her feet, sucking and tickling each of her toes with his tongue. Now the heat spread from her feet and traveled up her body to her thighs, embarked on the same journey as his talented tongue, which found its place where the fire burned brightest and hottest. He teased her little nub while she thrust her body upwards desiring more and finally she cried out with joy when the climax propelled her into total rapture.

She lay exhausted, heart with rapid beats, and gasping for breath. "You still didn't… "

This time his grin displayed pure lechery. "But I will… oh I will."

He reached down and inserted himself where her juices flowed, in the hottest part of her, and moved in the ancient rhythm of men and women, faster and faster.

Oh, I can't possibly — not again.

But she did and simultaneously, the lion roared with primal satisfaction.

***

Liandock stood by her door. "I must go to Penrow and prepare him for his trip home."

"I never expected to meet with you after I left Lanfair. This has been more than I imagined possible. Will we ever connect again?"

"I am not a seer, but I suspect we will. Not in Kaylin, however. How often I do not know. We are so well matched, Kat. I regret we are not meant to be permanent. I am convinced your return to your own world, when the time is right, is of vital importance. More important than any of us realize,." His faint smile, rueful. "But you and I must eventually part forever."

He doesn't want us to be over, I don't want this either.

Liandock lifted the pendant from beneath her clothing. The green, almost iridescent, glowed from within with the light of a thousand suns. "I've showed you how the stone regains the power needed. You can do this too."

Kat screwed up her face. "What? How can I do this?"

Liandock eyed her as a father might cast an exasperated eye on his child. "Kat." He shook his head. "Pleasure yourself, of course."

CHAPTER 47

Kat arrived at the courtyard shortly after her morning meal, and discovered Mouse, with two saddled horses and a third pack animal. Her duffle and backpack were stowed carefully, along with two other bags belonging to Mouse. The leather pouch containing her writing materials, she slung over her shoulder and she carried her young pyrock in the traveling cage, covered with warm fur.

"You possess a pyrock, Lady Kat?"

Kat nodded.

"What is she named?"

"I call her Wink. She kept winking at me, so I figured she wanted to give me a clue."

"She likely intended to suggest the name. Pyrocks are intelligent creatures, and we understand little about them."

The door from the keep opened, and Eduardo, accompanied by Wynneth appeared at the entrance.

Eduardo strode over. "A word with you, Mouse."

Kat strained her ears, eavesdropping shamelessly.

Eduardo stopped beside Mouse. "Did any of the Assassins realize your true identity?"

"They did not. I used the concealing charm."

"Excellent. Did you convey to Galdin she is on her way to Shendea?"

"No."

"Why not?"

"The risk, Eduardo. Particularly after the attempt to kidnap her."

"I am well aware of the risk. Remember, my heart is at stake." Eduardo sighed. "You must tell him, and soon. Your own situation is precarious as well. Give him no ammunition. We need you to have his ear."

"I will contact him when we are on our way."

"Excellent."

Eduardo walked back to where Kat and Wynneth stood.

Kat raised an eyebrow. "What was that about?"

"Nothing much. A few last minute instructions. You are aware, Kat, I maintain every faith in Mouse's abilities to keep you safe. He is an excellent guide, and knows more about the lands of Pridden than many others."

"Thank you. I am truly sorry about how I misjudged so many here in Kaylin. I promise I will perform the task you asked of me to the best of my ability. I regret I obviously didn't accomplish any of what you needed me to do here in Kaylin."

"On the contrary, Kat. You accomplished more than you realized. I receive reports from many people in Kaylin on a regular basis. In Trigoran a Kaylin man and one from Glowen are exchanging goods and occasionally meals. This one example may spread. People follow examples which work."

Kat blinked. "Oh."

"Not only this example, but a number of those in Trigoran approved of your defense of Mayda. I see other examples of small things you accomplished." Eduardo smiled. "Achieving substantial results are not done all at once, but in a series of small actions. You have begun the process. I am content with what you succeeded in doing thus far."

"Really?"

Eduardo nodded.

"I'm happy you think so. I'm also glad you trusted my judgment enough to find me another guide, even before you knew of Drainin's treachery. And thank you too, Wynneth for your help and your kindness." Kat reached forward and gave Wynneth a hug.

"You will be successful, child. You have excellent help." She glanced pointedly at Kat's chest area.

The stone warmed beneath Kat's clothing, and she laughed and hugged Wynneth again.

"Farewell Kat, I am sure we will meet again." Wynneth broke the hug, waved at Kat, and walked back into the keep.

Kat put her hand on Eduardo's arm. "I do mean to keep my promise, and I trust you will keep yours, because you gave me your word."

"I never intended otherwise." Eduardo took both Kat's hands in his. "Be safe."

Mouse called to her. "We are packed and ready to begin our journey to Shendea."

Kat began to walk towards the horses, stopped and moved back to Eduardo. "A question, please?"

"Yes?"

"Will you be the one from Kaylin who possesses the power to help me? And will you do so?"

"I am the Wielder here, and I will help you when the time comes. In addition, I will request Wynneth add her power to mine."

"Wynneth? I didn't know she possessed a power."

"She does, Kat. A valuable power indeed. She wields the power of Compassion."

J. M. Tibbott

DRAMATIS PERSONAE

NAME	DESCRIPTION & RELATED	FROM
Argelwyd	Original Lord of Pridden	Morden
Bannon	Caretaker of Pontis on Kaylin	Kaylin
Bardu	Praetor of Eduardo's guards Bond mate of Irina	Rifella
Brith	Seamstress for Eduardo's keep	Kaylin
Bronwyth	Head of functions for Eduardo	Shendea
Caleesh	Goddess for Pridden (except in Morden) Spirit only	Pridden
Carlo	Young designer/coder for Nick	Our world
Clune	Financial clerk for Eduardo	Kaylin
Dafid	Door guard for Eduardo	Kaylin
Deleth	Healer to Lord Rhognor Related to Wynneth	Shendea
Drainin	Counselor to Eduardo	Morden
Eduardo	Lord of Kaylin Related to Mouse	Morden
Galdin	Thane of Morden	Morden
Godrith	Tapestry Master in Shendea	Shendea
Haydar	Horse-Master for Eduardo Mayda's father	Baklai
Illian	Apprentice builder Penrow's daughter	Kaylin
Irina	Member of keep guards Bond mate of Bardu & sister to Liandock	Rifella

NAME	DESCRIPTION & RELATED	FROM
Kandu	Praetor Bardu's second-in command	Rifella
Karen	Friend to Kat Nick's wife	Our world
Kat	Katherine Karim - Mother a Scot, Father Arabic	Our world
Laylin	Serving woman for Kat	Kaylin
Liandock	Master Metal-Smith of Kaylin brother to Irina	Kaylin
Lanerch	Lord or Kaylin prior to Eduardo Adoptive father to Eduardo Eduardo	Kaylin
Rhognor	Lord of Shendea	Shendea
Makinti	Praetor for Thane Cathked Bardu's boyhood friend	Rifella
Mayrin	Wife of Horse-Master Haydar Mayda's mother	Baklai
Mayda	Serving woman to Wynneth daughter to Haydar & Mayrin Apprentice to Wynneth	Baklai
Morshag	Legendary horse thief Now a curse word in Baklai	Baklai
Mouse	Serves Galdin Related to Eduardo	Morden
Nick	Kat's supervisor	Our world
Penrow	Master Builder of Kaylin Father to Ilian	Kaylin
Salssin	Agent of Assassin's Guild	Morden
Sherwyn	Head Housekeeper for Eduardo	Kaylin
Souris	Waiter at hotel in Tortola	Our world

NAME	DESCRIPTION & RELATED	FROM
Ssarff	Leader of Assassin's Guild	Morden
Ssayleese	Snake Goddess in Morden Spirit only	Morden
Thontook	Master Weaver of Kaylin	Kaylin
Wynneth	Healer to Lord Eduardo Related to Deleth	Shendea

J. M. Tibbott

CREATURES OF PRIDDEN

NAME	DESCRIPTION	FROM
Cathnog	Large ferocious cat-like creature with huge canines resembles a saber-toothed tiger.	Shendea
Gornog	Pig-like animal, size of a jaguar, grey & black, covered in stiff bristles, two set of tufted ears, six clawed feet, 12 inch tusks in a warted mouth. Meat is tender, sweet and delicious, although causes gas in those who consume it.	Kaylin
Hissar	Rodent-like creature 1.5 feet, with the temper of a Tasmanian devil, three rows of barbed teeth, and the strength of a creature ten times its size.	Baklai
Horse	Almost the same as our world, except much larger in size.	Baklai
Hydodd	Large elk-like animal with huge horns, cantankerous and a match for the ferocity of the Cathnogs.	Shendea
Kithra	Dog-sized rodent with black eyes and needle sharp teeth and brown hair. Travels and attacks in packs.	Kaylin
Ponti	Resembles a horse, but with very large head for it's body size, large splayed feet, short legs, wide girth	Shendea

NAME	DESCRIPTION	FROM
Ponti cont.	very sure footed in mountainous regions. Pontis grow to about twelve or thirteen hands high.	
Pyrock	Small furry animal, with long tail and leathery wings can transport instantly, and locate any person anywhere on Pridden. Answers only to one person during lifetime.	Kaylin
Wullawerth	Sheep-like animal with masses of fine soft hair, excellent for clothing. Prized for eating.	Kaylin

ABOUT THE AUTHOR

J. M. Tibbott has been writing since childhood, but *The Arrival* is the first published novel. As a writer of magazine and newspaper articles, being an editor for an online newsletter, and a writing instructor, J.M. belongs to a community of local writers, all of whom are continually upgrading their own skills.

While the initial intention was to publish a myth/fantasy novel, as J.M delved further into the creation of a new world in which *The Arrival* takes place, it became obvious that the complete story required multiple books.

Thus, J. M. is hard at work on the next book in the series.

SNEAK PEEK

We hope you enjoyed the first book in the Pridden Saga, and just to entice you, we've included a peek into the next novel in the series, *The Healers of Shendea*.

The Healers of Shendea

The Pridden Saga
Book Two

J. M. Tibbott

CHAPTER 1

The path from Kaylin to Shendea through the Nordad pass, was disturbed only by the moaning complaints of the wind. The clop of the horses hooves on the hard rock surface, together with the hypnotic rhythm and sway of their mounts, lulled Kat and her companion. The pack animal, tied to Kat's saddle, followed silently. As they exited the pass, they paused at a fork in the road, when sudden cold from the green stone between Kat's breasts startled her. *What the... ?*

A guttural roar shattered the silence. Kat's horse reared, and all three animals danced backward, neighing frantically. With a further screech, an enormous cat-like creature sprang from the bushes beside the pathway and leaped for the pack animal. Vicious claws raked the horse, who reared and screamed in pain and fear, and attempted to run. Secured to Kat's saddle he pulled against the bit in his mouth, unable to free himself.

"Cathnog!" Mouse pointed to the path on the right. "Run, Kat." He whirled his horse to the left and screaming in fright, headed toward the thick grove of evergreens. The massive cat vaulted after him.

Her skin still prickling from the unexpected encounter, and furious with Mouse for abandoning them, Kat and the pack animal galloped up the right fork. *He ran and left us. The coward.* The stone on her pendant lay like a block of ice against her skin.

The cathnog roared again, fainter, as he followed the fleeing Mouse. Abruptly, a challenging bellow joined the melee.

Kat stopped, as she caught sight of a small building beside the road. *This will do. The poor pack horse needs tending.* She dismounted, and led both horses into the shelter. The pack animal's eyes rolled in terror and the poor creature's entire body trembled, as Kat struggled to control the horse and secure it to a post inside the small building. She retrieved the first aid kit, supplied by Wynneth, from her pack. She found an ointment in the kit and avoiding the thrashing hooves, applied the soothing mixture to the wound on the horse's flank. At once the animal ceased its trembling and nickered as if in relief.

Kat still caught the roars and bellows of the battle in the distance, between the enormous cat and the mysterious second creature. *What will I do if my cowardly guide is killed? Will I be able to find my own way to the nearest inn? Wait, I have Wink.* She removed the woolly covering from the traveling cage tied to the back of her saddle, and peered in. Two tiny bright eyes appeared from a ball of fluff, along with a grumpy peep. "I'm so sorry, Wink. I had to run, and I forgot you would be bounced around." With a sleepy chirrup, the pyrock's eyes closed and she became a roll of fur once more. Kat rewrapped the cage.

Unexpectedly a high pitched scream, and a bugle of triumph indicated the cathnog had met his match. The ensuing silence was absolute, and Kat waited, unnerved. *Should I stay here or make a run for it? I'm not sure if the pack horse can keep up. Is Mouse alive?* The sound of hoofbeats coming toward her, persuaded her to wait.

Mouse appeared outside the shelter, his robe ripped and his horse quivering in the aftermath of the battle. He dismounted and entered. "Are you alright? I saw the cathnog leap toward you."

Kat's words were laced with icy disdain. "I am, no thanks to you. I thought you were supposed to be my guide." *I knew he wouldn't be any help in the protection department. I'm right.*

"Lady Kat, I did not abandon you. I screamed to persuade the cathnog to follow me so I could draw him away from you."

Kat raised her hands to her mouth. *Ohh, crap.* "My bad." *Mouse looks confused.* She lowered her hands. "What I mean is… I… I misunderstood. I thought you were running for your life and leaving me. I apologize."

"It was a natural assumption on your part."

"I have to ask you. Even though I was fleeing, I heard some horrifying shrieks and bellows. What went on?"

"Fortunately for me when the creature had almost caught me, a hydodd appeared, an animal who is the sworn enemy of the cathnog."

"Oh yes, I remember Wynneth telling me about them."

"This hydodd was extremely powerful, and larger than most. He managed to dispatch the cathnog speedily." Mouse

359

ced as he waved his hand to indicate the size of the rious animal.

"Mouse, please forgive me, I misjudged you." She glanced at the blood seeping down the arm of his torn robe. "You're wounded. Here." She grabbed the ointment again. "Wynneth's ointment will help. Let me see your arm."

Mouse exposed the slash on his arm, and grimaced again with the effort.

Kate applied the ointment to his upper arm. *Wow, he's got muscles. How odd. He looks so small.*

"Thank you, Lady Kat." Mouse's face relaxed.

"You're welcome. Our poor pack horse also got slashed, and he certainly appreciated the ointment as well."

Mouse walked over and examined the wound on the horse. "The cut is not too bad. He will be fine. We should continue on to the nearest inn. He will have a chance to rest and recover, and we will spend the night. In the morning, we will exchange our animals for pontis, one star turn sooner than anticipated. You will be happy to know, cathnogs rarely appear this high on Mont Diffenna, so we are unlikely to encounter another."

"Mont Diffenna? Is this where Rhognor lives?"

"Yes he does. But Lady Kat, it is fine you that are less formal when speaking with me. But be sure to use Lord Rhognor's full title in the presence of others."

"Okay, okay. I'll remember. But perhaps when we are alone, you will simply call me Kat."

"Okay." Mouse grinned at her. "Wynneth told me this word means all is well. I too will be less formal when we are alone, Kat." Still grinning, Mouse mounted his horse and the three headed back up the roadway.

***

Mouse led them up the path of Mont Diffenna, cutting through a forest of deciduous trees which rained withered leaves on the three of them, and left behind bare branches like bones rattling against each other. The dried leaves pattered across the roadway, pursued by frigid winds sweeping down from the mountain.

Mouse glanced back, confirming Kat followed close behind. *How advantageous I defeated the cathnog out of her sight. If she had seen me take on the the mantle of a hydodd, she would immediately jump to the conclusion that I have the power to return her to her world. Even though I cannot achieve this on my own, Eduardo would be upset if I interrupted her task to visit every land in Pridden.*

"Mouse. How long before we reach the inn?"

He turned in the saddle. "Lady.. er Kat, we will arrive shortly after the mid-day meal. However, they will still be willing to serve us, as I imagine you are hungry."

"Exactly why I asked. I'm starving."

Mouse chuckled. "I do believe you will not perish before we reach our destination. You will soon be fed, and we will stay at the inn for the rest of this turn and over the night. Had we not been interrupted by the cathnog, we would have merely stopped for a quick meal and travelled to the next inn to sleep. We are traveling less fast than I expected, and once we change to pontis, the way will be slower than on horseback." He groaned internally. *I am not looking forward to an extra day on a ponti. I find them most uncomfortable. I suspect Kat will experience the same discomfort.*

Mouse rode on, caught up in his own thoughts. *Interesting. I have not found Kat to be as difficult as I imagined. Perhaps this journey will not challenge me as much as I anticipated.*

MORE REVIEWS

"Move over George R.R. Martin, J.R.R. Tolkien and J.K. Rowling. Another saga is on its way through the prolific pen of J. M. Tibbott. When game designer Kat Karim falls into a strange new world, she is confronted by ferocious beasts, fantastical realms and treacherous characters plotting against her. Who is her friend and who is her enemy? And how will she get back to her own world? Don't miss *The Arrival: Book One of the Pridden Saga*." — G. N.